THE COST OF VENGEANCE

"Leanne, what's going on here?" he asked.

She gulped the last of her drink. "It's—Tregare, you do things I can't live with. So I won't. Not any more."

She stood, and he with her. "You need any help moving out?"

"I'll manage. You go upship and make sure of your sneaky course change, Tregare. You wouldn't want to miss winning a trick."

He came close, then, to striking her. But he didn't. He said, "Maybe you think this is some kind of game, with UET. No such thing, and never has been." She started to turn away; he grabbed her arm.

"No. You listen. You realize what I *did*, here? I took us into Stronghold with a bum Drive and brought us out, alive, with a good one. And with fuel, and supplies, and the Admiral's stamp on a set of orders I can use to get us in and out of *Earth*, if I work it right."

"You, yes. You, you, *you*!"

"Look, I give credit all around. You and everybody else did great, executing the plans, but peace take you, they were *my* plans. This is my ship, and I have to be responsible for it."

Praise for F. M. Busby's Star Rebel:
"Fans who were caught up in the whirlwind adventures of Rissa Kerguelen will want this 'prequel,' the first of two volumes about the early life of Bran Tregare . . . Busby does a good job of filling in Bran's background, showing the making of a rebel in agonizing detail."
—Library Journal

And for The Alien Debt:
"Great space adventure in a richly imagined future world . . . It's crisply written. Human and alien, the people are real. The action moves fast."
—Jack Williamson

Other Bantam Books by F. M. Busby
Ask your bookseller for the books you have missed

STAR REBEL
THE ALIEN DEBT

Rebel's Quest

F. M. BUSBY

BANTAM BOOKS
TORONTO · NEW YORK · LONDON · SYDNEY · AUCKLAND

REBEL'S QUEST

A Bantam Book / January 1985

ISBN 0-553-24727-1

Published simultaneously in the United States and Canada

PRINTED IN THE UNITED STATES OF AMERICA

H   0 9 8 7 6 5 4 3 2

For all rebels who find themselves

Contents

1. Prologue:
Bulletin on Tregare

"Testing—one, two—all right, the recorder's working. Alden Bartlett dictating. Shelly, do this one up and get it into Distribution right away. I'll just rough it; you fill in from the files and streamline the chat. This hot number came down from Committee Chairman Minos Pangreen his own brass-bound self.

"What it is, is an All-Worlds, All-Ships Bulletin on Tregare the Pirate, so use official headings: United Energy and Transport, Presiding Committee, old Pangreen the Chairman, UET crest, all that. Do it up pretty.

"All right; subject, Bran Tregare. Born Australia, New Year 9 or 10—look it up—to Sean Tregare, citizen of North America, and Lisbeth Duggan. No surviving family on Earth or at any legitimate colony, so we don't have that kind of handle on him.

"Entered the Slaughterhouse—oops, Space Academy—at age thirteen, graduated in normal sequence at sixteen. Good scores but no outstanding cadet promotions. Two turns in the Special Punishment cell, which should have told somebody something.

"On graduation, did his cadet cruise on the *MacArthur*,

1

Arger Korbeith commanding. I hear the Butcher's still complaining he should have spaced that kid while he had the chance. Put four or five others out the airlock, that trip, but missed the kingsnake. Everybody guesses wrong now and then. . . .

"Back here at Earth, Tregare was transferred to the *Tamurlaine* as Third Officer. The ship went as directed to the Twin Worlds—Tweedle first—and then to Penfoyle Gate. Then lifted for Terranova but never arrived there, so it's assumed that's when the ship Escaped. At next contact it was renamed *Inconnu* and Tregare was captain. It's usual enough that the old captain doesn't survive a mutiny but this guy seems to have wiped out *all* his superiors. Boil this all down a lot, will you, Shelly?

"That next contact was with the *Hannibal* under Commodore Sherman. Tregare blew the ship apart, but its scouts got away and reached Johnson's Walk safely, which is why we know the story. And from then on . . .

"Some of these reports contradict each other. That is, unless someone invented a faster-than-light Drive and Tregare has it, he couldn't have been to all the places and done all the things listed in here. My guess is that when a ship or colony of ours gets creamed, they figure they'll look better if they blame it on the Bogey Man. But leave my guesses off, Shelly; this thing's going out over Pangreen's name.

"After the *Hannibal* incident, next contact was when he hit three ships off Shegler's Moon. He got the armed ship *Cortez* with a missile and his turrets crippled the *Goering*, so that it spiraled down onto Shegler's primary. That world is like Venus only a lot bigger, so there went the *Goering*. The *Charlemagne* got away to tell us about it.

"There's a lot more, but I have an appointment coming up, so could you crib the rest from the files? Don't bother trying to sort out what's relativistically possible and what's not; I can't figure the Long View of space-time myself and won't ask you to try it.

"But here's some speculations that haven't been filed yet. That Tregare's allied himself with some unknown species of aliens possessing FTL travel. That somewhere he's found or set up ship-building facilities, and is building a fleet of ships—

twenty, fifty, maybe a hundred. Well, to say the least, these things are unlikely—but the guesses have official sanction, so put them in anyway. Labeled *as* guesses, of course.

"Another is that he's the one who hijacked the ship with all the frozen sperm and ova and conceived-zygotes, and the Zoomwombs to hatch them in, and is force-growing thousands of Instant Troops to attack us with. If you put that one in, Shelly, look up the dates and add those, too. I think that ship disappeared while Tregare was still on the *MacArthur*.

"But it's not our business to tell our bosses they work too hard at scaring themselves. If Tregare did even half the real items they say he did, he's the single biggest menace our government faces. So just set down the facts and let our beloved readers, All-Worlds and All-Ships, do their own editorializing. Right?

"Hmmm—I see here that somebody wants Tregare boosted to the top Wanted slot: Escaped Target Number One. Could be a reasonable priority, at that. I mean, how long has it been—twenty years, maybe?—that anybody's heard anything about Cade Moaker and *Cut Loose Charlie*? But Tregare, we hear a lot about—enough that Upstairs gets nervous and we catch it. Actually, the way this Tregare operates—well, never mind that. Pangreen will either up the Target rating or he won't.

"End Bulletin draft, subject Bran Tregare known as Tregare the Pirate. Alden Bartlett out.

"And Shelly—if you can get this out today, tomorrow I buy you a three-drink lunch and we take the afternoon off."

A long time later, so long that the readout paper had yellowed and gone brittle, Bran Tregare read that Bulletin. Smiling a little, he shook his head. They had a few things right, UET did, but not many. The fake ID had held up, he noticed—UET had no idea he was the son of Hawkman Moray and Liesel Hulzein, and nephew to Erika Hulzein whose Establishment in Argentina was a major thorn in UET's paw. Not that those connections did him any good: Erika had been after his hide, and his parents had run off and left him to the nonexistent mercies of the Slaughterhouse. And had gone to the world called Number One.

UET had some of the early stuff straight. Yeah, he'd blasted the *Hannibal*. He hadn't known before that his second armed-ship kill was the *Cortez*, or that he'd also nailed one of the other two; he'd been too busy trying to cope with a crippled Drive. He wondered how the Escaped colony on Shegler's had fared after discovery by UET, but the Bulletin didn't say.

They couldn't know of his stops, once he was captain of *Inconnu*, at the Hidden Worlds of New Hope and Freedom's Ring, and his visit in between, to UET's base on Hardnose, was considered to be a hoax by someone else. On the other hand it had been Raoul Vanois in *Carcharodon*, not Tregare, who raided the mining colony on Iron Hat.

UET's speculations about alien alliances and FTL Drives made him laugh out loud. Well, the wilder their beliefs, the less apt they were to be set for what he *was* planning!

He did wish they were right about the shipbuilding part, but to his knowledge only one Hidden World had built any kind of ship: Number One had a cargo shuttle that worked fine for in-system work but lacked interstellar range.

He read more: yes, this escapade was his; the next wasn't. And so on. He wished to hell he *had* been the one to wipe out the slavers on Dixie Belle, but that was the work of a man named Dominguez, whom Tregare had never met but would like to, someday.

And of course the Zoomwomb-and-zygotes caper was long before his time. It had given the planet Number One its rather surprising population in a hurry, but by none of his own doing.

"Bran? I thought you said something about a drink. I am certainly ready for one." Still dripping from the shower, Tregare's wife wrung water from her long, dark hair and put a towel around it. To look at Rissa Kerguelen one would hardly guess that she and Bran had married in a dueling ring, after she had fought—naked and unarmed—with a man twice her weight, and killed him. It had been a long time since Stagon dal Nardo had any place in Tregare's thoughts; he didn't stay there long.

"Sure. A minute." A quick scan covered the rest of the Bulletin; he set it down. "You want some chuckles, look this over." He stood, and went to make the promised drinks.

Thinking: UET didn't know about his alliances, either—

Limmer on *Lefthand Thread*, for instance. Hell, they didn't even know that Kickem Bernardez had taken the *Hoover*.

And reminiscing: *Number One, yeah. That's where it all really started.*

2. Number
One

Tregare was dozing. Jargy Hoad, his oldtime Slaughterhouse roomie and now his Third Hat, had the watch as *Inconnu* neared the planet. Tregare had a lot of thinking to do, but right now he was too tired to do it.

Second Hat Erdis Blaine, his sometime lover, was leaving the ship at Number One. The trouble with Erdis was that she thought life should be played fair. She didn't realize, and couldn't accept, that fighting the monolithic tyranny of UET a man had to use whatever worked. In Tregare's view, treachery was rewarded by death. Back at Shegler's Moon, *Inconnu's* most recent stopover, Port Administration had tried to cover its ass with UET by selling Tregare out. After he'd fought clear of the ambushing UET ships—all three of them—he went back and blew Port Admin purely to hell. The word would spread, and the lesson needed to be made clear. But Erdis couldn't see that, so she was getting off. Well, if he was a monster, as she said, he'd had plenty of help. . . .

Before the breakup, Erdis had for some reason decided to get pregnant. That wasn't Tregare's worry, since she hadn't asked his consent. His problem was figuring how to buy out her officer's-shares in the ship itself. Might be best to pay largely in cargo bought, back at Freedom's Ring, especially for delivery here. But Freedom's Ring's contracts were with the Hulzein connection on Number One, and that meant Liesel Hulzein, Tregare's mother. And probably his father Hawkman Moray and his sister Sparline. Long ago, appalled and heart-broken when he knew they'd left him in UET's Slaughterhouse when they went off Earth, he'd vowed never to see or speak with any of them again. Thirteen he was, then; even now, maybe close to ten subjective bio-years later, that hurt was fierce.

But he'd figure something out, some way to handle things. . . . Bran dozed.

The intercom brought him awake. "Bran. Jargy here."

Getting his face out of the pillow and throwing covers back, Tregare sat up and flipped the talk-switch. "Yeah? Anything wrong?"

"Nothing at all. But come up to Control anyway. We're close to hitting air, and I don't think the view is anything you'll want to miss. I mean, on tape it couldn't be quite the same."

Tregare shook himself fully awake. "Sure. I'll be right up."

The view from Control was something, all right. With the downscreen on hi-mag, Tregare saw first an endless-seeming plain; just below the ship, now, was a huge water sink. He checked; as planned, *Inconnu* was coming down headed toward the Hidden World's arbitrary West—traveling with the terminator and expecting to land before crossing it from dawn into darkness.

Ahead lay several parallel ranges of hills. Jargy pointed. "Take a good look. I read about the Big Hills, on the data sheets, but now I believe them."

Still a bit sleepy, after all, Bran said, "They don't look so much." Then he checked the instruments. "We're still forty kilos up? I just changed my mind!" Because the slanting afternoon sunlight now showed him something of the sheer size of those rounded masses—foothills, they weren't.

"Aircars can't cross them," Jargy said. "Even with oxy for the passengers, the cars simply won't climb that high. And you notice how far they extend, north–south—not feasible to go around. So this perfectly good plain, less than a hundred kilos from the main port, is hardly explored at all."

Flipping through the info, noting the average height of the Big Hills, Tregare could see why. He said, "Gives me an idea.

Remember, I'm thinking of a base here? Well, how about on
this side of the Hills? With the ship and the two scouts we
could move supplies over—and sure's hell the locals wouldn't
bother us!"

The locals! Who was he kidding? His family, here on this
world, was what still worried him. Too many nights he'd lain,
shivering in fear of Slaughterhouse brutality, hating his parents
for leaving him there while they escaped to a safe world. But
so what? He didn't have to see them, did he? Maybe not—but
why was his body giving him all the sensations of panic?

Grimly he shook his mind loose from the problem. Those
people weren't his real enemy, UET was. And this wasn't
Airlock Drill on the *MacArthur,* standing naked in the line of
cadets and waiting for Butcher Korbeith to have one of them
spaced. Bran had vowed to kill that man someday; if he ever
did, maybe these flashbacks of fear would vanish. But to do it,
first he had to get on with the job at hand: gather ships under
his command, and *attack.* Not that the Butcher was his only
target; he was after any part of UET's cruel reign that he could
bite off. And here was where he planned to start it. . . .

The Long View—the fact that up near light-speed ships
might experience one year while planets went through twenty—the Long View made things difficult. The trick, though,
was to learn how to use it. By passing info to every Escaped
Ship met in space and to the Port computer of every Hidden
World he visited, Bran Tregare was building a longterm
communications net. He wasn't the man who'd first begun it,
but he knew a good thing when he saw one.

So someday, he hoped, there would be a rendezvous of ships
to join him, here on Number One. And he'd need a base to
service them and arm them—as many as he could round up,
but six or eight at the very least, or it wouldn't work.

So for now, get his base set up. And when he'd prepared it
the best he could, for the gathering he hoped to bring about
eventually, take off again on a two-purpose mission: to make
more contacts with Escaped Ships, and to bite UET's tail to the
bone!

Jargy Hoad's voice broke Tregare's fugue; for a moment he
couldn't remember what he'd been saying. Oh yes, about the
locals not bothering them, east of the Hills. Jargy's grin
indicated that he agreed, and he said, "You know, that's not a
bad idea." So, approaching the Big Hills the two men scanned

the terrain in search of a good site. At first Bran liked a ledge area to one side of a canyon, but a better look showed it slanting too much. Jargy picked a dry lake, but as Tregare pointed out, nothing said it was dry all the time. Then Bran spotted, on the long slope where the Big Hills themselves began, an ancient crater with a fairsized ringwall and a floor more flat than not.

"It's closer and it's better," he said. "I wouldn't risk landing the ship there yet, but a scout I would. Hang a bulldozer outside the scout, and in four, five days—a week, maybe— we'd have us a nice flat port."

He realized he'd said the plan in shorthand, but Hoad knew what he meant. "Sure. Except, do you know anyone who knows how to run a bulldozer?"

"Course not. That's what groundsiders are for. We hire some."

Radar confirmed eye judgment that the flatlands on the west side of the Big Hills were nearly a kilometer lower than the eastern plain. A little to the north of their path Bran spotted the major settlement: "The capital city, or whatever." One Point One, it was called, and it was bigger than any town he had yet seen on a Hidden World. Well, with the Zoomwombs and all, it would be. First Hat Gonnelson, doing pilot, swung course toward the place.

The port looked fairly large, too, and now held three ships, none of them armed. Earlier, at hailing distance, Tregare had talked with the port's spokesman-on-duty, and had been impressed by the way this place simply took incoming ships in stride. There was no hassle, no apparent anxiety. Finally he'd asked: "You people don't seem nervous about new ships, the way some places are. How come?"

A little bit, then, the voice flattened out. "Most places don't have our grade of missile defense."

A hard line to top, so Bran said, "Well, now I know." Certainly he appreciated the logic. Now as Gonnelson brought *Inconnu* down, drifting expertly toward One Point One's port, Tregare saw something odd, off to the north—across the Big Hills ran a zigzag mark. There wasn't time to do more than swing an aux screen's camera over that way, and put it on hi-mag and hi-speed, both, so he did that much. Later he'd have a look. . . .

* * *

On the landing circle the port had designated, Gonnelson brought *Inconnu* to rest without a jar. "Good job," said Tregare, and clapped a hand to the man's shoulder—briefly, because he knew that Gonnelson was no more comfortable with touching than with talking: a little went a long way. But a little couldn't hurt, either.

Bran watched Gonnelson run down through the grounding checklist; halfway through, realizing he didn't need to monitor, he turned to Jargy Hoad. "On the commercial stuff, you deal for the ship. The talking part, I mean. Anybody asks for me, I'm busy. And—"

"Wait a minute." Hoad waved a hand. "I don't know prices, any of that stuff. Bran, how can I—?"

"We have folks who do. Groden, down in Stores, for one."

"Ol' Gripin' Groden?"

"Not any more. Held back too long on promotion, was all. He's a lot different now. And anyway, you can punch most of the info out of Tinhead."

Jargy frowned. "Still, though—Third Hat, dealing for the ship?"

"Second. Didn't I tell you? Erdis, she's getting off. And rules or no rules—compared to you, Al Druffel just doesn't hack it." Before Hoad could ask anything, Tregare said, "The thing is, most of our cargo for here is consigned to Hulzein Lodge. I have my own reasons—tell you sometime, or maybe not—I'll deal with those people but I won't talk with them. So you handle that part."

After a pause, Jargy nodded. "If you say so."

To the port Tregare gave the correct protocol, both from upstairs and after landing. Such as "Bran Tregare, captain, speaking for the armed ship *Inconnu*." They wanted the ship's history and he gave it straight: nothing to hide, here. But when it came to commerce he said, "Our Second Hat, Jargy Hoad, is authorized to handle all that. Don't bother me with it." And mostly, nobody did.

He had one bad moment, going into Control while Jargy was on a direct circuit to Hulzein Lodge and dickering on delivery charges, to the Lodge rather than directly to the port. On the screen Bran Tregare saw his mother Liesel Hulzein, and noticed that now her crown of braided hair carried a lot more

grey in it. Behind her stood the tall man, Hawkman Moray—
he hadn't changed much. For seconds Bran looked to see if
maybe his sister Sparline might be in the group, then he shook
his head and moved to make sure that he himself wouldn't be
seen from the far end.

He was moving to leave Control entirely when Liesel's voice
cut through, saying, "I've had enough of this! Liesel Hulzein
speaking, and I know damned well that the captain of *Inconnu*,
the armed Escaped ship, is Bran Tregare. I want to talk to him!
I have the right—after all, he—"

Hawkman gripped her shoulder. "No, Liesel. He may not
want it known." Tregare gave a thankful sigh.

Voice disguise is easy: with one hand Bran pinched his
nostrils closed; with the other he grabbed a talkset. "Captain's
orders are that *Inconnu* deals with Hulzein Lodge through the
Second Hat. He says you'll know why."

He saw Hawkman frown before saying, "Yes. It's an old
grudge. Something we did, or didn't do, a long time ago. We'd
hoped—but apparently he still believes we had a choice."

Oh, hell! But he wouldn't open that can of worms again.
Tregare cut the circuit. He left Control. In fact, he ran.

After a cup of coffee to calm down with, he went back up to
take care of the business he'd had in mind. Immediately on
landing he'd fed all the news he had to the port's computer and
milked it of word from other ships. And had called the three
currently in port, asking to meet with their captains and giving
a guarded version of his own plans: ". . . and to our mutual
advantage I'd like to make agreements with any ship that's
willing. Call me back when you have time."

For none of the three captains had been available to talk
with him on the comm. One was Cade Moaker on *Cut Loose
Charlie*; to him Tregare added, "We had a close pass once,
when I was a cadet on the *MacArthur*; I was in Control at the
time and heard you tell Korbeith's hyena off. Loved it. And I
was lucky enough to survive riding with the Butcher. Just
barely, though."

The other two, Bran hadn't heard of: Rasmussen on
NonStop, who was down with some exotic brand of the flu, or
Krieg Elman who commanded a ship now known as *Stump
Farm*. That one's spokeswoman didn't seem to want to give

Tregare the time of day, much less any commitment for her
captain to meet with him.

Now, though, Moaker was willing to talk. On the screen the
man looked old but vigorous. He said, "What you say of your
plans, I like. But can't join in." He shook his head. "Old
Charlie's past it, pretty much. Not just the Nielson Cube,
which isn't all that close to crapping, but throughout. We're
good for two more hops, I'd say—but I'll settle for one. I take
the conservative approach. From here, where I'm loading up
on what I expect to need, we head for a colony that can use our
technical help, and set up in business there."

Bran scratched his head. "What's wrong with right here?"

Moaker grinned; he looked younger that way. "Too much
competition. I'm thinking of Fair Ball; ever heard of it?"
Tregare hadn't, and so indicated; Moaker fed him the coordinates. And then said, "Not all my people are ready to settle
down with the old man. And for this jaunt I don't need a full
crew. So if you can use any additional help? I won't send you
anyone I can't recommend fully."

"Why—thanks, captain. Happens I can use several. And if
you'll be in port a few days more, I'd be pleased to host you on
here, you and your officers."

"Thank you; we'll see. Pleasure talking with you, Tregare."
Moaker cut the circuit, leaving Bran with the thought: *I wish
that man could stay around for the big fight.*

He checked the other ships. Rasmussen was slightly up and
around but not very, and Krieg Elman was still unavailable.

So much for that. Tregare was hungry, and went downship to
fix that problem.

Commerce ran more smoothly than not. The Hulzein
contracts gave Jargy no problems; other cargo sold well, and
exchange rates were favorable. Not buying for future trade just
now, Tregare began loading up on materials for his base, across
the Hills. Alsen Bleeker, a thin hollow-cheeked man crowding
middle age, tried to push a little price-gouging, over and
above agreed terms—on pain of holding up the ship's refueling. But Tregare had seen his tanks filled—ship's and scouts'
both—first of all his dealings. So he told Bleeker to trundle his
goods back to the warehouse. "You're not the only source, and
maybe you can use the exercise. You come here again, figure to

deal square." Not even a quick offer of extra discount changed his mind. To Jargy he muttered, "A little rough on him, maybe. But I want the word to get around." And thought, *If my own side wants to gouge me, isolating the base is a damn good idea*.

Done with trade, for now, Tregare went offship. It was late morning, warm and slightly breezy; from his first exposure to local air and sky he'd liked this planet. As he neared the edge of the landing area a woman stepped out of a groundcar rental office. "You need some wheels?"

She was skinny, with short, shaggy red hair and a freckled complexion that could have used more care. Thirtyish, maybe. "No. An aircar, later. This time I'm walking."

Her grin was missing some bicuspids. "Aircars, I can get. Where is it you have in mind to walk?"

None of her business, but maybe she could help. "I want a bulldozer, including the operator. Stuff for a job where we have to lift the gear there, to do it."

"Lift? No aircar's going to lift a bulldozer, mister."

"Once I find the dozer, I'll take care of that part."

So she gave directions, then said, "You're off that ship there." Right. "How's your captain? A real sumbidge, like most?"

So she didn't know about officers' cheek tattoos. "You could say that."

Her directions worked, though. Following them he found a ramshackle setup with miscellaneous equipment sitting all around; the sign read "J. MacDougall & Assoc, Gen'l Contractors." MacDougall was scowling Black Irish but talked amiably enough. Assoc was Pete Aguinaldo who smiled as if he hadn't been unstoned in recent memory, but his answers made sense. Tregare hired them, and a dozer, and a portable "walking" hoist the scoutship could power, and some things he took MacDougall's word were necessary. "Day after tomorrow, then," said Tregare. "Midmorning?" Agreed; everyone shook hands, and Tregare left.

Heading back to *Inconnu*, the smells from a streetside food booth attracted him; he bought and ate, with considerable relish, two spicy concoctions of ground meat wrapped in some kind of leaves and served on a stick. Not bad at all!

When he passed the rental office the redhead wasn't outside, so he went in. "I got the equipment lined up; thanks for your help. Now—you said you could get me an aircar?" She could. He explained that he wouldn't need a driver; she agreed to provide a map and come along as guide. Tregare nodded. "Fifteen, twenty minutes, you said? Fine, I should be back from the ship by then."

Aboard, he brought Gonnelson and Jargy up to date. Erdis Blaine wanted to talk but now wasn't the time. "Tonight. Okay?" He ran and then reran the brief flash of tape, the zigzag line on the Big Hills. Either it was important or it wasn't—now he intended to find out.

Groundside again, Bran saw the aircar waiting. He walked over, climbed inside, and said to the redhead, "We okay to go? You got the map, and all?" He activated the propulsors.

"Right here." Pause. "My name's Keri Freling. What's yours?"

"Tregare." He began to taxi. "Point me north, will you?"

Looking startled, finally accepting that he wanted business, not chatter, she answered, "Sure. Sure, Tregare."

Neither reckless nor cautious, he took the car up. Pointing north, as he'd asked, she explained that here they were outside the city's jurisdiction, ". . . but don't fly over One Point One, below six hundred meters, without learning the altitude lanes." She gave him a pamphlet covering those; he tucked it into a pocket.

Turning east toward the Hills, Bran topped the first range and headed north again. Freling asked, "Where are we going?"

On the massive upslope to his right Tregare saw a complex of buildings dominated by a large, timbered structure. "What's all that?"

"It's Hulzein Lodge. Don't go much closer; those people don't take to uninvited visitors."

"I wasn't planning to." *Not hardly!* He looked from his unfolded map to the view ahead. Yeah—not too much farther now . . .

"What are you looking for?"

"Show you in a minute." A west-reaching headland blocked

his view. "Freling? You know how to use the oxy gear? I'd like to go up over this." He got his mask from under the seat.

"Why, yes. But—" Then she put hers on and shut up. And as Tregare lifted over the mass ahead, before him was one end of the Big Hills' zigzag scar that his screens had shown him from above. This end looked as if a giant axe had made it.

Freling grabbed his shoulder. "No! Don't go in there."

He eased his power back. "Why not?"

"It's a trap. Five aircars—six, maybe—have tried it. Not one came back."

"Maybe they didn't know enough."

Her grip jerked at him. "These were *experts* here; you've just arrived. What makes you think—?" Her hand shuddered. "If you want to try it, take me back to the port first. And post a deposit to cover the cost of the aircar!"

"Fair enough." He turned back, and dropped altitude until they could stow the oxy masks. Her silence gave him time to think. *Was* the place a trap? A blind alley, the end of it too narrow for turning back? Or maybe these "experts" hadn't seen it from topside, didn't know how sharply it zagged, and which way.

Tregare did, though. *And with the scout, I'll check it.*

He took them back in a moderate hurry, not really fast. Over the city he circled, well above the traffic limit, until the pamphlet and rooftop lane markers gave him a good idea how the system worked. He landed in front of Freling's office and paid her off. "Thanks for the guided tour."

"If you'd like more of them, we're here. There's a lot to see: the Slab Jumbles, for instance. . . ."

"If I do want more, you're first in line." But if he did need an aircar, it was simpler to buy one. Or better, two.

Walking back to the Port, at its edge he detoured for a closer look at something he'd heard about. Having bought a deteriorated spare Nielson Cube from a visiting ship, a consortium of oligarchs had set out to build a ship of its own. Not for interstellar use, or anywhere near full-sized. But for a hull with only a few times the bulk of a scoutship, and the short hauls of in-system freight runs, a half-power Nielson Cube should give safe service indefinitely.

Tregare looked up at the partially-completed structure. The frame girders were all in place; hull plates covered them, starting from the bottom, about halfway.

It all looked workable; too bad Bran couldn't be here to see the packet's first lift.

One more look, while he wondered what kind of share Hulzein Lodge might have in this enterprise. Then he turned away and walked to his ship.

Aboard *Inconnu* he found things going smoothly. He stopped by the galley, intending to ask for a tray to be sent to his quarters, but was told, "It's already been ordered, captain. I'll send it along in about twenty minutes." He acknowledged with thanks, and when he got to quarters he knew what to expect. Erdis Blaine, dolled up fit to kill and smelling great.

Arms outstretched, face turned up for his kiss. The big farewell scene; right? So she wouldn't have to feel any guilt or remorse, but rather, could feel generous and righteous, both.

Tregare wasn't having any. Firmly, though without violence, he moved her away and to one side. "That horse is dead. You shot it."

"But, Bran—"

"Dinner, we can share. But not bed." And by the time the tray arrived, and the wine, she saw he wasn't really listening, and dropped the subject.

Later, as she stood to leave, she said, "Bran, if you hate me so much, why are you being so fair in buying me out?"

The woman, peace take her, didn't understand *anything*. "I don't hate you." He suppressed the pang of bitterness. And wondered why good-hearted, decent people like Erdis here, couldn't get it through their heads that dealing with the monstrous *in*decency of UET, you had to take all the edge you could get. Inwardly, Bran sighed. As things were, it wasn't exactly that he was going to miss Erdis Blaine. What he missed already, and had for some time, was the real affection they'd had together.

His child that she was carrying did not—*could* not—concern him. All he had to do with it was a cell he'd given her with no such aim, without even his consent for its use in this fashion.

And with Blaine's ship-shares as Second Hat, the kid sure wouldn't be hurting for child support money.

Shaking his head, Tregare got back to now. "Hate you? Hell, even if I did—Blaine, on an Escaped Ship a captain *is* fair, or he doesn't stay captain very long."

Maybe she got the point, maybe not. Next morning, after he'd arranged her transportation to the hotel Maison Renalle, he did give her a goodbye kiss. But his mind was more than halfway stuck in what he needed to do next, across the Big Hills.

As she left, another worry hit him. Al Druffel, ever since he broke his leg skiing, back on New Hope, had been out of business as Third Hat. Now it turned out the ligaments needed extensive surgery, so Druffel was selling off, going groundside. And where was Bran going to find himself a new Third?

When MacDougall called, ahead of midmorning on the scheduled day, Tregare was well-breakfasted and ready to move. "An hour? Fine. See you." In finding Mac, Bran decided he'd been lucky. The man didn't dawdle.

Arrangements set with Gonnelson, Tregare went up to the starboard scoutship. The hatch opened; he took the small craft up and out. He had time for a short jaunt north; running higher than any aircar could, he headed for the zigzag gash through the Big Hills. And got his first good look at it.

He had no idea what forces produced the original cut, but later there had been lateral slippage along a fault line, to make the Z-turn near the top of the western slope. Going from the port it would be first a quick left and then almost as abrupt a right turn. To try this, without knowing the layout ahead of time—no wonder nobody came back!

But why *hadn't* anyone known the terrain? After a moment, Tregare had the answer: only ships' people could have seen the thing from upstairs, and they weren't the ones who would be interested, or mention it.

How about altitude? Checking his radar altimeter against the one calibrated with the Port as zero, he overflew the pass. And nodded: in this atmosphere, an aircar could take a medium load through, with a hundred meters to spare.

Unless there was something else he didn't know yet. . . .

* * *

Back to the Port. From upstairs Tregare saw a tractor
nearing *Inconnu*, towing two cargo flats. Among the gear he
recognized only the bulldozer and a hoist. MacDougall was
prompt—good enough. Bran landed, and went aboard ship,
where he rounded up some people to help with the heavy
lifting. Hain Deverel was senior, so Tregare put him in charge.
"We're going across the Hills. Pick two more to stay with you,
working with the contractor. About two weeks, I'd guess; then
I come get all of you, and the gear. Okay?"

"Two weeks?" Deverel didn't sound happy, and—*oh, hell.*
Now Bran realized: the man didn't want to be away, that long,
from his longtime lover Anse Kenekke. Tregare had never
understood that kind of thing, but these two men he liked and
trusted.

He said, "I'm sorry, Hain, but you *are* the best for this job.
And for quarters, now, there'll be only a couple of pre-fabs."

Deverel shrugged. "Two weeks. All right."

Deploying the "walking hoist," by degrees Mac and Pete
walked it up the scout's flank. In the open cargo hatch they
planted it for best leverage to raise the dozer. That mass would
have to ride sidesaddle, outside—but besides the hoist's own
cables, lashings were made around the scout's hull. Bran
nodded. "You've got it solid, Mac. It's not going any place
except where we do."

Inside the scoutship, all stowage checked, Tregare said,
"With the dozer hanging out there, this bucket's going to ride
weird. I don't want anybody hurt. So—Deverel, you ride
sidebar for me, and everybody else go down one deck and
strap into the accel couches. Okay?"

With the others gone, the two men strapped in. Deverel
said, "What am I here for? I've done no piloting."

"Time you learned, maybe." The Drive's hum built to
stability; from below came word the passengers were secured.
"You look like officer material to me, when the chance comes."

He hit the power switch; the scout lifted.

Lift took a bad slant; Tregare pulled a hard bias to get
straightened up. That done, he looked over to Deverel. "This
off-balance thing, with the dozer, pay it no mind. The rest of it,

running this crate, watch me and ask questions." But the man seemed to find no questions to ask.

Up crowding black sky with stars in it, Tregare drifted his unbalanced load across the Hills, then southeast toward his crater. Short of it by maybe twenty kilos he spotted an east-slope plateau that gave him an idea. An aux base, a home-office retreat apart from the jangle of activity when other ships arrived. Base One, with the crater as Base Two. It could work. . . .

To the north, a glimpse of the zigzag pass reminded him of something. "Hain, why I wanted you up here and nobody else, is I don't want the rest seeing some things from upstairs."

Slowly, the man said, "But you don't mind if I see."

"Why should I? You trusted *me*, didn't you?"

The crater floor wasn't all that level, but at the southeast part Bran found a flattish spot and set down. When the tilt subsided, he could exhale without making noise.

With everybody up, then, they moved the dozer and other gear groundside. Once the talus slope was dozed down and leveled, the prefab huts were erected near the crater's west wall. Shouting over the dozer's roar, Tregare told Mac, "Give the site as much clear space as you can manage, level, and stomped down hard with the treads. Get the middle really firm; the edges aren't so critical." Because ships, landing, needed more solidity than buildings did. And to move things faster, he had to cut every corner he could find.

Near the scout was a gap in the crater wall; the floor sloped off into a gully. Ideal place for fuel tanks; next time he'd bring explosives to blast the shape of hole he needed, and cross-filament synthetics for his tank liners.

So far, so good. On a portable talkset he twiddled frequencies until he hit the right skip to bounce above the Big Hills and connect him with *Inconnu*, where Gonnelson reported all was well. To Mac, Bran said, "This HF stuff may take some fiddling. Up freqs daytimes, down 'em at night is the rule." He shrugged. "Pretty soon I'll bring in stuff that uses scatter, and can ignore skip. But this week, here's what we've got."

Then, making sure his instructions were clear, Tregare left his three ratings and two employees, and took the two extras back aboard the scout, heading for *Inconnu*.

Without the dozer's lopside weight, lift-off went better.

* * *

Back aboard ship, after scrubbing up, Bran checked tapes of incoming calls. He found an invitation from Rasmussen, captain of *NonStop*, to bring a colleague or two ". . . and join me for dinner here. I don't quite understand your proposal but we can discuss it. Answer at your convenience."

On screen the man was wedge-faced, dark-haired, pleasant of voice, and sounded reasonable. So, checking his chrono, Tregare called in an acceptance and rounded up Jargy Hoad to go with him. They arrived in good time.

Rasmussen was a good host and *NonStop*'s galley had at least one superb chef, but no deal was closed. ". . . like your plan, Tregare. Getting a fleet together, looking to take the fight to UET. But just now I have other commitments."

Bran shook his head. "*Later*, I'm talking about." And explained the loose data network operating on the Long View, to set the rendezvous of allies here on Number One. Hoping his arsenal setup on New Hope was in gear by now, he said, "For your help on the mission, I arm your ship for free." He leaned forward. "On that mission, though, I don't share command. So what do you say?"

Rasmussen liked it but couldn't promise anything. "If I *can* make your rendezvous, I'm with you." So as Bran and Jargy left *NonStop*, everybody shook hands, and Tregare had to settle for that. Better than nothing, he supposed. . . .

Up in Control on *Inconnu*, Bran found messages waiting. The first of any importance was from Cade Moaker on *Cut Loose Charlie*. "You said you could use some people. If you have a Hat berth open, my Second's looking for one. Decided she's not ready, just yet, to settle down groundside on Fair Ball."

Since he needed a replacement for Druffel, Tregare called back, and soon Moaker was onscreen. Beside him stood a young woman. "Ola Stannert," Moaker said. "Captain Tregare."

Nodding greetings, Bran looked at her: medium height, slim, bio-age in the twenties. Good cheekbones, generous mouth, eye-color probably distorted by the circuit. Straight blond hair that fell behind her shoulders, so he couldn't tell the length of it. She said, in a low-pitched voice that still carried well, "I think I'd like being on an armed ship."

Within five minutes the deal was made: given Moaker's recommendation, Tregare felt no need to ask a lot of questions. Her shares in *Charlie* bought her in as Third Hat and left her a surplus; she didn't seem to mind having to drop one grade. Her cheek bore no tattoo, so she wasn't a Slaughterhouse graduate—not in officer grade, anyway. These things ascertained, Tregare said, "Move in when you're cleared with *Charlie*. And in advance, welcome aboard."

"Thank you, captain. A day or two, I expect." He cut the circuit.

"I'm glad you filled that Third slot. I'd been wondering."

Tregare looked around. "Hi, Jargy. Didn't hear you come in. Hang on a sec, while I check the rest of the input backlog, and I'll buy you a drink."

When the screen lit again, the pictured woman looked familiar but he couldn't place her. Fairly tall, he thought, if she'd been standing. Strong features, highlighted by dark eyes under challenging brows. Midnight hair, bulked out with the waviness that indicated frequent braiding. Age? Not too far off his own, likely.

The voice resonated. "This is Sparline Moray and I want to talk with Captain Bran Tregare. I have good reason; there are things to be said, and we are, after all—um, somewhat related. I'll accept a return call, any hour, at Hulzein Lodge."

Tregare's face went hot. To his comm-tech he said, "Tell Hulzein Lodge there'll be no return call." *So they'd sicced his sister on him, had they?* He stood; the rest of the incomings could wait. "Come on, Jargy. The drink. My digs." Damn, though—with the puppy fat gone, Sparline was one striking woman.

Down in quarters, drinks poured, Jargy said, "Tregare, you never mentioned being Hulzein-related. I know a little about those people, and—"

Tregare used sipping-time to think how to put it. "You heard what she said: somewhat related. But not closely." *Not now, anyway.* "And that's how I intend to keep it." Satisfied or not, Hoad pushed the matter no more.

Al Druffel, his ship-shares paid off fairly, left the ship on crutches; Tregare noted that the young ex-officer made sure to tip the unrated crew members who carried his gear. Maybe Number One's medics could fix the leg; Bran hoped so.

Back in quarters he found the intercom chiming. "Some-body here to see you, captain, from *Stump Farm*. It's not their skipper."

"Yeah?" He yawned. "Show'm up here, in five minutes. Whoever does that, bring me a snack, too. The galley knows what I want. If our visitor's hungry, double it."

The crewman escorting *Stump Farm's* envoy brought a single-sized snack but double coffee, so Bran poured for two but ate for one. "Talk in a few minutes. Okay?" As he ate, he looked at the woman.

Average height, a little sturdy, with a pleasant face under short curly dark hair. Age youngish, but grown-up, not a kid. Done eating, he poured them both more coffee. "Krieg Elman send you? About time our two ships talked some."

She shook her head. "He doesn't know I'm here. He's crazy. I want off that ship! I can't get my First Hat shares out of Elman, but if I have to, I'll ride unrated. Because I don't want to be on *Stump Farm* when that maniac blows the Drive."

Changing his mind about four times in five seconds, Tregare said, "You know who I am. Now what's *your* name?"

Leanne Prestor. First Hat since Escape, which no officers had survived; Elman had held Chief's rating. "Oh, he can handle the ship all right, but he thinks everybody's out to get him." A shaky laugh. "Not just UET, which *is*, of course. Any other Escaped ship, anyone groundside—even here, on a Hidden World. Everybody wants his ship; that's his obsession. He doesn't trust any of us, his own people. And his standard reaction is, seeing threats that aren't there, is to start yelling that he's going to blow the Drive." She shuddered. "And one of these days he'll forget he's bluffing, and really do it."

Tregare thought. No Brooks Marrigan here, so wedded to *Spiral Nebula* that he'd take it out in obviously unsafe condition, but unable to defy Tregare's threat to blow *Nebula* apart, rather than let Marrigan lose it in space for lack of repairs. Bitter as hell about his own helplessness in the face of Tregare's ultimatum, Marrigan had sold off, so now Derek Limmer had a refurbished ship, *Lefthand Thread*, and Tregare had an ally. Back on Freedom's Ring, that hassle had been.

This mess, though, was different. *Damn!* All four ships were grounded close together. If Elman did go apecrap he'd take out the whole lot.

Several ideas came and went, then one stuck. Tregare said,

"Prestor? You leave anything you really need, on *Stump Farm*?"

"No. If I went back, I probably couldn't get off again. Captain—do I have a ride on here?"

"Sure. No Hat berths open, though. Will a Chief's rating do you?"

Her relief was evident, but Tregare had no time to listen to thanks. "Then let me figure this." He had separate scramble codes set up with each ship so he didn't need to warn Rasmussen or Moaker. Calling Control he got a call put through to *Stump Farm*.

"Bran Tregare for *Inconnu*, to Captain Krieg Elman. Listen quick; no need for answer, and maybe no time, either." He gave Prestor a wink. "Elman, hear me! We all have to lift off fast. I can't for a few minutes so I may get caught; I hope you can go right away. Because there's UET ships coming in. And you know what that means.

"Get your ass upstairs fast, Elman! And good luck."

Less than fifteen minutes later, *Stump Farm* lifted. Then everything went to hell. Because Port Admin announced that a ship *was* coming in. No names, no ident, just the fact. Tregare hauled Prestor up to Control with him and aimed an aux screen topside, waiting. The action didn't take long.

Shaking his head, wondering just how bad a person's luck could get, for a while he hardly noticed Leanne Prestor's queries. When he did notice, he told her, "I don't know who the hell that was, coming in, but now it doesn't matter much. Because whoever it might have been, your Krieg Elman took care of it. He rammed.

"And blew *both* Drives."

3. Bases
Loaded

Being depressed, Tregare decided, really got him down. He alternated between guilt and anger, and was comfortable with neither. Dammit, was it *his* fault for taking Prestor's warnings seriously and spooking Elman to lift scared? He couldn't have known that there'd be an incoming ship to trigger the man's paranoia.

And yet, if he hadn't been so quick to make his smart move, maybe two shipsful of people wouldn't be plasma, now.

So when Deverel called to say the crater site was leveled and ready for more equipment, Tregare welcomed the distraction; he went out and bought two aircars. He left one for Gonnelson to test-drive; the other, he'd wring out himself to find out if that zigzag pass would really work. Because if it did, the project could move a lot faster.

And if the pass turned out to be a trap he couldn't handle, maybe he deserved it. But that was no conscious part of Bran's thinking as he headed north, then across the first Hills range well clear of Hulzein Lodge, and north again.

In the way his blood pulsed, he felt the challenge ahead.

The giant axe-cut looked no less awesome than before. Flying past it for a quick preparatory scan, he caught whipsaw from turbulent air. He circled away, then cut in, pointing directly at the gap. Climbing, he gunned the car hard.

At first he thought he had the handle, but once between the towering walls his car was caught by gusts that lifted and dropped him, threw him to the side and nearly into one jagged scarp. He swung the car's nose down and away, hit full power and pointed for the most room he had, up ahead. Pulling for height, hoping the car could take the stress.

It shuddered like coming apart, but then he was past the turbulence. Now he needed altitude; he pushed for it and got it.

But ahead—when suddenly he saw only a wall there, he gave it what time he could afford and then swung hard left; at both sides he missed death by not very much. The abrupt swing right he was ready for, and made with no real difficulty. Then he concentrated on keeping proper distance from the rising ground below and cleared the summit easily. After that, down the Big Hills' eastern slope, he could coast and enjoy it.

But two things were for sure. One, for saving a lot of time and fuel, this pass was the edge he needed. And second, anybody who got through it the first time needed some luck.

At the crater, progress was good. The floor was reasonably level, the prefabs set up around the edges, and all loose gear stowed away, out of the weather. Tregare congratulated everyone, and set them to gathering their duffel for a ride back to town. Mainly he didn't want to try the pass in less than full daylight, but no point in worrying people, so he didn't say so— he just rushed them some.

Westbound was easier because the wind was on his side. He had more altitude, up where the zigzag notch was wider. It still made a hairy passage, but nothing like the first time. When he could, Bran sneaked glances at his passengers. Deverel, narrow-eyed, tried to watch terrain, instruments, and controls, all at once. The two lesser ratings looked to be trying to decide whether to be scared or not. White-knuckled, Mac likely didn't know his face held a fighting grin. Aguinaldo's smile showed only bliss. "Nice," he said, as the car shot past turbulence and turned, high over flattish lowland, toward the Port.

Visibly, MacDougall forced himself to relax. "You did that

well. I'm good with aircars, but I'm not sure my coordination's still fast enough for that run."

"Mine is," said Pete.

Mac turned on him. "Maybe if *I'd* just smoked three drugsticks, I'd think the same of myself."

The lazy smile didn't change. "Sure, I like the sticks. But not when it counts. I didn't say I'd want to try it *now*."

Avoiding the western ridge, Tregare skirted its northern end for a straight course to the Port, and dropped Mac and Pete off at their business. "When the next load's ready, in a day or two, I'll call you." Then he made the short hop to his ship.

Boarding *Inconnu*, Tregare and Deverel hit the galley for coffee, and Bran got filled in on the fine points of how the work had gone. Then Deverel said, "Something puzzles me. Going over there, you didn't want the others to see anything. Coming back, though—"

"Why'd I change my mind? Didn't realize I had. Didn't think about it at all." But why? Then he knew. "I ran into a true paranoid. Fella used to be named Krieg Elman. And must have decided I don't want to be one."

Then they discussed further details of the new base.

Ola Stannert was aboard and in Third's quarters. Tregare put her on a split watch, half with Jargy to teach her the ship, and half with Gonnelson so she'd learn how to communicate with Gonnelson. She learned fast; Bran was gratified.

The blond hair, he noticed, reached in full mass to well below her shoulders. Tregare found her attractive, but he was a little late; Jargy Hoad already had the inside track.

Cordially, but without naming his destination, Rasmussen made his farewells and lifted *NonStop*. Forty minutes later he made an urgent call to *Inconnu*. Bran ran upship, hotfoot, and took the comm. "Tregare here."

Screen showed Rasmussen standing by his own screen, which gave an outside view: the dark of space dotted not only with stars but with moving objects, dimly seen. ". . . debris, Tregare, from *Stump Farm* and the ship Elman rammed. I can't afford to slow down, collect any of this stuff and land it. But maybe one of your scoutships—" He gave the figures: coordinates and approximate drift factor. "In case you want to check it out, and see who it was that Elman wiped off the books."

And it's my fault. "Yeah, I'll do that. Thanks, Rasmussen. And again, good landings to you."

Signing off, Tregare turned to Jargy, who had the watch. The first half, it was now, before Stannert was to join him. Well, change of sked: "Tell the Third she's taking Gonnelson's watch. All of it, by herself. No problem, I think. Okay?"

"Sure, Bran. Care to say why, though?"

"What you heard. I'm taking the aboard-ship scout upstairs. And try to pick up enough scraps to figure out who I killed, when I sent Krieg Elman off with his head up his tail."

Only Tregare would be walking space, but Gonnelson needed a suit, too. Because if they salvaged something too big for the scout's airlock, they might have to hang it half-outside. Tregare wasn't planning to ride an open lock when they plowed air, so to get him inside they'd have to dump the scout's own air. He didn't say all that: just "We'll both need suits," and the First nodded.

Suited, then, both men clambered through the airlock, past hastily-loaded clutter of cables and fasteners; in case they needed to salvage something really big, Tregare could hang it on the outside. Figuring to waste fuel coming down slow, and preserve any outside cargo unburned.

When Gonnelson got them upstairs, Tregare navigating, the main drift of debris was easy to find, and to match vee in. Outside the lock Bran anchored the longest lifeline he had, took his best jump, and corrected with energy-gun bursts. He found plenty to salvage, and hooked each item to the cable with wraparounds. Some of the things surprised him, but now was no time to think about them. When he came to something too big to handle but too good to leave, he used the gun to cut it down to manageable size for outside transport. Then he hauled himself, and his collection, back to the scout.

Stowage and tying took him nearly an hour; going back inside, he was pooped. In the lock he signaled Gonnelson to dump the scout's air, and held on through the decompressive blast, then went on in and closed the lock behind him. Sitting, then, and strapped down, he said, "I wish I could have got more, but this is about all we can get through air, safe. So let's do it. But slow."

* * *

Groundside, because they couldn't possibly dock with *Inconnu*, they let air into the scout, climbed past the gathered litter, and boarded the ship. With his helmet off, Tregare gave orders. "A work crew to get all that salvage off the scout and spread out for looksee." Then he called Cade Moaker. "Got some things to show you. A turret projector, for starts. That ship Elman rammed was UET, and armed."

"I'll be over. Mind if I bring the Port Commissioner? I think he should be in on this."

"Sure." Tregare hadn't had occasion to meet Layne Ingalls, "the Commish," but had heard well of the man. Now, though, Bran needed to get out of his suit and wash away the stink a suit built so fast. Soon, no longer poisoning the air downwind, he went groundside again.

A little on the elderly side, Ingalls moved well. Shaking hands: "Glad to meet you, Tregare. Now what's all this stuff you've brought down, eh? I know about the two ships that smashed, upstairs, but—"

Cade Moaker interrupted. "The idea, Commissioner, is to determine the identity of the incoming ship."

Tregare's turn. "Right. And we have it." He showed the remains of the heterodyne projector, then a mostly-legible insigne on a scrap of hull plate. "The *Pizarro*, sir. An armed ship, as you can see. More important, though—" He held up readout sheets from his prize exhibit, the *Pizarro*'s core files, the item he'd burned loose from its surrounding framework. "The *Pizarro* took, in space, an Escaped Ship I'd never heard of before: *Swing Low*."

Ingalls cleared his throat. "I know the ship; it's been here."

Tregare frowned. "That's the problem." At Ingalls's startled look, he said, "*Swing Low* didn't quit easy; at capture, it was hopelessly crippled. The *Pizarro* spaced all survivors, then gutted the ship of information and supplies. And using that info, came here."

Ingalls went pale. "You mean—?"

"I mean you better hope the *Pizarro* had no chance to spill your coordinates to any other Uties, between killing that ship and coming here. And I mean, maybe your missile defenses can handle an armed ship's attack—but because Krieg Elman was insane enough to ram on suspicion, you don't have to find out. For a while, at least." *And my own guilt*—UET or no

UET, he'd still triggered a lot of death. But this way, he could live with it.

His handtalker pinged; from shipside, Jargy Hoad told him that some of Number One's oligarchs were coming to join the session.

"Yeah? Like who?"

"Varied folks. A Harkeen, which I think is a clan title, not the individual name. And somebody from something called the No Name Cooperative, carrying two swords I don't see how anyone could swing, so let's hope they're ceremonial. And a tall gent named Hawkman Moray, from Hulzein Lodge, and—"

Forcing himself, Bran unfroze. "Jargy! Get down here right away, and take over. I'll come up and do your watch." He cut circuit, gave Moaker and Ingalls quick goodbyes without explanation, and headed for the ship. *That was close.*

Upship in Control, Bran put an aux screen viewer on the groundside confab. Jargy had it in hand okay. Dammit, why couldn't his family leave him alone? They'd done it before. . . .

As the new delegation, all five of them, joined the group below, Tregare listened to the signal from Jargy's talkset. The No Name fellow, with the absurd swords, was trying to run things. But Hawkman Moray's great height gave him a psychological edge; with a few quiet words he got the session on track, so Commissioner Ingalls could report the new information.

At the end, Hawkman said, "How long since *Swing Low* was here? Five years?"

"Six, maybe," said Ingalls. "I can look it up."

Running through the t/t calculations, Tregare watched Jargy work his own hand-calc before Hoad said, "The *Pizarro* had to catch *Swing Low* not more than two-point-six lightyears out." He cut through attempted interruptions. "So unless, on the way here, the *Pizarro* passed another UET ship within talk range, UET has no word of you. The odds are good. And—" Jargy grinned. "Even if they did, it'd be twenty years before UET could get here in any real force."

"We have to think ahead!" A nasal voice, Alsen Bleeker's. "We need an armed ship, for defense. Why not this one, right here?"

"No," said Hawkman Moray. "I—I used to know its captain. You won't be hiring that man to sit guard on a mudball."

Too right, Hawkman! Tregare punched Jargy's beeper and told the man what to say, then listened. "While we're here, you can count on *Inconnu's* help if you need it. But when we leave, that's up to the captain."

Bleeker and Big Swords tried to make a fuss. The Commish merely shrugged. Hawkman, looking up at the ship, nodded. *He still knows me. Too bad it can't help.*

Next day, wanting to expedite delivery of some supplies, Tregare rented one of Keri Freling's groundcars and drove across One Point One to the Harkeen warehouse complex. He parked near the office entrance, went inside, and found that business face-to-face went faster than over a phone. He dealt with a chubby man, Harkeen by name as well as by affiliation, and soon cleared the paperwork and saw the first consignments loaded and headed for the Port.

So he shook hands, thanked Neyford Harkeen, and went outside. Beside his groundcar stood a tall, bulky young man, scowling and dark-browed. Tregare veered to walk around and past him, but the youth grabbed Bran's arm. "Just a minute, you!"

Tregare restrained his first impulse and made no move. "Yes?"

"Your damned groundcar. That's where *I* park."

Three adjacent spaces were empty; Bran couldn't see what the problem was. "There wasn't any sign up. Sorry," and he waited for this lout to let go of him.

But the left hand came to clench on Tregare's jacket while the right, releasing his arm, made a ham-sized fist and drew back. The hell with it—Tregare took two fingers of the grabbing hand in each of his own, stepped back abruptly, and leaned down. A moment he stood, his would-be assailant kneeling and howling; then one more tug put the youth's face in the dirt.

When the other got up, Bran saw no intent of further attack. He said, "Maybe you did own a grievance. But you got too quick with your hands."

"I'll get you for this! I'll see you dead! My family—" The hulking boy spat, but the drops fell short. He turned, cradling the injured hand in the other, and limped away.

From behind Tregare, Neyford Harkeen said, "No idle threat, I'm afraid. Though with due precaution you should be relatively safe from the dal Nardos."

"Who?" Neyford repeated the name. "They're big around here?"

"On the way to being. Not nice people, I'm afraid. No one says so publicly, but the dal Nardos progress largely by extortion and assassination."

"And nobody does anything about it?"

Harkeen shrugged. "Some try; they turn up dead, and by coincidence their heirs are named dal Nardo. You see, there's no overall organization here. Oligarchs work independently, and—"

Tregare nodded. "Feudalism. But you *could* gang up."

"Or hire outside help. Captain Tregare—"

"No. People have to clean up their own mess."

"It might be yours, too. If young Stagon complains to his father—"

"He's the honcho?" Harkeen nodded. "Look—you said we got nothing to worry about. Make up your mind!"

Neyford Harkeen waffled. Yes, but. If. Maybe. But still. So they went back inside, and Harkeen put a call through to dal Nardo HQ. When Lestrad dal Nardo came on circuit, Tregare told him what happened outside; carefully, he made sure he had all the details right. Dal Nardo answered, "That's not the way my son reports it. You've made yourself fair game, captain—you and all your people. Guard yourself, if you can."

Allowing himself no laughter, Tregare said, "Looking at an armed ship and two armed scouts, you say a stupid thing like that? *Listen*, now—" And he detailed what could happen to any or all dal Nardo holdings if that clan bothered Bran Tregare enough to notice. Adding: "Stomping overgrown kids isn't my line, but that one of yours is bigger than I am, and needs some manners."

He cut the circuit and turned to Harkeen, who didn't seem to realize his mouth was open. "What you do with people like that," said Tregare, "you explain why they're not going to mess with you."

Then he left. Going back to the ship, his car was followed by two larger ones, the armored kind. He guessed he knew whose they were, but all they did was follow. And if Lestrad dal Nardo wanted to *look* tough, who cared?

* * *

The scout was loaded, with the makings of three prefabs lashed to the outside. Mac and Pete brought a crate of explosives and the gadgetry needed to use the stuff. This time Bran was ferrying a bigger work crew, with Deverel again in charge. And what with the extra huts, Anse Kenekke was also in the group.

At midafternoon Tregare set the scout down in the crater he thought of as Base Two, though his plateau above as yet bore no trace of the projected Base One. Unloading and planning took longer than he expected, especially laying out the fuel tank sites. So instead of flying and landing in dark, Tregare slept over. The scout's bunks were hardly luxurious, but comfortable enough.

Back at *Inconnu* next morning, Bran got bad news from the Commish: one of Mallory's Drive techs had died in a Port-area bar fight. Tregare's first thought was that it could be a dal Nardo move, but Ingalls said the other fighter was a loner, fresh in from hunting bushstompers south of the Slab Jumbles. "Just an ordinary fight, over a woman who wanted no part of either of them."

So when Ingalls asked if Tregare wanted to add punitive charges to the Port's court docket, Bran shook his head. "My crewman and your hunter, they were both unlucky." Feeling old and tired, he added, "It's the Port's case; I'm out of it."

Lestrad dal Nardo might be backed off, but he hadn't quit. Everywhere Bran went in One Point One—arranging for supplies to be loaded in the ship and scouts—he was followed. Blatantly. After a time he got tired of it. He waited his best chance, though; in the area of small shops and food booths one day, he noticed he had only one bloodhound, a hulking bruiser behaving like the Menace on Tri-V. All right. Tregare picked his spot, turned a corner quickly, and stood waiting.

When the man, hurrying to catch up, came around the building's corner to see Bran facing him, he stopped short. "You following me, or going someplace?"

"I—going someplace. What'd you think?"

"Then go there. Me, I think I'll hang around a while."

No fast thinker, this one. "You can't tell me what to do."

"Wrong. I just did. Move it."

"Let's see you *make* me move." The man pulled out a knife,

and pointed it—weaving in what he probably thought was a pro stance—at Bran. "I'm staying, smart guy."

Enough of this crap! As he spoke, Tregare took the knife away and heard elbow ligaments rip loose. Slapping the empty hand up against an exposed corner-beam, he drove the blade through flesh and deeply into wood.

"Yeah. Stay right here. Long as you want." He walked away, not heeding the man's suddenly-shrill cursing. Bystanders gawked, but no one interfered.

Apparently the lesson took; after that incident, Bran spotted no more followers.

One more time Tregare took the scout across the Hills, to check that his fuel tanks were ready for filling and to have landing circles marked on the crater's leveled floor. Those matters seen to, he lifted *Inconnu* and brought that ship to his developing Base Two. Gonnelson followed in one scout, Jargy Hoad in the other.

In a couple of days the camp shook down into an operative routine; Bran felt the base was coming along well. When the major projects were on track he went upslope in one of the aircars he'd brought along in the ship's starboard scout bay, to have a closer look at his cliffside plateau. Coming in over the lower dropoff he taxied through sparse, grasslike ground cover, almost to the westward-rising cliff. And got out, and walked around.

The place wouldn't need much bulldozing, just some minor leveling of the inevitable talus slope, for building foundations. He stood, maybe fifty meters out from that slope, and looked eastward. Ahead and to his right the ground hummocked a little, but mostly the shelf made a gentle slope. All right—storage buildings close under the cliff, and a headquarters cabin—where to put that? Some of the oligarchs' infighting included bombing from aircars, and the zigzag pass wouldn't be his personal monopoly forever. Turning, he looked up, estimating the angle to the cliff's edge. And laughed. Right where he stood, a car couldn't drop over and land a bomb on him, without slowing enough to be dead meat for ground fire. Some smallish missiles . . .

He piled loose rocks to mark the spot, and took the aircar back to Base Two.

* * *

With one storage tank complete and secured, Tregare pumped much of *Inconnu*'s fuel into it and took the ship across the Hills for a refill. "I'd like to stock up for half a dozen ships," he told Jargy when they were back again, "but even watching for price dips, I can't afford it."

"You shouldn't need to. Any ally who meets rendezvous in shape to join up can probably buy its own."

"I know," said Bran. "I just want to make sure."

Jargy cuffed Tregare's shoulder. "You worry too much."

With the walking hoist, MacDougall was pulling the dozer up the side of one scout, to ride outside. When everything was cinched down properly, Bran got the work crew aboard and lifted to the plateau. Gonnelson, with Ola Stannert to talk for him, could handle things for a while at Base Two.

The bulldozing went fast; so did erection of storage buildings, mostly prefab but some timber-framed. Number One's trees, taken from the plateau's south end where cliff eased into a gentler slope, gave good lumber. Using the energy gun from his disabled power suit, clamping it under an improvised chute, Tregare shaped square timbers by having the cut logs pushed through. "And everybody keep your hands on *this* side, so's you don't lose any."

He wanted the cabin to be a mini-fortress, so it took longer. Thick walls and roof of solid wood, metal-reinforced. Windows with no ground-level look-in from outside—the one facing uphill looked at blank cliff face. Under the building an escape hole dropped to a tunnel ending in a ravine to the south, and partway along that tunnel was an upward egress to a brushy hummock. "I'll make a pillbox there. Use it to cover the front entrance."

Jargy shook his head. "To defend against *what*?"

"I don't know. *Anything*, I guess." But after two more supply trips to the crater and one to the Port, Tregare figured his little Base One to be fairly well secured. Especially with the small defense missiles he'd bribed out of Alsen Bleeker's warehouse without that gentleman's knowledge; those were now installed at the plateau's outer edge, ready for hookup.

Some of the small detail was a bother. Time wouldn't allow bringing and burying enough pipe to get sewage wastes off the plateau completely. So, since the place would have to depend on a water table rather near the surface, Tregare settled for building a fancy outhouse and heat-fusing the pit to keep it sealed; three times, he had to recharge the energy gun.

Once the cabin's double-plastic windows were in, he took the work crew down to Base Two and began loading the scout with some appliances and fittings he needed, plus a fair amount of food and drink. He was bringing his final load offship—no point in bothering the help with this little stuff— when Leanne Prestor said, "Captain? I'd like to talk with you."

He turned around to her. "That'd be fine, except right now I have some work to do, upslope. Later, maybe?"

"Why couldn't I go along? And help with the work?"

I don't need any help. But this woman was the only person who had recognized the danger of *Stump Farm*'s paranoid captain *and* had the initiative to get away; it might not hurt to get to know her better. So Tregare said, "If you can arrange leave off your watch in the next ten minutes, come along."

"Right." Sturdy legs pumping, she ran up *Inconnu*'s ramp. Tregare put his gear aboard the scout, went back to collect a few last-minute odds and ends, and returned to find Prestor waiting in the co-pilot's seat. "I'm covered for tonight's watch. If necessary, I can arrange for tomorrow's, too."

Tregare didn't let his brows rise in inquiry. "That's fine. But I expect we'll be back then." He warmed the scout's Drive and lifted. Flying to the plateau they didn't talk. Bran had some questions, but he figured they could wait.

Once landed, he and Prestor carried supplies and equipment, mostly to the cabin but some to the storage sheds. Then they got to work on the plumbing, so he could start the pump and fill the attic water tank. Next he hooked up to the kitchen facilities, and the folding tub in the bathroom. Prestor made a good helper; she understood instructions, and talked only to the point at hand. She didn't need to know that the tub could pivot to expose the trapdoor leading to his tunnel, so Tregare didn't tell her.

Under the west-rising cliff, sunset came early. Wiping sweat from his forehead, Bran said, "The rest of it can wait; let's call it a day. You getting hungry? I am."

"Why, yes." She pushed at the hair over her forehead; her own perspiration made it curlier than usual. "I hope you can cook, though. Even if I knew where things are, here, I'm not very good at it."

"No problem—there's frozen stew." He saw she didn't know which way to take the remark, so he said, "You watch, while I figure how this combustion stove works, and learn from my mistakes." Then she smiled, and wandered around the cabin as though trying to memorize it. There wasn't that much; one entered through the only door, at the right of the front wall, into a room that took up half the building. Its left front corner held a wooden bedframe with two bunk-sized mattresses, and now a pair of rolled-up sleeping bags. The cabin's rear half was kitchen and dining nook on the right side, bathroom on the left. Not a lot to keep in mind, but Tregare let her look all she wanted until the stew came to boil; then he gave chow call.

The slab-topped table he'd built himself; the chairs were cheap flimsies from One Point One. The stew was good, and the small cooler he'd brought along worked fast, so they had cold beer, too. When he piled the used utensils into it, the compact dishcleaner also worked. He hoped the water heater wasn't too slow, because a hot bath felt like a good idea.

First, though, seeing through a front window that day had begun to turn to twilight, he said, "Come on outside and see something." He went out, and she followed.

The way the cliff shadowed the plateau, no sunset was visible now. But looking eastward the two saw sunlight leaving the Big Hills' lower slopes, and shadow chasing that light out across the plain below, before the bright reflection shimmered on the horizon a moment and disappeared. Then, suddenly it seemed a lot darker.

Cooler, too. So indoors Tregare lit up the front room's combustion heater. As the place warmed, he checked at the sink and found the water hot. "Prestor? I haven't found the shower gear yet, but if you want firsts on tub dunks, go ahead."

He liked the smile she gave him. "Why, thank you." She entered the bathroom. Looking for something constructive to do, Bran settled for unrolling the sleeping bags and arranging them, each on its own mattress. Then he sat, thinking, for only a brief time until she came out, hair damp and face pink. "It's all yours, captain."

He took no great time at it, himself. And came out to find

Leanne Prestor lying at the far side of the two sleeping bags she'd zipped together to make only one.

Until now, he'd had no sexual thought. Slowly, he said, "You don't have to—I didn't intend anything."

Again she smiled. "I did."

"Why?" Yes. Why me? And why so fast? And was he ready, so soon, to deal again with someone's else's feelings? The physical part, sure. But still . . .

He waited, and she said, "Because you don't just dither, you *do* things and you know what you're doing." Now she frowned a little. "You're dangerous; I know that. But maybe that's part of it—like having a tiger that I know won't hurt me." Pause, then, "You wouldn't, would you?"

"No." But—*Erdis!* "Not on purpose, I wouldn't." He thought about it. "You got to realize, people don't always have the choice. But if you still—"

"I still. Come *on*."

For Tregare it had been a time, so sleep had to wait until they'd had "seconds," and next morning saw more activity before they arose.

The only eggs were freeze-dried; Bran served them scrambled. Along with toast and juice and coffee, he figured it made a damn good breakfast. Down to coffee, Leanne said, "I should tell it straight. Onship I'd *like* to move in with you, but I don't have to."

This one talks up fast. "You're ahead of me. Spell it."

She pouted cute, but Tregare waited for the words. "We're good here. On the ship, though . . ."

"On the ship, *what*?"

"Sometimes officers and ratings can roomie and sometimes not. On *Inconnu*, which way is it?"

"Well—" He stalled, partly because he hadn't really thought about it and partly because his instinct went against being rushed. Was this too soon? And distracting him further, a kind of buzzing started inside his head. No—not *in* his head—he was really hearing it. And now it built to thunder, and he knew—a ship was lifting, crossing above him while still plowing air. Not *Inconnu*; the direction was wrong. This ship was coming from the Port at One Point One. He hadn't known any were there now, but if one had landed from westward, the sound might not have been noticed here, with the Big Hills between to deflect it.

He started to sit back, to put his mind to Leanne's question, but from above the sounds changed. Not just the ship, its thunder softening with distance and climb into thinner air, but something approaching, now.

An aircar. No, more than one, and not far off. *How the hell did they get over here?* And then came the *ssisss* of a falling object and a clanging explosion too close not to jar things. Why, the bastards were bombing him!

There wasn't time for anything, so he didn't take it. "Get under the bed!" and he saw her go in that direction. All he wore was pants and socks; they'd have to do, as he realized the damn missile-control panel wasn't hooked up yet so he'd have to try to get to the scout. He was out the door and running, feeling the sharp rocks cutting at his feet, while he tried to think how to jigger the scout's control frequencies to launch some missiles. Once they were up, they'd seek heat and metal, but what the *hell* were his launch codes?

Sound and shadow passed above him; something hit his leg and hurt a lot; he heard the rattle that meant a whole batch of needle projectiles had hit the ground behind him. He didn't look at the leg—it was still working, so it could wait. Then he was up the ramp and into the scoutship.

For seconds that seemed longer, he paused. *The launch codes!* He was too hassled to be able to remember anything about them. He put the viewscreen on and saw two aircars circling; one dropped a bomb and all too soon the scout rocked to the blast.

Hell with it—if he waited, he was dead. So he hit the Drive switch and took the scout up cold. Well, not quite; it hadn't wholly cooled from its last flight. But still a risky move.

The scout made it, though. Tregare got off the ground alive. And went up past the two aircars and made a sharper turn than he really should have, and came down in one elegant S-curve that put his projector fire across both cars, blowing them into nothing much.

Then he landed, right about where the scout had sat before, and went back into the cabin.

* * *

She probably hadn't gone under the bed at all, for what good that might have done her. Leanne Prestor sat on that bed, drinking what looked like a cup of coffee. She said, "You want some?"

Wrung out all to hell, Tregare didn't appreciate anybody trying to show how nothing bothered. He took the cup. "Yeah, gimme that."

First she was silent, then she said, "I'm sorry. You're so damned competent; I was only trying to keep up a little. Tregare—what *did* happen? All I know is, there was a lot of shooting, and I was scared out of my skivvies."

Put that way, he could understand. "Me too. Two aircars with bombs and needleguns, it was. I don't know how they got here. I took the scout up and wiped them." He felt the blood on his leg. "Hey—take a look here? I guess I got hit some. Not too bad?"

"It doesn't seem so. The needle went straight through, nowhere near the bone. Where's your first-aid kit?" And when the wound was patched to Bran's satisfaction, she said, "You never did answer my question."

He was going to ask "Which one?" but then he remembered. And said, "I'd purely enjoy you moving in with me. Don't let anyone accuse you of trading on my rank, though. Which means, don't give 'em any excuse to."

She nodded. "Yes, of course. I won't cause trouble."

Not that he figured on any more attacks right away, but Tregare wanted those missiles in working order. Leanne asked why he had no such things down at Base Two and he explained that not only did *Inconnu* have its own missiles ". . . makes these here look like kids' firecrackers . . ." but also its projector turrets had traverse capability, which the scout's lacked.

She couldn't help him on the hookup, except with fetch-and-carry work; circuitry wasn't her specialty. But he found himself enjoying her company anyway; she seemed to know when it was okay to talk and when to shut up and let him think.

Originally he'd planned for manual launch control, with radar and sonic alarms to alert the operator. Now he decided to jigger that setup a little, adding the option of letting the alarms do launching automatically. "Not all at once," he said, explaining to himself as much as to Prestor. "Send up two, first.

When they blow, either on impact or burnout, if the target's still there, then another two fire. And so on."

This was one of the times for talking. She said, "So how do *you* come here and land in one piece?"

That answer he already knew. "The system's either on manual or automatic; I can switch it here or by a coded signal when I'm leaving or coming in." He made half a grin. "Just so nobody forgets the drill, is all."

There were a few more things he wanted to do before leaving. Most of them got done but some would have to wait for another time. At midafternoon he said, "Time to pack it in," and they put tools and apparatus in some sort of order and boarded the scout. When they were strapped in he called *Inconnu* and got Jargy Hoad.

"It's going well here, Tregare. How's it with you?"

"A little flap, nothing serious. Tell you later. Just wanted to say, have somebody cover Prestor's watch again tonight."

Hoad acknowledged; Tregare cut the circuit. As he waited for the Drive to warm up, Leanne said, "I could stand my watch."

"Not from One Point One you can't. That's where we're going."

When he lifted, Bran first cruised the downslope below his plateau. He saw some fragments of aircar wreckage but, he decided, nothing big enough to identify—even if he could have landed, or taken time to investigate on foot. So forget it . . .

He took the scout high, crossing the Big Hills, and tilted to get a good look at their overall contours in this area. He landed in the open space nearest the Port Admin building and said, "I'm going to talk with the Commish. Want to come along, or stay here?"

"I'm coming with you. Tregare, this is why you brought us here, isn't it? I certainly don't intend to miss it."

Tregare called the Commissioner, whose secretary said that Layne Ingalls was in conference but should be free in half an hour; could he call back? "Yeah, sure," and Bran confirmed his call codes and primary frequency for that purpose. Call closed, he turned to Leanne Prestor. "Dry work. We have some time to kill. Fix us drinks, maybe? Bourbon, ice, for me."

She said, "Half an hour? You know, we could—"

"Drinks. Please. Or I could fix 'em."

"Tregare—I'm not supposed to ask? Is that it?"

His hand slapped his seat's armrest. "Hell, no. Asking's okay; it's fine. Just, this time I have to say no. Two reasons. One is, I killed some people this morning and I'd kind of like to find out who they were, if I can. The other—well, in bed I don't like time restrictions. Now—"

But she was already moving. "Drinks coming up." When she handed him his, she said, "I like knowing the reasons for things."

Ingalls called back on schedule; a few minutes later Tregare introduced Chief Rating Prestor to the Commissioner and they all sat. "And what's on your mind?" Ingalls said.

All right. "What ship lifted off this morning, heading east?"

"Only one has departed all week. This morning, yes. That was Dominguez on *Buonatierra*."

"Damn! I wanted to meet that man." For a moment, Tregare forgot his present concerns. "Did he check the data grapevine, where we all leave word?"

"Yes, he took full computer readouts. But the man was in a hurry. Refueled, restocked, and left. Something about a rendezvous, though how you people can compute such things in the Long View—"

"Yeah. It's not easy." But right now was a shorter view. "Dominguez, though. You know if his cargo included any aircars?"

Ingalls nodded. "Yes. Two. And that's odd. Because they weren't packaged for stowing. In fact, when I saw them, not long before *Buonatierra* lifted, those cars were simply sitting just inside the cargo hatch, and the local pilots who delivered them seemed to be doing routine maintenance."

Tregare leaned forward. "Those pilots. They belong to anybody in particular? Some clan, some oligarch?"

"Mmm, no. They hire out. Not particularly savory characters, I might add. They work for—"

"The dal Nardos, maybe?"

"Sometimes. And the No Names. And last summer one of them did a month of chasing poachers off the fishing grounds that young Fennerabilis is trying to develop. More legitimate than most of their enterprises, that one. I'm just as glad they're

gone with Dominguez." *Not with Dominguez, but gone, yes.*
"Why—"

Tregare stood. After a moment, so did Prestor. Bran said,
"This morning a ship went over where I was and two aircars
came down bombing and shooting. Anybody wants to investigate, I can tell 'em where the pieces landed. How the
investigators get there, across the Big Hills, is their problem."

Briefly, Ingalls looked startled. Then he nodded. "Quite so.
I assume that if I asked your cooperation—?"

"You'd get it. But hardly anyone else would."

"Yes," Ola Stannert answered. "The floodlights are working."

"Good," said Tregare. "Expect us pretty quick now." He
lifted the scout, started toward the Big Hills and then swung
back. On his comm-panel he punched a call into the local
system for Layne Ingalls's office and got relayed to the
Commissioner's home. "Tregare here. I think I know which is
the dal Nardo estate"—he gave the coordinates he'd spotted
on the map—"but I want to be sure. Confirm?"

"Why, yes; that's correct. But, Tregare, you can't just—"

"I know, Ingalls. I'm not certain they hired the bombing—
just positive. And they didn't kill me, so I'll return the favor."

"What are you going to *do*?"

"Teach Lestrad dal Nardo something he can't learn any
younger."

Prestor was gasping and protesting but Tregare didn't have
time for it. He'd spotted the dal Nardo mansion, and drifted
toward it, while he talked with the Commish. Now he dropped
near to ground level; the scout tilted, its Drive raising hell
with the immediate landscape. All around the great house,
twice, he walked the small craft, turning the ornamental
grounds to pure chaos. Then he lifted the scout high and took
it across the Big Hills slowly. Because he figured he had some
talking to do.

He looked to Leanne. "What's your problem? You said you
liked me because I know what I'm doing, but when I do it you
get all shook up. You having second thoughts, maybe?"

Her head moved, not decisively. "But you—you just took
this scout and *smashed* somebody's property. I—"

"Not somebody's. Lestrad dal Nardo's. Case you didn't

notice, it's his people tried to bomb us out, at the cabin; nobody else here had reason to." He overrode her attempt to interrupt. "He's leaned on me before; I *told* him what would happen if he kept it up. He did, and I did. Any more questions?"

She had none, but he gave answers anyway. "It's close to time for lifting *Inconnu* off Number One. What I need here is almost done, and it's years before I—" No, he didn't have to tell her about the fleet he wanted, or when rendezvous could occur. "—before I come back here. What I do is, I use those years on fast time, *ships'* time—making contacts I need, and plainly raising hell with UET any chance I get. I don't waste that time sitting here and getting old." His right fist clenched. "I want UET scared, up to its neck in puke. So I have to go *hit* the bastards. And I can't leave some scorpion behind who thinks he can go eat eggs out of my nest when I'm not looking. You understand that?"

"Yes."

"Good." But another thought came. "From now on, when I do something, why don't you just figure I have a reason for it? And do the asking later."

Her smile came a little shaky. "Yes, I think I can do that."

The remaining twilight let him land, with no need for instrument work, alongside *Inconnu*. In that ship's galley, because he and Prestor hadn't eaten since leaving the cabin, he talked while he ate. "What I want to know, Jargy, is how they knew where I was."

"MacDougall. Aguinaldo." Gonnelson said it. "Their—"

Needing to swallow before talking, Tregare shook his head. "No. Mac and Pete wouldn't cross us."

Jargy Hoad said, "Their crew, he means. Moved back and forth a lot, in the other scout, to have days-off in town. So somebody got to one of them. More, maybe. Right?" Gonnelson nodded.

Tregare could see it but he didn't like it. "How soon can we dump most of the outsiders and do our own work?"

Hoad grinned. "Yesterday. Mac and Pete stay and three they vouch for. The rest are superfluous now, anyway."

"Yeah. Good, Jargy." Bran thought ahead. He needed talk with MacDougall and Aguinaldo, but tomorrow would do.

Right now, he turned to Prestor. "How long you need to get your stuff together?"

"Twenty minutes, maybe thirty."

"All right. About then, I'll come help."

As she left, Jargy Hoad said quietly, "You have a new roommate, Bran? Funny thing; I'm not at all surprised."

"Funnier still," said Bran Tregare. "*I* am."

Next day in his quarters he hosted Mac and Pete to lunch. His point was that when he took *Inconnu* off Number One, fairly soon now, he needed reliable caretaker service for both his bases. "And some missiles here, too, of course, with a control booth, and control capabilities for both places, from either one."

No problem on any of that; the big question was: "All right; now can you two arrange a setup to keep these bases in shape for me while I'm gone? Even if it's twenty or thirty years?"

Mac shook his head. "I can't handle something like that. The administrative part, sure. But the on-the-spot stuff—I'll be in town with no ship or scout for transport, and I don't intend to risk my neck in an aircar, as often as I'd need to, crossing that pass of yours."

Even without drugs, Pete Aguinaldo's smile was lazy. "That part's mine. Okay, Mac?" And the other nodded. "Then we have a deal."

There was more to it: contracts to be filed with the Port Commissioner's office, legal arrangements for the long term (privately, Tregare had little faith in those, but as a matter of form he negotiated and finally signed).

Then there was a certain amount of commerce back and forth across the Big Hills, until Bases One and Two were as complete as Bran could manage, and *Inconnu* primed to lift. The ship would run crowded, because he wanted supernumeraries just in case, after having to scrounge for troops to man Derek Limmer's ship.

Tregare enjoyed the ride when Pete Aguinaldo first took an aircar through the pass from the coastal side. The man eased in toward the "chimney" at medium speed and altitude; when the turbulence hit he went with it, mostly, letting it bounce him to the sides of the cut but not quite into disaster, and steadily increasing push to gain height. Bran had to admit that Aguinaldo was doing this with less effort than he had used.

And when the dogleg loomed, Pete swung the car at an angle well ahead of time, then hit max thrust to take an economical diagonal across that zigzag. Straightened out after the second turn, the car made its final climb easily. Tregare said, "I like how you did that. The dogleg. How'd you gauge it so well?"

"I noticed, before. On your right, just at the turn, there's a pile of white boulders. Maybe some aircar wreckage in it, too. Anyway, when I saw that coming up, I—well, it's like putting a groundcar into a sideways skid, and then pouring on the traction."

"I never got fancy with groundcars," Bran said. "Just ships and scouts. But the way you took that zigzag sure works fine."

"Going back should be easier."

When Pete left, after dining on *Inconnu*, Tregare considered his arrangements and found them good: the maintenance skeds for skeleton crews at both bases, the funding arrangements through the Port, with MacDougall working the investment side, on commission. As good as could be set up, he decided, when you have to go with absentee management. If only his plans didn't need so much *time* . . .

He was tired, needing sleep before morning lift-off from Number One, but he checked the comm for messages. Most, his watch officers had handled—but Stannert told him one was personal so he played the tape. It was Sparline, his sister, and his gut knotted so hard that for moments her words made no sense to him. Then, "*I* didn't leave you there, Bran! Peace take you, I was only twelve years old. I had no—"

He couldn't listen any more. Shaking his head, trying to dislodge its sudden ache, he said, "Stannert, tell them there'll be no answer." And more to himself than to her, "I *can't*. When they left me at the Slaughterhouse, that door closed. It stays that way." And how could he do this to Sparline? He *had* to, was all.

He said, "We lift at oh-six-hundred. For Target Place." *And about* time *we got this show on the road!*

4. Deuces
Wild

Ola Stannert had been Second Hat on Moaker's *Cut Loose Charlie*, so Bran figured to let her do the lift-off. But at nearly the last day, Chief Engineer Mallory came up and said, "Tregare, I'm getting too old for this deadly game you're into. I have some good years left and I'd like to spend them on this world; I've asked around, when we were over at One Point One, and I can do well here as a consultant. Will you buy me out?"

"Well, sure. Sorry to lose you, Mallory, but I see your point." It took some figuring but there were no real problems. For one thing, with Tregare leaving investment funds at the Port, Mallory didn't need his shares all paid off right now. So the two men shook hands, and Mallory and his belongings rode the scout's last trip to One Point One.

The trouble now, though, was that Ola Stannert couldn't always decipher Junior Lee Beauregard's accent, which he himself described as "mushmouth Southron." Redheaded, freckled Junior Lee was a competent Chief Engineer, but his speech patterns did take some getting used to. Tregare had learned to ignore the differences consciously, and listen to what Junior Lee *meant*. So Bran did the lift himself.

"Drive ready, Chief Engineer?"

46

"As ever will be, skipper."

"Then here we go." And whoever had tuned *Inconnu's* Drive, Mallory or Beauregard, the ship lifted on a rock-steady thrust.

Target Place itself wasn't all that desirable as a destination, but starting from Number One it lay not too far off a route that hit several Hidden Worlds without much zigzag, and passed within reasonable detour distance of some UET colonies. "In case we get the itch to check one of those out," said Tregare. "Just for instance, if we make a turn to bend around Franklin's Jump on the way to Target Place, we'd have our vee down enough to decel and raid if we wanted to."

"Would you want to?" Leanne asked. They were in quarters, and Tregare got the idea she wasn't paying much attention.

So he said, "Depends; we'll see." Then, looking at her, "Your mind's on something else. What is it?" It couldn't be sex, he thought, because they'd had that before dinner, and were still polishing off the coffee and wine, after.

She fooled him, though. "Bran? If I wanted to spend a night with somebody else, would that be all right?"

Jolted some, he said, "Somebody you have in mind?"

She shook her head. "Not really. But if I did, could I?"

He thought about it. "Sure you could. Right after you move out of here."

"But, Bran—!" She looked startled. "I didn't think you were possessive. Or monogamous, so to speak. And how many women have *you* roomed with, anyway?" He wasn't in a mood to count back; he waved the question away. "Well, at least you've never gone in for permanence. So why—?"

"Give me a minute." He had to think; he knew he had a reason but he didn't have it quite figured out. Then he nodded. "If I was Third Hat, Leanne, or Second, this wouldn't apply. You could do what you want and still be with me. But I'm captain, and that's different."

"I don't understand."

"So listen, and maybe you will. Captain's woman can change, leave to go with somebody else, that's okay—but she can't play around. It's—I guess it's a matter of dignity. Something silly like that." He looked closely at her. "You understand now?"

After a time, she nodded. "I think I do."

"And you'll go by my rules, on this?"

"Yes. Yes, I will, Tregare."

"That's good. Here, let me pour you some more coffee." But she couldn't let it go. She asked what he'd do if a woman—not her, especially, but any—broke those rules. He had no idea, but she wanted an answer. So finally, half seriously, he said, "I'd throw all her gear out the airlock, and let her new fella find her some clothes."

She smiled. "That's reasonable, I guess."

Inconnu built vee to the point where someone had to decide whether to bend course over past Franklin's Jump or head straight for Target Place. Tregare met with his Hats and took a vote: three wanted to scout the Jump and Gonnelson didn't care either way. So Bran sat shotgun, off to one side at a monitor position, while Ola Stannert fed vees and vectors into Tinhead and got back Drive coefficients she could call downship to Junior Lee. "And for each change, act on the count, Chief. Understood?"

"Purely shall, ma'am," and Stannert seemed to get his meaning.

Through the stages—swinging ship a little, easing accel, coasting, taking sights, swing some more, all of it—Tregare followed the action because he didn't know Ola Stannert's grade of skill yet and needed to check her work. So far, so good—his mind drifted to other concerns. . . .

Monogamous, Leanne had said. Well, was he, or not? In practice, he guessed he had been—in principle, he didn't know. But since he'd put that onto Leanne Prestor, then while they were together he'd do the same by her. Not that he'd had any other ideas.

"Complete, captain," Ola Stannert announced. "Course should put us past Franklin's Jump at the edge of detection range; vee roughly point-one c if no corrections are made. Confirmed?"

Startled back to now, he took a quick scan. "Seems like it. Any changes we need should be small. Good job, Stannert."

Running the ship crowded, Tregare found, seemed to cause a lot of small hassles. People got in each other's way, and tensions sometimes popped. Fights happened; accusations were made. Bran hadn't had to hold any kind of ship's court before; now it looked as if he needed to.

Well, *when in doubt, delegate!* Tregare didn't remember who'd told him that, or when, but it seemed like a good idea. So he said to Jargy Hoad, "Screening this crap, you're in charge. Set up a complaint desk—Ola Stannert running it, maybe. Prestor says she'll take it for a quarter-shift each day; see who else you can get."

Any time Jargy looked solemn, Bran Tregare got wary as to what the kicker was. Hoad said, "And what do *you* do?"

Bran sighed. "You know that, if you think a minute. The desk handles the easy ones, you interview the remaining bitchers and try to get them to settle out of court, or whatever. If they won't, *then* I hold Captain's Court and my verdict is peace-take-it *final*."

Jargy Hoad grinned. "Not bad, Bran. It might even work."

When he finally had to sit court, after stalling as long as he could, Tregare showed up with a bad mood and a lousy headache. After an uncharacteristic bout of indigestion the night before, he hadn't slept very well. The galley seemed too informal, so he held the session in his own quarters. And sat, sipping coffee with Leanne, while the people involved took their own sweet time getting there.

Finally Jargy came in with two men who glowered at each other a lot, and a red-haired woman who ignored both of them. The place was fairly well filled so they had a little trouble finding seats. Bran said, "This the first case?"

"That's right," said Jargy, and named the complainants. Gaines, the short, dark man, had come aboard at Shegler's Moon. Lanky, sandy-haired Martin was new on the ship, from Number One. Item at issue was that when Martin's wife, the redhead whose name was Sheila, left Martin for Gaines, she took along some jewelry. "Family heirlooms, he says," Hoad added. "They won't give 'em back."

Tregare cleared his throat. "You folks know you have the right to counsel, if you can find anybody knows how to do that?"

No counsel; they'd all speak for themselves. And did, at length, until Tregare wished he'd never heard of any of them. Finally he shook his head. "*I* can't say how the gift was given or who has rights to it now. So I'll tell you how it's going to be."

Everybody stayed quiet until Tregare said, "Spread the disputed goods out there in front of us. Then you have five minutes to decide who owns what." Leanne was whispering to him that he couldn't *do* that; he shushed her and could sense her outrage. "*Later*, dammit!"

Gaines spoke. "But that's just it; we haven't been able to agree. What if we still can't?"

"Don't worry about it," said Tregare. "Anything you can't agree who owns it, goes out the airlock."

Well, he'd read something like that when he was a kid, from a book of one of the old Christian sects. It worked for Suleiman. . . .

Now Martin was hollering. "I'm a citizen of Number One, and under that world's codes I claim the right of challenge!"

This was new to Bran; he leaned forward. "Challenge to what?"

"To a duel, of course," Martin said. "And to the death. Being the challenging party, it's my right to specify that."

Sheila whispered to Gaines, and that man spoke. "And as the challenged party I get to name the weapons!"

"Not on Number One you don't!" Martin again. "The referees decide which is the disadvantaged party, and that person—"

"Everybody shut up!" said Bran Tregare. "On this ship, I make the rules." He paused: don't be *too* bossy. "Let's hear your choices, for weapons."

Gaines wanted energy guns. Martin preferred the needle-throwers. Bran shook his head. "Neither of those. Not on shipboard. You want to cut through a bulkhead and wreck circuitry in there? Or bounce those needles around the audience?" Before they could answer, he had his solution. In early North American history there had been a frontiersman named Bowie. . . .

". . . so what we do, you see, is tie your left wrists together and then give you knives to use with your right hands. Unless one of you is left-handed, in which case that'll be your knife hand. Now whether you want this with clothes or without 'em—" Then Martin and Gaines and Sheila were all yelling quite a lot, and Jargy Hoad was trying not to laugh.

The settlement was, Martin got about two-thirds of his jewelry back, and everybody promised to leave everybody else alone.

* * *

"You really know how to pin people into a corner, don't you?" Bran and Prestor were alone in quarters now, and he could see she wanted to argue some more, hours after the "court" was done.

He shrugged. "You saw how it was. You got a better idea?"

Pausing, she said, "I—right *now*, I don't have an easy answer. But what you did was sheer barbarism. There has to be something better, and I—"

"Barbarism, yeah." He didn't want to get angry but he was, anyway. "Now look. Everything I have, Prestor, including my life, I got the hard way. At the Slaughterhouse, riding with the Butcher, and taking this ship. So now don't try to tell me how to handle it."

Her eyes teared and she turned away. Before bed there was no more talk, and in bed, no contact. Tregare didn't like what was happening between them but he didn't know what to do about it. He got up and had a drink and smoked one of his infrequent cigars; none of it helped much but he did feel a little better. Maybe . . .

Next evening they made it up, more or less; at least he screwed his brains out, for what that was worth. And he did like Leanne Prestor, and in many ways respected her. But in some others he had to think her brain was half cornflakes. So what he did was try to keep their talk where she made sense. And mostly it worked.

Going in toward Franklin's Jump, Tregare watched Gonnelson bring *Inconnu*'s vee down to the point that gave all the options: slow and land, up the vee and leave, or anything in between. The ship's beacon was turned off and approach was at the far end of detection range from the planet; coasting, *Inconnu* wouldn't look like much of anything from groundside.

So they coasted, and time passed, and Tregare tried to find something to help him decide what to do here.

And then they saw a ship lifting from Franklin's Jump. Lifting like a real bat.

"What's its course?" Tregare asked, and the comm tech said it looked to be heading not far off their own. Figures for vee and accel first varied and then came clearer. Tregare said, "Gonnelson, let's go after that ship. I want it."

* * *

Surprisingly, the chase wasn't easy; initial course divergence cut the hell out of *Inconnu's* velocity advantage. By the time Bran had his ship chasing on-line he'd lost overhaul capability. For now, anyway. The other ship was gaining distance, it had the edge in vee, and accel was about even. When Tregare asked Tinhead for the third derivative of distance with respect to time, it came out as near to zero as made no difference.

So the way things were, he wasn't going to catch up. "Damn all!" he said. "On accel, we should have the edge. That ship's not armed, and UET always arms the ships that turn up with the best Drive coefficients." Because, mass-production or not, some Drives simply wound up with more oof than others did.

"Loading," said Gonnelson, and suddenly Bran knew what his First Hat meant. *Inconnu* was hauling close to max load; if the ship ahead was running light, even a considerably less powerful Drive could give it an advantage in boost.

"Yeah, right," and he called the Drive room. "Beauregard? We need some more push."

There was a pause, then Junior Lee said, "Cap'n, you got you all the Drive they is."

Tregare scanned his instruments and spotted something. "At this level of excitation, you're right. But we still have safety margin on the exciter. Junior Lee, run that thing up to redline!"

"Redline? For certain sure, you want that?"

Curbing an impulse to sarcasm, Bran said, "Yes, Chief. Do it."

The third-derivative indicator got off the zero pin. *Inconnu's* accel grew; its vee approached and then surpassed that of its quarry, and that ship's lead in distance decreased. Instruments showed the Drive working near its limits—but not, Tregare hoped, too close to the edge. Accel leveled; third derivative hit zero again. But second derivative was on his side now; *Inconnu* was gaining. He queried Tinhead some more. Catching up would be futile if he simply flashed past the ship ahead; he had to match vees so that no matter how fast they were going, they'd be nearly at rest with respect to each other. Well, he knew how to extract those parameters, and after a while he got them. And put them on the auxiliary display board for Gonnelson and succeeding watch officers.

Tinhead set the forced rendezvous at ten hours minimum. "Gonnelson, I need a snack and some sleep. Carry on."

The man nodded, and Tregare left Control.

Back to quarters after eating, Bran found Leanne in bed but awake, reading. She said, "Will you catch that ship, do you think?"

"I'm working on it."

"And then what?"

Distracted, he shook his head. "Take it, if I can. Bring it over to the Escaped side. Install my own cadre, with an alliance agreement for when I get my fleet together. You know that."

"I know you think it can be done. And I hope you're right."

"Then why ask?"

"It's the details I was wondering about."

Without volition, he laughed. "Those, I haven't figured yet." Thinking about them, though, had him strung out too tight for anything more than a little cuddling then, before sleep.

He woke feeling better, knowing his plans in rough if not in fine. In the galley he said "Light and quick," ate that way, and went up to control.

Jargy Hoad, on watch, said, "We have their beacon. It's the *Peron*, and they're headed for Stronghold. I don't know who's commanding; we're not in talk range yet."

"How about our beacon?"

"By it we're still the *Tamurlaine*. Is that how you want it?"

Bran nodded. "For starters. Until we're up close, anyway."

And *Inconnu* was closing. Tregare watched as Jargy eased the accel back slowly, working toward a least-time rendezvous. When the two ships came first into talk range and then into firing distance, Bran opened his ship-to-ship circuits. Voice only, at first. "Hello, the *Peron*. The armed ship *Tamurlaine* here, Bran Tregare commanding. As authorized by the Presiding Committee I direct you to cut Drive for rendezvous and boarding. Will your captain acknowledge, please?"

No answer, so he repeated it, then added, "What's wrong with you people? You know the standing orders. Either you respond and comply or we are compelled to fire on you. So answer me!"

The voice that came, then, sounded breathless. "Sorry, sir. The captain's not available just now. We're having some trouble on here." Tregare saw the *Peron's* Drive nodes flicker and their field die, and Jargy make moves to match the change. "If you'll give us a little time—"

Tregare quit listening; he cut his send switch and on another circuit gave orders. "Boarding party. Get suited up; no time to horse around with a connecting tube. Everybody armed." He heard answer and said, "As many as can get in the airlock, jammed up. Yeah, I know some suits are redlined for maintenance. All you need is about five minutes over and five back—pick the marginals on that basis."

When he had the operation underway he cut back to the *Peron*. What had the man been saying? Oh, yeah— "Well, time's what you don't have. Here's how it's going to be. When we match up close, open your airlock. If you don't, I will. My boarding party's armed and doesn't want to see any guns at all on your people; you understand me? Have *all* your personnel in the galley; coasting, you don't need a watch officer. Anybody found anyplace else gets shot down."

"Our Drive crew—"

"Get 'em upship, fast." Here he was on thin ice and knew it, but couldn't think of a better idea. Then he did. "Either I take that ship over, for sorting out, or I blow it. That's up to you. But spread *this* word: no one who follows my orders will be killed or punished. Any resistance, though, can get folks dead. You got it?"

At the other end of the circuit he heard argument, but one voice overrode the rest. "Don't you understand? There's no damned *choice!*"

"Glad to hear somebody's smart. We're matching now, so get on with your part of it." And Tregare cut the circuit.

He looked around to see Jargy Hoad standing. The man said, "Request relief from watch, skipper."

"Sure. I'll cover. You better hurry, though."

"Right. Before all the suits are taken."

"When you have the galley over there, put that viewscreen through to here. Two-way. I'd kind of like to sit in."

As Jargy left, Leanne Prestor came over to Tregare's seat. "Bran, what's he doing? Do you know?"

"Course I do. He figured it out, without me telling him. We take this ship, it's his, and we're allied. So naturally it's his place to lead the boarding party."

* * *

When the aux screen lit, Tregare saw that the *Peron*'s galley was wall-to-wall with standing people. To one side stood most of Jargy's spacesuited contingent, the majority with helmets tipped back so they could hear better. The screen at that end must have come alive at the same time, because Hoad looked up at it and nodded. "Ship secured, Bran, except for a few diehards. Had to shoot a couple on the way upship, and two, three more are being hunted in the cargo area. We have Drive and Control solid, though." Bran released a sigh; it takes only one fanatic to blow a Drive. He gave Jargy a quick acknowledgment and commendation, then shut up and listened, as Hoad addressed the group.

"We've interrupted an Escape attempt, I gather. Well, I have my own ideas, how to handle these things—and they don't include murder." Tregare grinned—*nice going, Jargy!* "So I want the leading activists in the attempt to come over here." Silence, no moves. "You might as well; if you don't, someone else will point you out." Then, from various places in the room, three men and one woman began moving toward Jargy. When they reached him, he said to the overall group, "You people stay put here, for now. I'm taking these four upship for a private talk."

When Hoad and two guards escorted the four out of the galley, Tregare waited until the screen switched to a view of the *Peron*'s control room. Then he said, "Jargy? You hear me?"

"See and hear you both, Tregare."

"You want to tell 'em the real situation, or should I?"

"You give the overall; I'll handle the detail." So Tregare explained that the *Peron* had been taken not by UET but by an Escaped Ship, and that now the idea was to sort out the Utie loyalists and put them away safely in empty cargo area until they could be grounded in isolation on a Hidden World. "So we need your help, telling us who's safe to run loose and who needs locking up. And the trick is, none of 'em knows what's happening until we have all the nuts and bolts in the right bins."

"Thanks, Bran," said Jargy. "I can take it from here."

The *Peron*'s computer log had data Bran could use; he fired it into Tinhead, ran correlations with stuff he already had, and came up with some interesting ideas. Some of those, of course, would have to wait on the Long View and some long chances.

The *Peron's* mutiny or Escape, depending on who was telling the story, had been less bloody than most. Partly, of course, because of Tregare's intervention while everything was still up for grabs. The captain, caught unarmed, had fled upship to take refuge in the topside airlock; then, desperate, he went outside in a suit. And when the Drive was cut, his lifeline came loose.

All three Hats were in on the Escape effort and had survived. In fact, there had been only a dozen fatal casualties, and four of those fell to Jargy Hoad's boarding party. Surviving Uties numbered slightly under forty, and Tregare refused to take any of those aboard *Inconnu*. "You might's well go on to Target Place, Jargy. You can dump 'em there."

"Why couldn't you?"

"Junior Lee isn't sure we can get there."

"What—?"

"Oh, we'll get *some*place. But to make that kind of bend in our course, and still land—he says maybe so, maybe not."

Between the two ships, now, came a certain amount of personnel transfer. Tregare had supernumeraries, Hoad was shorthanded and could use a cadre of people he knew. Ola Stannert was of course leaving *Inconnu* with Jargy. But on the *Peron*, Second Hat Frei Relliger wanted to leave, so the Hat berths evened out pretty well.

First, though, Bran had a talk with the tall, blond young man. Hosting the session in his quarters, Tregare saw Relliger seated and furnished with a drink, then said, "It's nice you want to join my ship. But I'm curious. Why is it you want to leave the one you're on?"

The man shrugged. "Woman trouble. Which is to say, about three months ago I lost mine to the First Engineer. I thought I'd get over it—but seeing them together on the ship so much, it just keeps getting worse for me. You understand?"

Tregare didn't, but he nodded anyway. "This kind of thing happen to you much? I mean, any part of life you care to name, we all win some and lose some. What I want to know: is it, you just can't stand losses?"

Chewing his lip, Relliger paused. Then his expression cleared. "No, sir. That's not it. Thinking back, I've had my

share of lumps, and taken them. Including some in the
romance department." He sighed. "This was different. I really
thought—but then it all fell apart, and I'm not handling it
well."

"How bad?"

"Killing bad. I never felt that way before, and I don't like it.
It's not the way I *am*."

Tregare thought about it. "Maybe it's the way you're
turning."

"No, sir. Or I'd have done it. Just being off that ship, now,
the pressure's gone."

"All right. Welcome aboard."

Relliger's *Peron* shares bought him a Third Hat on *Inconnu*,
near enough to work out, so Tregare staked Leanne Prestor to
the Second's berth. He didn't ask where Jargy was going to fit
Stannert into the *Peron*'s hierarchy of officers, and Hoad didn't
volunteer the information.

Now connected by a transfer tube, the two ships drifted for
several days while all these matters were settled and a certain
amount of stores were shifted both ways, to forestall shortages
on either vessel. And when these chores were done, Bran and
Jargy met to share a farewell drink in Tregare's quarters.

"You have all the computer stuff," said Bran, "on our
rendezvous some day, when I get the big job figured out."

"That I have. Cheers." Each man sipped a little. "And I'll
keep in touch, best we can over the Long View, and leave word
myself, of course, whenever I can."

Tregare leaned forward. "Who do I leave word *for*?"

Looking puzzled, after a moment Hoad laughed. "Oh, yes.
Not the *Peron*, you mean. Well, it took a lot of thinking, but I
finally have it. The gamble, Bran, when we overtook the *Peron*
and I led the boarding group." He shook his head. "Anyone
who played poker with those odds would be an idiot."

"It was all we had, Jargy."

"I know. But it wasn't figurable; it was all wild cards. So that's
how I'm naming my ship, Bran Tregare. It's *Deuces Wild*."

They drank to that while impatience rioted in Tregare, and
he thought, *first Kickem, then Limmer, now Jargy. It begins to
move!*

* * *

From the *Peron*—now *Deuces Wild*—came one other item of possible future gain. Eda Ghormley, *Inconnu's* chief medic, told Tregare about it. "I talked with this woman on the other ship, one of their medical aides. She's a sleeper from the Underground, and she's going to do the cheek tattoos for Mr. Hoad and his new officers, so they can fake it at any UET colony."

Immediately interested, Bran said, "How about for us?"

"For us, she gave me a kit, and instructions. So if you want me to fix up Mr. Gonnelson and Ms. Prestor, and the new man—"

"If they're willing." Because about Leanne, he wondered. Would she go along with having her face marked?

Ghormley might as well have read his mind. "What I have here is new. For one thing, it's removable."

Tregare rubbed his own cheek. "Suppose you could fix this for me, where three promotions all look the same but don't match my first marking?"

She shook her head. "No, sir. That permanent stuff I can't do anything about. I'm sorry."

"Not your fault." *Comes to it, I'll have to think of something else, is all.*

The only other problem he could think of, along those lines, was that Frei Relliger wore a Second's tattoo but was Third on *Inconnu*. So Leanne Prestor, now Second Hat, would have to settle for being marked as Third. He hoped it wouldn't bother her much.

The Relliger part made no sweat because young Frei's promotion was recent and his tattoo was the erasable kind. Prestor, though, disliked the entire idea. "Why should I? Why do we have to? I don't *want* my face marked up."

At the moment, other worries on his mind, Tregare was close to having had it with Leanne. "In case we hit a UET colony, is why." Then he said, "If you'd stayed with Krieg Elman, you wouldn't have to worry about this small stuff, would you?"

In seconds she went pale, no doubt thinking of the debris and plasma that Elman's *Stump Farm* had become. "That's dirty, Tregare. That's really dirty. I—"

"You came on here and I took you in; you joined the team. Now it's one of two things. You take that damned tattoo—that *temporary* tattoo—or Relliger's my Second Hat and I find me a new Third who's not so picky."

"And what happens to me?"

He shrugged. "Chief rating, I guess."

"And do I stay here, or not?"

Oh, she was pushing! Narrow-eyed, he said, "That's up to you. For now."

He watched her absorb what he said. She made a sort of smile. "I guess I can put up with the tattoo."

"Good." He came to his feet. "I have to check some things."

He'd waited to go up to Control because he wanted to match with Junior Lee Beauregard's stint down in Drive. He was a little ahead of the Chief Engineer's sked, just long enough to take one more good look at the rather discouraging Drive data. He called down for Junior Lee to call back when he came in, and not long after, that intercom channel sounded. "Beauregard here, cap'n."

"Right. Tregare here. Chief, I've been punching figures out of Tinhead, but I want you to tell me what they mean."

Junior Lee cleared his throat. "Well, 'em numbers, I know 'em good. Can't talk in 'em much, though. What y'all need?"

And that was the problem; Bran wasn't sure what he did need. All right, go in with what they both knew, and work from there. "Chief, I stretched the exciter and Nielson Cube both, chasing the *Peron*. Efficiencies are down, on both units, and once the drop starts it keeps dropping."

"Glad you know that, cap'n, same as I do."

"But I don't know how fast either unit loses efficiency. What the curve is. I tried a negative exponential but it wouldn't hold. So—"

The engineer cut in. "That ain't it. It's—lookyere, sir—what we do is, I punch you up 'em numbers to read. Better'n any try talkin' 'em things."

Hell, yes. If Junior Lee could "talk" with Tinhead's keyboard and readout, there was no need to put this stuff into words. Bran watched as the numbers began to emerge. On another input-output circuit he ran trial calculations, trying to find a curve that would match. And finally he had one, or almost. Starting with normal top Drive boost he found that once the effects of his abuse of those units began, the dropoff curve was a reciprocal log function. He told Beauregard as much. "Varies according to how close we push max, and there's a couple of constants I'm rough-guessing for now, but that's about it."

Silent for a time, Junior Lee said, "Put some numbers in that?" So Tregare did, and Beauregard's next answer was, "Then cap'n, either we coast us a whole bunch, or with the speed we got now, we don't turn course hardly at all."

"I agree," said Tregare. "When I work out which it is, I'll let you know." Already he was running star charts on his nearest aux screen. "And thanks, Chief."

He returned to quarters nearly an hour later than he'd said he would, and found Leanne, wearing a light robe, dozing curled up on her left side.

The clink of ice cubes, when he made a drink for himself, woke her; she sat up, and he saw the small bandage on her left cheek.

He smiled. "Been busy, have you? I appreciate that."

"Yes. Temporary or not, though, the process still hurts and draws blood." She leaned forward. "So will the removal, if ever. Ghormley told me how the temporary part works. It's simply that the Underground developed dyes that can be neutralized by tattooing *again*, with a special fluid." She stood, and came to him. "Bran? What took you so long, up in Control?"

"Trying to figure where we go next." He told her of the Drive problems. "We need to get someplace where repairs can be made, and getting there we have to nurse what we got."

"Have you decided? Our destination, I mean."

"Not yet. It takes figuring, maybe even talking." He had his hands to either side of her waist. "Before I went upship you had a mad-on at me. You still do?"

"No. I thought it over. For UET an officer *does* have to look the part." She leaned up to him, and they kissed.

"Fine. I'll go sluice off a little sweat, and be right with you."

The trouble with the weakening Drive was that Tregare had to guess right the first time, what to do; a wrong guess meant drifting to eventual starvation. He'd already ruled out their original goal, Target Place. Chasing the *Peron* had put *Inconnu* far off course from that world; he could make the turn, or the decel and landing, but not both.

Terranova was a possibility, but he'd have to change course

"immediately if not sooner" and even then it'd be close. They'd need to cut Drive and coast most of the way, until time for a slower, more extended period of decel than usual.

That's where the Long View came in, the time-dilation that came with high vee: Einstein was long dead, but his ideas still governed ships that chased light. The difference between running point-nine of c and point-nine-nine didn't make all that much difference by planets' time, but by ships' clocks it made a lot. With a healthy Drive, Terranova was maybe eight ship's months distant. With *his* Drive, Tregare was looking at more like two years. He wasn't sure his supplies would hold out that long.

Up in Control, when he thought he had it figured, he called council, presiding over his three Hats and with Junior Lee sitting in. He gave them the figures: Drive efficiency dropping on a reciprocal log curve ". . . active time, that is, and any time we run at less than max, helps stretch our reserve out." Requirements for a course change to point at Terranova. "Doesn't leave much leeway on the decel end, but maybe enough." He cleared his throat. "That's not the problem, though," and he gave them the time-stretch part. "We might make it, we might not."

"Choice?" That was Gonnelson, and Tregare caught his meaning.

"There is one, yes." He flashed the star chart on the aux screen. "I'm skipping one other UET colony and two Hidden Worlds we might reach, because none of them have Drive repair facilities the last I heard. Or likely to develop any such thing by the time we could reach those places."

"Some idee, though," said Junior Lee Beauregard, "you got up your sleeve. Ain't that so, skipper?"

Tregare nodded. "Sort of, Chief." With a light-wand's dot of brilliance he traced a path across the screen's chart. "The course we're on, we came to by chasing the *Peron*. It was going to Stronghold. Of all our possibilities, that's the most distant. But in ship's time, it's the place we could reach the quickest."

He watched their individual reactions to the idea. Stronghold: UET's fortress outpost, set up to guard against the alien Shrakken, lest those creatures come to avenge UET's murder of a Shrakken crew and taking of its ship. Well, that was the rationale Tregare had heard for Stronghold's existence.

Frei Relliger half stood, then sat again to speak. "I don't—sir, a Hidden World would be best, or even a UET colony. But Stronghold—it's a UET *military* outpost. What chance would we have there? How could we get away with it?"

It was about time, Tregare thought, that somebody made that point. Because it needed answering, and the answer seemed to be his own job. Carefully he kept a straight face as he said, "For one thing, we lie a lot. I grant you, Relliger, it'll take some study."

Gonnelson nodded. "Stronghold."

5. Stronghold

The long haul into Stronghold, with Junior Lee pampering the touchy Nielson Cube and Drive exciter, gave Tregare time to figure and rig the ship's cover story. Working from the data from Kickem Bernardez on UET's list of ships scheduled for Stronghold over the years, he picked a name. In council with his officers, Control and Engineering both, he said, "From here in, we're the *Alexander the Great.*"

So the ship's talker-beacon gained an *Alexander* program. Outside on the hull, the insigne was changed—not totally, but the name was overlaid and the symbols altered. Leanne Prestor designed the necessary decals, and Hain Deverel went outside in a standard suit to place the polarized-electret plastic overlays, which would withstand plowing air on landing. Floating out on a lifeline, Deverel relayed views of the new insigne to an aux screen in Control; Tregare said, "Yeah, good job, Hain. Come on in—I owe you a drink."

So the ship's outside would bear UET's scrutiny. The inside was more difficult. Hiding the ship's true log under a couple of levels of code-groups was no problem. Working up a fictitious log to fool UET's command at Stronghold—well, for a time there, Tregare missed a lot of sleep.

There was no use trying to begin the *Alexander*'s history at any real point of truth. But nothing wrong with working in a few truths concerning ships and persons; the trick would be to come up with items that UET's own records might confirm, while keeping the log free of entries subject to disproof. What made the job possible at all was that customarily ships gave only taped summaries at their ports of call. And personnel records in those summaries began with the date a person joined the ship plus citing the previous duty station. For ratings and unrated crew only the bare bones were required—UET was mostly interested in officers.

So Tregare began by having the *Alexander* detached, long before lift-off, from its Stronghold-bound fleet, which was due to arrive a year or two after Tregare would with luck be there and gone again. For its "original" officers he threw in names he knew UET couldn't check on—some real, some phony.

He checked the timing and decided that this hop should be the *Alexander's* third. All relatively short ones, and he had to run t/t through several times to make it come out right. He put himself aboard for the second one, as First Officer off the *Hoover*, at Terranova. The next fictitious stop, at Johnson's Walk, logged Cleet Farnsworth off the ship to a new command, the *Pizarro*, with Tregare succeeding to the captaincy. Then he had to juggle his other officers' records, both to fit the dates and to seem credible.

When he thought he had it right, he called council again, ran the summary and called for criticisms. Except for a few details, most of his work drew approval. Hain Deverel chuckled once. "A nice touch, captain, having that Utie turncoat Farnsworth promoted. Wherever the bastard is, I hope his soul appreciates your charity."

Tregare grinned back as Leanne said, "The summary's fine, Bran—at least I think it is. But what if someone coming aboard wants to snoop the full log. And finds there isn't one?"

"That's right," said Bran. "I guess I haven't told anybody about that part yet. So now I will, because we'll need to get into practice first."

Approaching Stronghold, Tregare studied the data Bernardez had captured and passed on to him, and learned the rigamarole required before landing at the fortress outpost. Of course he had it in mind to ring a few changes.

A little less than three days out, the hail from groundside

began to come clear. Frei Relliger had the watch, and per orders he called Tregare. "You'll want me to hold off answering, I expect?"

"Right. The way we're coming in, there's enough stellar wind that it's feasible we couldn't read them yet. Tape everything, though, and monitor while you're doing it. If there's anything you think I need to hear, tell me right away." The intercom went silent as Tregare reflected that the young man off the *Peron* was really a lucky acquisition.

Tregare got up from bed. He hadn't been asleep, just waking and dozing comfortably, almost ready to rise but lazily delaying the act. Now, though, he might as well start his ship's-time day.

The talk had wakened Leanne; she, too, sat up. "We're close now, aren't we? Pretty soon the danger begins. How soon?"

Begins? He thought about it, and said: "The day you were born. And for me, the day I was."

Roughly thirty hours short of touchdown, Tregare decided he had all the info he could get from Stronghold's greeting-tape routine, and that he'd better start answering. As near as he could tell, Admiral Saldeen on Stronghold wasn't worried much about anything in the way of ships coming from human-controlled space, but he was getting a little impatient for an answer from this one. Not that the admiral came on the circuit himself, but whoever did the talking sounded more brusque and demanding as time passed.

At the comm-panel in Control, giving the comm-tech an extra break for snack or coffee or both, Tregare opened communication with groundside. First the standard chatter: "the armed ship *Alexander*, Bran Tregare commanding . . ."

In council they'd argued about using his own name. "But what if word's gotten there already, about you?"

Bran shook his head. "I've figured all that. The interval—"

"The what?" Frei Relliger's brows were raised.

"You didn't learn that? It's Pythagoras and right triangles, applied to the way ships chew time. Distance is one leg, time's the other, and interval's the hypotenuse."

Headshake. "If you say so, captain."

"Not me. Einstein said it first." The Third Hat nodded, and Tregare went on. "I checked the times UET learned anything about me after Escape, and figured time and distance from those places to when we get to Stronghold. And the odds have a lot of zeroes on them that the info won't be here yet."

Relliger still looked doubtful, but nobody argued.

Now, talking to Stronghold, Bran had covered all the standard stuff. The groundside spokesman said, after the wait for signals at lightspeed to reach Stronghold and return, "Then you'll be landing at about nineteen hundred hours. So let me give you the drill we have here. First you—"

Tregare quit listening, because that wasn't how it was going to be. When it was his turn, he said, "There'll have to be a few changes. Unless—is your garrison there, the entire personnel complement, inoculated against the Grey Plague from New Canada?"

The answer was a time coming. "Why, no. I don't think so."

Tregare wasn't much surprised. Because both the Grey Plague and New Canada were his very own inventions.

". . . quarantine procedures as worked out and applied by the medical departments . . . have proved effective and totally safe." Tregare read out the quarantine rules. They sounded most official. Both Leanne Prestor and Hain Deverel were good at helping paraphrase Tregare's ideas into official-ese.

What it boiled down to was that only in spacesuits would ship's personnel leave the *Alexander* or groundsiders come aboard. And any time the airlock's outer hatch was opened, the lock would first be fumigated with a guaranteed disinfectant. Eda Ghormley had come up with an aerosol spray that smelled bad enough to be credible—it was normally used to kill moths, something like that. "Of course this means," said Tregare, "that except for fuel and water which can be piped directly, all supplies must be loaded onship by way of the main airlock, since we have no way of using the cargo hatch without fear of contamination. But then, nothing's ever perfect, is it?"

Then groundside's Chief Medic had a lot of questions, and Bran was glad he'd worked out some answers ahead of time. "No, sir; we were never given the planet's coordinates. Out somewhere past Far Corner, is the impression I got." And, "No, we had no deaths aboard ship. No cases, even. What happened, there'd been Grey Plague at Johnson's Walk and everybody had to be inoculated, including us. Because the problem is, the shots make *you* safe enough, but they also make you a carrier for a long time. So that's why the quarantine measures were imposed." He ventured a short laugh. "It's going to make for lousy liberty, here, but this crew knows how to obey orders, right enough."

"This Grey Plague. What are the symptoms?"

"Nobody seemed to want to talk about it, much. A grey color to the skin. Uncontrollable dehydration. Convulsions. Fever. Delirium. A lot of screaming, so probably it's very painful, but at that stage there's no ability to communicate. So—"

After transmission lag, groundside asked, "Can you provide us with samples of the inoculant?"

"The what?"

"Vaccine, serum, whatever it was in the shots *you* received."

This question, Tregare had been waiting for. He said, "No. We asked, but they wouldn't give us any. Said it was too dangerous to keep around, without someone special-trained to handle it. We thought our medic knew enough, but Johnson's Walk said no."

"I see. Well, I hope you won't mind if, any time your airlock opens, we douse it with our own antiseptic spray, also."

They were still too far out for the screen to show picture, but still Tregare repressed his grin. "Not at all. Sounds like a fine, sensible idea."

The conversation ended; Bran cut the circuit. Relliger said, "All well and good. But still—what happens when they board and somebody exercises authority to snoop in our computer files?"

Tregare didn't laugh at his Third Hat. All he said was, "You ever try to punch a terminal keyboard, wearing space gloves?"

So it was all working, but some misgiving nagged Tregare. He couldn't figure what it was, until he decided he needed a shave and saw himself looking back from a mirror.

The damn tattoo, was what! The parts that didn't look right. Sure, he'd got by with the discrepancy at Hardnose, but that was a piddling little colony with no firepower to speak of if someone *had* got suspicious. And they hadn't been there long, and half the time he'd fixed himself some grease smears on clothes and cheek and forehead, ostensibly from double-checking maintenance work. Here on Stronghold, though, once the ship set down he'd be up against people who

outranked him and forces that hopelessly outnumbered him.
And he couldn't get away with being grease-smeared *all* the
time.

He couldn't think of a good idea so he asked for some.
Leanne tried touching the circle up with surface paints; the job
looked fine, but the stuff smeared too easily. "Thanks," said
Tregare. "It'd work just fine on a viewscreen closeup, but—"
And for that purpose, close now to Stronghold, it served
admirably.

Frei Relliger suggested a faked injury, covered by a
bandage. Bran shook his head. "Somebody'd want to look at it.
A medic, maybe." Damn! There had to be some kind of
answer. . . .

Gonnelson cleared his throat. "Shiner."

For a moment, Tregare didn't understand. Then Prestor
said, "Oh! Like a black eye, you mean." And the First Hat
nodded. "But that would smear, just like—"

"Real one."

With admiration, Tregare looked at his First Hat. "That'll
work. If there's time for it to bloom—" He shook doubts loose
from his head. "We just won't entertain guests on here 'til it
does. And offship, through my helmet nobody can make a
really picky inspection." He stood. "All right, Gonnelson. Get
up and do the honors."

"Me?" The man looked horrified. "*No!*"

"Sure, you. It's your idea, you get the privilege. Why, just
think—this is probably the only chance you'll ever have in
your life to slug a captain and get away with it!" But the jollying
didn't work at all, so Tregare went serious. With a hand to
Gonnelson's shoulder, he said, "I've never seen you fight, but I
heard about a thing that happened when somebody in a bar got
to bullying you and wouldn't stop. You hit hard and you're
accurate, is how I heard it. And I want this done right."

Slowly Gonnelson stood, his face paler than usual. Bran
said, "Wrap something around your hand. We don't want any
busted knuckles." When that was done, Tregare turned a
little. "This about the correct angle?" Then, "I'd better shut
my eyes. Otherwise I probably couldn't keep from ducking."
He saw Frei Relliger move off to one side, out of his line of
vision. He closed his eyes, and waited.

The impact dazed him; he stumbled backward and found
himself held and supported from behind. At first the voice

there made no sense, then he understood. ". . . way he wound up, I didn't want you slamming back against the bulkhead, skipper." Relliger . . . .

The lights wore halos; so did everything and everybody else. He wanted to say something, but words wouldn't form. He waved a hand, meaning to signal that he was all right, but the people crowding around him and easing him into a chair didn't seem to pay much attention. Gonnelson—Gonnelson was *crying*.

Tregare couldn't have that. With great effort he put words together. "The hand—it's awright?" Massaging that one with the other, the man nodded. Now speech came better. "Good job, feels like," as he winced from the movements talking made. "If that doesn't do it, we'll need a sledgehammer. Thanks, Gonnelson."

First Tregare had himself a robust drink, then he ate. Chewing mostly on the right side—his jaw hadn't been struck, but the left side was sore, anyway. As much as possible, he ignored it; he was working on his cover story. "Small abortive mutiny, I think," he said to Leanne Prestor. "A little coup group—maybe three—been planning Escape and got desperate as we came closer to Stronghold." She started to interrupt but this was *his* story and he was still embroidering it. "—jumped me coming out of quarters, knocked me around some until I could get my gun out. Then, of course—"

Playing along with his scenario, she said, "What happened to them? And who were they? On the records, I mean."

Spreading his hands wide, Bran said, "Spaced 'em; what else? One dead, one hurt bad, one plain scared spitless. Names I'll pick from those dead in this ship's real mutinies and feed 'em into the log summary all the way, up to now. And next move, I go down and scar that corridor's bulkheads a little. Energy gun—that'll save me having to splotch blood around; they mostly cauterize."

Leaning forward across the table, Leanne clasped his hand. "But what if they—UET, I mean, on Stronghold—interrogate the crew about all this? How many people can you rehearse on it?"

He grinned. "No need. Nobody was there to see. All there are is rumors. And besides, UET never asks about anybody but officers. So *we'll* have the story straight, and that does it."

* * *

He went on viewscreen to Stronghold, next, with no bandage but a smear of colorful antiseptic over his swelling bruise. To the groundsider's question he said, "A little problem on here, yes. It's taken care of, and you get a full report when we're down."

Inconnu disguised as the *Alexander* was closing fast on Stronghold. Twice that world's rotation showed Tregare the main fortress and its spaceport. The first time he couldn't distinguish much, even on high-mag, but next exposure showed him that the Port held fourteen ships; nearly half of these would be armed. Well, this caper wasn't depending on muscle, anyway. Because if it did, Tregare was in deeper than he could handle.

It was about time to see how Frei Relliger could land a ship, so Tregare assigned him the job and rode sidebar for him. The new Third Hat seemed a little twitchy when the ship began plowing air, but he brought it down steadily and met the landing circle with only the slightest of jars. Seeing the man's apprehensive look, Tregare said, "Good sitdown, Frei. It buys you a drink." And as soon as he saw the log brought up to date, he took Relliger to captain's digs and paid off.

When he went groundside, Tregare took along Hain Deverel and two other ratings, all briefed on the "mutiny" story and all, of course, in suits. In the airlock they waited while nozzles installed by Junior Lee's people fogged the chamber with aerosol mist. Then the outer hatch opened, and using a hose running up the ramp from a tanker car, spacesuited UET personnel gave men and airlock another spraying. It was all going to be a big nuisance, Tregare thought—but the inconvenience and its supposed cause should distract UET's attention from other matters.

So the four of them left the ship. The suited groundside squad returned to their vehicle, leaving the hose in place. Tregare's group was beckoned to a large open groundcar. Its driver and its one passenger who wore captain's insignia were not spacesuited. Tregare thought they looked a little nervous. Well, that wasn't such a bad idea. . . .

Looking a little sheepish, too, the other captain reached to shake Tregare's gauntleted hand with his own bare one. "Welcome to Stronghold, captain. I'm Jase Hogarth, adjutant to Admiral Saldeen." He didn't introduce the driver, a youngish woman who wore Chief rating's stripes and a sandpaper haircut, but Bran did name his own people. Then they got into the car, moved off toward the nearest buildings, and Hogarth began pointing out the sights of the place.

To the left, "That big grey pillbox, it's the powerhouse. Most of the installation underground, of course, to save on shielding for the fusion cycle. Only fourteen years old, the plant is. Probably obsolete on Earth, though, by now." Bran mumbled something noncommittal; what he knew about power research on Earth he could stick in one ear.

They skirted the rest of the landing area, passing through shadows cast by the tall ships. Stronghold's sun, a fierce actinic dot so distant that Stronghold's year made fifteen of Earth's, had risen less than halfway from horizon to zenith. To one side Hogarth noted the communications complex; its growth of antennae, in all shapes from spidery to disclike, made his identification redundant. Bran made approving comment anyway—it didn't cost him.

Up ahead, then, minimally sheltered by foothills beyond, stood the Headquarters complex, officer and civilian quarters, troop barracks—the one with the flagrant display of defense weaponry had to be the Committee Police contingent, but Tregare didn't state his deduction out loud. Instead he paid attention while Hogarth indicated the locations of other facilities: the warehouses and related supply functions, the fuel refinery sited well away from the main area, the storage tanks, main reservoir, crop lands off to the far side where Tregare couldn't really see them from here. All very interesting—because riding in this groundcar, not yet twenty minutes on this world, Tregare was getting himself one hell of an idea for future reference!

Peace take me, it can be done!

Admiral Saldeen was the far side of middle age, but his voice and movements showed vigor. Coming around from behind his desk, to shake hands, he grinned. "Glad to have you here, captain. Tregare, is it? Seems a shame, your having to wear that suit, but plague's nothing to fool with. Now—your report, sir?"

Deverel and the other two ratings were cooling heels in an outer room. They, and Tregare also, had been checked for weapons; no one entered the admiral's presence armed, except his personal bodyguard. Naturally Tregare and his group had brought no overt handweapons. Unarmed, though, they were not. Some of their suits' "air" tanks contained other substances, such as cough smoke and puke gas. Not that Tregare expected to need any of that stuff, but having it at hand made him feel a little more confident.

Now, handshake done with and both men seated, Bran answered, "My summary log is already sent into your computer files, sir. And that's about all the report I have. Actually, Admiral Saldeen, I'm here to get *your* report." Before the admiral could interrupt, Bran said, "Overall estimate of probabilities of Shrakken activity, for one thing. Morale situation: improving or deteriorating, here where we—" *We.* That's important to say. "—where we can only wait and watch. And that's another thing." He paused.

Saldeen frowned, then said, "*What* is? Explain, captain."

"As you'll see by our log, my mission has an option. In any case I receive your full report and return it to Earth as soon as possible." He tried to look apologetic. "*I'm* not being pushy, sir, but my orders came from the Presiding Committee itself." The admiral seemed to relax, so Bran continued, "The option is that if *you* think it's a good idea, then on leaving here I first take a loop out toward Shrakken space and scout for alien ships there. Now whether—"

The admiral shook his head. "We've done that. No sign."

Tregare leaned forward. "Of course, sir. But how far?" Saldeen told him. Bran pretended to consider the datum, then said, "It's the Long View, sir. When these orders were sent out, the Committee didn't know you had explored so extensively." He nodded. "Then I guess all we need to do, if, as I expect, you have my fuel and supplies replenished in short order, plus the Drive repairs I've listed, is for you to countersign the original orders and add your recommendation." Seeing the man's brows rise, he added, "Simply have it punched in by comm channel; no need to handle possibly contaminated readouts." He smiled. "And then we can get this damned Grey Plague worry well away from you."

"Yes. Hmm—not much of a rest stop for you, is it, captain?"

"No, it isn't. But already a few of our people are testing negative as carriers. By the time we reach Earth again, we should all be safe for normal folks to associate with."

"Umph. I certainly hope so. Now which level of report are you expected to receive and return? Total, redundant-reduced, edited by selective importance, or summary?"

Run that one past me again! How long since Stronghold had been established here? And on *Inconnu,* how much of Tinhead's memory space could be spared for this stuff, without cramping normal functions? Tregare made a guess: "Make it redundant-reduced for the first and latest decade of Stronghold's existence, summary for everything in between." What UET's Presiding Committee might want to see, Tregare had no idea. But the early days might have some clues for him personally, and the latest data he *had* to have.

A little more talk before leaving. "Sorry, captain, that those suits don't have facilities for me to feed you a drink. It's been a pleasure, though I must admit I'll be glad to see you take that damned Plague away safely." Then, after another mismatched handshake, Tregare collected his people and they got a ride back to the ship.

On the way, between reminding himself of the basics of Stronghold's layout, Tregare found himself thinking. Not everybody in UET was rotten. Admiral Saldeen, for instance. Too bad they were on different sides. Because Tregare *liked* that old rooster.

What made Tregare antsy was his Drive problem, but that work got underway immediately. The only tough part was not being able to use the cargo hatch, so that the exciter had to be broken down into components in order to get through the airlock.

The Nielson Cube made another problem. The thing itself was only about a meter each way, but its cryogenic crate measured twice that. Junior Lee Beauregard solved the difficulty—his crew pulled the old Cube and wrapped it in a blanket of thick, efficient insulation while at the same time at the foot of the ship's ramp a UET gang did the same for the new replacement unit, tapping it into flow from a portable tank of liquid helium to make sure it wouldn't warm enough to go sour between uncrating and installation. "Purely fast, we done gotta move, skipper," he said, and Tregare saw to it that extraneous personnel were kept the hell out of the way during those moves, until the new Cube was safely in place and the old one snugged into UET's crate groundside.

But the job did get done, and less than two hours later Junior Lee announced, "She balance real fine, cap'n. Rarin' to push, any ol' time."

Not all Stronghold's people were as helpful as Admiral Saldeen. For instance, Tregare wasn't exactly fond of Commodore Peldon when she came aboard with the announced intention of snooping into Tinhead for more details. What she looked like, Bran didn't know, because her suit's helmet was one-way opaque. Her voice and manner, though, held all the subtle charm of a backrub with a handful of poison ivy.

First off, the Commodore demanded full access to Tinhead's data banks. "All of them, captain. There'll be no secrets here."

Her advent had routed Tregare out of bed about three hours ahead of schedule, so he didn't feel especially conciliatory. "Course not," he said. "For starters, let's see your authorization."

"But I'm Commodore Peldon!"

"Anybody in that fishbowl mirror could say as much. What's on paper, to show me?" She handed over a flimsy, and ordinarily he'd have accepted it, but now he nitpicked three minor omissions on the authorization form. "Go get it done right; then come back." The Commodore used some surprising language then, but dutifully waddled her bulky-suited way off the ship.

"Are you sure," said Leanne Prestor, "that chasing her offship was really a bright move?"

Taking her arm, Tregare started them moving back toward the galley. "This time of morning I'm not sure which year it is. Come on." And when he'd had coffee and breakfast and more coffee, he said, "That's the hatchet lady, I chased off here. I don't know how or why, but she's trouble." He got on the intercom to Control, checking on progress of fueling and resupply. Four hours to completion, the answer came. "But I could cut upstairs earlier if we have to, right?" At Gonnelson's confirmation, Bran nodded, and turned back to Prestor. "See? We stall her, is all."

He couldn't stall the admiral, though. When Saldeen called to get Tregare's acknowledgment of receipt for Stronghold's report, Bran had to check with Frei Relliger to make sure the data was all logged into Tinhead. At the same time, with no audio going offship to the admiral, Tregare checked on fuel and supplies. The latter were complete, but a balky pump had fueling behind sked. "Another hour to top us off? Okay, thanks."

Then he got back to Admiral Saldeen, and the man's next request shocked him. "A passenger? But, sir—?" Because one goal of the Grey Plague story was to make sure no personnel could be transferred off or onto the ship. UET's custom, Bran knew, was to shuffle crews around a lot; in this case he couldn't let such a thing happen. His people didn't want to be tossed back into UET and he didn't want any Uties aboard, either.

He thought he'd beaten their system, but now Saldeen said, "That's right, captain. One passenger, to be delivered to Earth."

"Dead, that would have to be," Tregare said. "Nobody can live in a suit that long, even if you fit it with input and output plumbing. Just the effects of isolation on sanity—"

"Captain, you are talking when you should be listening." So Tregare shut up; he was still in hostile country, and outnumbered. The admiral said, "Your cargo manifest shows that you have vacant area in your Hold, Portside Lower, which contains only sealed items that can't be opened without proper tools. That hold also is equipped with access to water and with one-way vented sanitary facilities, for the convenience of the loading crews. Do you follow me, so far?" Tregare nodded; the admiral grinned. "The passenger in question is a prisoner, a traitor. Drug interrogation proved that much, but Earth HQ has the new truth-field equipment; it is imperative that our people get *all* the information about this possibly dangerous conspiracy. Do you see?"

"Of course, sir. But the Plague—"

Saldeen frowned. "The prisoner boards your ship—suited, of course—along with those carrying the necessary supplies of food and so forth, all sealed. Once this person, baggage and all, is in the hold, you seal *that*, and spray it thoroughly with both your germicidal agents and our own. Leaving a plague-free environment in which the suit is no longer necessary."

Thinking fast, Tregare said, "And at the far end?"

"You've already told me, captain, that by the time you reach Earth, you and your people will no longer be carriers."

Tregare had run out of valid-sounding objections, so he said, "Then send the prisoner aboard, sir. We'll be ready."

And besides—*a prisoner, huh?* Or, just maybe, a sleeper.

Up in Control later, he knew when the prisoner was brought aboard and stuck into Hold, Portside Lower, after which the UET escort left the *Alexander*. He couldn't pay too much attention, though, because signals were coming in from offworld—signals that UET was also receiving. And the news wasn't good.

It was UET's biennial fleet from Earth approaching. Bran hadn't expected it to get here for another year, maybe two. Now he checked some figures (t/t∘, 1/x, Arc, Cos, Sine), shook his head and cursed a little. Gonnelson said, "Problem?"

"Yeah," said Bran Tregare. "I keep forgetting how just a little change in vee, up crowding light, affects time-dilation. Like the difference between twenty-to-one, and maybe twenty-two instead. In the fourth decimal place, is where it matters, and our instruments aren't that good. So what we have coming in is a bunch of ships we can't afford to hang around and meet."

Gonnelson's "Why?" was gesture, not word, and Tregare answered. "Because this is the fleet that includes the *Alexander*. The real one."

So to top it all off, here came Commodore Peldon, or somebody wearing a mirror helmet and using that name. The voice was the same, though. Tregare took the papers from her but didn't bother reading them; he used the time, pretending to look at the flimsies, to think fast. He sat the commodore down before a console and said, "I'll get somebody up here, so as not to disrupt my watch crew, on account of they're busy, to punch data for you. Here—let me plug you in an audio feed," and he did, because that feed preempted what she could hear from outside her suit and he didn't want her hearing what he needed to say to Junior Lee Beauregard.

"Ready as ever will be, cap'n," replied Junior Lee. So Tregare sat back while a comm tech arrived and began retrieving, for Commodore Peldon, computer data that in UET's hands would hang Tregare. Not that Stronghold likely used hanging as a method of execution, but the principle held.

"Junior Lee," said Tregare now, "get the fuel input valve closed."

"Right now?"

"Five minutes ago. We're topped off, near as makes no difference."

"You fixin' to lift? Best I advise groundside—"

"Advise, hell! We tear the feedpipe loose, it gives them something to do besides trying to intercept us. Especially when our Drive-node ionization ignites the fuel spill."

Junior Lee's cackling laugh wasn't his most lovable feature. "Sure 'nuff, cap'n. That there valve, she is now—close off!"

The offship intercom made its piping call; onscreen appeared the admiral. "Captain, I have a communication from the incoming fleet. It contains certain confusing items of information. Until the contradictions are resolved, I must ask you to consider yourself under arrest. You will not—repeat, will *not*—attempt to lift off and escape, or the fleet will blast you out of space. I—"

The hell with it. Push come to shove, Tregare answered, "No, it won't. You'll order that fleet to swing well clear of my lift-off path, leaving me a safe corridor. Or else—" Or else *what*? He looked around and saw Commodore Peldon nodding as the comm tech began to feed her Tinhead's information. Okay—"—or else I will remove Commodore Peldon's helmet and expose her to the Grey Plague. And then I will set her down safely on Stronghold. But my airlock's tied up right now, so I guess I'll have to let her out the cargo hatch. So there goes your Plague security. Sir."

Silence, and then, "Tregare, you're a devil!"

"Yes, sir. I missed my calling."

"Eh? How's that?"

"I should have been on UET's Presiding Committee."

Escape wasn't all that easy, because nothing ever is; plan all you want, but something will screw up. On Tregare's topside screens he saw the hi-mag image of the incoming fleet sheering off from its direct approach; a few more minutes and those ships couldn't intercept him, if he timed it right. He had his fuel, his supplies, his Drive working. So why didn't he lift? Yet he didn't. And finally he realized what the problem was. It was Commodore Peldon, still busy accreting data. What to do with *her*?

The simple answer was take her upstairs and space her, so she couldn't deliver *Inconnu*'s history to UET. But although he thoroughly disliked the woman he'd never seen, Tregare wasn't quite prepared to kill her. So he gave Gonnelson certain instructions, and the two of them grabbed her. In the suit she wasn't easy to handle, but it didn't take long to strip away all the electronic hardware and leave her with nothing of Tinhead's data except what she might have heard and remembered. Then Tregare reached for the clamps that secured her helmet.

"What are you *doing*?" It was Prestor—and what *she* was doing here, peace only knew. "Bran—you can't!"

"Oh, for—!" Savagely, he shook his head. "I'm sending this Utie bitch off without a helmet. We need the diversion."

"They'll flame her dead! Anybody would, in this situation."

"And who cares? One Utie more or less, what's the difference?" But once she'd spelled it out like that, he couldn't do it.

So, helmet intact but suit's speakers smashed, the woman got marched downship to the main airlock. Leanne Prestor helped Tregare with that chore. At the top of the ramp, airlock opened to the ship's interior but sealed toward groundside with the spray routine ready to go, Tregare said to Commodore Peldon: "When you're cycled through, run down fast and get you some distance. When I lift, there won't be time to find cover." She didn't answer, so he said, "Do you understand?"

"Yes. I think so." Even leaning close to her helmet, he heard the voice only faintly.

"Then do it quick." Running upship to his own job, Tregare found Gonnelson ready to raise off. All right; the First Hat could do it—but Tregare sat in to make some changes once *Inconnu* got upstairs.

Then, as Bran watched screens and meters, the ship lifted. Some UET vessels tried to cut over for intercept, but the vectors gave them no chance. *Inconnu* got away from Stronghold, free and clean.

Entering his quarters, Tregare found Leanne sitting on the side of their bed and looking glum. "What's the matter?" He felt good, so when she didn't answer right away, he told her *why* he felt good. "This Drive—the new Cube, and Junior Lee's tuning every bit as good as Mallory's—we've got close to ten percent more oof than we ever had." He couldn't stop grinning. "Just the same, though, when we go behind the big gas-giant I'm going to swing course hard and then cut Drive."

"I don't understand." No wonder, she didn't look as though she were really listening.

So he explained. "They'll chase us anyway. And one of those ships might be a hotdog just like us. But they'll come scooting out, tailing our course the last they saw it; they'll do their scoot right on past us and diverging fast. With our Drive and beacon off they haven't a prayer of detecting us. And once we see they're gone by, building vee in the wrong direction, *then* we pour it on for Earth." At her frown, he said, "Oh sure, we'll still go there. Only thing is, I'll be fudging the orders some."

"I'm sure you will. Can I have a drink?"

"Coming up." And with one for himself, too, he sat and looked at her, wondering. And finally said, "You never did say what's wrong, Leanne. Something is, right?"

"That woman. What you did to her."

"The commodore? I didn't hurt her any. All we did—"

"You were going to kill her. If I hadn't—"

"I wasn't going to hurt a damned hair of her. I—"

"You'd have *sent* her to her death, and you know it!"

He knew she was right and he didn't like it, so he said, "Aw, she's high brass. And what she remembers from Tinhead's readouts is the only dope Stronghold has on us." He snorted. "She has any sense, she'd've used that info for leverage."

"As you would do, of course."

"Hell, yes." What the— "Leanne, what's going on here?"

She gulped the last of her drink. "It's—Tregare, you do things I can't live with. So I won't. Not any more."

She stood, and he with her. "You need any help, moving out? You have a room picked out yet?" Or a roommate? But that would be none of his business.

"I'll manage. You go upship and make sure of your sneaky course change. You wouldn't want to miss winning a trick."

He came close, then, to striking her. But he didn't. He said, "Maybe you think this is some kind of game, with UET. No such thing, and never has been." She started to turn away; he grabbed her arm. "No. You listen. You realize what I *did*, here? I took us into Stronghold with a bum Drive and brought us out with a good one. And with fuel, and supplies, and the Admiral's stamp on a set of orders I can use to get us in and out of *Earth*, if I work it right. I—"

"You, yes. You, you, *you*!"

He saw what she meant, there, and said, "Look, I give credit all around. You and everybody else did great, executing the plans." One deep breath he took. "But peace take you, they were *my* plans! And they will be at Earth, too, most likely." He made a snort. "Oh hell, it takes all of us to do it right; I know that. It's just—this is my ship and I have to be responsible for it. No matter what anybody says, it's my load."

She started to say something more, but he'd had plenty: "I'll get out and let you do your moving. Log your new quarters assignment in Control so the watch officer can reach you if necessary. And—no, I guess that's all."

As he turned away, she said, "Am I still Second Hat?"

"Long as you do your job. So far, you have; keep at it."

She tried to smile but it didn't quite work. "You're angry."

How else? The very banality broke his tensions; Tregare laughed. "Don't worry about it. I'll save it for UET." He left her then and went upship.

The plan worked. When *Inconnu* emerged from the gas-giant's shadow it ran dark. Hours later the UET pursuers, building vee rapidly, flashed past along Tregare's former course and soon were out of contact range. Then Bran swung ship and set course for Earth.

About that course, people had some questions. At the next Hats' council, Tregare tried to figure out his answers. "For starters, right here we have a perfectly good ship's ID all countersigned by Admiral Saldeen, along with his orders to *go* to Earth. Now what we do about all that, how we fudge it, is something else. But—"

"Why?" Gonnelson.

"Why Earth?" The First Hat nodded.

And that was the hard question. Tregare thought about it and then said, "I don't know, really. It's a hunch, is all. That getting a chance to get in and out of Earth at all is a peace-taking miracle, and I don't want to waste it."

Prestor spoke. "But what good will it do you, to go there?"

Shrugging, Tregare grinned. "Maybe I just need to find out what the place—the situation, I mean—smells like, these days."

Frei Relliger scowled. "To what purpose?"

Junior Lee Beauregard laughed. "Don't never ask a houn' dog that."

And Tregare decided that maybe Junior Lee had the answer.

6. Earth

Living alone made Tregare edgy. The split-up with Leanne frustrated the hell out of him. Getting cleanly away from Stronghold, bilking UET out of a new Drive and the rest of it, called for a celebration. What he really needed to do was get flatass drunk, but under the circumstances he couldn't afford to. He settled, the third day out of Stronghold, for hosting a moderately boisterous party, attended (off-and-on, so as not to disrupt the watches in Drive and Control) by all officers and senior ratings. Tregare took about half the booze he really wanted, reached a medium state of cheer, and was so nice to everybody that he could hardly believe it. To Leanne, even, but in her case he didn't exactly go overboard with cordiality.

So it was a relief to get away from her and talk with his Chief-rated Medic, Eda Ghormley. The thin, grey-haired woman was sipping on a surprisingly stiff-looking drink as he asked her, "You been keeping tabs on our prisoner?"

She nodded. "By the monitors, yes. I do look in occasionally. What do you plan to do about that one? And when?"

Bran checked his chronometer. "When? Let's say eighteen hundred, ship's tomorrow. Gives me time for some sleep and breakfast after this party winds down in a little while. Now as to *what*—"

He told her, and she said, "Why so complicated? And how do you keep it all straight in your head?"

"Fancy, because all we have is UET's word that this is any kind of rebel. When we're done, we'll know for sure. And how I keep it straight is, I plan my whole story on the basis that the Grey Plague is real."

Ghormley said, "Yes. You'd have to do it that way."

Tregare woke healthy, called for breakfast to be delivered from the galley, showered and ate and so forth, and dressed for the day. Then he called Eda Ghormley and had her listen while he spoke to the prisoner in Hold, Portside Lower. After three days, he figured that person could use some company. He said, "Get your suit on; you're being visited. We'll come in suited and then spray for safety so you can unsuit for discussion. You understand how it works?"

The answering voice was husky, almost a whisper. With no picture, Bran couldn't visualize the person speaking. "Discussion? You mean interrogation, don't you?"

"A few questions, sure. You'll be ready? Twenty minutes?"

"Yes, of course. Oh, yes."

Tregare cut that circuit and said to Ghormley, "You need any help with the gloves?"

"No, sir. And the drug kit's already packed."

"See you down there, then."

At the door to Hold, Portside Lower, Tregare and Ghormley met. Both were in space suits, but instead of gauntlets the medic wore surgical gloves, taped at the wrists to the suit's sleeves. Approving, Tregare nodded. "Let's go in."

Cradling the canister of foul-smelling antiseptic spray in one arm, he opened the door; they entered and he closed it again, to face another suited figure, and Tregare said, "All right, now we'll spray this place so you're safe, and then—"

But before he could finish, or do anything, the prisoner unlatched the suit's helmet and threw it to the deck. From a youngish haggard face the husky voice almost screamed. "You won't take *me* to Earth! You can torture me some more, but your damned Plague will make it stop, sooner or later. You don't have me forever. Not now, you don't!"

Eda Ghormley started to say something, but Tregare shushed her: dammit, this could *still* be a UET plant, if someone had gambled that the Plague was phony. So he grabbed the prisoner, and then Ghormley helped him wrestle

the top half of the space suit off and get the person tied down,
and somewhere along in there Bran realized that the stubble-
headed, burn-marked prisoner was female. No matter; he
gestured, and the medic gave the shot of the so-called "truth
drug."

Then Tregare began asking questions.

She was a plant, all right, a "ringer"—but not from UET.
She'd been planted *on* UET by Earth's Underground organization as a sleeper, and had performed well until betrayed and
caught. Renni Lofall, age thirty-two—well, that was her official
cover name and the age was probably close—thought the
betrayal was a matter of ignorance rather than malevolence.
Tregare had no way of knowing and no reason to give a damn;
the woman had caught hell, but Stronghold was back *there,*
and not apt to catch up.

The burns on scalp and cheek and breast and torso—first
he'd thought they were from simple hot iron, but not so. UET
used electric torture and some sadist had run the voltage up.
Either way, Bran could understand why Renni Lofall had
decided to take her chances with the nonexistent Grey Plague.

Lofall, now, was coming awake from the drug. She blinked
and said, "Whatever you got from me, I hope it does your
superiors no good at all. And *I* won't live to see them."

"Too right, you won't," said Bran Tregare. "Because I don't
have any superiors." It took a while, before he got through to
her that *Inconnu* was Escaped and Renni Lofall was, too. And
that the Grey Plague did not exist. Then he and Ghormley
took the woman upship to *Inconnu's* small infirmary, and put
her to bed.

"Earth, now," said Tregare, to the group assembled in his
quarters. "To skim there, the story has to be perfect." Yes, he'd
told Leanne he intended to fudge Admiral Saldeen's orders,
and of course that's what he'd have to do—but all his thinking,
to date, gave him no clear or complete idea *how* to do the
fudging. So it was time to get his best people thinking loose,
and kick some ideas around.

"The Grey Plague was fine for Stronghold," he said now,
"because their medical facilities were limited. Earth's aren't.
They'd be all over us, quarantining us aboard or even ordering

us to evac for groundside isolation. We'll have enough problems without that kind of hassle."

Frei Relliger spoke. "Skipper, I don't see how we can chance it. Once we're groundside—"

"Don't land," said Gonnelson. Looking at his First Hat, Tregare nodded. Sure! He outlined the idea, fast: refuel and resupply from the pods in sync orbit, same as the near-Earth patrol ships would. To save on time and fuel, both. But to justify the option, and bar any exchange of personnel on or off the ship, what kind of mission orders could he fake?

"We're still the *Alexander*," he said, thinking it out. "And coming back immediately from Stronghold."

"Exceptin'," Junior Lee put in, "we got us a whole new crew. How you gone fix *that*?"

"Yeah," Tregare said. *How?* Yeah . . . "All right. Saldeen's recent files show several ships coming to Stronghold from colony worlds, not straight from Earth. The summary log we have to provide shows only a person's *latest* previous ship. Prestor, Relliger—check Saldeen's ship listings against our true log and try to frame capsule entries that could fit." Another thought. "Our people who joined us from groundside, just log them in off UET worlds, to whatever ship we say we got them from."

He grinned. "And I'll check you later, to be sure we don't need faster-than-light travel to explain any entry."

The "mission" parameters were still to be defined, but the session had run past some mealtimes and Bran was overdue to check the watch log, so he adjourned the meeting with thanks.

When Ghormley reported that Renni Lofall was out of shock and appeared resonably healthy, Tregare invited Lofall up to his quarters for a private dinner. Even if this Underground agent's Earthside data was a decade or two obsolete, she'd still have information he needed. And her desperation, when she thought she was choosing a slow, painful form of suicide, had touched him more than he liked.

So now he welcomed her into captain's digs and fixed her a drink. Wearing a plain jumpsuit that almost fit her but not quite, she walked stiffly and sat with caution. Well, he'd seen what UET had done to her above the waist—he hadn't asked Ghormley about the rest. Not thinking, he said, "Comfortable?"

She half smiled. "No, but improving." His face must have shown embarrassment, for she said, "None of *your* fault, captain." Now she did smile. "It's still hard to believe I'm safe now."

He had to say it. "You're not, really. None of us are, until we figure a way to get in to and out of Earth." He leaned forward. "Maybe that's where you can help."

So while they sipped drinks and snacked on appetizers, he told her his very tentative plans, and asked for suggestions. "Let me think a little," she said, so when their dinner arrived and as they dined, he didn't push it. They made only light conversation, and not much of that.

Over coffee and liqueurs, though, she began to talk. The Shrakken, the possible alien menace—that was what Stronghold was there for. So perhaps . . . and by the third round of coffee, Tregare had the bare bones of his plan. "Warn Earth, yeah. And then the priority mission to alert wherever we decide the Shrakken are heading. The Twin Worlds, maybe, and Terranova."

"You have to high-code this warning," Lofall said, "and choose a code that fits the right year. They change them, you know."

"Sure. The Long View. Well, the Q-code still fits; all I need to figure is the progressive permutations." He laughed. "And to throw in a few glitches."

"I don't understand."

"Errors in the code paragraphs every so often. So the rest is gibberish until they computer-analyze. Slow 'em down a whole bundle. Time they figure it, with any luck we're gone."

"Then you think you have the problem solved, at Earth?"

"No. But we have us one good head start on it."

Lofall had other interesting facts to offer. Such as how to communicate with the Underground on Earth, how to do it from high orbit, how to decode the apparently random signals Tregare could elicit from groundside. Sitting by his keyboard terminal, Bran punched all these items into Tinhead. Finished, he said, "You must have a pretty good rank in the Underground. Or even in UET, for that matter. Communications is your specialty, right?" She nodded. "Mine too, until I got into the captain business."

"From our talk here, I'd gathered as much." Her brows

lowered. "Rank, though. The Underground's so different, a comparison wouldn't mean anything. And on Stronghold, between spacers and groundsiders—well, I guess I outrank your Chief ratings but your officers outrank *me*." She looked at him. "Does it matter?"

"Not except for quarters assignment, now you're fit to move out of infirmary. Officers' digs are full up right now, and so are Chiefs' rooms. There's a couple of Firsts' cubbies open, so you could either take one of those or bump the least senior Chief. It's up to you."

She shook her head. "I'm not bumping anyone. I'm riding as supernumerary with no assigned duties. As yet. Certainly I don't want to throw my weight around. The cubby will be fine."

"All right. I'll walk you there. Stopping by the infirmary first, if that's where you have your gear stashed."

She stood. "Do I *have* to keep the space suit?" Noting how she said it with a straight face, Tregare decided he liked this Underground agent.

Over the next few days Tregare stayed busy. First he "adjusted" his orders from Admiral Saldeen, to allow for the phony Shrakken warning and the orbital refueling. Then he ran the permutation-updates on Q-code to the actual time he'd been at Stronghold, and coded the warning itself, not omitting the parts addressed to UET on the Twin Worlds and Terranova. He considered the computer image of the admiral's signature: his copy had to look nearly like the original but of course no two signatures are identical. Finally he ran the data-bits through a digital-to-analog converter and then put that signal through a distortion net until he came out with something just slightly different from his model. Then back to digital mode and into Tinhead. *If that doesn't fool the bastards* . . .

His plans were coming into focus now, but still a lot more risky than he liked. He'd put a lot of urgency and all the admiral's authority into that faked warning, and Stronghold itself gave evidence that the Shrakken scared UET spitless— but still, hanging around Earth very long invited meddling by UET groundside. He kept working on ideas. . . .

He needed a fake name and ID for himself, he'd decided, and certainly he couldn't simply invent one and hope to get

away with it. So he asked Renni Lofall. "Is there anybody at
Stronghold, looks somewhat like me, who'd be the right rank
to command this ship by now?"

Thinking about it, she squinted at him, poised her hands to
mask off first one part of his head and then another, and finally
nodded. "Deet Armiger. Deet for Dietrich. He's been on
Stronghold about six years, so he's perhaps sixteen out from
Earth, groundside time. His record's good, and he's worked up
to First Officer. A captaincy now would be plausible."

"And the resemblance? How close?"

"Around the eyes and nose, rather good. Not the same
jawline at all. But if you had Deet's red hair and red beard,
you'd pass."

Tregare thought, then laughed. "I have time to grow the
whiskers. And if somebody on this bucket doesn't have some
red dye that matches close enough, I miss my guess."

He located the dye, all right, and the bleach that would be
needed first. He tried the stuff out on his sideburns, and Lofall
okayed the results. Since the supply was limited, Tregare held
off doing the full treatment until *Inconnu* would be nearing
Earth. Lofall explained that to avoid an artificial, too-uniform
appearance he should vary the bleach: "The beard's darker,"
she said, and, "I can't cut hair myself, but I can tell somebody
else how Deet should look. For one thing, he has less
forehead." She drew a rough sketch, and Bran saw what she
meant. No problem.

Meanwhile, once she'd helped him pick the name, everyone
aboard was instructed to use it at all times. "It's a nuisance, but
we don't want any slips." By the time they reached Earth, he
figured, the usage should be habit. Maybe even Junior Lee
could get over snickering when he said it.

Renni Lofall's own hair was long enough, now, to hide the
burned spots; except for one, burned too deeply, they showed
only as shorter patches. On her cheek the scar was visible but
fading. About any other marks, Tregare didn't ask.

She had, after calling first for permission, come to his
quarters. She sat but declined a drink, and said, "There's an
officer's cabin vacant, and—"

"You want it?"

"I wanted to ask whether anyone would be moving into it.

And if so, whether it would be the senior Chief, or possibly me."

"You want it, it's yours. Need any help?" He knew she didn't, with the few things she'd brought aboard and hardly more she'd drawn from Ship's Stores, but it was polite to ask.

She shook her head, thanked him, and left, now moving smoothly and without stiffness. Bran looked at the closed door, thinking that Leanne could have told him herself. Because a vacant cabin meant somebody had moved in with somebody. It would hardly be Gonnelson, so Prestor had moved to join Frei Relliger. Or more likely the other way around, her digs being the roomier.

Well, the hell with getting his feelings hurt. Maybe for morale and maybe for old times' sake, next chance he had, Tregare threw a small party for the new couple. Everybody seemed to enjoy it.

The plans for the Earth maneuver were as good as Tregare could figure them, but still he worried. Something was missing, and he couldn't guess what it might be. He knew what *kind* of thing he wanted and didn't have: some kind of edge, was what. But how to get it?

He was up in Control when *Inconnu*—or rather, the *Alexander*—met the UET patrol ship, some days short of Earth. Tregare had put his ship on decel early, taking longer at it than usual and staying well below redline; he needed all the options he could get, and coming in slow was one way to expand his choices.

The patrol ship obviously wasn't on station, and said so. "We've been back to the new refueling depot," its captain said. "Well, ten years is new enough, if you take the Long View. Anyway, the *Il Duce*, heading for Stronghold, had orders to take post at our station while we went for a refill. Did you meet the *Duce* on your way in, Captain Armiger?"

Tregare hadn't; he must have passed just outside detection ranges. For this meeting he hadn't bothered with the red dye; his new beard cloaked his jaw well enough, and any patrol ship skipper would have been still short of puberty when the real Deet Armiger left Earth. So Bran passed polite chat with this other captain, briefly since they weren't within talk range very long, and they parted with mutual well-wishings.

The one thing Tregare gained from the exchange was a

handle on UET's refueling outpost. He had its coordinates, the characteristic signals of its beacon, and a couple of good ideas.

Maybe this was the edge he needed. Because damned few people understood how relativity's Long View really worked. And Bran did.

The orbiting depot wasn't hard to find; this far out, its natural Solar orbit took very little adjustment to keep the installation essentially at a sidereally constant position—that was to say, more or less on the line from Earth's sun to Stronghold's.

The thing had a haywire look to it, but why not? Out here it had no stresses to withstand. Approaching, on hi-mag Tregare saw an ungainly framework, a skeletal construction to which the major components were secured. He counted three large fuel pods, one full and two not quite. The one rigid-looking construct had to be the supplies warehouse, and probably quarters for station personnel. Off to one side floated an ice asteroid at the end of taut guying cables; it sprouted several plastic funnels ending in feedpipes. Inside those funnels would be the heating elements to melt the ice, and the pumps to supply ships with the resultant liquid. No ships were here now; the station's complement was two scoutships, moored to the base structure. Bran hadn't heard of this project before, but it looked like a workable design.

And for his purposes, it was perfect.

Still not bothering to recolor hair or beard, he hailed the station as Captain Dietrich Armiger of the *Alexander*, out from Stronghold and heading for Earth. "But we had a little chase back there, off our course and slowing enough to cut our t/t₀ some. Which is why we're here a little early."

The man at the other end of the circuit, not pictured too clearly yet at this distance, shook his head. "I've never understood that stuff too well, but I'll take your word for it." *Damn right!* "And how can we help you, captain? And what was the chase about?"

"Sorry—that last question—it's what you might call Top Clam. But I can say this much: you know why you're out here, and our diversion was highly related. Now what we need— well, we have less fuel, because of the side-trip, than we should have at this point. Maybe it's safe to go on in as is, maybe not; the computer gives us marginal figures. So we'd like to top up some."

"Certainly, captain. And welcome to the *Arachne*." The man smiled. "The name's unofficial; comes from our structural makeup."

Well, the thing did look a little bit like part of a spider's web, with the solid components doubling for trapped insects, and folks in this kind of isolation needed all the in-jokes they could invent. Briefly, Tregare regretted having to hoodwink these people. But only briefly. What the hell—they were UET, weren't they?

If there was any hassle, it would be over fuel, and he really had enough, already. So he left that for last, maneuvering *Inconnu* to couple with a loading dock on the warehouse. He picked the side nearest the "iceteroid," so as to take on water at the same time. Agee Benbow, his contact on *Arachne*, seemed a little surprised. "Nobody's tried to double up those loadings before," he said. "It makes sense, though, if you're in a hurry."

"Which we are, and thanks for the cooperation." Tregare was watching the water feed. These orbiting ice cubes, he knew, were never plain ice; there had to be other components such as solid methane and ammonia. Finally he figured out how it worked. At the funnel's apex, just before it met the cylindrical feedpipe, valves gave streams of vapor to space. Well, the temperature differential wasn't touchy; he couldn't recall the boiling point of ammonia, but methane's was something like minus one-eight-four, Celsius. Neither compound was likely to get mixed up with liquid water, given enough heat to drive them out of solution at low pressure. So the water would be fit to drink; good. Tregare's chemistry wasn't all that accurate, but he thought he had it right.

If he didn't, that's what the filter system was for.

When water and other supplies—mostly food—were taken care of, Bran watched the disconnections and then shifted his ship over to the nearest fuel pod. When that feeding was begun, he accepted Benbow's invitation for a brief social visit to the depot's personnel areas. Along with him went Relliger, Prestor, and Deverel. Gonnelson was left to hold down Control. The visiting party was not unarmed, but you wouldn't know that fact by looking. It wasn't that Tregare expected any real trouble; he liked to take precautions, was all.

The depot's "scooters" were small chemical-reaction rocket craft, used to get the working crews from one part of *Arachne* to another. Max thrust might have lifted one off Earth's moon for a quick hop, but not much more than that. Here in no-grav space, range was limited by air supply; Tregare's casual questions determined that a work shift in a scooter shouldn't run into overtime too much. The thing seated up to ten, but not in comfort. Moving awkwardly in their controlled-magnet shoes, Tregare and his group met the two from *Arachne* at *Inconnu's* small topside airlock, because coupling the scooter there was easier than at the larger main lock.

Waiting in the scooter were Agee Benbow and a woman who was somewhat older than her voice and movements indicated. "My Exec," said Benbow. "Lacey M'Guinness. Mac, for short." So Tregare, with handshakes all around, introduced his own people. Then everybody sat down and strapped in, and Mac did the uncoupling routines, pointed the scooter toward the warehouse, and applied thrust. Tregare felt the gentle push build.

By design he was sitting where he could watch every move she made at the controls. Probably he'd never have to fly one of these things, but just in case . . . well, it looked simple enough, as she took the spacesled a little wide and then slowed toward a docking point, touching with hardly any jar.

Then they all went inside. Into bare, unfinished-looking corridors for a time, but finally into a more cheerful room where another man and woman rose to greet them. Tregare heard the names but promptly forgot them.

So everybody sat down and had a few drinks, plus some snacks that accumulated to become a moderately-sized meal, and Tregare asked (with genuine interest) about the history of *Arachne*, which Benbow and Mac were quite willing to tell.

The depot group wanted to hear, in turn, about the *Alexander's* travels. With a warning glance to his own people, Bran set off with a ship's history that made a few concessions to truth, but not many. Any time he caught himself talking his way into a hole, he had the easy out of invoking Security. And of course, in UET, that word slammed the door on any further inquiry. So, sneaking an occasional look at his wrist-chrono, Tregare strung out his story as long as he could stretch it.

Finally, though, Agee Benbow also checked the time and said, "Oh, I'm sorry, captain! It's been so pleasant, talking, that I hadn't noticed. But your partial refueling must have been completed hours ago, and I'm sure your crew is wondering what's happened to you. That is—you did say you were in a hurry?"

Nobody looked suspicious yet. Tregare said, "The hurry isn't just here, Benbow, it's on our overall assignment. So I thought, long as we're stopped here and hooked up, why not fill the tanks all the way? And save time at our Earth stopover, you see." He paused, and tried to remember how to look embarrassed. "Uh—I'd appreciate it if you all forget you heard that last part. I mean, I wasn't supposed—"

He paused, and Mac M'Guinness said, "Of course, captain. We didn't hear a thing. Did we?" She stared around the room, and the *Arachne* contingent shook their heads. "All right?"

For moments, watching Benbow's face take on a stubborn look, Tregare tried to rehearse the threats and arguments he'd have to improvise if things went wrong here. But that look passed, and Benbow said, "Yes. I should know better than to quibble about Security matters. But now then—" And whatever else, Tregare saw that the other man's previous cordiality had been rubbed dry. "—now, Captain Armiger, I don't wish to be inhospitable, but you know when your refueling will be done, and I don't. And I have duties to perform, which I've been happy to postpone in favor of this visit, but—"

"But now you'd like to know," said Tregare, "just how long we'd be hanging you up, here." *Say it right, now.* "My fault, I guess. Thinking back, I didn't make our fuel needs as clear as I thought I was doing." He knew the time, but for show he looked at his chrono anyway. "Okay." He raised his drink and without haste downed the last of it. "If we leave now, when we get to the *Alexander* it'll be time to start buttoning up and make ready to head in-system." He reached out a hand and Benbow accepted it. "And we do appreciate your welcome."

M'Guinness drove the scooter. This time Bran didn't watch the controls; he watched the woman. She wasn't young, but her lined face had vitality and her moves showed superb reflexes. When she docked at the topside airlock, Tregare waited while the rest of his party went into the ship. Then he stood, saying, "You're good with this scooter."

As they shook hands, she answered, "And you're a phony. I don't know what you're up to, but I don't believe a word."

"Then why—?"

The woman smiled. "Armiger—it takes one to know one." Then he went inside his ship and watched while she undocked and took the scooter back to *Arachne*.

Upship in Control, Tregare watched while *Inconnu* disengaged from the fuel pod and turned to initiate the curving course that would meet with Earth-orbit. The comm-tech expanded Gonnelson's usual monosyllables into precise instructions, and *Inconnu* began to move. Monitoring, Bran saw that the figures were right.

He nodded to Gonnelson. "Good job." Then he headed down to quarters. As he opened his door he turned to see Leanne Prestor coming toward him. "Hi. Something you wanted?"

"Yes. Do you have a minute?"

"Yeah, sure. What's on your mind?"

"What you did, there at the depot. I liked it."

"I didn't do anything. Faked 'em out, was all."

"That's what I *mean*. Our situation—I expected some kind of shoot-out, or violent bluff, at the least." Face flushed, she clenched a fist. "Things you'd done before—I expected—but this time you handled it without hurting anyone. If only you could have—"

So he knew what she meant. She liked things to work "nice." Well, so did he, but sometimes they wouldn't. Leanne didn't realize the difference; for peace' sake she thought it was *his* choice. And was she trying to come *back* to him, now? *Not that* . . .

He said first, "I always do what I have to." And then, "You and Frei, you getting along all right?" Then he waited.

Until she said, "What? Oh, yes. Just fine." Finally she left.

After Gonnelson's course had had time to put a few numbers into Tinhead, and Tregare had grabbed a few hours' sleep, he went up to Control and checked the situation. As he'd expected, the First Hat had set things up right. The trick was to start from *Arachne*'s "orbit," feed in the various gravitational influences—Sol's and Earth's being preeminent— and coast in on a compromise between least-time and least-fuel.

Near as Bran could tell, Gonnelson had it about perfect. So there wasn't much for a captain to do, up here just now. He hadn't had breakfast; now was a good time for it.

Entering the galley he met Renni Lofall coming out. "Captain—I'd like to talk with you."

"Sure. In here, though. I'm hungry." So while he ate she toyed with coffee she obviously didn't want, until he said, over his own second cup, "Okay, let's talk. What's the subject?"

"I want some work to do, on this ship."

Surprised, he said, "You're a comm-tech, aren't you? So—"

"You already have surplus in that specialty. Oh, I've filled in a few watches, learned things I didn't know about shipboard comm. But in that capacity I'm a fifth wheel."

He looked at her, seeing that a lot of strain had left her face. "What capacity you got in mind, then?"

"I'm an administrator, too. I can monitor the *systems* that keep an organization going, and make sure they're working correctly."

"Such as what?" Seeing her take his question as negation, he added, "Specifically, is all I mean."

Running fingers through her short, still uneven hair, she said, "What's your latest ship inventory? And how accurate?"

He thought about it. "I guess—well, I leave that up to Tinhead. We log supplies in when we load, and people are supposed to keep track of what's used. Like Groden, down in Stores. And—"

"And you know as well as I do that people sometimes forget. There's bound to be slippage. So, to be sure you don't someday find you're all out of some necessity you thought you had plenty of, it's imperative that regular inventories be conducted."

She was right, of course. So he told her she was, and thanked her, saying then, "Okay, you're in charge of inventory, just now. Ask Groden to line you up a work crew to help check. Take it easy on him, though; he tends to have a sore back, and I don't mean his muscles."

Lofall smiled. "Mr. Groden and I get along quite well in these matters." At his raised eyebrows, she added, "Job-related, I mean. I'm making this proposal on his behalf as well as mine."

Tregare laughed. "All right, Lofall. You have yourself a job."

* * *

Passing through the Solar System's outer reaches, *Inconnu* passed two more patrol ships and—as the *Alexander*—exchanged greetings with them. Tregare tried to wangle some Earthside news but got nothing useful from either contact. Passing wide of Jupiter, though, *Inconnu* cleared that planet's interference-shadow and began picking up all sorts of miscellaneous signals from Earth and the inner System. So with Renni Lofall deciphering some of the fancier codes that were new since Tinhead's Earthside programming, Tregare got an earful of UET's local planning.

And some not so local. For instance, another fleet of ships was preparing to leave for Stronghold. Bran tried to count by Long View terms—how many years would this be, at two years between fleets, since the one he'd dodged at the fortress world? He couldn't decide—five, probably—but one thing came to mind: UET was using a lot of its substance to guard against the Shrakken. Even though a lot of ships that went to Stronghold didn't necessarily stay there. *I can still take the place.*

But to plan for that move, he needed more info. He'd questioned Renni Lofall a little bit on that score, but not in detail. So when Renni brought the completed inventory summary to his quarters, he decided to get down to cases more.

First, though, the report. *Inconnu's* supplies were mostly in good shape, but a surprising number of unglamorous necessities were running toward the low side: stuff nobody had the specific responsibility for keeping track of. But she'd logged the whole summary into Tinhead, so it would all be on the order readouts for the orbital resupply station at Earth.

"Good job," said Tregare. "Let me top up your drink."

"Haven't we finished our business, for the moment?"

"The inventory business, sure. But for a time now, I've been meaning to hear some more about Stronghold." So she agreed, and he started asking. And, of course, making notes.

He'd guessed that Stronghold's personnel complement was something less than ten thousand—and planned to grow slowly, as support facilities also grew. He was interested to learn how many were civilians, including nonworking "dependent" family members, how many troops—and the size of the Committee Police contingent. The latter was larger than he'd thought, but not enough to change his estimate of the forces *he'd* need. Because UET never allowed arms to any but Police and military.

"No problem," he muttered, and didn't realize he'd said it aloud until Lofall asked him *what* was no problem. "Oh, nothing. Not right now, anyway. Well, I guess that's all for this time, and thanks." He stood, ready to see her out.

She stood also, but came toward him instead, and put her hands to his shoulders. Puzzled, all he said was, "Yes?"

"Tregare—don't you get tired of living alone? I do. Unless you have a little something going on the side. I don't."

The trouble was, he hadn't been thinking of her in this way. And, maybe because first Erdis and then Leanne had rejected him, his first instinct was toward caution. So while he was still trying to find an answer, she pushed off from him. "Sorry. I forgot I'm all scarred and ugly."

On twin thoughts, that she'd been hurt a lot and that sure's hell he knew he could trust her, Bran's self-absorption broke. Moving fast, he caught her at the door. "You're not; no such thing. This was a little quick, is all. Grabbed me off guard. You want to talk some?"

"All right." So they sat. He expected her to say something; when she didn't, he asked two questions. Why him, and why now? Speaking carefully, she said, "You, because you accept me fully and were the first who did, aboard here. Now, because earlier I was too damned sore, but I think I'm healed well enough. And also because once we reach Earth you'll be too busy."

Oddly, her rather clinical manner aroused him; for the moment he tried to soft-pedal that reaction. "There's after, too."

She shook her head. "Maybe not. At Earth, I may go groundside." He wanted to know how and why, and she said, "Responsibilities, that I have to the Underground. Family I'd like to see, even knowing what the Long View's done to respective ages. Things like that. As to how—" She grinned. "You'll see. And I won't risk your security in any way."

"How about yours? UET Earthside has no handle on you now, but—"

"And won't. I have a solid cover identity." When he protested that living on phony ID could get tiresome, she said,

"You don't understand. *This* is my cover ident. Once I get groundside, I'd take it off and blend back into the woodwork."

He didn't ask her real name because he had no need to know it. In fact he didn't ask much of anything, because now she was taking her clothes off, and it wasn't polite to let her get too far ahead of him in that activity.

To anyone who hadn't attended UET's Slaughterhouse, the woman's scars might have shocked arousal out of being. Bran had seen worse, though; in fact he *wore* worse. Not so cruelly and deliberately placed, however. At any rate he made no comments, and when she came to him, met her more than halfway.

About her state of recovery, it seemed she'd been a little optimistic. In the face of "too long since last time" Bran was *trying* to be easy with her, but saw her face contort with pain. So they switched to a position he found somewhat awkward, but it worked for both of them.

Anyway, sitting up after a while, Lofall looked as pleased as Tregare felt. She didn't talk about it; what she said was, "Your hair and beard. Earth's not far off now. Would you like me to do the coloring for you? I'm quite good at that, and can get rid of the excess curliness, too. Though as I said, someone else should give you the necessary haircut."

So after Tregare ordered them up a meal and they had that, she smeared him with one and another evil-smelling paste and eventually washed away each of them. Bran looked at the result and ran a finger across the lank red hair that fell over his forehead. "Why'nt you just chop this back so I can see better? That ought to do it." When she protested, he said, "After all, who says Deet Armiger always goes to the same barber?"

She tried it, and made several successive corrections. Finally Tregare said, "Let's quit while we're ahead." And at her startled look, added, "On my appearance, I mean."

With the urgency off, he was able to make love in the fashion he was most used to, and still keep it gentle enough for her.

A day or so later, *Inconnu* began to draw direct calls from Earth; the ship had been detected and groundside wanted some contact. Tregare didn't stall for long. He looked over his plans and went ahead with them, announcing the imminent arrival of the *Alexander the Great*, Dietrich Armiger commanding. He said, "I won't put the coded report and mission directive off to you until we're in better reception range, but part of it you need to know before we arrive. Which is, we refuel and resupply at whichever orbital station you assign us, and then move out ASAP on the next leg of our mission. Time's important and this crew is a briefed team so Admiral Saldeen has ordered that no personnel transfers be made at this stop. The Admiral sends his apologies for any apparent high-handedness but says you'll realize the urgency when you see his coded report."

Tregare cut the circuit and wiped sweat from his forehead. He hoped his spiel, which Prestor and Deverel had helped phrase, carried the grade of conviction that would sell UET Earthside.

From the answers he got, after transmission timelag, it was going pretty well, so far.

Somebody groundside, though, seemed to need to put a spoke into the wheel of anyone citing any authority but his very own. This person was a Colonel Missouri (or something that sounded like Missouri, and the nasal twang surely fit). The colonel dictated that being an unscheduled arrival, the *Alexander* would take its turn at Station Five, and never mind that Station Five was preempted by the fleet for Stronghold.

Since there was no point at all in arguing, which would merely draw unwelcome attention, Tregare warped course so as to jump the line ahead of two ships, making a more leisurely approach, and settled into a holding pattern immediately following the Stronghold ships.

He did ask Missouri's assistant, when the colonel left to exert his authority on some other caller, how come the ships for Stronghold needed refueling. "I mean," said Tregare, "they just now lifted off Earth." He was told that he was asking about a Security matter, so he apologized and cut the circuit.

"I can tell you that," said Renni Lofall, sitting in at comm. "Some years back, the first ship to lift in one of these fleets just swung off the wrong way and kept going. Never *was* caught."

Bran nodded. "So now they herd 'em a lot closer?"

"That's right. You'll notice, out there, two armed ships and four not. The armed ones came up first, almost fully fueled, and merely topped off. They're waiting while the other four, which lifted almost empty, refuel at Station Five. So—"

"Mother hens giving the chicks no chance to get lost." He shook his head. "With that grade of mistrust, how do they run their show at all?"

Lofall shrugged. "The only reason it works, Tregare, is that actual rebel activity is about a tenth of what UET's geared up to fight."

Tregare thought about it. "That situation needs correcting."

Not right now, though. Current drill was to minimize contact with UET but keep necessary dealings all smooth and nice. Coasting in Colonel Missouri's specified holding pattern, the *Alexander* accepted the airlock-docking of two courier craft, and in his digs Tregare entertained the midrange groundside brass commanding those little buckets, and sent them away happy. He didn't have to give them any coded reports because they lacked proper clearance, but he put the matter in a more face-saving way: "I expect you'll see all this stuff, groundside. It's just that *I* don't have authorization to release the info, except direct to HQ." Leanne Prestor, he could see, was truly impressed at his "tact." Her trouble, he decided, was that she'd never been at the Slaughterhouse.

And just as well. She'd never have lived through it.

When you have to wait, you might as well enjoy it. Tregare made a point of getting all the Earthside Tri-V channels monitored and taped. He had the major news circuit piped into the galley, because he wanted the whole crew to get a good look at what UET said was happening on Earth. And compare that with Underground data.

The latter, Renni was helping him with, readjusting one transceiver pair and its tape-handling accessories to handle the Underground's "wideband burst" method of secret communication, which traded bandwidth for time at an astonishing ratio. The principle was an old one; the Underground's trick was that each burst carried the coded key to shift the system's base frequency for the *next* burst. Without the codes, no one would be apt to intercept more than the occasional burst—and wouldn't know what to do with it, anyway, since each burst carried parts of several different data blocks.

So retrieving the info was tricky, but with Lofall's help Tregare was getting the stuff into coherent order. He didn't much like the results, though: UET had North America in worse shape than ever, and still pushing. If the UG's observations were at all accurate, something like thirty percent of the continent's population now existed in Total Welfare Centers. And Bran knew what Total Welfare "clients" really were: government-owned slaves.

The rationale sounded reasonable. If you couldn't support yourself and your family, kindly ol' UET took over all your assets and liabilities, and placed you in a Welfare Center where you were fed, clothed, and housed. And sent out in work gangs hired by private industry or by UET itself. A small amount of your contracted wages went as "credit" into your personal account, and theoretically you could earn enough to buy out of Welfare. But damn few ever managed to reach that goal.

And of course it wasn't only bankrupts who went to Welfare. The Centers now probably contained more dissidents than any other category of client. Everybody knew it, but don't say so out loud!

Bran shut down the readout and turned to Lofall. "What say we grab some lunch?" So they went down to the galley. As they began eating, somebody turned up the Tri-V news monitor.

"Hey, let's see this," said Hain Deverel. "Some Welfare kid hit it big in the monthly lottery, and she's being interviewed."

"It's a replay," someone said. "Happened last month. The story now is that she's disappeared." Several people shushed the talker, and the newscaster could be heard.

Busy with his food, Tregare half listened. Several weeks ago, on her sixteenth birthday, which gave her adult status, a young Welfare "client" named Rissa Kerguelen had won the state-run lottery's grand prize, built to its largest-ever size by the drawing of a series of ineligible winners over previous months. Approximately a hundred million Weltmarks, the man said. Or maybe twenty-three million, Bran estimated, after taxes. A hell of a lot, anyway!

Now, it seemed, this record-high winner had disappeared. All possible means were being used to find her, and make sure of her safety. *Safety? Oh, sure, Mike!* Toward that end, then, her media interview on the day the prize was awarded was being shown again on Tri-V.

Tregare leaned forward and to one side, to see better. This

could be interesting. The screen showed a drab auditorium; a surprisingly large press turnout half filled the place.

A fattish man with a lot of blond, slicked-down hair led in a young girl who wore a red dress. Somebody else's dress: it was several sizes too large and hung on her like a sack. Just guessing, Tregare bet she had nothing on except the dress.

Under Welfare-stubbled dark hair her face was so blank that Bran couldn't decide if she were pretty or ugly. Well, a Welfare kid—coping with something like this could freeze her.

The fat man took her up onto a small platform, with mikes. He smiled and smiled; Tregare tried to think where he'd seen that smile before. Certainly not on *this* butterball . . .

Then he remembered: "Plastic Smile" on the *MacArthur,* Butcher Korbeith's sadistic bodyguard. But Bran had killed that one. . . .

This one's name was Supervisor Gerard. When he got done talking about himself, he introduced his supervisee: Rissa Kerguelen, age sixteen just today, daughter of David Marchant and Selene Kerguelen, both unfortunately deceased, of a city Bran didn't recall hearing about before and promptly forgot.

As Gerard stepped down and left her standing there alone, the kid started to say something, but stopped when a question came from the floor. "What's your reaction to winning the big prize?"

Pause. Then, "Naturally, I'm delighted."

Another voice. "How does it feel to grow up in a Welfare Center?"

More quickly this time, Rissa Kerguelen said, "I can't answer that; I've never grown up anywhere else. How does it feel to grow up outside?" Laughter came, and Tregare thought, *good on you, kid!*

"The last big winner called it an utter miracle. Do you agree?"

Obviously gaining confidence now, the girl shrugged. "No. Why should I? Every month, as long as I can remember, it happens—with the winners announced on Tri-V. This time it's me, is all."

After a moment, "Who will you vote for in the next election?"

Kerguelen shook her head. "I don't understand."

"Which bidding conglomerate has your support?"

Slowly again, she answered, "I can't say—I don't know enough about any of them."

"Does that mean you don't favor the present Committee?" Some menace in that question? Maybe . . .

She was flustered; on the screen a close-up showed her biting her lip. "It doesn't mean *anything* yet. Give me time to learn."

A harsh voice. "You better learn fast, kid."

The implied threat stalled things, then the camera swung to a grey-haired woman: "What do you intend to do with the money you've won? And with your life, from now on?"

Not hesitating, Rissa Kerguelen said, "Buy my brother out of Welfare—my Uncle Voris, too, if he's still alive—and share with them. That's the money." Now, for the first time, she smiled, and Tregare decided she was better-looking than he'd thought. "My life? Well, I'm going off Earth and I'm going to grow my hair down to my butt—and the rest of it's my own business."

While Tregare chuckled at the kid's feisty answer, he heard gasps from the media reps, and one said, "You resent your present hairstyle?"

Again no hesitation. "What's to resent? A few sets of clippers are a lot cheaper than combs and brushes always getting lost and wearing out—anybody can see that. I don't get to like it, though, and I never did."

She'd slowed them down some, all right. Now someone asked, "What are you going to do, off Earth?"

"I don't know yet. What are *you* going to do, *on* Earth?"

Whether or not that reply ended the interview, now the screen cut back to the first newscaster. ". . . and that's all we have for you on the missing lottery winner Rissa Kerguelen. If anyone has any information leading to—uh, making sure of her safety and well-being, please contact us here at . . ."

Tregare quit listening; he knew bullshit when he heard it and that 'caster was full of it up to here. The kid, though—wherever she was, he hoped she was all right.

Renni came along to his quarters. Before anything else, she filled him in some about UET's lottery winners. "Those wins are UET's carrot, Bran. So they get lots of publicity. For a time, that is."

"And then?"

"Then it tapers off and disappears. And the winners, very quietly with no public mention at all, are taken in charge again."

"What—?"

"Arrested on any flimsy charges UET cares to make. The remaining prize money confiscated. And it's back into Welfare."

Until she yelped, he didn't realize how hard he was gripping her arm. "You mean, *that's* how the kid disappeared?"

Rubbing the arm, Renni said, "No. Not this time. Or they wouldn't be doing any of this on Tri-V. No, she got away. And I think I know how and where."

"But didn't you just now first hear of her, same as I did?"

"I'd seen earlier mentions, Bran—brief ones. But they didn't apply *here*, you see, so—well, anyway, some facts in that case clicked with some equally irrelevant material off the UG circuit. Irrelevant to this ship, I mean. And—"

"Are you going to *tell* it?"

She sat up straight. "Right. *Yes*, sir." Okay; he could put up with a little clowning, until she went on, "Young Kerguelen was taken from the Welfare Center by a reporter who is one of *ours*. The UG, I mean. Where she was taken is not important. *But,* from that place, a few weeks later, another of ours put a young woman on a low-level SST to Buenos Aires."

"And all that means what?"

"Put it together yourself. And add in Erika Hulzein's Establishment, which operates somewhere out of Buenos Aires and is most influential in keeping UET's fingers off that whole country."

Aunt Erika? Not thinking, Tregare said, "If the kid's with *that* old tiger, UET can go piss up a rope."

Lofall narrowed her eyes. "What do *you* know about the Hulzein Establishment?"

Now when Tregare took hold of her, it was gently. "More than I intend to tell you, Renni. Except that we're on the same side but never got along. All right?"

It must have been, because for quite a while there, everything else was.

For the rest of that day, in the back of Tregare's mind, the mystery of the Kerguelen youngster's fate nagged him. At one point he even toyed with the idea of trying to route some kind of illicit call through to the Hulzein Establishment in Argentina, and asking about the kid. But such a move would be just plain asking for trouble, and he was already surrounded with enough potential for that. So he didn't.

Instead he kept his ship waiting in line while the Stronghold fleet went, one ship at a time, through the supply feeds. He greeted and hosted two sets of couriers from groundside, who brought him flimsies of info that UET hadn't cared to trust to the airwaves, and in turn he gravely handed over printed (but still coded) readouts of the report that had Admiral Saldeen's slightly-edited signature on it. Groundside had had Tregare rerun that report to them, over tightbeam link, several times. But they couldn't seem to get the glitches out of it. Somehow Tregare wasn't too surprised.

When the second group was ready to leave, someone came running to join them. Panting a little, she said, "Catch a ride groundside with you? I was on the earlier shuttle and missed it going back. Met an old friend, we got to talking." She turned to Tregare. "Captain, I owe you an apology. May I speak with you a moment?"

Everybody was standing at the main airlock's inside hatch. Tregare motioned the others into the lock and drew Renni Lofall off to one side, out of earshot. "What the hell you think you're doing?"

With bright-colored lapels, epaulets, sleeve and leg stripes affixed to her jumpsuit, she looked the perfect courier: no denying that much. How had she done it? No time to ask. She said, "I told you I might be getting off. This is my move. You won't spoil it?"

He grinned. "Couldn't if I wanted to. Hope it works, is all." He looked around. "Nobody's watching. Kiss good-bye, Renni." They did that, and again; then he said, "Groundside, what'll you do? Do you have contacts to help you, once you land?"

"All set, yes. And—" She hugged him. "It's been good, Bran."

"Yeah. Same here." What else? "You—" But no more time. From the airlock someone was beckoning; she had to run. "Good luck, Lofall." Then the inner hatch closed, and she was gone.

* * *

Finally the *Alexander* was signaled ahead to a supply dock. Tregare sat monitoring Tinhead's record of the loading process. As he watched he felt grateful to Renni Lofall for insisting on taking inventory. It wasn't that *Inconnu* had been short of anything in a way that could endanger the ship—but he'd have felt stupid if, halfway between someplace and no place, he'd run out of soap or something. Now, thanks to Lofall, he wouldn't.

The input of solid supplies was nearing its end. So now was where push came to shove. Because having topped off fuel and water tanks at the *Arachne*, he couldn't accommodate much more of either item. And when that fact became evident, someone in UET HQ would want to know *why*. He had his story, of course: the Admiral's orders. But on a hunch he'd held it back, and he wondered if maybe the hunch had been wrong.

Now, as the ship undocked and instructions came for the *Alexander* to move ahead and take on water, on the forward screen Bran saw a triangle of three ships approaching. What he didn't like was that their path wasn't far from his own intended course for leaving here.

And then Bran *really* didn't like it. Because on hi-mag, his main screen showed one of the nearing ships to be the *MacArthur*. And over a monitor came Arger Korbeith's gravel voice. "*Alexander*, hell! That ship is the *Tamurlaine!*"

And Korbeith's ships cut abruptly toward intercept.

There wasn't time to tell the supply station anything at all. Cutting his offship-send, Tregare told Gonnelson which way to point *Inconnu* and said, "Junior Lee. Fire the Drive, redline max. Now!" Slowly at first, *Inconnu* turned and moved.

It wasn't the comm-tech's fault; lacking other instructions the man obeyed Korbeith's transmitted order for two-way visual. The Butcher hadn't changed; that craggy yellowed face would probably look much the same in its coffin. Tregare could see Korbeith squint and blink at what he saw in *Inconnu*'s control area; then the man nodded and yelled, "Damn it, *all ships!* You've just resupplied an Escaped ship. And your Captain Dietrich Armiger is the pirate, Bran Tregare." Glaring, he yelled, "I see you, Tregare, you snot! Once, you got away from this ship alive. Not again, though." He cut voice-send, but Bran saw him barking orders. To his own crew and to his other ships, they'd be.

So Bran gave a few of his own. "Cut Drive to half-max, Junior Lee—I need some time before this fight." And, "Gonnelson, head us straight for the center of their triangle." Tregare moved to another console, one that gave him more tools to work with. On intercom he called, "Anybody in Scout Bay Two, say so fast and get out faster." He activated the enabling circuits that would let him run that scoutship as a remote-control drone, then as no answer came to his order, opened the bay and fired up the scout's Drive. Only on idle, for the moment, and now he told Junior Lee Beauregard to run ship's Drive at redline again. Well, a little under, he wanted, but Junior Lee knew that.

There hadn't been time, what with all the rest of it, to get gunners up to the projector turrets, so Tregare slaved all his projectors to his own console. Hoping the turret controls were sitting on neutral, because from here he had no heterodyne control but only traverse and override capability, he fired three energy bursts straight ahead, just to get his heterodyne up toward peak range. Then, watching Korbeith's delta of killer ships approach, he waited.

Not for long. Korbeith's group opened fire early. This near to Earth, ionization of attenuated gases made coruscating tracer lines where the convergent lasers tracked—glowing streaks that dazzled vision. So under cover of that glare, Bran launched his scoutship from Bay Two. First hesitating, he decided its best use was to go directly between two of Korbeith's ships, the *MacArthur* and one of the others. When he had it pointed right, time came to use his own projectors— on the third ship.

Everything happened in a hurry. He got the third ship, all right. When the scout was between the other two, Tregare blew its Drive, and one ship blew along with it. Not the *MacArthur*, though; obviously damaged, it still held course, almost.

But Bran Tregare was past now—past the lot of them, and away clear.

7. South Forty

When it came to escape routes, what Tregare liked about making a sling turn and cutting Drive was that the pursuit could be expecting it and still couldn't do a damn thing about it. "Here we go," he said now, some days out from Earth. "We're out of sight behind Saturn—I'm swinging course. When the posse comes past the planet, we're dead-Drive coasting—about as easy to spot as a flea on a sheep dog." He laughed, then settled down to set course. "How many chased us, anyway? I've been too busy to check."

"Four," said Gonnelson. "Nothing fast." Tregare nodded.

He'd picked Saturn for his pivot because Jupiter was in the wrong direction, while Saturn lay within a radian of his chosen course and gave him leeway for the swing. Prestor thought the rings would be a problem because *Inconnu*'s closest approach obviously had to be well inside their spread. Tregare, though, simply went "under" them, below the planet's ecliptic. Which meant that the turn gave the ship a slight vector toward zenith. Well, that was all right—he'd be crossing a number of UET's regular shipping routes, and passing "above" them meant he'd be in a skew pattern with any Uties if he chanced to cross paths. Hard to intercept, that was the point of it.

* * *

Once they were back on Drive and well away, Bran held council; in captain's quarters he provided drinks and snacks while the group had a chance to look at a star-chart readout.

After a while, when everybody had settled down pretty well, he stood. "Okay, people: here's what I have in mind and I'd like to hear your thinking on it." He used a pointer at the chart. "Mostly I think we should stop in on Hidden Worlds—gather info, all that. Besides trading, of course. But it wouldn't hurt to raid a UET colony or two, if that option turns up handy by location."

He spelled it out, and some of the group had comments and some didn't, and the upshot was that *Inconnu's* next stop should be a Hidden World called South Forty. It was off any major UET route, its settlements were well established, and it was fairly well in line for a considerable choice of second stops.

So, excusing himself with a gesture, Gonnelson went upship and set course.

Bran sat, after the others left, brooding over the tag-end of his drink. The knock startled him; he opened his door to a youngish woman whose jumpsuit bore no indications of rank. "Captain?"

"That's me." The odd thing was that he didn't recognize her. Well, maybe the short red hair, frizzed fluffy on top but tapered smooth at sides and back, was a new look for her. "I don't seem to recall your name," but he gestured her inside and to a seat. "How long have you been on this ship?"

"Since about twelve hours before we left Earth orbit. I came aboard as a courier." Pert-faced as she was, she had more age to her than showed at first—but the movements of her slim body showed an athlete's coordination.

Tregare frowned. To cover his surprise, he said, "Courier? Where's your fruit salad?" But then he saw, on the slightly faded suit, the darker places on sleeves and legs and shoulders where those decorations had been. *So that's where Lofall got all that stuff*. He moved a hand. "All right; I know where it went. I saw it go off the ship. But now then—who are you, and what the hell are you doing here?"

"My name is Tanit Eldon. I'm an Underground agent with roughly the same rank as the woman who left ship wearing my—" She grinned. "—my fruit salad. For about three months, since taking some brief training at the Hulzein

Establishment in Argentina, I've been working undercover for UET at the main spaceport. And at the moment, since my report is long and dry, I'm waiting for you to offer me a drink, captain, sir."

Working undercover, was she? Maybe—*but who for?* Drinks made and served, because he could use a new one himself, Bran Tregare asked questions. A lot of them, and cutting back and forth from one subject to another, trying to trip her up.

Most of it fit—maybe all of it, but he didn't *know* all of it. She had code words, she had names—info that Renni Lofall had picked off the wide-burst channel for him. She described the layout and setup of Erika Hulzein's Argentine base, and maybe she'd been there and maybe not, but Bran hadn't so he could only go by what little he did know.

"How did you and Lofall get together?"

"She was loitering around where she could make eye contact with the couriers, or anyone else that came aboard, and now and then giving an Underground code sign." Again the grin, and Tregare felt he should be noticing something. Finally he did; occasionally her right thumb, the hand resting quietly in her lap, made an inconspicuous triple twitch: toward the back of the hand, forward, and again back. When he nodded, Tanit Eldon said, "When I responded, we did the usual drill— greeted each other like old friends and arranged to meet and talk in her room." She shrugged. "I wanted onship and she wanted off, so the details were easy. The only way it could have been easier would be if we wore the same size suit."

"That's nice." But one thing her story didn't explain. So he asked. "*Why* did you want to get on this ship?"

"Because word got back, from your wide-burst contacts with the UG, to Erika Hulzein. And she wants to make an alliance."

An alliance? *Erika?* Tregare said, "Just who is it, she wants to team up with?"

Eldon leaned forward. "Well, any Escaped ship would be better than none. But the way I was told, when Madame Hulzein put it together that here was a ship that was Escaped *and* armed, she said it had to be Tregare's *Inconnu*. And that's when I was pulled by the roots out of my previous assignment, and ordered to get on here at any cost." Pause. "Which I did."

He thought about it. Whether his aunt Erika knew who he really was, or whether Eldon did, made no difference. Because either way, no "alliance" could be made operative during Erika's probable lifetime (and how was his sickly cousin Frieda, Erika's daughter, doing these days?). Regardless, that stuff would have to wait.

What couldn't wait was finding out if Eldon told any truth.

Shrugging, she accepted being interrogated under truth drugs as a matter of course. "Now if you were UET I'd be trying to claw my way out of here. But at the port I didn't have that problem; the UG rather neatly got me into a job that didn't carry a high level of Security precautions."

So Eda Ghormley brought the kit upship and administered the injections, and Tregare ran his questions—or as many as he could keep in mind—through the mill all over again.

Tanit Eldon's story held up solidly. So Ghormley left, and Bran waited until the drugs wore off so that the woman came back to herself and knew where she was. Then he personally took her down to Stores, where Groden issued her the standard necessities, and finally Bran escorted her to the quarters lately vacated by Renni Lofall.

Still looking slightly whacked-out, Eldon said, "I can't simply *ride* this ship; I'll need a job. I don't know ships' needs, but I've worked as a junior administrator."

Tregare couldn't help saying, "Too bad we don't have any juniors to administrate," but then he smiled and said, "How are you at keeping track of inventory, monitoring actual count against the computer's version?" Because he didn't have time for that stuff, himself, and Renni Lofall had shown him the need.

She nodded. "I've done that kind of thing, yes."

"All right; tomorrow, show me a trial run. If you pass—" Suddenly he realized she couldn't know all the complicated stuff about rankings and owning shares in the ship; no time for all that, now. "If you pass I'll buy you a Chief's rating and you can pay me back out of work credits." She wanted to ask more but he shushed her. "I'll explain later; for now, don't worry about it."

Then he left, trying to figure what Erika's angle could be.

* * *

Danger seemed to unify the ship, and keep down the incidence of hassles. Since *Inconnu* first headed for Stronghold, Tregare had needed to hold court only twice, both for minor matters. So he'd nearly forgotten about that chore, until one day his Third Hat appeared at Tregare's door with a scowling Chief Rating named Sven Dahl, one of Junior Lee Beauregard's Drive techs. "We have a problem, skipper," said Frei Relliger.

Bran sighed; if he wanted problems he'd ask Tinhead for one. "Come on in." It didn't look like a social occasion, so except for seats he offered no hospitality. "What is it?"

"He gets his say first because he's brass; right?" said Dahl. Tregare looked at the man; the Chief was a "black Swede" or maybe Norwegian, swarthy with dark hair and high cheekbones. Big, and probably good-looking enough except for a nose that must have caught one fist too many.

And now the squarehead was spoiling for a fight. So Bran said, "If that's how you want it. All right, Relliger. What's the beef?"

Obviously embarrassed, the Third Hat tried to keep his story short but couldn't seem to manage. Since he and Leanne worked separate watches, they each had a lot of lonesome time. Dahl had started hanging around Leanne every chance he got, and making suggestions. And then—

"Just a minute," said Tregare. "Shouldn't she be here herself, to tell this part? You saying it, it's hearsay evidence."

"I asked her to. She wouldn't come, unless you make it a direct order." Tregare nodded; he'd hear these people first. Relliger continued. Finally Dahl had propositioned her outright, and she'd turned him down. "At which point he turned on her and was grossly insulting. He's not going to get away with that."

"You charging insubordination, or what?" Relliger shook his head, so Bran didn't wait for a verbal answer. "All right, Chief Rating Dahl. What's your side of it?"

"Sure I made a try, there. Where's the law against that? Or against striking out, either. But she set me back *snotty*. Like I wasn't good enough for her." Brows raised, Tregare waited. "So I told her she wasn't so much, shopping around like she does. First you, skipper, then him, so why too upnose for a Chief? I mean, it's not like she did the Slaughterhouse and brought her tattoo from UET." Arms folded, Dahl sat back.

"There's more than that," said Relliger. "He called her names."

"A couple, maybe," Dahl said. "But nothing real bad. I—"

"I do not *care*," said Bran. "I want to know one thing here, and one thing only. Exactly what is it that I am supposed to decide, about this?"

"It's not deciding," Relliger answered. "Just give us permission to fight; that's all."

Then it came to Bran, what they were after. After Escape he'd filed UET's Ships' Regs away and written a very brief paper entitled "NEW Ship's Regulations, by order of Bran Tregare." Looking back, he figured he'd put in some silly stuff, out of sheer smart-aleck bravado. But he remembered the first three; they came first because he meant them:

I. *Orders will be obeyed first and argued later.*
II. *No drinking or drugging on duty.*
III. *No fighting without captain's permission.*

All right. Now he said, "You want to fight?" Both nodded. "You'll each tell me why." He paused. "You first, Dahl."

"I want to show him I'm the better man. And her, too."

"It's debatable that winning a fight proves that, but I understand your point. And you, Frei?"

"He's not going to get away with insulting Leanne!"

Tregare thought about it, and weighed the odds. On the face of it, Dahl had the physique and quickness to make short work of Relliger. Dammit, Bran couldn't *afford* to lose another officer just now—and if he didn't specify otherwise, he knew this fight would be to the death. Yet if he shielded his Third Hat from danger, the man's usefulness would end as the crew lost respect for him. And the whole stupid mess over nothing more than a pair of bruised egos. . . .

There wasn't any good answer, so Tregare made one up. He made a show of thinking hard, but he was only figuring the details of how to say it. Let 'em wait a little . . .

He cleared his throat. "Scout Bay Two is mostly empty. First you stow the loose gear away; there'll be nothing used as weapons. Unarmed combat, and unclothed—no watches or rings, even."

"Wait a minute!" Dahl. "What are the rules?"

"Make up your own." Nobody answered; Tregare decided

he was beginning to enjoy this. "What happens in there is your business. When somebody knocks to be let out, and not before, the door opens again." *Now the kicker.* "Don't take more than ten minutes at it, though. Because that's when I let the air out."

"But you said, no watches!" Both men protested.

Tregare shrugged. "*Your* problem." He saw the two of them looking at each other, and was pretty sure what they were thinking: no referee, no seconds, no cheering section for the winner . . .

Then Relliger said, "Dahl? Maybe if you'd apologize to Leanne—"

The Chief Rating shrugged. "I could do that. I guess I was a little rough. Got sore, you know, and—"

"Sure. But she'd appreciate your telling her so."

Talking almost like friends, the two men left. Bran Tregare poured himself the drink he'd been wanting, and grinned.

South Forty was a long haul from Earth and seemed longer. Twice *Inconnu* passed UET ships within shouting range, but Bran kept his beacon turned off and didn't bother to answer their hails. Since he couldn't spare time and fuel to try intercept, why give them any data about him? A further point was that even if intercept had been possible, he had no officer cadre to put onto a captured ship: Gonnelson didn't want command, and Tregare saw neither Prestor nor Relliger as command material. Not yet, anyway. And he wasn't exactly overstaffed with ratings, either.

He could have sidetracked to raid any one of three UET colonies not too far off *Inconnu's* route. Bored, he figured the costs in fuel and time, and decided none of them were worth stretching the trip by months of ship's time. Heavenly Isles would have been the most economical side-jaunt, but as Tregare said in council, "It's a fairly new colony and the planet's mostly ocean. Likely all we'd get from a raid would be the fuel we'd waste stopping there." So they skipped Heavenly Isles; Tregare had t/t₀ still riding above six by then, and would have hated to waste it.

Slowing toward the system where South Forty orbited, Tregare detected no other ship traffic. Not surprising; his data bank showed this Hidden World to have little commerce. But it was a place he wanted to check out, for future possibilities. A little isolation could be a good thing.

The sun was more orange and less bright than Earth's, but South Forty's orbit averaged only about point-eight of an A.U. so temperatures would be reasonably comfortable. Coming in past the usual gas giants, Tregare got a good hi-mag look at South Forty. His approach angle, by luck, showed the planet side-lit; checking the movement of planetary features on time-lapse tape, the degree of axial tilt was evident. About one-third radian, Bran guessed; slightly less than Earth's but not much. Looking, Bran Tregare nodded. The habitable zone on this world would cover a lot of latitude—and in that zone was plenty of land area.

But so far as he knew, there wasn't much habitation yet.

Closing so near that he'd spotted the major settlement and its spaceport, still Tregare got no hail from groundside. Finally he got on the horn and initiated the action. With straight talk, since this was a Hidden World: " . . . armed ship *Inconnu*, an Escaped Ship, Bran Tregare commanding, request landing instructions . . ."

Eventually an answer came. No screen picture, just a woman's voice, saying, "South Forty responding to *Inconnu*. Sorry to be such slow pay, but we get so little action these days that the port isn't manned full time. Please be welcome here. Pick any landing circle you want, but it'd be helpful if you'd burn the weeds off one that hasn't been used lately." She paused, then answered Bran's next question before he asked it. "We're well-fixed for fuel and supplies. In fact we had to shut the refinery down because we ran out of storage volume. So—"

"Right. Thanks for telling me." And in fact he *had* been wondering if this backwater could make it worth his while to expend the fuel needed for entering and leaving its gravity well. "See you down there pretty soon."

Two more orbiting spirals: then he plowed air and went in.

Number Six landing circle looked most overgrown. When *Inconnu* came to rest, the growth was gone. Leaving Gonnelson to hold down Control, Tregare's group waited in the main airlock until most of the smoke and dust had settled, then the hatch opened and the boarding ramp moved out and down.

Tregare led the way groundside. Following him were Frei

Relliger, Hain Deverel, and a couple of other Chief Ratings.
All wore their usual sidearms but no heavier weapons.

From the modest-sized Port Admin building, a party of
three came to greet their visitors. The tall, lean woman in the
lead looked to have about forty Earthyears, bio. When she
gave a hail, Bran recognized her voice from the circuit contact.
Then the groups met and everybody shook hands. "So you're
Bran Tregare. We've heard about you, more than a little. And
we have some messages for you, left by other ships."

"That's good; thanks." Distracted a little, Bran tried to keep
the names straight. This blond woman, slightly greying, was
Mayo Tolridge. The man was Theo-somebody, and the youngish brunette was somebody-Corelli; maybe he could fill the
rest in later. "Who-all left messages? You happen to remember?"

The names rang few bells, so he decided the stuff would be
mostly info from people he did know, relayed by some he
didn't. And inside the building, that's how it turned out. Raoul
Vanois had been here with *Carcharodon*, and left an uncoded
voice tape for Tregare. "It's two as sends word for *Inconnu*."
Contrasting with the odd grammar—and now Tregare recalled
that Vanois was a Backwoodser and touchy about his planet's
mode of speech—the voice itself came clear and sweet, like a
child's. "I has first from Derek Limmer. He have your note is
label Delta Five and say will or does mission at New Hope. I
does not understand what year he says, but he meets you at
Number One." There was more, but from it Tregare got little
meaning.

Well, though—Limmer had agreed to visit the New Hope
arsenal and pick up ships' weapons for delivery to Tregare's
base. Long View or not, the network was beginning to
function!

Two other tapes had been brought here and entered in the
original versions. Kickem Bernardez, at time of recording, was
still maintaining the *Hoover*'s UET facade and visiting colonies
with impunity. He didn't yet have Tregare's planning on hand,
but "given any luck at all, Bran Tregare, I shall hear it from you
in person, some landing, over a great untidy lot of drink."

And Jargy Hoad had raided a UET world and not only got
away clean but came near to capturing a UET ship, groundside. "But I must have tipped our hand, Bran. With a quarter
of his crew stranded groundside, and before he had his ramp

up and his airlock closed, that skipper lifted off." A pause. "I just wish I could figure what I did wrong, there. So I wouldn't do it again."

None of the other material was anywhere near as interesting. Bran heard it through, recorded it in case some parts might be important later, and then spent another hour composing and taping messages *he* wanted to leave here. For the data net to work in the Long View, it needed all the input it could get.

On Hidden Worlds, Tregare's business rarely involved him with the ways their governments were organized. So he never did bother to find out Mayo Tolridge's position in the hierarchy at South Forty. She was, though, apparently in charge of all dealings with *Inconnu*, and that was fine with Bran Tregare. Because the woman stated her wishes clearly, made reasonable trade offers, and settled any given individual deal without undue bickering. Bran was used to more shuffling, but found it easy to get used to her style of commerce.

South Forty was at disadvantage because the Port's main computer had troubles. Nearly half its memory storage wouldn't access dependably; some days it worked, other times not. Tregare offered to take a look, but found the problem was beyond his grade of skill. He wished Renni Lofall were still available, but wishing didn't help much.

When he mentioned the difficulty later, in *Inconnu's* galley, Hain Deverel spoke up. "Mind if I have a try, skipper? If it's all right with groundside? I have a sort of knack with 'intermittents'—I get hunches, and sometimes they're right."

Well, Tregare had the same kind of ability in other fields, so he got Tolridge's okay for the attempt, and Deverel found and fixed the glitch in less than two hours. Notified, the woman said, "That's worth something in our trading. A bonus to your ship. I'll have to think what's suitable."

"Not the ship," said Tregare. "Pay Hain Deverel. He did the work." He wasn't quite sure why he put it that way; if he himself had found the trouble, he'd have assigned any bonus to *Inconnu*. Finally he decided it was because he held captain's shares and Deverel didn't.

A side effect of the incident was that the Port bought quite a lot of spare electronic hardware. "For backup and expansion both," Tolridge said. Then she and Bran looked over their respective inventories to see what else might be swapped to mutual advantage. Until she exclaimed, he'd forgotten the seed grains he'd picked up at one of *Inconnu*'s early landings. Some he'd traded at Number One as planned, but there was a lot left. Now Tolridge looked excited. "That's a problem here. Anything we plant, fertility's fine for some years, then starts dwindling. So we do need new stock."

Okay; the deal practically made itself, and this day's work seemed to be wrapped up. They'd been consulting in Tregare's quarters, so he invited Tolridge to share dinner with him there. She'd mentioned throwing a spread for him and his officers, but so far the event hadn't happened. Now, apologizing for that delay, she accepted his hospitality.

From the galley he ordered a moderately festive meal, featuring bushstomper steaks from Number One, and opened some wine from that planet. They ate leisurely and drank the same way, talking widely varying subjects that had nothing to do with trade—or, indeed, with here-and-now. "Tell me about your life," she said, and he gave her a much-edited version: the overall flavor of UET's Slaughterhouse but none of the grimmer details, the same treatment of Butcher Korbeith and of the triple mutinies leading to his Escape.

"Since then," he said, refilling her glass, "I've been here and there a lot. Ships don't give detailed itineraries, you know." She nodded. "Since UET already knows it by now, though, I don't mind admitting that I got in and out of Stronghold—and also Earth, though only in orbit; we didn't land."

Looking at him with an odd intensity, she said, "You take it right to them, don't you, Tregare? I suppose that's why you're becoming so notorious." She waved off any reply. "Oh, yes— nearly every ship leaves some kind of word about you and your doings. Some of it secondhand from UET worlds. Do you know what *they* call you? "Tregare the Pirate"—as though you were the only Escaped Ship that ever raided. I wonder why—"

"Simple enough, I'd think. Last I heard, *Inconnu*'s still the only Escaped Ship that can shoot at 'em. And has done it."

She blinked. Maybe a little on the drunk side, but not much, he thought, and restrained his hospitality, pouring her glass only halfway full, as she said, "How long, now, will you stay here?" Now that the trading and supplying were pretty well done, she meant.

"A few days. My crew's been working long hours; those people deserve some groundside leave, a chance to walk around and scan sky." He grinned. "Not to worry; they don't rampage a whole lot." Some, of course, but he expected she'd know that much.

"Another thing," he said. "I need some more computer time. Because in that blocked bank there could be some stuff for me that I couldn't access until Deverel got the jinx out."

"Of course. Any time. Tomorrow—or is it today, by now?"

He checked his chrono. "Close to it, but not quite. You like some more coffee?"

She laughed, then hiccuped. "No coffee. Who needs a wide-awake drunk?" Working at it, after a moment she stood. "I don't usually—" She shook her head. "Tregare? If you could walk me home I'd appreciate it. It's not all that far."

"Sure," so they went downship and out the ramp. The night held a bit of chill but not much. The sky showed bright stars, with a twinkling cluster low on the west horizon, but no sweep of galactic haze.

Not leaning on him greatly, of a sudden Mayo Tolridge stopped and held him back. She was looking up as she said, "You've been a lot of places, Tregare. A *lot* of places."

"Well, a few more than most, I guess."

"And what do you think of the universe?"

He didn't know, so he said, "Mainly, it's *there*."

She laughed. "Right. And I've figured it out. Bran Tregare, the whole damn universe is one big Rorschach test!"

"If you say so. It's a new thought, anyway. Which way, now?"

"To our left, here," and soon they reached a fair-sized house, built all on one level. Tolridge couldn't find her keys, so she knocked, and after half a minute or so, a man opened the door.

"Mayo? Are you all right?" He squinted at her. "Carrying your cargo alist, eh?" To Tregare, "She doesn't do that often."

"I know. She told me. We were feasting a little, onship, after winding up trade arrangements; Ms. Tolridge has been a big help, so—"

"Oh, yes; you're Tregare." Bran accepted the offered handshake, heard the man's name, and promptly forgot it. "Well, thanks for escorting Mayo home. Care for a drink or anything?"

Politely, Bran declined, said his good nights, and headed back toward his ship.

* * *

His way took him through a grouping of small shops and other businesses. One place looked like a bar, and when he walked into it, that's what it was. Not crowded, this late, but several people sat in booths at either side of the aisle leading to the bar. Sometimes, Tregare decided, a man can use a drink just for the hell of it. So he walked the gauntlet of booths, bought his drink, and started back to find a booth of his own because the barstools didn't look all that comfortable. He paid no heed to the seated people; he wouldn't know any of them, anyway, and he wasn't in search of company.

But as a party of four came in, laughing and half-running, he stepped aside to let the group go by. And as he began to move again, someone took hold of his right sleeve. "What's the matter, captain? Are you stuck-up, or something?" The woman's voice restrained his first urge to pull away; he looked down to see, seated alone in the booth, redhaired Tanit Eldon. She said, "Twice you've walked past me. Don't you associate with Chief ratings, off duty?"

Come to think of it, he hadn't seen much of this woman *on* duty, either, once her inventory readouts and Groden's reports assured him of her competence. Well, Erika Hulzein wouldn't waste training on stupid people. . . . Tregare said, "Wasn't expecting to see anyone I knew, so I wasn't looking. This seat taken?" She shook her head, so he sat, and took a sip of his drink. The taste wasn't what he'd expected.

Probably his face showed surprise, for Eldon said, "Is something wrong?"

"No, the drink's all right. But I ordered bourbon."

She laughed. "I had the same problem. On South Forty, that stuff *is* called bourbon."

"No place else would." Then they were both laughing.

After that drink, Tregare switched to beer, which even South Forty hadn't managed to turn into something else. Eldon was on a talking jag. ". . . the original Tanit was some kind of fertility goddess, back in Carthage or Babylon or someplace. I read about her, but somebody had cut all the sexy parts out of the tape." Sitting in the dim part of the booth, eyes shining in the shadow of her face, she looked at him. "My mother named me. Do you think she wanted me to be good at mating?"

* * *

Back onship in Tregare's quarters, he decided she probably thought she *was* good in bed. She had all the complex moves, and put considerable energy into them, but after a time he began to anticipate the routines, and it put him offstride. So he stopped moving, and waited until she did, too. "Tanit?"

"Yes?" Panting, she said, "Anything wrong?"

"Course not. Just, because you're such a good learner, I want to suggest something." She nodded. "Okay. This is a little tricky but I'm sure you can do it."

And she could. When asked, she could relax and do nothing except what her body's own reflexive responses dictated.

Then, for both of them, things worked a lot better.

Later, sitting up, she said, "I could learn a lot of things faster, Tregare, if I had more time to work with you directly."

"We could bend schedules that way, sure."

She blinked her eyes in the way he was learning to recognize. "I hear you're rooming alone now, captain. I could—"

"No." Too fast, that; he should explain more. "You're too new aboard. No matter how you behaved, some people would say you were trading bed for status. And *being* new, shipside, you'd make mistakes and give the gripers something to chew on. So I'm afraid the word has to be no."

"Well, I didn't mean—"

"Sure not. Play it safe, is all."

She agreed, so he was off *that* hook. And not much after, late time or not, they tried bed again. She did remember what he'd told her before, so he found the occasion quite an improvement.

Next morning, waking alone, Tregare arose short of sleep, but all things considered he felt better than he probably had a right to. Well, being lovers with Tanit Eldon didn't hurt his morale any. He wondered—had he, maybe, got himself into this situation too quickly? No preliminaries, just jump to it? "Peace knows," he muttered to himself, "being hard up doesn't suit me a whole lot." Maybe it made him a little *too* vulnerable, too open.

But to make such decisions fast had always been his pattern. Well, almost always. And, for totally non-related reasons, he'd questioned Tanit under truth drugs; he *knew* her mind and liked it.

What else drew him? The red hair, short but still echoing the glorious mane of Phyls Dolan? Tregare shivered, hating to be reminded of that poor woman drifting all these years, space-frozen. If only he'd been able to move faster! . . .

He brought his mind to now, where it belonged. Dressed and ready to start his day, he headed upship, to the galley.

After breakfast he went groundside to dig further into possible ship data and messages. Mayo Tolridge had offered to set up a data link for *Inconnu*, but Tregare knew Tinhead's keyboard and control codes differed somewhat from those in Port Admin; he didn't want to chance throwing in errors without realizing it.

He found a certain amount of additional info which the malfunction had previously blocked away, but nothing crucial. Starting to leave, then, he passed the comm room and heard Tolridge's voice. Talking, apparently, to an incoming ship: ". . . helpful if you'd burn the weeds off one of the more overgrown ones." Tregare couldn't make out the answering words, but then Tolridge said, "*Inconnu*, yes. Leaving in a few days, I think." Turning back to the room's door, Bran caught something about hoping to talk with him, and then Tolridge said, "We'll see you down here soon then, *Graf Spee*."

He walked into the room; the woman looked up. He said, "Who's upstairs, you were telling all about me?"

She looked startled. "*Graf Spee*. Ilse Krueger commanding."

The name rang a bell; after a moment he snapped his fingers. "Got it. I've heard of her, here and there. Smallest person ever to survive the Slaughterhouse. Hadn't heard she was Escaped, though." He scowled. "You sure it's not a UET trick? I mean, what name did the ship have, before?"

"Why, I don't know! But a woman, commanding—"

"Or claiming to command. Well, never mind. I'm going aboard ship now, and either way, I'll take care of it."

On *Inconnu*, up in Control, Tregare put his forward screen on hi-mag and monitored the incoming ship's descent. From this angle he couldn't see if it was armed or not, but coming down its weapons made no difference anyway. He had his own turrets slaved to the console in front of him; if that ship so much as twitched its Drive blast in his direction, the next second it would be a cloud of plasma. And to be certain, he warmed the projectors with a few harmless blasts into atmosphere, to bring his heterodyne into peak energy range.

Then he waited.

Circumspectly, with no way of knowing that Tregare's projectors tracked *Graf Spee*, that ship landed—a civil distance from *Inconnu* and never hinting any threat of Drive blast. When *Spee*'s ramp was down and the South Forty delegation came out to give greeting, so did Bran Tregare, accompanied by his First and Second Hats. Gonnelson didn't want to come along, but Bran told him he could merely shake hands and fake it.

Not far from either ship the three groups met. Tregare, waiting while Mayo Tolridge did the hellos and introductions, took an evaluating look at Ilse Krueger. Peace take it, she *was* small—a meter and a half, maybe, if that much. Slim but not fragile, and she moved well. Closer up he saw blue eyes with a barely discernible slant to match the Slavic cheekbones. Her blond hair, too short to hold a curl, lay smooth with only a slight hint of wave. Maybe that hair covered scars, but otherwise the Slaughterhouse experience showed only in a pale mark from above her right eyebrow back toward her ear. Of course, Bran reminded himself, limbs and torso no doubt carried worse souvenirs, because the woman *had* survived and graduated.

The introductions had got around to him and her. Her handshake didn't try to do anything much, but it wasn't limp, either. She smiled slightly, and said, "Tregare, eh? This is a fine occasion."

"Right." Then he said, "Congratulations on your Escape and command, Krueger. I don't think I know all the history."

Obviously she knew what he meant because she nodded. "I see. All right; under UET this ship was the *Bismarck*. Captain was Garrett Trumbull. Doul Falconer was First Officer and I was Second; Doul and I, we—" She shook her head. "I'll never get over missing him." Tregare watched her put her poise back together. "It was Doul who took charge of organizing Escape. I helped. The Third—hell, I don't *want* to remember the name of that little hyena. He's the one who got Doul killed." For a moment her face went pale and gaunt; then, quite matter-of-factly, she said, "Once I had the ship secured, I found time to cut his ratty little throat."

For once, Tregare had nothing to say. Krueger continued, "If it were up to me, I'd have named this ship *Falconer*, after Doul. But he'd picked *Graf Spee*, a joke he understood and I don't. So I've kept the name."

"Sure." Time to change the subject, so he asked where the ship had traveled since Escape, and what other ships she knew about. And mentioned the overall info net; she knew of it but had had only a few chances to feed it or draw on it. "Well, I put quite a lot of stuff in, here. You'll be getting it."

Then he accepted her invitation to dine aboard *Graf Spee*.

Gonnelson and Prestor didn't like the idea of his going aboard this stranger ship solo, but he went anyway, saying that an unarmed craft in need of refueling was in no position to pull anything tricky. "Not with *Inconnu* here, and two armed scouts."

"One," said Gonnelson.

"*They* don't know that." Anyway, Tregare's hunch said he faced no danger, so he went with it.

Krueger's Second Hat, an older man sporting no UET tattoo on his cheek, met Tregare at ramp-top and escorted him to captain's quarters. Wearing a light-blue outfit, something between a uniform and a jumpsuit, Krueger greeted him. She didn't have bourbon, but her Terranovan brandy was pretty good, and later Tregare enjoyed the dinner a lot. The main dish was a kind of stew or goulash; some of the blended flavors were new to him, but he decided they could be habit-forming in rather a hurry.

He was saying as much when the corridor door opened and in barged two large, sweaty young men. The sweaty part was easy to see because they were wearing only brief gym trunks. And they looked to be identical twins, obviously much involved with muscle-building routines. One pushed back his damp blond hair and said, "Done with our workout, captain."

The other mimicked the movement, but lefthanded. "A shower will feel good. Then, may we join you for dinner?"

"Yes—may we?"

Ilse Krueger shook her head. "Not this time, Helmuth—Gregor. Captain Tregare and I have business to discuss."

The two went into the bathroom, and Tregare said, "Couple of brawny lads there." Deliberately he refrained from asking any questions, or so much as raising an eyebrow. She'd tell him or she wouldn't; he didn't care which.

She did. "They live here. With me. Would you like something more? There's quite a bit left."

So Tregare ate again, slowly now for he was filling up. He wished the two youths would finish their stint in the bathroom—he had need of it himself. And finally he went in, anyway, to find Helmuth and Gregor fully dressed, just standing there.

He said hello and went to do his business, but Helmuth or maybe Gregor grasped his arm. "A word, captain."

"Yes?"

"Do not involve yourself with Captain Krueger."

"No?"

"No," said the other. "We belong to her. You do not." Then they left, and finally he could relieve himself.

When he came out, Ilse Krueger had poured coffee and some more brandy. She talked and he didn't, until she paused and said, "Is something on your mind?"

Tregare shrugged. "Not particularly." Then, "Well, yes, now that you mention it. Why did Ajax and Hercules think they had to tell me to keep hands off you?"

"They did that?" She laughed. "Because they know me, I suppose." Her eyes narrowed. "Are you going to obey them? Are you afraid of them?"

"Yes, and no." She waited, so he said, "If you and I messed around, they'd sulk on you for a month. But they don't scare me."

"Why not?"

"Same reason they don't scare you. Those little trunks don't hide much. People with Slaughterhouse scars make me cautious. Those boys don't have any."

Again Krueger laughed. "I should have known. But we won't tell them, will we? It would hurt their pride."

The charade began to irritate Tregare. "Let's cut the games. I have something important to discuss." And he told her of his plan to gather a fleet of ships, the rendezvous at Number One and the approximate timing, and asked, "You want to be in on this?"

She paused, frowning. "I'll have to think about it. Offhand I like the idea—getting this ship armed, twisting UET's tail. But I have some commitments first. This network of yours—can I let you know by leaving word at message drops, and with any Escaped ships that pass within talking range?"

He shrugged. "That's how everybody else does it, who's not around to talk in person. Don't take too long, though, making up your mind. Rendezvous sounds like a long time from now, but don't forget how a trip or two *chews* time."

"I won't." Now Tregare stood. "Leaving so soon?"

"'fraid so. I need to run through my checklist and set the hour for lift-off. No point keeping the troops in suspense any longer than I have to."

She stood also, put her hands on his shoulders and leaned against him. "Some other time, Tregare."

"Could be, at that." He knew she wanted some sign that he found her desirable, so he leaned down and they kissed. She was really damned good at it; for a moment Bran was tempted, and the hell with the muscle twins. But then he disengaged. "Some other time, Krueger. Yeah."

Out in the corridor he was glad of the choice he'd made; both of the large young men were standing there, and he'd bet a stack that they'd been listening. They still didn't scare him, but not since boyhood had he taken pleasure in combat. Not since being introduced to the Slaughterhouse version.

Half-blocking his way, one of them said, "Leaving, captain?"

"That's right." Bran stepped and looked straight ahead. The man moved aside, and neither tried to stop him.

8. Fair
Ball

A few hours later, picking his exact time to add the best resultant of planetary motion and rotation to his chosen course, Tregare lifted *Inconnu* off South Forty. He did it himself because all the Hats had done it since his last turn and he didn't want to get rusty. In the direction he headed, he had several choices of destination. After a while he decided to look in on a small colony named UETopia. It was pretty well in line with several choices of a second stop, and the best part was that these shorter hauls wouldn't hurt him too much when it came to making rendezvous deadline on Number One. *I just hope to hell enough of us get there on time!*

The only trouble with UETopia was that it wasn't there. Either that or someone had entered the coordinates wrong, or the computer hiccuped on the readout. Whichever way, no UETopia. Well, the name irritated him, anyway.

Heading away from that empty space by Tinhead's guidance, *Inconnu* was up to point-two c when the comm-tech on Relliger's watch caught a beacon signal from about a radian off the ship's course. Advised, Tregare got out of bed, into shoes and pants, and grabbed a shirt which he put on while running upship.

When he got to Control, he shut up and listened. Long

127

enough to learn that the beacon was from UET's colony Muspelheim. And that without consulting Tregare, Leanne Prestor (who wasn't even on watch, officially) had opened communications using the *Alexander the Great* ploy. Waiting until the long, transmission-delayed conversation ended and the circuit was cut, Tregare said, "Prestor. What do you think you're doing?"

She smiled at him. "Keeping our options open."

"You just closed down a bunch of mine. Why?" Mad as hell, he said, "Nobody but me decides for this ship. *Nobody*, and you know that. So tell me, fast and clear, why I don't unrate you where you stand, and pick me a new Hat."

"Pick two, then," said Frei Relliger. "We knew you were busy, and identifying us as the *Alexander* was the simplest alternative, whether you choose to land at Muspelheim or not."

It made sense, but Tregare didn't *like* it making sense, because he couldn't let these two get away with trying to run the ship on their own. Stalling, he said, "You back her on this, Relliger?"

"I do, yes."

"Then you can share the penalty." *I'm not armed. Are they?* Hell with it; either he was captain, or—"You're each fined a month's share-earnings." He paused. "Do you accept that?"

After a moment, both nodded. Hoping his relief didn't show, Tregare said, "All right. Past is past. Now let's see how we clean up this mess and turn it to *our* advantage."

Prestor wasn't done yet. "Captain, do you know what Muspelheim means?"

From childhood reading the answer clicked. "Sure. Norse myth; the land of the fire giants. Lots of vulcanism here, right?"

Prestor looked abashed. "Why—why, yes."

Abruptly, Tregare nodded. "Unless you got more questions, Leanne, what you say we get on with it?"

On points, landing didn't seem to be too bad an idea. The settlement wasn't big enough to support any large UET garrison, and the only ship currently groundside—the *Patton*—wasn't armed. Muspelheim's surface gravity was only about point-seven g, so even if refueling turned out to be a problem, *Inconnu* would have no trouble reaching any of several next-stop choices. Bran gave instructions—more detailed than were really necessary—on future contact with Muspelheim as the ship approached that world. Then he went back down to his quarters.

Eldon had been angry with him for leaving so abruptly, and when she saw him enter, she began again. He said, "Shut up, Tanit." He didn't say it loud but he didn't say it twice, either. "I had a problem upship and it couldn't wait. You could." He paused. "If you still want to. Do you?"

She looked more like wanting to sulk and argue, so he turned away and fixed himself a drink. When he sat facing her, she said, slowly, "Yes, Tregare. I do."

"Fine," said Tregare. Because, so did he.

Muspelheim's settlements, as they showed on *Inconnu's* forward screens, lay on a narrow coastal plain. Behind that plain rose jagged-topped mountains, and Tregare saw that a number of them indeed bore smoke plumes. Evaluating the several towns and villages—plus areas obviously under cultivation—Bran guessed Muspelheim's population in the mid-five-figure range, with maybe a third living in or near the spaceport town. The port's Admin complex wasn't up to Number One's but looked about average for most colonies—UET or Hidden Worlds, either one.

He left the approach to Gonnelson, who had the watch, but reserved the landing for himself. Sitting beside the First Hat, ready to take over, Tregare watched the port move offscreen as the ship turned in preparation for sitdown. And for a moment, something caught his attention: the antenna setup on the main Admin building. Briefly he tensed, then relaxed—hell, a colony this size would naturally have missile defenses!

But now he was edgy, listening as groundside talked him in and the comm-tech on watch translated Gonnelson's monosyllables into English for the port's benefit. Absently, he noticed the squiggles on the visual monitor for that ship-ground frequency. And then, not so absently, saw squiggles that monitored frequencies he was *not* hearing.

So he remedied that lack, found the right scramble code on his second try, and caught himself an earful.

" . . . to Port Control: of course I'm sure! The message just now . . ."

"Port Control to the *Patton*." Seeing the squiggle timed to be an answer, Tregare put that freq on audio, too. "You're saying that the incoming ship isn't the *Alexander*? Then what ship is it?"

"Dammit, I *told* you! It's *Inconnu* now, but it used to be the *Tamurlaine*, before the pirate Bran Tregare usurped command. And it's armed!"

"Armed?" Groundside sounded nervous. Gonnelson muttered something, and console lights showed Tregare that the First Hat had switched control over to him. The strained voice, distorted by less-than-perfect circuit tuning, continued. "Is he too close to blast with our missile defense, without endangering your own ship?"

"That's chancy." The *Patton*'s speaker hesitated, then said, "Let him land. As soon as he's near to touching down, I'll lift. *Across* him; you see? Lift, hover, and land again. Then your ground troops can attack, and clean up what's left."

Tregare cut the sound. Seeing startled looks, he said, "I heard all I need to." He hit another switch. "All-ship broadcast! Everybody strap in or hang on! Now!"

Then he attacked.

Inconnu had been coming down slow and easy. Taking his best guess, Tregare cut the force of his braking Drive and let the ship drop free; groundside's missiles would play hell tracking his angular velocity at this range. Then, closer to ground than he'd intended, he hit the preempt and fired Junior Lee's Drive close to redline max: *Inconnu* shuddered and stalled, as Tregare tipped nearly a radian to one side. He had the *Patton*'s audio signal on again, and by the yells and screaming he knew he'd made his point; that ship had caught Tregare's Drive blast at an angle and was toppling sidewise into crashing ruin.

Bran wasn't done yet. He hadn't spotted the port's missile sites, not for sure, but its guidance antennae sat atop the main Admin building. So with *Inconnu*'s Drive churning up the ground below it, but at much less than max now as the ship built altitude by mere meters, he kept the ship on a slant and walked it across the Port, across the Admin building, then with twitches that changed both the tilt and its direction, back around the area that probably held most of the missiles. And what that blast hit, it pulverized.

He looked at Gonnelson, and shrugged. "No point landing here, would you say?"

"No point."

So Tregare headed *Inconnu* straight up and lifted. Two missiles followed him, but not closely enough to worry about.

Before Muspelheim on the back screens had time to shrink from disc to point, Tregare told Gonnelson and Deverel to assemble all personnel with comm-tech training. "In the galley." When the two men looked puzzled, Bran said, "The *Patton* said something about a message. Which couldn't have come from anywhere except this ship. Which means somebody sent it. So wear your sidearms."

As they left, he began digging into the comm consoles' tape facilities. The aux positions held nothing that didn't belong there, but the main panel revealed an unlabeled tape container. With care, he withdrew it, and found it had been played to the end—and now would not rewind. The thing was warmer than it should be, so he knew the magnetic information-content no longer existed. In a hurry, he broke the box open; he wasn't surprised to find a small expended heat capsule, triggered by the tape's ending to disrupt the magnetic patterns and half-melt the plastic into a solid mass.

Hell with that, then; he went to the galley.

At least one of his people had used some initiative; besides the comm people, Eda Ghormley was there with her truth drug kit. Tregare explained the situation, then said, "I'm sorry, but to find one rotten Utie I have to inconvenience all of you. There's no other way." He heard some mumbling, but most of the group made a nod or gesture of assent. So Ghormley began her injections and Tregare asked questions.

One after another, the ratings checked out clean. Partway through, Bran was surprised to see Tanit Eldon receiving a shot. "Hey—you're not in Comm."

"I've had training, though; it's part of the UG routine, for people who might get onto ships."

"But you've already passed this stuff."

She smiled. "Under the circumstances, I prefer to ensure that there's no question. In *anybody's* mind."

Under the circumstances, yeah. The captain's lover, new on the ship, maybe needed more confirmation than most; he could see that. So in her turn he put her through the same questioning as everybody else.

The trouble was, she and everybody else passed. So over the next two days he ran *all* the crew—including Control and Engineering officers—through the interrogation. And, having heard a weird rumor that *he* was the culprit, had Ghormley run him through the procedure. Before witnesses.

He passed, too, though. So he had the ship searched for stowaways. But there weren't any.

Tregare stewed. Because of his experiences—desertion by his family, then surviving the Slaughterhouse, Butcher Korbeith and his guard Plastic Smile, the Utie Cleet Farnsworth's countermutiny—he found it hard to trust people, and he knew it. But here on his own ship, after all this time, to find a Utie traitor! Except that he *hadn't*; he knew there was one, though.

But *who?* He caught himself watching people, wondering. Then he'd shake his head; he had to trust his own people, or he'd go around the bend paranoid, like Krieg Elman.

In quarters with Tanit, both undressed but Tregare feeling no urge for sex, he talked about the problem. And ended up with no answers at all.

Frowning, she looked over to him and said, "Maybe there isn't the answer you're looking for." She cut into his protest. "No—I mean, maybe the person who fixed that tape isn't *on* the ship now. You've had people leave, haven't you, at one Port and another?" He nodded. "Then the tape could have been there for some time." Her brow wrinkled. "You had a closet Utie in your crew, let's say—someone who left ship at Earth or even before." Personnel did go groundside sometimes, though right now he couldn't put names to all of them, so he nodded.

Then shook his head. "No. Who arranged to *send* that tape?"

"Groundside did, is my bet." He knew he looked incredulous then, as she said, "The UG could have managed a similar hookup, a prearranged code group to trigger transmission *if* the proper circuits were set up in Comm."

He stood and reached for clothing. "I'm going up there and check that idea out."

"Forget it, Tregare. Those input circuits would be set to disconnect, totally, as soon as their job was done." So he flung the clothes across the room, and sat again.

His mind still gnawed the bone she'd thrown him. "Why didn't the tape do its trick at Earth?"

Her eyes widened, her brows rose. "How could I know that?"

He was thinking better now. "Two reasons I could go with. One: with all those UET ships milling around up there in orbit, nobody'd *expect* a lone Escaped maverick to show up. And two: we'd just come from Stronghold and had Saldeen's orders with us to prove it."

She smiled. "There's another possibility. Maybe your Utie didn't want any fireworks until he or she was safely offship." Her eye-to-eye gaze moved lower. "You're feeling better now, aren't you?"

And he was.

In council, three days out from Muspelheim, Prestor was at it again. "Yes, I know it took some action to get us out safely—but all *that* killing? Tregare—what could be worth doing it?"

Exasperated, Bran found no words. Gonnelson said, "*Your* life?"

Then Tregare could laugh, as he said, "Leanne, when they're out to get you—and Muspelheim was—you don't just piss around. You give it your best shot, and hope to hell it's enough."

Tanit Eldon, first time he and she talked after Muspelheim, gave him no such crap. What she said was, "Tregare, when your neck's on the line, or your mission, you do what you have to do. The Underground taught me that." She made a one-sided smile. "And I guess UET taught *you*. But not the way they intended." Relieved, Bran dropped the matter and got on to more pleasant business.

Now, though, when Frei Relliger cleared his throat, Tregare had no idea which way he was going to jump. And was relieved when the man said, "The captain's right. He couldn't afford to take chances."

So much for that. "Next order of business," said Tregare. "Where we go from here." As he pointed out, the impromptu lift-off hadn't given *Inconnu* a very good initial vector toward several of the possibilities for next choice of destination. "I punched up a holo-chart, and our best bet for fuel and time is Fair Ball." He told what he knew of the place, which wasn't much more than any member of the group could have dug out of Tinhead. Then he added, "The last I heard, Cade Moaker was heading there. And Moaker's a man I'd like to talk with again."

Since no one had any better ideas to propose, *Inconnu's* course was swung toward the Hidden World known as Fair Ball.

Somewhat larger than Sol, the planet's primary shone whiter. Fair Ball itself, riding farther out than Earth did, had a longer year. Its orbit was tilted but its axis wasn't, much. Seasonal temperature changes were mostly due to the orbit's eccentricity. And, "Smallish radius, high average density," Tregare said. "Which puts surface gravity closer to one-gee than I'd expect." He shrugged. "Well, that's what the tape says."

Maybe because *Inconnu* was coming in on a slant from zenith, it was only about two days from landfall when Fair Ball hailed it. With a loop tape, repeatedly asking the ship to identify itself, and so forth. "If you haven't been here before, a few references might be in order."

Why bother with tape, replying? "The armed, Escaped ship *Inconnu*, Bran Tregare commanding. Did Cade Moaker make it here all right, with *Cut Loose Charlie?* If he did, he can confirm that it was on Number One he told me he was headed this way."

After the two-way transmission lag, groundside's loop tape stopped. Then a woman's voice came over the circuit. "I'm afraid Captain Moaker died a few years ago. He did mention you, though." She laughed. "Most ships' people do." A pause. "But as a double-check, to *prove* who you are, could you cite a few more names? For instance, do you know Sten Norden? Ilse Krueger? Malloy or Bernardez or Hoad or Quinlan? Rasmussen? And their ships?"

Now it was Tregare's turn to laugh. "Kickem Bernardez and Jargy Hoad I *roomed* with, back at the Slaughterhouse. Malloy and Quinlan, then, were running scoutships for summer training; I didn't know they'd Escaped." He thought back. "*Pig In The Parlor*, Malloy was going to name his ship. Krueger and Rasmussen I've met, and Derek Limmer—hell, I *got* his ship *Lefthand Thread* for him, on Freedom's Ring. Jargy has *Deuces Wild* and Kickem hasn't renamed the *Hoover* yet, far as I know."

Again the wait; then the woman, sounding impressed, said, "That's sufficient, I'd say. Now, captain, do you have any questions? And what is your estimated time of landing?"

He checked with Tinhead. "Roughly forty-eight hours from now, give or take a little, depending on where your port's longitude has rotated by the time I get there." Questions? Hmm. "What ships are in port now? And I could use some coordinates for that Port."

"You missed Quinlan's *Red Dog* by about a week, and *Strike Three* lifted yesterday, under Cyras Adopolous. So there's only *Charlie* here now. Grounded permanently, with the Nielson shut down and the nodes practically burned off in the landing here. Cade incorporated the ship as a business, and his people have done well."

Thinking about it, as the woman fed the coordinates along, then signed off, Tregare saw how a ship could operate as a going concern, groundside. Given fuel, which any spaceport had, the Drive's power systems could function as a generating plant for a fair-sized city. And few settlements had the kind of machine-shop, fabrication, and maintenance facilities a ship could muster. The skills of ships' personnel, hired out on groundside jobs, would bring in a fair grade of income. And for a ship that didn't need to fuel and resupply for space—liftoff and accel and decel and landing, and life-support systems now redundant—any reasonable cargo was good for years of profitable trading. Sure's hell, it would work!

Not that Tregare had any such ideas, but still it was interesting.

Now Bran checked the planetary data. Fair Ball had two major continents, antipodally located and both mostly in their respective temperate zones, semi-connected by strings of island chains. Baseline Port was on the northern land mass, about the middle of it in longitude and a few hundred kilos north of the southern shore. Most of that distance was desert, which was why no attempt had been made toward the more usual river-mouth settlement. The port was on the major north–south river, though, so it had waterborne access to the highlands farther north, where the rudimentary charts indicated such activities as mining, herd grazing, lumber harvesting, and (nearer to the port) agriculture.

Not a bad setup, Tregare thought. With a population of close to six figures, even spread out a lot, this place could prosper. Well, he'd seen all he needed, for now.

A little over twelve hours before *Inconnu* was due to plow air, Tregare was visited in quarters by Leanne Prestor and Frei Relliger. Maybe feeling in need of mutual support, most of the time they held hands. White-knuckled, Tregare noticed. Not the least bit at ease, obviously.

He offered drinks but got no takers. Well, the hell with it; it's their shoe so let *them* drop it. Relliger couldn't seem to decide what to say but eventually Prestor got it out. Yes, they both wanted off, groundside, and hoped Tregare wouldn't make any difficulty about whatever pay-off shares they might have coming. "No problem," said Tregare. "You figure 'em, I'll check 'em. If there's any real difference and a rerun doesn't straighten it out, there's always arbitration."

He thought Relliger would argue but the man didn't. Instead, Leanne began talking, high-pitched, about her feelings. "I know it's awful, us both deserting you like this. But we have to—well, I—" Bran gathered that the two planned to get on another ship someday. Not hardly right away, Tregare thought, because Leanne was pregnant by purpose, and most ships didn't favor officers who were pregnant or in charge of infants.

Bran said nothing of that side of things. "You're not deserting me. You're looking for where you fit better." Not allowing them a word in edgewise, "You're both competent, able ship's officers, but you don't belong on an armed ship and never did. Not one like this, that has to fight UET any way it can. Any way *I* can. So you can get off here with my blessings." They looked skeptical. "I mean that; you've both done good work."

Leanne Prestor shook her head. "I don't understand you. You can be such a mean, ruthless bastard—but now at the last minute we tell you we want off and you're *nice* to us. Why?"

He grinned. "Not nice. Fair, is all." Why was he always having to explain simple facts to people? But he did: "Outside of UET, captains who aren't fair don't last very long." He didn't want her getting soppy on him, so he said, "But against UET I can't afford fair. Just mean. Mean as I can think of, and the more the better." He looked at her. "You got it?"

"Maybe. I guess so." Changing the subject, she asked who might be replacing her and Relliger in the Hat berths.

"One I've decided, one I don't know about, yet. No idea, I mean. But that's my problem, not yours. Maybe there'll be a candidate waiting, groundside."

Then the two relaxed, and Relliger did have a drink. Leanne, being pregnant, settled for fruit juice.

When they left captain's digs, Tregare felt mostly relieved. Now he had his *options* open. Whatever they might turn out to be.

Coming in for the approach, Tregare checked the numbers and put on a little extra decel, to allow Baseline Port to pass the terminator and be well into daylight before *Inconnu* got there. Then he moved over to the aux pilot position and gave Gonnelson the landing chore. It was either Relliger's or Prestor's turn, but they were getting off; Gonnelson could use the practice.

Inconnu's main forward screen showed Fair Ball's primary off to the left; thus, Tregare was nearing the planet from "behind" but landing against its rotational velocity. Tanit, sitting beside Tregare at an extra comm-panel position because she'd never viewed a landing, asked why he wanted to buck the rotation instead of going with it.

So he had to explain. Not that he minded; he could use a little distraction. "Far as need for decel goes," he said, "yes, sure, we have rotation working against us, but orbital velocity *with* us. So—"

"Why can't you have both?"

"On account of I want us to land in daylight." Using both hands, he gestured the layout of the vectors and hoped he was getting it straight—knowing something, and telling it, were sometimes different. But she seemed to understand. So he added, deciding it was too much work to get the exact figures out of Tinhead right now, "If that was Earth out there, the ratio of orbital velocity to rotational is about two hundred to three."

That part she got, just fine. And then pretty soon they were plowing air and setting down, Gonnelson's touch being as smooth as always.

Gonnelson didn't want to go visiting, and Prestor and Relliger were no longer connected with ship's business, so

Tregare took Hain Deverel with him groundside to meet the
"local admiral," Captain Gannes. Nobody said what he was
captain of, but the stooped, elderly man greeted the two men
in his office in Admin, and introduced his assistant, Marisa
Hanen. The woman, round-faced and blue-eyed with a high
forehead that looked to be going higher before too long, stood
nearly Tregare's height and probably outweighed him. Her
soft, clear voice belied the heavy-boned bulk of her, as she
said, "I suppose you'll want, first thing, to make a search of all
our computer entries from visiting ships. And I hope you'll
have data to give us, in return."

With a smile, Tregare nodded. "Yes, I think so. Do you have
a system of cross-checking all the entries, to give an overall
picture of ships' movements in space-time?"

Gannes answered. "We're working on it. Cade Moaker gave
us the idea, when he brought *Charlie* here. It's a complex
problem, though; I can't say we have the system running
smoothly as yet."

Shrugging, Tregare said, "And what with the Long View,
ships' times differing so much, maybe nobody ever will. But
whatever you do have, I'm sure it'll be a help to both of us."

Then he asked about local customs regarding trade, refueling, and such. Gannes shook his head. "Out of my bailiwick.
That's the Board of Trade, Suth Fairgrave's group. They meet
down on the second floor, but they're not in session again
until—let me see—three days from now. I hope the delay
won't inconvenience you."

"Depends. Do I have to dicker *with* this Board for everything, or can I set up tentative deals for their okay, assuming
they do?"

Gannes looked embarrassed. Hanen said, "A little of both.
Officially you can deal freely. Unofficially, if Fairgrave doesn't
like it, you may have a problem."

The situation felt entirely too damned familiar; Tregare felt
himself tensing up, but said only, "Is his word final?"

Two headshakes. Gannes said, "Carries considerable
weight, though."

Rising to leave, Tregare hoped his smile looked nicer on the
outside than it seemed on the inside. "So does mine."

Then he said polite good-byes, and he and Deverel left the
building to walk under Fair Ball's pale sky that held a great
amount of haze and only a touch of blue.

* * *

Back on *Inconnu*, after a quick lunch, Tregare arranged with groundside for a direct feed from the Admin computer to his ship. Needing nothing more than a word-readout display, he routed the feed down to his quarters and went there to browse at leisure.

Some of the entries were interesting but for a time he found nothing that seemed important. Quinlan on *Red Dog* had left the barest of info; obviously the man was a loner, so no point in trying to make contact with him. Ilse Krueger had been here, but some time ago, before he and she had met in person. Other people he knew—news of them was being relayed secondhand at the nearest. Well, that's how it *would* be. . . .

The ship *Strike Three*, that he'd missed by only a few days, interested Tregare. Its entered log was more detailed than most but still only hinted at the outlines of some obviously important events. At one entry he whistled—the *captain* of this ship had been bought out and got off here. Zelde M'tana: not a name he'd ever heard. So he thumbed the readout back a way; maybe this ship's history could use some looking into.

Strike Three was the ship's fourth name. It had started out, under UET, as the *Great Khan*, and its last UET commander had been Emilo Czerner. Hmm. All right—Tregare recognized another name or two. Escape had put command to Ragir Parnell, and the ship became *Chanticleer*. Tregare recalled, from Slaughterhouse days, the tall, serious cadet captain under whom Jargy Hoad had served after Jargy's transfer. A good man, yes. And then—the log got a little mixed up, there, as if entered by someone not used to the chore. Hmm . . .

Some more names he didn't know, and then this Zelde M'tana showed up as Third Hat. Tregare checked back. At first the woman wasn't on the roster at all; then, after Escape she was sharing captain's quarters. In between, she'd killed a Utie who wore a power suit! And then she came up with a Hat berth. He grinned.

Then he didn't. There had been a UET countermutiny, cat's-pawed by a UET hideout who had shipped as cargo. Cargo? Oh, yes—a hold full of women consigned to the cribs on UET's mining world, Iron Hat. *Cargo, huh*. Eyes narrowed, he read on.

Cyras Adopolous: after Escape, Parnell's First Hat. Disabled in a brawl in Parleyvoo on Terranova. UET country. What happened to the rest of the chain of command, Tregare couldn't figure, but all at once there was Zelde M'tana as Acting Captain, and a while later the adjective got lost. M'tana crushed the countermutiny but Ragir Parnell died; the log didn't say just how. And while she commanded, the ship was called *Kilimanjaro*.

Tregare punched for side-data on M'tana. It looked clear enough. She'd been bought off *Strike Three* and was looking to buy a Hat berth on some other ship. Well, he was short a Hat. It couldn't hurt to see and talk with her.

That evening, Bran and Tanit dined in his quarters and later took themselves to bed for a while. He was thinking, now that she'd had time to make a place for herself among the crew, to establish her bona fides, she might as well move in with him—assuming she still wanted to.

Their lovemaking varied a lot; on this occasion, when things were getting close to winding up, they switched to her being on top. To get some synchronizing feedback for their moves, Bran grasped her forearms as she braced herself on them. "Ow! That *hurts*, dammit!" It was a real yelp, she made then.

Startled and distracted, "What? *What* hurts?"

"My arm. I burned it today; the heat-marker slipped when I was marking some cargo crates."

"Sorry." In the dim light he couldn't see the burn but he took her word for it and shifted his grip toward the wrist. "Better?"

She nodded, but the momentum was broken. Eventually Tregare came to climax, but Tanit couldn't. "It's not your fault," she said afterward. "I can't take pain much; it spoils my concentration." Sipping the drink he'd fixed for her, she said, "Maybe it's just as well I'll be groundside the next few days."

"Groundside? What—"

"Yes. What's the point of leaving Earth if I don't get to see anything of the other worlds? Please, Bran?"

He didn't like the idea much, but in fairness he had to agree.

Over the next three days he took care of ship's business that didn't need Board of Trade approval, at least not in the preliminary stages. He set up dickers for cargo *versus* supplies, got *Inconnu's* water tanks topped off, put in tentative offers for new cargo, and got the John Hancock of Captain

Gannes on his schedule for liberty parties. Actually that was his first concern; the other matters were less urgent. And in all the dickering, the only item that seemed to trouble anyone was fuel for the Drive. Everything else, Tregare gathered, the Board would rubber-stamp. Fuel, though . . .

He couldn't figure it out, so he decided to wait and see. Meanwhile, Relliger and Prestor were packed to leave ship, so next morning Tregare requisitioned a groundcar and small open trailer, and drove them to a wood-built inn called River House, on the outskirts of the town of First Base. He left the trailer there, and Relliger to unload it, and took Leanne Prestor to City Hall where she could register herself and Relliger with Immigration. Tregare hadn't been into First Base before but Hain Deverel had, and had given Tregare a good description of where the main points were. When Prestor came out again, Bran drove her back to the inn and rehitched the now empty trailer, as Relliger emerged from the building and said, "In case we don't see you again, join us inside for a farewell drink or two."

"Thanks, but I need to get back to the ship now." Tregare shook the man's hand. Prestor looked to be feeling kissy but also settled for a handshake. Smiling then, glad to be done with all this ritual that didn't *move* anything, Bran said, "Good luck to both of you." And got into the car and drove it back to the Port.

Back onship, he felt restless. He missed Tanit; of all his ship's people, she was the one he could *talk* with best, to keep from brooding his way back into paranoiac suspicion. And she'd gone off to see some mines and some herd-grazing camps; wasn't due back for several days yet.

He checked his chrono. Nearly an hour until he had to be at the trade meeting. Time for a drink. He made it a short one, though.

Although the Board of Trade began its meeting shortly after noon, *Inconnu*'s business didn't receive consideration until nearly four hours later. Working up a slow burn, Bran Tregare sat and watched the proceedings. Especially he watched and evaluated Chairman Suth Fairgrave, a heavy-set, red-faced man with thinning sandy hair and a loud, ponderous voice. At their initial handshake Tregare learned that Fairgrave was a knuckle crusher; Bran gave him no leverage and assumed a poker-faced grin to mask the effort needed to withstand the crushing grip. Equally deadpan, the Chairman showed no disappointment at his failure to bully *Inconnu's* captain.

Throughout the afternoon Fairgrave did most of the talking, at great and unnecessary length. Even the simplest, most routine items, it seemed to Bran, took hell-and-forever for Fairgrave to understand and approve. Yet clearly the man was not stupid; rather, he seemed to enjoy making everyone else hang by the thumbs.

Fairgrave's age, Tregare couldn't guess. He was a youngish-looking man who somehow gave the impression that the appearance of youth wouldn't last much longer; his physical movements had more speed than precision. All in all, Bran disliked him more than not.

After the first half-hour, Tregare dismissed the other seven Board members from serious consideration; whatever Fairgrave said, most of them went along with him. Bran did catch and recall some of the names: Zinsmann was the gaunt one, the balding Farley smiled a lot and said very little, Horner was the dark-haired woman who might be interesting on a more personal basis, Chavez made a few comments that showed quickness of mind. The other three, including the spectacular redheaded woman teetering on the far edge of her prime, bore names Bran couldn't remember. And after a while Captain Gannes' assistant Marisa Hanen joined the group but didn't say much.

Boiling inside, trying not to show it, Tregare waited through the tedious session. Finally his bladder called recess on him—coffee was at hand and boredom had made him drink too much of it. When he returned to the meeting, Fairgrave said, "*Well*, captain. We've been waiting for you."

Tregare's patience, never one of his strong points, stretched almost to breaking. He took one deep breath and said, "Then I'll try to cover my part of the agenda as quickly as possible." He'd brought his own readout sheets and now, sitting, rattled off the first items.

Fairgrave interrupted. "One at a time, captain; one at a time. Now the matter of water: you took it upon yourself to top off without Board approval?"

I don't believe this! "Excuse me, Chairman. Are you saying that there was any question of my ship being *denied* water?"

Headshake. "No, of course not. But—"

"But nothing moves here until you say so. Is that it?"

"Well, there *is* the matter of protocol, and—"

"If you'd been available, I'd have asked. You weren't, not to me, until I got back from the john just now. Fairgrave, a ship's needs take some time, and they can't wait on one man's preset schedules. You understand that?"

Face redder than usual, the man half rose. "Do *you* understand, captain, that I—" He looked around the table and corrected himself, "—that *we* are responsible for trade at this port? And that we do not take our responsibility lightly?"

Frantically, Bran tried to think of an answer that would be logical without being totally insulting to this bureaucrat. *Oh, the hell with it!* "It's your *authority* you take so seriously you take it to bed with you." Overriding Fairgrave's protests, Tregare slammed a fist to the table. "Well, you've run into something, Fairgrave. What it is, is that you will approve this readout or you will give me a counter-offer on the whole list, and I'll consider it, and we'll dicker. But the whole thing, not one dinky piece after another." He handed the readout over. "Look at it, and fast. It's simple enough." *Even for you!*

Now the Chairman did his quibbling, item by item, in mumbles to himself alone; the process took nearly as long as before but Tregare could see no reasonable way to protest. Foot-draggers always have the edge. . . .

And eventually, nearly an hour later, Suth Fairgrave stated his reservations—one at a time, naturally, until Tregare barked out, "The overall figure, peace take you!"

"Well, for everything except fuel, which of course must be treated separately—" and while Tregare was digesting that one he followed the man's figures with the top of his head, decided the percentage of gouge was too small to argue about, and nodded.

"All right. Seal it approved and get your people moving stuff right now. Nightshift rates will be paid, but because *your* stalling makes it necessary, the Port pays half the differential."

He thought Fairgrave was going to buck that point, but the man didn't. So Tregare said, "Now let's get to fuel."

Some hours later he wished they'd done that part first, when he wasn't so tired.

* * *

They'd talked and yelled it and done a certain amount of cursing back and forth; now, several hours past normal time for eating dinner, stalemate held. Standard rates for the fuel Tregare needed were sixty thousand Weltmarks; Fairgrave was demanding twice that, *unless*: "Tregare, we have to begin hitting back at UET. With your ship you could take the Far Corner colony and hold it against them. If you'll agree, we can—"

It was stupid; it was all wrong; Bran tried to explain why. During the times when the Chairman recited his piece, over and over again, Tregare thought about his options. He didn't *have* to go along with this crap; if necessary, he had enough fuel to wipe this Port and take what he needed by sheer plunder. Or, using his remaining scout, he could accomplish the same thing with much less damage. Except that he didn't *want* to have to do any such thing to a Hidden World. To his own people, who were all he had to work for. Even *this* clabberhead . . .

So he gave it one more try. Standing, to give himself that much extra impact, again he whomped fist to desk. At vision's edge he sensed a tall figure entering the room, but had no time to glance aside and see who it might be. "You *will* refuel me, just as the Compact states. Or I'll orbit a beacon, blacklisting you with every ship that comes into signal range."

Fairgrave played his vocal record again. ". . . matter of price, same as with the food. Now if you'll undertake our mission . . ."

Tregare sat down. "Your *stupid* mission." By this time he hardly listened to his own words. ". . . hold Far Corner against UET?" A little cussing, and then, "You think I'll waste my life on that mudball?"

It went on and it went on, Fairgrave saying how the taking of Far Corner was *important*, and Bran answering, "You wouldn't know important if it bit you on the leg. I—" Seeing a shadow on the desk in front of him, he looked up to see who was casting it.

She was tall, big-boned, and very black. Her strong-featured face betrayed her age not at all, and her ships-issue jumpsuit outlined a trim figure, definitely female but still ripening. As she stood over him, saying nothing, he noticed that one earlobe carried a heavy-looking gold ring—and that the other ear had no lobe at all. Those features were obvious because her tightly-curling hair was clipped to the semblance of a tight cap of black felt. "You!" Tregare said. "Who are you? What's your business here?"

"Zelde M'tana." Deep-voiced for a woman, still she spoke softly. "My business, it's with the computer terminal over there. Go right on yelling—it won't bother me none." And without waiting for an answer she stepped past, toward the terminal.

Fairgrave began talking again, Bran cutting in now and then, trying to reach some kind of understanding. Possibly because of M'tana's gibe, they kept the noise level down now. But none of it helped matters, and when the tall woman came back past Tregare he welcomed the distraction. "You get done what you wanted—M'tana, is it?"

She looked down to him. "Some part of it, yeah."

Marisa Hanen began to protest that a very important meeting was being interrupted, but Tregare cut in. "What else you need, M'tana?"

"To talk with you. Stay all night here, you still get no place— and you know it. I bet nobody's had dinner, though it's late for that." True enough, and Tregare's stomach confirmed it. "Tregare—buy me a drink on your ship, and a meal with it. We need to talk."

Predictably, Suth Fairgrave began to shout. "—most arrogant, ridiculous thing—you walk in here and—"

That did it; Bran slapped the desk, and stood. "If *you* don't like it, it has to make sense." He declared the meeting recessed. "Come on, M'tana—you just bought yourself some drinks and dinner."

"*And* talk."

He touched her shoulder. "Yeah, that too." And they left.

Outside the building she detoured to a waiting aircar; near as Tregare could see, she handed something to the man inside it, then came out carrying a travel case. Rejoining Bran she said, "Ole, my pilot. Flew me down from upriver a ways. I was paying him, just now."

"Sure." He walked her over to *Inconnu*, up the ramp, and then straight to his quarters. On the intercom he ordered their dinners from the galley and offered drinks. She chose bourbon; they clinked glasses and sipped.

It was about time, Tregare thought, to get down to business.
"First now—tell me who you are." What he wanted was *her*
version of what he'd read from *Strike Three*'s computer-
entered log. What she handed him was an envelope; inside
was a letter of recommendation signed by Cyras Adopolous,
Captain. Knowing part of the facts already but not prepared to
admit it, Tregare scanned the sheet. ". . . joined ship at
Earth . . . chosen for training . . ." Communications, navi-
gation, weapons, the power suit: these things caught Bran's
attention, and so did her test marks, scored by Adopolous and
the late Ragir Parnell. ". . . appointed Third Hat, then
Acting Second; assumed command in emergency and so
functioned for the duration of the trip. Under trying circumstances, performed all duties effectively."

So far, so good—but now, maybe, a little pressure wouldn't
hurt. Handing the papers back, he said, "Yes. I've skimmed
the bulletin-board circuit. So you're the one who wants a Hat
berth." She nodded, and he sank the hook. "Worked up from
cargo, did you—all the way to captain, for a while—by way of
the skipper's bed?"

She looked puzzled, not angry, as he explained that her
ship's log didn't list her—and a number of others—at all, until
after Escape, and then suddenly she was in captain's digs with
Parnell.

Unsmiling, she shook her head. "It wasn't like you think.
Tell you sometime, maybe. For now, I'll stand on what
Dopples wrote."

Delivery of two food trays interrupted Bran's reply. He
handed one to her. "Eat now, M'tana. Talk later."

Afterward, sipping tart wine with a tangy afterbite, they
talked. Yes, she wanted to buy into a Hat berth; well, he had
one open, and briefly he explained why. Then he went to
questions: her background, knowledge, experience, ships she
knew about. All of it.

The background surprised him. He'd heard of the Wild Kids
on Earth, gangs of fugitive children who roamed semi-
deserted towns and countryside, forming their own societies
and dodging UET's Welfare roundups. Zelde M'tana had *been*
one of them. "The worst was the Committee Police their own
damned selves," she said. "I got one of those, with a spear gun,
but the raid went wrong; that's how come I got caught." She

was skipping a lot of it; he could see that. But anyway, she wound up as cargo on the *Great Khan*, headed for the cribs of Iron Hat to service miners and keep them happy for UET. And then, instead, Escape . . .

They were out of wine; he opened another bottle. "Yeah. I wondered what training you had. Now I know—from UET, nothing. Out on the loose, though, you learned command before you were fourteen. But if Parnell hadn't logged it, that you by yourself took out an armed man in a power suit—"

"It took me luck; he stood at the edge, when I jumped to kick." She told how the armored man had slammed back and forth, falling, how it seemed his shrieks would never stop. For a moment her young eyes looked haunted.

So he changed the subject. "The thing is, you won. Now tell me, what ships did you meet, or speak?" Well, after Escape they'd had a skew pass with Bernardez, but neither he nor Parnell admitted they were Escaped. At Parleyvoo on Terranova they'd barely missed Malloy, and his message hinted that "soon there'll be a pig in the parlor." Tregare explained the reference; Malloy had then been preparing his own Escape. Zelde herself had spoken Ilse Krueger on *Graf Spee*, in space, and Ilse had confirmed that she would join Tregare's effort. "Well, I figured she would." Then he had to explain the loose information net a little more.

And, feeling that maybe he'd had a drink too many, Tregare spoke his own mind a little. "Fairgrave's idea—he has the wrong place, is all. Stronghold! That's the key." *I'm talking too much!* So he went back to asking questions.

Her answers came freely. "No, I never lifted off or landed for real, yet. Showed good on the sims, though." On weapons, "You know we wasn't armed, the ship. I know just portables."

So far, she sounded good. One more thing, though, Tregare needed to learn. "How did you get up to captain? Tell it all."

"Ragir's hurts brought him down," and in the saying, her own face showed pain. "Then Dopples, out flat so long. He took a knife in the gut at Parleyvoo. Went after the bandit that cut my ear—" She touched the lobeless one.

"He saved your life, did he?"

She frowned; he could see she was trying to figure how to say it. "Not that. The other two I killed, myself. What he did, Dopples he brought me back that part of my ear, and the ring in it. And killed him the one that tooken it. But that gutstab brought him real low, a long time." Her mouth twitched, almost to a smile but not quite. "And that there was when he didn't even *like* me. But still we was shipmates; you see that?"

"Yeah. I do. Then what happened?" It got complicated. M'tana told a story pretty well, except that Tregare got lost in sidelights that were obviously important to the woman but bogged him down in more unfamiliar names than he could keep track of. Especially since he was busy dealing with the fact that Zelde M'tana impressed him a lot more than anyone had in quite some time.

"Tzane was in line for Acting Captain but wouldn't take it, so that put me leapfrogging her. Some didn't like that; I had to kick ass a lot—like before, with Honcho, a time back." Tregare couldn't remember who Honcho was. Somebody from when Zelde was still with the Wild Kids, he thought.

"Carlo never got over me making Third when he was bumped for screwing up. So when he had it again, that's how Franzel, the Utie hideout, stuck her hooks in him to try the takeover." Peace on a mountain—the *intensity* of her, now! Blinking back tears, she said, "If I hadn't of had to go fight, right then, maybe Ragir'd not've died." She shook her head. "Anyway, I got to the power suit we had left—it worked good enough, except no way to use the projector that went with it, and—and I took the ship back, is all."

Not meaning to, Tregare laughed. She looked at him; he reached to squeeze her hand, then refilled her glass. "Hell, M'tana—in a way we're *twins,* you and I!" And he told her of the *Tamurlaine's* Escape and Cleet Farnsworth's counter-mutiny, and how Bran himself, in a power suit, pretty well cleaned the ship of Uties.

Looking more relaxed then, she continued. "Well, when we got to here, nobody except me to run the ship all that way, too many couldn't live with it. Cargo to captain, me. I had to sell off. You see it?"

"Sure. On *Inconnu,* though, you wouldn't have that problem. All I'd log for record is what Adopolous gave you to show around." He paused. "I could use you on here, M'tana. But the question is, can I afford you?"

"What's that mean?"

"Weltmarks—I need a lot, maybe you gathered, and I have only the Hat berths to peddle for them." He thought he knew what she'd say next so he didn't let her say it. "Don't offer to come aboard as a rating—I'd never ship an ex-officer in a pride-hurting job. Too risky; you people found that out with—what's his name?"

"Carlo. Carlo Mauragin. But I—"

"So if you can't afford to buy a berth, you're out. I'm sorry."

"Sorry, yeah. What kind of figure you got, on Second Hat?"

"Two hundred thousand. Do you have it?"

Her headshake wasn't a simple "negative." "What I got, or what I don't—seems you're pricing kind of high, though."

With impatience, he gestured. "You heard what they're trying to do to me here! I *need*—"

No hesitation; she said, "One-forty, I'll go. Out of that, I'll see you fueled."

"No." It wasn't enough. He swallowed some wine. "That leaves me only twenty thousand fluid credit from the deal. I need more than that, a lot more."

Totally surprising him, the woman laughed. "You *got* more." She handed him a printout sheet, and while he tried to figure it, she said, "See? I *own* that fuel—bought it at regular price and you get it the same way. Leaves you—"

"Eighty thousand clear, yeah!" Hmm, she'd bought a fair amount of food, too. He looked more closely. "You—the time code on this tape—"

"That's right." For the first time she smiled freely. "Heard the argument, you see, and—"

Not meaning to, he slammed his glass down so hard it broke, and leaned back, laughing. "*That's* what you were doing on the computer? Buying up fuel before Fairgrave changed prices officially?"

She nodded. "Seemed like a good move."

Twice Bran pumped his right fist up and out. On the intercom he called Control; Gonnelson had the watch. Tregare told him to advise Port Admin that *Inconnu's* business with the Board could wait until next day, midmorning. Then he signed out and sat back. "All right, Second Hat M'tana—and when I have the fuel and the eighty thousand that's who you are on this ship, long as you can hack it—let's have a drink."

They were back to bourbon; a deal like that, Bran thought, deserved more than wine. After the first sip he said, "You want to stay here tonight? Or do you have things to take care of, in town?"

She didn't—or nothing that couldn't wait. "No—Second Hat quarters on here sounds fine."

But that wasn't exactly what he'd meant. Tanit was gone off someplace and this woman *stirred* him. Without quite lying, he implied that the Hat quarters weren't available yet, and said, "What I had in mind, M'tana, was right here."

First she paused, but before he could say more: "You said you was shorthanded—means you got space. Somewhere I can be, for now." Her hand waved off any interruption. "One thing you should know, Tregare. My men—*I'm* the one does the picking." While he thought that one over, she said, "This change anything? I mean—you want some other Second Hat— and get your fuel someplace else, too?"

For a moment, anger came, but then he saw the tension in her face, and felt his own relax. *She's been through a helluva lot!* "No problem. You're right—there's space. There's time, too."

"Wasn't out to mad you up. Just had to say it."

And Tregare had to laugh. Both of them standing now, he gripped her arms, holding her face to face with him. "If you couldn't stand up to me, M'tana, how could you stand up *for* me?" Now he touched the lobeless ear. "Tell me about that sometime, will you? The whole thing, I mean."

"Sure. It wasn't so much."

"I'll bet." Hands on her shoulders now, he shook her, but only gently. "Stick with me, M'tana, you'll have your own ship again someday. And maybe more."

Talk time seemed to be over. He showed her to a clean, freshly-supplied Chief Rating's cabin and left her there. Back in quarters he had a small nightcap and thought about the entire evening, deciding that except for the one disappointment it could hardly have gone better. *That one's a tiger.* And tomorrow he'd promote Hain Deverel to Third, and have a full quota of watch officers again.

9. The Islands

The Board of Trade meeting took twenty minutes. Fairgrave didn't like it, but nothing said he *had* to like it. For the next two days matters moved fast and without interference, and on a sunny, characteristically hazy midmorning, the day after Tanit Eldon returned on sked, *Inconnu* prepared to lift.

At council, held in Control, Tregare had jockeyed coordinates out of Tinhead and maneuvered them on one of the aux screens. He wished he had a holographic projector working, but the ship's had been inoperative since someone's energy beam slagged its innards during Escape. So Bran made do with what he had, trusting Tinhead to follow directions and swing perspectives correctly.

Noting the distances and angles between various UET colonies and Hidden Worlds, translating these into time and costs and fuel and risks, the group reached a consensus. Most of it, Tregare liked. Their first destination, though, a UET world listed as The Islands, he wished he knew more about. All Tinhead had to offer was that the planet's surface was mostly water with nothing you could really call a continent, that its major resource seemed to be fuel ore, and that it was obviously the most time-efficient stop they could make. So, with some reluctance, Bran agreed to it. And out in this part of

151

space he figured they could still get away with the *Alexander the Great* schtick.

The liftoff he assigned to Zelde M'tana. When she protested "But I never done this!" he said it was time she tried. He didn't mention that sitting alongside her he would have the takeover switch in case of need; she would know that much.

Before she could ask for instructions he said, "Just take it up the way you'd prefer to ride it," and tried not to show his delight when she boosted exactly the way he himself would have done if he were in a little hurry but no real emergency. Straight up, then bending half a radian toward rendezvous with the gas-giant Bran had pegged to give them a sling-turn boost. When she finished setting course, she turned to him, and he said, "Rock steady, M'tana. Not a wobble." And before she could answer, added, "On the sims, now, you might want to practice landings." First she looked puzzled, then nodded, and grinned at him.

With two new Hats to acclimate, Tregare wanted to bring Hain Deverel along fast, too. But the slingshot turn was trickier than Bran cared to load on someone with Deverel's limited experience. Instead, he took it himself but put the new Third alongside him, using controls that didn't affect the ship's moves but made a record of what the ship *would* have done. "That way," Bran said, "we can compare after, and see which of us made the least mistakes. Okay?"

Deverel nodded. "It's a good training system."

The turn ran on tracks. Then, comparing Tregare's tape with Deverel's on splitscreen, they saw that the Third had overcontrolled early-on but made quick recovery and came out as close to exact course as Bran had. "All right, Hain. Next time you do it yourself, while I take a nap."

Deverel had to know Tregare was joking, but his expression showed he appreciated the compliment.

Once course and timing were determined, Tregare went down to Stores to see what shape the ship's inventory was in. He got a pleasant surprise; after working first with Renni Lofall and then with Tanit Eldon, Storesmaster Groden had begun to learn the new inventory system and was doing well with it. The stooped, middle-aged man had shed the grumpy manner Bran had accepted for so long; now he was accommodating and even cheerful. So Tregare hinted, broadly, that another promotion was in store.

"Well, thanks, cap'n; I'd like that. Could you stretch that and boost my assistant, too? Mayly Dunbar—she's not here right now—she's still only a Second rating. And she may have to fill my job, not too long from now."

Tregare's brows raised. "You want off the ship, Groden?"

Headshake. "Not me. I'm happier on here than I ever was. It's my arthritis, wants off. The gee-changes, see? More and more, they give me pure hell. But I'm good for a while yet."

"I hope so. Have you seen Eda Ghormley about the problem?" Ghormley, *Inconnu*'s closest answer to a full-fledged medic, might be able to help or might not.

"No, not yet. But maybe it's a good idea, at that."

Until *Inconnu* was set on a straight-accel heading, Tregare had had little time to be with Tanit Eldon: briefly, the night of her return, they'd been together, but not since then. Now, though, Bran could relax a bit; he and she arranged a dinner and evening in his quarters, and, as usual, she arrived on time.

After the hug-and-kiss greeting, after he'd changed two empty glasses into full ones, they sat. He said, "What did you learn about Fair Ball? That interested you, I mean?" But he didn't listen too closely, as she talked about commerce along Main River, and mining and agriculture and the herding of meat animals. He was looking at her, trying to see her as he first had done, to see if she had changed, and how.

Well, the hair was different; hair grows, and gets chopped back. The top frizz and short back-and-sides had changed to a full smooth cap, neat at the edges. And she wore less makeup now. But, as always, she looked good to him.

So he was puzzled to realize that somewhere along the line he'd decided *not* to ask her to move in with him. Not just yet, anyway. He liked her; he needed her to talk with; nowadays she made bed a delight. But still . . . he decided that maybe the problem was, it still bothered him that she'd insisted on being away from him for over a week when he really felt need for her.

So for now he said nothing about the roomies idea. After dinner, though, Bran enjoyed their activities very much.

* * *

Officers didn't usually work projector turrets, but Tregare wanted M'tana checked out on them anyway. "On account of when it hits the fan," he told her, "nobody ever knows who might have to do what." In her usual quiet way, she agreed. And by now he knew the woman well enough to realize she didn't bother to disagree about small stuff, but when she did balk, she truly meant it. He conducted himself accordingly.

On the firing-run stimulations up in Turret Six, at first the tall woman couldn't seem to master the problems of coordination: when she kept her heterodyne indication to a circle the range lights got away from her, and vice-versa. Finally Tregare cut the sim in mid-run. M'tana turned to look at him as he said, "What's the matter? Do you have any problems seeing?"

"Not like you mean that, I don't think." She scowled. "But, I watch the circle, I lose the range lights. Or t'other way 'round."

Tregare's sigh was relief. "Oh, *that*. I should have told you. Don't look back and forth. Unfocus your eyes a little, so you see it all at once."

She nodded. "Makes sense. You want to start that thing again?" And after a run that showed flashes of accuracy and another that improved it a lot, she seemed to have the knack. Bran ran her through the rest of the series; her scores weren't great, as yet, but he saw that with practice she could be one hell of a gunner.

Shutting the sim down, he said, "That buys you a dinner. My place, in half an hour. Okay?"

Climbing down from the gunner's seat, she said, "Sure. I—" And just as one foot touched the deck, *Inconnu* gave a lurch. Not a big one, just the watch officer making an accel correction, but it caught her off balance and she fell against the console's rounded corner, hitting her head.

Before Tregare could get to her, she was standing, but her eyes didn't look focused. He saw the skin at the right side of her forehead coming back from an indentation, leaving a red mark but no cut, and the red fading slowly. He put an arm around her shoulders, in support. "Hey! You're all right. There's no—"

No blood, he was going to say, but surprisingly she shoved at him, separating them. "Don't never do that!"

"Do *what*? All I—M'tana, *are* you all right?"

"Trying to ease me, you was. Don't never. I can't—dunno

why, but it puts me dizzy. Can't think straight. A long time I didn't know what done me that way. Learned a while back, though. So—" She touched the bruise, winced a little and shook her head.

Carefully, he said, "Is dinner still on, Zelde?"

"Sure." She grinned. "Can't hurt a Wild Kid, hitting her in the *head*."

During and after the dinner, Bran didn't feed his Second Hat too much booze. Possibility of concussion, and all. But she seemed to be tracking fully. Several days later, when she racked up an average score of 60 in the turret with a top run of 68, he repeated the invitation and this time didn't ration the bourbon. Well, by now he knew that Zelde M'tana was good at holding her liquor because she knew how to *monitor* herself. Tregare appreciated that skill, since it was one of his own, too.

Still curious about this woman with the unorthodox background, he asked questions. Some she answered, some she wouldn't, and some she simply didn't know. Such as her ages, either bio or chrono. "Back on Earth, what year it was, nobody never told me. The Utie woman, one as put me on the *Great Khan*, she guessed me fourteen or fifteen, maybe. Could of been wrong, and said so. And from there, bringing it up to now—" Her brow furrowed. "Eighteen, maybe twenty bio, best guess I got." Shrugging, "Ain't like it mattered."

She seemed so much older, so matured by experience. But that happens, Tregare thought, when you're up against the Long View.

Now she talked more freely. Tregare began to wish he'd known more of Ragir Parnell, the man she still obviously mourned. She'd saved his life at Escape, moved into captain's digs to care for him, overcome total ignorance of ships' ways to earn a rating and then abrupt, unexpected elevation to Third Hat. "And weren't Ragir, put me up for it. Dopples done it, Dopples not even liking me then, 'cause he hated women as dealt on their men's rank." Shaking her head, "That, I never done. And finally Dopples knew it."

Other events on the multi-named ship, Tregare couldn't get so clear. It wasn't that M'tana couldn't do brief, solid reports, but now she was ranging back through memories that held a lot of feeling. There was something about a Policebitch at

Terranova who bluffed her way aboard ship just at liftoff time
and turned out to be an Underground agent making her own
individual Escape. Tregare couldn't figure that one out, but
decided he didn't need to.

With *Inconnu* on decel toward The Islands, Bran keyed
Tinhead to the fake *Alexander* log and did a little creative
updating. Then he gathered his Control officers plus Junior
Lee Beauregard, to look through it for discrepancies and
suggest improvements. Junior Lee was a couple of centimeters
shorter than M'tana or Tregare. On first meeting her he'd said,
"New Second Hat, you are? My, my—y'all *are* a big one."

Eyes narrowed, Zelde said, "That all right with you?" But
Junior Lee's wide grin and quick reach to shake hands made it
clear that the Chief Engineer, in his own way, was being
friendly.

Now, as the update reading ended, Beauregard sat back.
"Looks spit-slick to me, cap'n." Hain Deverel suggested
deletion of some questionable details of the "*Alexander's*" visit
to a colony none of them knew except by report, and Tregare
accordingly put that section into vaguer terms.

After a few other comments were discussed, the meeting
broke up. M'tana had the watch. Tregare went to the ship's
infirmary, to talk with Eda Ghormley.

He found the thin woman sorting through medical supplies,
making an inventory sheet. As she greeted him, Tregare
noticed that the chronic frown was almost gone; maybe
working in an Escaped ship felt better than doing the same job
under UET. And it probably hadn't hurt matters when he'd
decided, a time back, that a Chief's rating wasn't prestigious
enough for the Chief Medic. Back at Number One his council
had okayed raising Ghormley to officer status, roughly equal
with Second Hat.

Now he asked her: "How's the lame duck business? You got
many in residence?" He knew from the log, but asked anyway.

"Just Schroeder from Drive, and she'll be up on crutches in
a day or two. Maybe next time she won't try to skip a landing
going downship, late for watch or not."

Tregare laughed. "Not while she has the cast on, she won't.
But what I came for—are you having any luck yet, rigging
something that looks like UET's cheek tattoos and won't

smear? Because coming into The Islands, we'll need that pretty soon."

She nodded. "I think so. Let me show you." And a few minutes later, after she peeled the decal off the hairless underside of his forearm and the colored design dried in place, she showed him that no amount of scratching or soap-and-water would smear the pattern. But the special solvent took it off clean. "So any time you want, bring your Hats in and I'll do them up properly."

He fingered his own cheek, where the later-added segments didn't match well with the quadrant originally received from UET. "Could you cover *this*, you think, so's it'd pass better?"

"Well, let's try." It took a little doing, getting everything to match, but he found the result hard to fault.

Still well out from The Islands, Tregare began growing his Dietrich Armiger beard. Zelde M'tana found it funny; in fact, once it gave a case of the giggles to that extremely ungiggly woman. "Come on, M'tana," he said. "Chuckle at the whiskers some other time. After all, this is *your* fake history we're trying to feed Tinhead and make it look good." So she sobered down, and the resultant entry was a fictional masterpiece, if Tregare did say so himself!

He held off the bleaching, trimming and dyeing of hair and beard as long as possible ("For one thing, it itches"), but made and aired a loop tape to the planet they were nearing, well before *Inconnu* came into detection range.

"Deet Armiger calling The Islands. Captain Dietrich Armiger, for the armed ship *Alexander the Great*. Homing in with ETA approx ninety standard hours. Come in please, The Islands . . ." And every hour, the comm-tech on watch stopped the tape and changed the number.

With sixty-eight standard hours to go, The Islands responded.

Entering Control, Tregare motioned his comm-tech to stay seated at the main panel and sat at an aux position. The voice from groundside was live, not tape, and the male speaker sounded youthful. Tregare cut his own tape's transmission, idly watching the indicator show silence as he framed his own first reply. But before he'd spoken a word, the indicator came to life. His panel was *sending* something!

Only for about two seconds, though, before Tregare slapped the Off switch and cut transmission. It took him a little longer to find which tape drive had been operating; he rewound the short bit that had been sent, set the unit's output to local audio with no scramble or offship signal—and as an afterthought, put on a headset and plugged it in to preempt the speakers. Because this kind of thing had happened before, back at Muspelheim. And this time, Tregare wanted first listen.

He started the tape. And heard, "First, let me identify myself. I am——" All right—that's as far as the message could have played; he restarted it. "——an agent of the Committee Police. My cover name on this ship is Tanit Eldon."

Long enough to determine the betrayal would have been total, he listened. Damn *all;* how could it be? *But peace take me, it* is! Deverel was watch officer; Tregare turned to him. "You handle the palaver, Hain. Something I need to do."

"But, captain——"

"You're up to it; punch up the *Alexander's* log and tell it like you believe it." He clapped a hand to the man's shoulder. "Sorry, but I'm in a hurry right now."

He checked his chrono, and nodded. Tanit should be asleep now, so he went to her room. But not taking anything for granted, Tregare went in fast, without knocking. And a good thing, too, because if a mat hadn't slipped under his foot, her clawing lunge would have taken his left eye.

He didn't have time to wonder how she'd known what the situation was, but something in the back of his mind told him she would naturally have monitors hooked up here, to check on how her treachery was going. Right now, though, he fended off the fierce, *expert* attack of the woman he'd made love with, only a few hours before. She knew moves he didn't, and his emotional shock took away any physical edge he had.

So she got in a few good ones on him, but the range was too close for any blow or chop to have much speed to it. As he realized he'd better do something fast or she would, by all the flavors of peace, *kill* him, he remembered Murphy, the scarred, one-eyed female combat instructor at the Slaughterhouse. *When in doubt, get closer; guard your eyes and balls; a woman's wrists are her greatest disadvantage.*

So, trying to ignore some jabs and gouges that would probably leave him hurting for a month, he *got* in close. His thigh blocked her knee; she had nothing to bite but his jacketed shoulder, and finally a hand came where he could grab the wrist. He took it, and twisted hard; it might be unfair that the female wrist had less width and leverage, but fair was for games, and this situation wasn't one. Ten seconds later he had that hand up behind her in a hammerlock and heard her shoulder creak near to dislocation.

And *then* she said, "Bran? What's this all about?"

He didn't figure the question deserved an answer. Right now, the questions would be going the other way. And since Tanit had obviously beaten the truth drugs, twice, he was going to have to use less sophisticated methods.

He didn't like it, but what choice did he have?

A chop to the neck half-stunned her; he kept it short of killing force. Off came her clothes; he used some of them in tying her to the room's armchair: forearms flat along the chair's arms, feet secured to its front legs, ties around waist and neck because she shouldn't be able to move much.

Then he thought about it; *now* what? He'd never tortured, and even now the idea nearly made him throw up. He knew the theories: not *just* pain or mutilation, but fear of it and of its results. Go too far with disfigurement and the victim simply abdicates; nothing you do will have any further effect. Yet you can't afford to bluff and have that bluff called, either. Why in the name of peace did this have to happen to *him*?

Or, for that matter, to her. Looking at her, even now he found her semblance dear. No, he couldn't destroy the beauty of that face or body. Stymied, suddenly he noticed he was rubbing his right thumb over the nail of that hand's middle finger. And remembering the agony of a childhood injury, he felt a grin forming. A very mean grin. Because he looked at that fingernail and saw no marks at all, from the earlier trauma.

"What are you going to do?" So Tanit Eldon, whatever her real name, was back to full consciousness. Ignoring her, he got on the intercom.

"Ghormley?" At her response, he said, "In about fifteen, twenty minutes, get here to Eldon's quarters with your medic kit. Make sure to bring some anti-shock stuff." He listened to her startled questions, and said, "You'll have a shock patient, all right. Take my word for it. Tregare out."

* * *

When a sharp piece of iron smashed nine-year-old Bran's fingernail and punched a vee-shaped segment under the rest of it, to put agonizing pressure on the bruised nerves, the boy had felt the worst pain of his entire life and nearly died of shock. So now he couldn't think of a simpler way to get the most impact with the least damage. Tanit Eldon was tougher than the boy Tregare had been; it took two fingers on each hand, and occasional harsh tapping on first one damaged nail and then another, before she gave up on pleading and began talking.

He had most of it from her before shock hit and he had to wait for Eda Ghormley to come up and counteract the effect. "Hypnosis, Tregare," she kept repeating. Automatically he ignored the screams and curses, listening only to the words that made sense. "The chemical *presence* of any truth drug in the bloodstream triggers the hypnotic implant; whatever my cover ID is, my cover story, under the drug it's *true* for me." Was she the only one like this? She didn't know, except that the technique was fairly new. And only one such agent would be slipped into any given ship.

Eldon hadn't been to the Hulzein Establishment in Argentina; she *had* been infiltrated into the Underground, though. Her story of Erika wanting an alliance was sheer improvisation; when she boarded *Inconnu* she didn't know its identity or status; she was one of an experimental group designed to go onto ships and be monitors. It wasn't her job to blow an Escaped Ship's cover immediately, but first to gather data, such as coordinates, on Hidden Worlds. "And I had two, now, so it was time. One's plenty, but Muspelheim went wrong." Then, for a time, shock took her.

Knowing the disabling effects of that reaction, before Ghormley arrived Tregare had Tanit Eldon untied and even clothed. Seeing the injuries, the medic gasped. "What *happened* to her?"

"I did." And then, "She's our traitor, and I had to know *how*." Further, "Twice she beat the drugs; I knew that. So—"

Shrugging, Ghormley punctured the blood-blistered nails to relieve the agonizing pressure, then administered the hypo to bring the woman back to consciousness. Tregare said, "Give her some pain-killing shots, too."

"Why—?"

"I've got most of what I need; the rest's not important. And just because she has to die in a few minutes, doesn't mean she has to hurt, up until I space her."

Bran didn't need any words then, from Ghormley, to know what kind of monster she thought he was.

Tanit didn't resist his further questions; she said, after answering them, "I wish we could have been on the same side."

Him supporting her, because drugs and trauma had her shaky, they were heading downship to the main airlock. "If you'd wanted to switch, you could have."

Headshake. "Couldn't. More hypnosis. I don't remember it, of course, but it's standard for field agents. Total loyalty to UET, total animosity toward its enemies. No choice." What her face did, then, was probably trying for a smile. "So you don't have to feel badly about spacing me; it's your only option."

"Thank you, Tanit." For what, he wasn't quite certain. But remembering Butcher Korbeith he forced himself to watch as vacuum drew her out the lock to death. She didn't scream or struggle or void her body wastes in panic; Tanit Eldon met death with dignity.

Heading back up to Control, Tregare wasn't sure whether her stoicism made him feel better or worse.

Almost, but maybe not quite, Tregare had himself back in gear. *I killed Tanit.* But he forced himself to listen to the playback of what Deverel had said to The Islands, and of what groundside had said back.

It smelled good. This place sounded less paranoid than most places Tregare had visited, UET *or* Hidden. Relying on M'tana's data, Deverel had cited Terranova as the ship's most recent stop, and near as Tregare could tell, The Islands believed everything Deverel had said.

When Tregare turned off the tape and said as much, Gonnelson cleared his throat. "Sure?"

"Sure as I *can* be, from up here. I've learned to judge these communications. Any time the other end hesitates, except to look up data, somebody's thinking something over—or up. On Deverel's tape, counting-in the decreasing range and transmission lag, the only real pause was when Hain asked for longitude, of their port with respect to the terminator, for our ETA. And that one, they had to look up."

"Hope so."

When Tregare entered his quarters, he found Zelde M'tana waiting, sipping a drink. There was one for him, too. As he sat, she said, "Heard what you had to do. Thought I might could help some." He felt his face go tight. "Bad, huh?" He nodded. "I done a Utie the same once. Carlo Mauragin. All the way downship, he yelled."

"This one didn't. And Zelde—I'd *loved* that woman. Or damned close to it, anyway." Honesty forced the qualification.

"Pretty one, too. Not a big skinny giraffe like me." Startled, not knowing what to think, he watched her pull her blouse off over her head. When her face came clear, she was smiling. "But I'm what's here. You want to see if it helps?"

One deep breath he took. "Yeah. I think I'd like that."

His prediction was quite correct.

Up again, both seated and clothed, they looked at each other. She said, "That settle anything? About today, or the want I seen, all along, you got for me?" Her eyes narrowed. "That how it is with you and any woman? Take us all to bed, you have to?"

Shocked out of any semblance of defense, Bran shook his head. "Sure I wanted you. You're not like anyone I've ever known, and I guess the difference made you a challenge. I can't help that, Zelde; it's just how things are." He shook his head. "But today—now—I wasn't after anything, and all I want to do is thank you. Because you didn't have to—"

"True's all hell I didn't. Tregare, it's not like you're Parnell. Him I needed, *had* to have. Same with Honcho, when I run a division for him, back on Earth. Biggest Wild Kid gang UET ever busted, and tooken 'em a nuke shell to do it." And Bran realized that while he'd survived risks and ordeals this tall black woman hadn't, the reverse was also true.

"All right," he said. "Just so we know how we stand."

"I ain't done yet. What I need you for is different. It's what you *are*, and what you gonna do. And except for this here, today, and sometimes we could both feel like it again, maybe that's what you need me for, too."

For seconds, the words silenced Tregare; then he said,

"M'tana, you impress the total hell out of me. And I think you're right." Assessing himself, his state of being, he added, "How did you know what could put me back together? And why did you want to?"

He liked her grin, then. "Hell'sfire, Tregare; a little screwing helps damn near anything. And we're *friends,* ain't we?"

"Right. And peace knows, I'm glad of it."

But that night, the nightmares returned: the Slaughterhouse dorm was somehow in space, and part of the time Bran himself was Butcher Korbeith, and the redhaired woman who went out the airlock was Phyls Dolan and Tanit Eldon both at once, so he had to try to space her and rescue her at the same time.

Going in toward The Islands, it seemed that Bran's reassurances to his First Hat had been correct. At the planet's one spaceport, situated on its largest island, *Inconnu* landed just after sunrise and met a friendly welcome.

Only one other ship sat groundside: the unarmed *Erwin Rommel,* captained by Lane Tysdale, a heavy-set swarthy man close to twice Tregare's age. They met as Bran came out of Port Admin, having settled the necessary fuel-and-supplies transactions. Tysdale invited him aboard the *Rommel:* drinks and lunch, the usual. Normal drill would be to take a sideman along, and although Tregare could find nothing remotely suspicious about the situation, he felt edgy and could have used the confidence of some backup.

But inwardly he shrugged. If he let himself get scared of shadows, haunted by Tanit Eldon's betrayal, he could wind up like Krieg Elman. So he made do with informing *Inconnu,* from Tysdale's quarters, where he was and when he expected to be back on his own ship. "Anything needs asking, call me. Armiger out."

Having come directly from Earth, Tysdale was well stocked with bourbon. With ice tinkling as they sipped, the two men traded small talk. Tregare wasn't as relaxed as he hoped he looked to be, because he had to concentrate on keeping his story straight.

It didn't matter for long, though, because Lane Tysdale had something on his mind, and starting his second drink he told it. "Armiger, I've got one hell of a mess on this ship, and I don't know what to do about it." Politely, Bran gestured that he was willing to listen, and the man said, "They put me sixty women on here, Welfare clients, as cargo for Iron Hat. Sixty, in a space fit to hold half that many. And then, an hour before we lifted, changed the orders to come here *first*. I asked permission to unload the women—some of them, anyway—or to follow my original orders to Iron Hat and *then* come here." One side of his mouth quirked. "I guess you know, Armiger, how far I got, trying to argue with the Port Commander."

Tregare thought about it. "Couldn't you put some of them in freeze?" Or maybe the *Rommel*'s chambers, like *Inconnu*'s, were unreliable.

But that wasn't the answer. "Preempted. The reroute, here, was to deliver some VIPs. The new governor and his two secretaries, and their families, filled those chambers. And now the old governor's group has them." His voice went from bitter to more so. "We lost a crewman, Armiger—because we didn't have a spare chamber when there was a medical emergency too big for my medics." He shook his head. "And those poor damned women down there—what's left of them—"

Running figures through his head, Tregare felt shocked. Earth to Iron Hat was maybe eight months, ships' time. Earth to the Islands was a year or more, easily—and from here to Iron Hat nearly the length of the originally-planned trip. "Some of them have died? Why?"

"Jammed in, like I told you. Poor sanitary facilities, no exercise, short rations—no shorter than the rest of us had, but what with the other problems—well, you see it."

"No exercise? I'd think you could—"

"Let them out a few at a time, under guard? Worth the guards' lives, that would be. Armiger, we're the only people they have, close enough to be worth hating."

Tregare tried to think of suggestions, but they all fell flat. Tysdale couldn't unload the women here because UET orders said they went to Iron Hat where the Miners' Co-op would pay the *Rommel* for transportation costs. He couldn't give them more living space because he had none available. He couldn't improve sanitation because any work force going inside to do so would be attacked tooth and nail. "Hell, Armiger. Two of the deaths were women charging into energy guns protecting the food delivery crew."

Finally Tregare gave it up. "How soon you leave for Iron

Hat?" Ten days, was the answer. "Well, if I think of something I'll let you know. Thanks for the drinks."

Walking back to *Inconnu*, Bran felt depressed. In quarters he sat, brooding, then had an idea. He called the Second Hat's cabin. "M'tana, you had enough sleep you could have dinner with me?" And before she could take the implication that his motive was sexual, he added, "Something I found out, I need to talk over."

When she arrived, after he poured drinks—a light one for him because they weren't starting even-up—he told her the story. "You rode cargo, yourself. Tell me about it."

"Wasn't like *that,* none. Crowded, sure, but not bad crowded." Brow wrinkling as she thought back to that time, she said, "Hold Portside Upper, we was in. About the same size as on here. And sixty of us didn't rattle much. Shared bunks, some of us. And—" She described the facilities. "Plumbing over where it tapped into Drive's, I expect. Three crappers, the squatover kind. Two shower closets. Four basins, two-way faucets, wash or drink, either one. Four-decker bunks along the side bulkheads. A sort of shelf with three slots over it; that's where the ration packets came out, twice a day. And a trash chute under it for the empty packets." She squinted a little. "The door out, it was two of 'em with a space between. Like an airlock, only not for vacuum. Security. And the rations—not great, but better'n I'd got in the UET lockup, earlier."

Bran paused to call the galley and order dinner, then he said, "Doesn't sound wonderful, but not any death trap, either. I—"

Leaning forward, Zelde grasped his wrist. "Tregare. Why don't *you* buy them women off him? One of the holds on here, we could fix it up good enough, and—"

He shook his head. "Zelde. You can't think, seriously, that *I'm* going to deliver a load of slaves, to whore for free in Iron Hat's cribs? Even if my schedules allowed time to go there?"

"Iron Hat, my ass! You—"

"And the ship simply can't *afford* to free those slaves and ferry them to some other world, a Hidden World, with no way to recoup the cost. I'm sorry, but—"

"Give a listen, damn you!" For moments, Bran almost expected physical attack. "Not Iron Hat. Find a ship going to

Farmer's Dell, and make you a swap. The Dell—I heard on it, back in Hold Portside Upper on the *Great Khan*. Always been short of women, so they don't mind paying to get some. But then they're *free* women, treated right." She had a stubborn look, as she said, "Well, that's how *I* was told it."

He nodded. "I heard it that way, too. But—"

"You got to, Tregare. You *got* to!"

Caught between anger and frustration and peace knew *what*-all, Bran took refuge in an unconvincing laugh. It didn't get him off the point of M'tana's fierce stare, but gave him time to sort out what he felt. "Slavery, Zelde. I hate it, same as you do. UET—it's a slaveowner *system*. Total Welfare, women as cargo, the whole thing. I—"

"You gonna *do* it, then!"

His scowl went tight enough to pain him. "Damn all, quit *crowding*, just a minute."

Surprisingly, her expression softened. "Sure, Tregare. You need some time, you got it. But—"

Without volition he shook his head. "Human cargo on *my* ship? No better than U E rotten peace-fucking T?"

Almost like iron, her hand gripped his. "No such a thing, Tregare. Wouldn't be like that, on here. The hold, yeah, but not how they get treated. And come to money, I could—"

A knock interrupted her; their meal was delivered. Hardly paying attention to his food, Tregare said, "Let me think about it. The way I've traded, we're low on high-bulk cargo; I could clear most of Hold Portside Upper. What's left would be crates nobody could break into, bare-handed." What else? "Clothes. No way do we have enough extra, and what they may have now—"

Startling him, M'tana laughed. "Clothes? They got none. No more than we did on the *Khan*. So—"

"So that takes care of the laundry problem, which was the next thing bothering me." He nodded. "All right. I'll try to dicker with Tysdale. Is that good enough?"

"Being as I go with you, sure. And I'll set a gang up, move things, get at the plumbing and stuff, try to make it no more work for you than got to be. You—"

"Zelde. Get these matters *planned*, the materials located, all that. But don't move Crate Number One until we have a deal.

"If we can manage one."

A quick Hats' council agreed the ship could afford the venture, so that was that. So far . . .

Tysdale couldn't seem to believe it, and even if he did, foot-dragging was his specialty. First he wanted the full compensation he had expected to receive at Iron Hat, along with ironclad documentation to prove to UET that in essence he had made delivery as ordered. The papers didn't bother Tregare any; Dietrich Armiger could swear to anything Tysdale wanted.

The money was something else. "You've got how many still alive, you say? Forty-eight? You guarantee they'll all live? And how about the fact that I'm transporting them a considerable time and distance, and deserve compensation for my expenses?" So Tregare haggled the *Rommel's* captain down to about half his original demands. And figured to lose money anyway—but that beat hell out of facing Zelde's reactions afterward, if he *didn't* make the deal.

Only after the papers were signed did Tregare let *Inconnu's* captain and Second Hat see his human cargo. Part of the view camera's lens was smeared with something, and Tregare had a fair idea what it was. Even so, he could see the wretched creatures huddled in much too small a space. They lay listless, filthy, some with festering sores on limbs and torso. Forty-eight? He tried to count but gave up; for the moment he accepted Tysdale's estimate. He could count the bunks, though. Twenty, or originally one for every three confined persons.

And he saw one crapper and one drinking tap and no showers. Nothing that looked like feeding arrangements, so he asked. "They have bowls and spoons—at least those were issued to them. Once a day my galley people take down a kettle of stew. It's set down in the open doorway and they have half an hour to dig in. But as I said, I need armed guards at that doorway."

"Don't surprise me none." M'tana's usually quiet voice held an edge Bran hadn't heard before. "Tysdale, you got a way to talk in at that place, a screen they can see who's talking?"

"Why, yes. Do you want me to announce the arrangements?"

Tregare was going to take the job on, but Zelde said, "Not so's you'd notice. I think that's for me to do."

* * *

It was loud and ugly and painful. When the prisoners saw the screen light up, they pelted it with excrement, which they had no trouble finding. Tregare said, "Peace take me, I've never seen such a pigsty."

"Be glad you can't smell it," Tysdale said, and Bran hoped he would never receive such a look as M'tana gave that man, then.

One deep breath, and she shouted, "Shut the hell up, down there!" To Bran's wonder, they did. "All right, who runs things? Somebody got to, anyplace. Whoever, say your name and hear the news I got for you." Silence. "Speak up, goddammit!"

A woman, probably young and once vigorous, but now looking neither, moved to the forefront. "What can *you* tell us? Why don't you kill us and get it over with? Who are you, anyway?"

"I'm Zelde M'tana and one time I rode cargo, same as you." *Oh, hell! I hope she doesn't blow cover on us.* But it was her show so Tregare said nothing; he checked that his knife was handy, though. "Not all shitty like they done you here, it wasn't. And that's the news. You're coming out of there, to another ship. A clean place, like you'll be, too. Only you got to come peaceful, not try to fight, and all." As the shouting began again, Zelde cracked the volume control high and said, "Talk it over. I can wait."

Bran could see the woman below, shushing the others, before she said, "My name is Cherisse Frisco. Before the Presiding Committee confiscated everything I had and Welfared me, I could have bought and sold this ship twice over. Now all I have is my own will to live by. And what's the point of living if we end up on Iron Hat, anyway?"

Tricky question, that. Tregare held his breath, until Zelde said, "You ain't there yet. And while you ain't, you rather live clean, or dirty like now? Like I said, take your time, deciding. I got plenty, too, except mine smells better."

Below, the discussion was loud again, too many talking at once for anything coherent to come through the circuit. As Lane Tysdale said, "Armiger? I'll provide guards, to get them off this ship and onto yours. You can clean them up, there."

"Like bloody hell I will!" Bran found himself glaring at the man. "That's your job. I expect they came on here clean; you send them off the same way." Overriding the other's protest, Tregare waved a hand. "You let this mess happen; you clean it up and I care not apeshit if you have to dirty some of your facilities a little. Otherwise the deal's off." M'tana gave him a stricken look; then her face cleared, so she must have guessed he was bluffing from strength.

It all took a while. Some of the women couldn't walk without help, so two who could supported one who couldn't. Luckily the proportion of invalids left no one unaided. And two or three at a time, the women went into the three shower cubicles made available and scrubbed each other down. The first trio had no luck trying to cleanse hair so matted and filthy it simply couldn't be made clean in a reasonable time. Zelde took over, commandeering some hair clippers; stubble washed quickly.

Tregare began to see why his Second Hat, coming from cargo, had earned the steps of command so quickly. She *acted.*

So while she seemed to have the mechanics of the situation under control, Tysdale's armed guards standing by as safeguard but not needing to do much of anything, Tregare decided to lean on the other captain. Well, first he called *Inconnu* and told the leader of Zelde's work gang to start moving cargo and installing plumbing plus fixtures. Some of the stuff would need fabrication in the ship's machine shop, but the needs were simple enough.

Then Bran said, "Tysdale? While we're waiting, you might's well have some of your people go down and take out those bunks, fittings and all. Steamclean 'em and deliver them to my ship." Tysdale balked, until Bran said, "You wouldn't want me to walk out of here now, would you? With all those slaves on the loose?"

So he got that one. And then, "Sixty women came on here wearing clothes. What's left goes off the same way. Dig 'em out." And he realized that the reason Tysdale caved in, once again, was that he hadn't been paid yet. And wouldn't be until Bran Tregare was damned well ready to do so. On *Inconnu,* as agreed.

Once the women, bathed and clothed, were herded across the spaceport into *Inconnu* and then to Hold Portside Upper,

Tregare made payment to Lane Tysdale and gladly saw the last
of the man, going down the ramp to groundside. Bran went to
the hold; Zelde was there, flanked by two armed guards. The
prisoners, some wearing clothes and others only holding the
folded garments here in warmed space, seemed bewildered.

Bran could see why. The hold's personnel-sized door was
open and members of Zelde's work gang went in and out. One
shower closet was in place and the other halfway erected. The
crappers were in, and two of the washbasins with drinking-tap
option. A small crew was installing bunks, and Tregare saw
that the Shops had produced new ones using the pattern of one
from the *Rommel*.

Bewildered these women might be, but still, Bran saw, wary
and resentful and potentially very dangerous. The sickest of
the lot lay on newly-installed bunks, but even they looked
around the place like caged animals.

So he went over to Zelde, and said, "Time I talked, you
think?" She nodded, so he made a shrill whistle to draw
attention.

"Welcome aboard. I captain this ship and it's time you
learned you're a lot better off than you've been thinking. For
starters, you won't ever see the cribs on Iron Hat. There's a
colony called Farmer's Dell—"

A shout interrupted him. In the press of women moving
forward, he couldn't determine who was shouting. "That's what
they told us on the *Rommel*, first. And before, when we signed
up."

Zelde spoke. "Same on the *Great Khan*, when I rode cargo.
But this here man, you can believe." She had them quiet now
and went on to say, "How you think I went from cargo on there
to Second Hat on here? Captain, even, on that other ship for a
time. So you—"

The woman who pushed forward then, Tregare recognized
as Cherisse Frisco. "Second *Hat*, you said? Not Second
Officer." She turned to face the other women. "What she's
saying, this Zelde M'tana, is that this is an Escaped Ship. So
we're Escaped." She looked back, now, to Zelde. "Or are we?"

Tregare answered. "We are, and you are. So you'll understand why, until we lift from here, I take no chance of any word
getting off this ship." Some didn't seem to like that, but Bran
had more to say. "Frisco, I want you to organize, if you hadn't

already, a peacekeeping squad to keep your whole outfit in line. Which means you stay in here because otherwise you'd get in the way. And nobody jumps the people who bring your food. I could use armed guards but that's a waste; I'd rather not. I could build a security 'airlock,' but if we won't need it, why bother? You have folks here that need medical attention, and I'd like it if our Medical Officer and her helpers could come in and work without needing protection." He paused. "Can you promise me those things?"

He saw Cherisse Frisco look to three or four women, one after another, and draw a nod from each. Then, to Tregare she said, "I can promise all of it. Anyone who breaks the rules, it's my responsibility to correct the matter."

Tregare grinned. "Frisco, we have a deal." He checked his chrono. "And you're all due a meal, too, about now. On here we'll feed twice a day, not once. For starters. Three would be a load on our galley staff, but if you need it, we'll do it. Then after chow, I think Ghormley and her medics will be geared to come down here and start work." He raised an eyebrow. "Any problems?"

Frisco said, "We guarantee your people perfect safety, here."

Before answering, Bran said to his two armed guards, "Why don't you folks go for a coffee break?" When they were gone, he told the sick, tired group of women, "No matter what happens, keep in mind—long as I can trust you, you can trust me."

Then he and Zelde went upship. He expected her to go to her own quarters but she accompanied him to his. Inside, she began to disrobe. "Tregare, you done great. Even Ragir—I don't see how he could of done better." She looked at him. "Get them clothes off, right now." So he followed suit, and they hugged. She pushed him back and said, "Why not in the shower?"

That much was fine and so was the talk later, while they ate. But when Zelde finally left and Bran was alone, suddenly he dreaded sleep. He was right, too: in his dreams, Hold Portside Upper, looking more like its counterpart on Tysdale's ship, was on Earth as a component of the Slaughterhouse. In fact, it was what he found when he opened the door to enter his squadroom—the women, naked and diseased, lying in filth, cried out to him, some with invitation and some threatening with jagged clawed nails. From one side, Jargy Hoad said to join the party. "Channery says he'll be along soon; he wouldn't want to miss you. . . ."

Sweating and shaking, Tregare found himself sitting bolt upright, half awake, but not totally. *Channery*, that goddamn rapist of junior cadets! Bran hadn't thought of the rotten bastard since he couldn't remember when. *Things must be really getting to me*. Well, seeing those women, the way they'd been on the *Rommel*, could get to anybody. . . .

He got out of bed and poured himself a slug of whiskey, twice a size he'd normally take, let alone at this time of night. And downed the whole thing; he might suffer for it tomorrow, but right now he needed to shut down the dreaming-function.

It worked. When he slept again, if he dreamed he woke with no memory of it. And got up feeling not half bad at all.

Probably there were rumors around the Port, but once the *Rommel* lifted off (for where, Tysdale didn't tell "Armiger"), Bran figured they would die of malnutrition. Most of his official transactions were done; mostly he was waiting for the work on Hold Portside Upper to be completed. But when it was, he got a call from Port Admin: a ship had come within detection range but not close enough to speak. Custom was that no ship deliberately missed groundside contact with another if only a few days' wait were involved; those contacts were too infrequent as it was. So Bran agreed to await the unknown ship's arrival.

Not unknown for long, though; it was the *Bonaparte*, commanded by Chalmers Haiglund. First Officer was Jimar Peralta.

The information came through Port Admin, not ship-to-ship direct contact. Tregare turned away from the comm-panel.

"Figured he'd have that ship by now," said Zelde.

"*You* know Peralta?"

"At Parleyvoo spaceport, on Terranova. The *Bonaparte* come in there, Tregare, while we was still working on the Nielson Cube, loading up supplies, mainly out fishing for some kind of Underground contact, so as to find us a Hidden World next."

Wondering, Bran shook his head. "Why haven't you mentioned this before?"

"Thought I did." A frown. "*Sure* I did. Well, the *Bonaparte*, anyway; Jimar Peralta, maybe not." She looked at Bran. "Why? You know that one too, maybe? Then I don't need to tell you, watch your ass all the way. Else he might could walk off with it."

Tregare chuckled. "Not likely. Though he has a claim, at that, having possibly saved it for me, a time or two."

So he told her about Butcher Korbeith and "airlock drill" where the Butcher might or might not put a naked cadet out into space, and how Peralta had twice intervened. And she told him how on Terranova the man had pressured Ragir Parnell toward trying to help him take the *Bonaparte*. "We drunked him up on trair, though, so he showed his hand. Then, 'till next day we knew he was safe to let go, we didn't do that."

Tregare didn't quite understand. "Zelde, back in UET's Space Academy, the Slaughterhouse, Peralta was one of the few decent people who had any authority. Ambitious, yes, but—"

"Ambitious, yeah; that's the worry. Wants command like a thirst-dried man wants water." She paused. "But how we knew he could be let loose, was what he said—why he couldn't take the rat way to command."

"Turn in an Escaped ship, and receive command of it from UET?"

She nodded. "He said like, all right, supposing he done that. Then when *he* Escaped, *where would he go?*" Zelde laughed. "He said, when *you* heard, you'd hunt him down if it tooken you all your life to do it. So might be you could still trust him."

"I'd hope so." He felt himself frowning. "That's not the problem." He stood. "Zelde, we haven't checked out this Port's missile defense and garrison facilities; there's been no need. But now—"

"You want I should send out some security snoops?" He nodded. "I will, that. But howcome?"

"Because I want to know the odds on *our* helping Jimar Peralta take a good healthy ship for himself." Thinking: *if he'll agree to my terms, I couldn't ask for a better ally.*

* * *

Right on its announced ETA, the *Bonaparte* landed. On Zelde's advice ("this Haiglund, Ragir said, is all by the book, and sure seemed Ragir had him right") Tregare made a formal call to the other ship and, as the junior of the two captains, accepted his senior's invitation to bring his First Officer along for a drink or two on the *Bonaparte*. Bran thought to spare Gonnelson the ordeal but Zelde said, "Ragir took me last time, on account Lera Tzane knew Peralta from early and was scared of him. Anybody with you excepting First Hat, that Haiglund he gonna ask *why*. And *me*, on a new ship and all—"

So Tregare bulldozed Gonnelson into going along. "Now look! You've done this before and got by with it." So the First Hat, without any show of sulkiness, accepted the inevitable.

The ramp guard and the airlock guard who escorted Bran and Gonnelson upship were courteous and businesslike. Captain Haiglund, admitting the visitors to his quarters, smiled and shook hands with both. A tall, broad man, Haiglund was, looking younger than his grey hair would indicate. "Welcome aboard," and all that routine; then, inside captain's digs, Tregare found himself face to face with Jimar Peralta.

Only one way to play it. Tregare moved to shake hands. "Mister Peralta. I've heard of you. Favorably."

Peralta's eyes narrowed; Tregare couldn't be sure whether his disguise held, or not. "Captain Armiger. A pleasure indeed."

The ritual seemed to run on tracks: exchange of data on other ships met, drinks neither stingy nor prodigal, dinner that kept balance between stinting and opulence; the food was quite good. And through it all, Gonnelson made semblance of communication with one word for ten of everyone else's. It was strange, Tregare thought, how nobody else seemed to realize that Gonnelson didn't *talk*.

While Tregare, trying to analyze, watched Peralta. The man hadn't changed much, to look at—he was still lean and taut, and moved like a caged cat. His face showed few lines of aging, but Bran saw shadows forming at brow and mouth-corners. All in all, though, Tregare thought, the other man had stood up well against the pressures and frustrations of shipping with UET.

The one thing Tregare couldn't risk doing was to leave the *Bonaparte* without hanging a lifeline out to Jimar Peralta. Whether or not Peralta saw through the Armiger disguise, Bran had to assume he had done so. All right; when time came to accept Captain Haiglund's polite dismissals and leave the *Bonaparte*, midway through the handshakes and farewells Tregare said, "Mister Peralta? I think we know a lot of the same people in the Service, and might enjoy trading stories about them. Not suitable to do that here, we juniors—but if you'd like to drop over to the *Alexander* in a day or two, informally if Captain Haiglund can spare you for a few hours . . ." Bran looked to Haiglund and got a nod. ". . . then give me a call and come aboard, with my welcome."

Peralta signed assent; Tregare and Gonnelson went downship and left the *Bonaparte*. As they walked back toward *Inconnu*, Gonnelson said, "Why?"

"If it's at all possible," Tregare said, "we're going to take the *Bonaparte* for Peralta. Because we need that ship. Peralta's a fox. If I make sure I can trust him, I need that man."

First chance he had, Bran told Zelde about his visit in fullest detail, and also his own intentions. "What do you think?"

She finished the last spoonful of her dessert, then, with the spoon, she gestured. "You'll have him here, I expect?"

"Right. Captain's digs are proper courtesy. But you haven't answered."

"Well, say you do bust Peralta loose of UET. Dunno if he'll serve second to you nor any other—but sure's hell you set UET up for a good mess of trouble."

Tregare nodded. "Too right. But I think I have the bait that will hook Jimar to join me. Long enough to get the main job done."

"What bait?"

He grinned. "Sit in when he gets here. You'll see."

Next day, after a voice-call to set the appointment, Jimar Peralta was escorted to Tregare's quarters. Bran waited there alone. When the guard-escort left and the door was closed, Tregare did the obligatory handshake and said, "Welcome aboard. A drink should be in order. Bourbon all right?"

He busied himself preparing the drinks, aware that Peralta was watching him. They clinked glasses. "Cheers."

They sat, and after a moment Tregare said, "This room isn't bugged. And there's only one latrine in all of UET."

"Bran Tregare!" The two were up and hugging, pounding each other on the back. As they sat again, Peralta said, "I *thought* it was you—but it's been some years, and with your hair dyed, plastered down over your forehead this way—"

Tregare laughed. "It's a fair disguise, at that. Didn't fool the Butcher, though." And he told of his incursion at Stronghold, and of barely escaping the refueling orbit at Earth when Korbeith arrived and blew his cover. He told all these things because either he could trust Jimar Peralta or the man would never leave *Inconnu*. Then he said, "I think we have some business, you and I. You mind if my Second Hat sits in on that?" Peralta nodded, so Bran called Zelde's cabin. Without speaking her name, he said, "Mr. Peralta's here. I'd like you to meet him."

Then he waited, and when Zelde entered, Peralta's reaction was worth the wait. The man went from sitting to standing in one motion. "M'tana!"

"That's right." Shifting a bottle from right hand to left, she came forward to shake hands. "Brought you some trair, seeing as you liked it last time."

Peralta shook his head, not in negation but apparently to clear his thoughts. "I'm surprised. To see you here, I mean. I hadn't thought you'd ever leave Ragir Parnell."

"Wouldn't have, was he still alive. Tell you later, maybe."

"I'm sorry." From the look of him, and his voice, Peralta meant it. "He was a good man."

"The best," M'tana said. "Not meaning a thing against you two here, either one." Then, "You like a little trair?"

This headshake *was* negative. "Not until you explain how that delicious stuff put me out of orbit, *twice*, while you and Parnell stayed well on course."

Zelde, Tregare thought, sometimes had a really mean grin. "Guess you should know, yeah. Trair, it's got something in it, you drink and feel great but not drunk, so you keep going. But the stuff, keeps you sober, it wears off quicker'n the booze part does. So there you are, all've a sudden, ory-ass blasted. Whilst Ragir and me, we went slower, and waited you out."

First Peralta began a slow chuckle, then his laughter doubled him over. Finally, wiping tears away, he said, "So that's how you whipsawed me. Thanks for telling it."

"Sure. Well now—you want we have us some?" At his wary look, she said, "All starting even, this time, I mean, and we none of us take a whole lot." So he nodded, and she poured.

When they'd clinked glasses and were sitting, Tregare said, "Now, the business. Peralta, on Terranova the situation was that Parnell didn't dare try to help you take your ship. Bad odds. Let's talk, and figure out what the odds are here." He waved off any answer. "First, though, we need to set terms."

"What terms?" The other man looked puzzled.

Tregare leaned forward. "I have a job planned. The terms are that if I help you take the *Bonaparte*, you owe me service. On that mission only, and the key word is Stronghold. Before and after, the ship is yours free and clear."

"And *on* that job, it isn't?" Peralta's eyes were narrowed.

"It's still your ship, even then. But during that time, it and you are part of my command."

This was the touchy part and Tregare knew it. "Of the two of us, I'm well senior. Why should I serve under you?"

Tregare shrugged. "I could say, to pay me back for getting you a ship." Oh, the hell with it—*be honest!* "But I won't. Because we both know I owe you, for saving my life once and maybe twice, on the *MacArthur*. And we both know I want you free and loose, on our side, to bite UET's butt, almost as much as you want it."

Grinning, Peralta spread his hands. "So where's your leverage, Tregare?"

"You're getting a ship. How'd you like to have an *armed* ship?"

"Armed? But how—?"

It was Bran's turn to grin. "I'll take care of that part. You come join me on Number One, date to be determined, on *my* terms—and I'll arm your ship for you." He paused, then said, "Is it worth what I ask, Jimar?"

He could see the imperatives warring in the man. Then Peralta nodded. "To have an armed ship—Tregare, it's a deal!"

The planning got a little tricky. Obviously both ships should lift off as soon as Peralta had the *Bonaparte* safely in hand, but

Inconnu had held only to wait and exchange information with the other ship—so Tregare had to ask Junior Lee Beauregard for some faked malfunctions, to justify delay.

More hellbent for command than ever, Peralta might be, but still he held the same scruples he'd shown at the Slaughterhouse. "Haiglund's a stuffed shirt and a Utie loyalist, but he's an honest man and a fair one; I don't want him dead. And when it comes down to cases, once we have the ship I want to put the surviving Uties groundside here, not space them. If we can."

"Yeah, Jimar. I remember; you always did hate waste."

The important parts. Things had to happen when Peralta himself had the watch in Control and one of his people held the Drive room. There was some talk about the power suits—since both Tregare and M'tana had used those decisively in takeovers—but Peralta said, "I'd rather the *Bonaparte*'s were disabled. Few of Haiglund's people are armed, and I can see that more of mine are; that should be enough force. A power suit—that way, it's too easy for killings to happen by accident."

So Tregare, with some misgivings, had to agree.

When they had it all figured, best they could, Bran again went over the parameters for the later rendezvous on Number One. "I'll have the ships' weapons there. You just be sure the *Bonaparte* arrives in plenty of time."

"It won't." Tregare blinked; then saw Peralta's grin. "What will arrive on time, Tregare, is my ship—*No Return*."

A few hours before *Inconnu*—or rather, the *Alexander*—was due to lift, a roistering band of its crew, led by a tall black woman, came back from town and insisted on boarding the *Bonaparte* to share a few drinks with their counterparts on that ship. From Control, Peralta gave orders to humor the intruders and avoid trouble. Bottles were passed around; Peralta's man in Drive told his watchmates to leave there and help maintain order, then locked the place from inside and reported "All secure." Captain Haiglund, alarmed by the commotion and getting no answers from Control, went charging upship and was taken into custody by strangers who didn't seem to be drunk, as had been reported.

Drumming knuckles on his own control console, Tregare had to make do with brief, fragmentary reports from Peralta, plus occasional items from Zelde whenever she was someplace where communications could get through. He knew she'd said a lot of things when she was in shielded areas, but now: ". . . gave up, so we locked 'em in a service cubby. Going downship now. M'tana out."

Well, so far, so good. But Tregare wished he could *be* there.

When his downview screen showed people coming down the other ship's ramp, Tregare began to relax. And on the scrambled channel, Peralta said, "Ship secured, Tregare. Superfluous personnel being herded groundside. We had some casualties, both sides, but less than I'd feared." Then, referring to an offer Bran had made earlier, "I'm accepting your contingent of volunteers, so we won't lift too shorthanded. Fourteen, I believe, and all to be upgraded one step for today's action." A pause, and then, "As soon as my discards and your people are clear of the safety perimeter, *No Return* lifts. Good landings, Tregare."

Below, not much later, Bran saw Peralta's "discards" milling off away from the danger area, and then *Inconnu*'s own people moving briskly aboard. He said, "Good landings; right. I'll look for you on Number One, Jimar."

"I'll be there."

He'd thought of putting the scout up to cover the liftoffs, but Peralta convinced him that if they timed it right they'd have both ships off before UET groundside could know there was any kind of problem. So why bother? He didn't.

Now Tregare watched *No Return*'s Drive nodes turn dirt to dust and steam as the ship began to rise—oh, so slowly, at first!—and then cant to one side and throw ionization into the missile-defense antennae. Not blasting them away, merely jarring them into temporary ineffectiveness.

For a moment, Tregare chuckled. But he didn't have time for it, because now it was *Inconnu*'s turn to lift; he gave Zelde M'tana the high-sign and felt his own Drive build and start to lift, moments behind Peralta.

And then on the downscreen a movement caught his eye. Someone, somebody groundsided from *No Return,* was running headlong *into* that ship's liftoff blast area. And ran, and ran, and hit the field's edge and turned into running flame, and fell.

As that view fell away, Zelde M'tana said, "Captain Haiglund, it was. We should of knowed he would. Tregare?"

"Yeah?" Bran tried to ignore his effort, not to throw up.

"Peralta, he don't need to know that."

"Right." So in the brief exchanges before the two ships went their different ways, Bran didn't tell him.

10. The Backslid

Figuring schedules the best he could, Long View and all, and realizing that no amount of urgency could hurry matters, Tregare decided how many junkets he could manage and still make it to Number One in time for the rendezvous he was arranging.

His next raid on a UET colony was the one that later made him Escaped Target Number One back at Earth. He got lucky that time; two armed UET ships were groundside, and coming down he wiped them both with his Drive before they could lift out of air. Then he plundered the place, and before leaving he blew its fuel refinery, so that any ship coming there would be grounded for a considerable time. His reason for being so punitive was that this colony ran to slavery; he wanted to turn the whole rotten mess upside down, and was fairly sure he'd done so. In fact, the remaining population seemed to think they were now Escaped, the equivalent of a Hidden World. He hoped they were right, but kept his next two raids a lot more modest. And then . . .

He went to Terranova using a totally improvised fake ID for the ship, and got away with it. But from that planet, he decided, he should start heading for Number One. And looking at his star charts, with the holographic projector still

out of action, he decided that his best bet was to go by way of
UET's small colony on the planet Far Corner.

So he lifted for there. The only trouble was that before
Inconnu passed $t/t_\circ = 2$, or maybe the other way round, in
came incoherent signal from a beacon circling a world that was
on no charts at all.

Not only incoherent, that signal, but intermittent as well.
First it came on abruptly, rather than emerging gradually from
the noise level. It stuttered, wavered, died, came on again—
long enough for Hain Deverel to get a bearing on it—then
died once more. "Old equipment," Tregare said. "Not maintained. On its last legs." Looking around at his Hats, gathered
hurriedly in Control, he said, "Should we give a look?"

Consensus was in favor, so Deverel changed course—not
more than a quarter of a radian, no great cost in fuel. Going
with Gonnelson's distance estimate, Tregare had Junior Lee
schedule Turnover.

Bran hadn't expected that he and Zelde would bed regularly
or frequently, and indeed, now and then was the name of the
game. With no coquetry or other emotional games, sometimes
the occasion called for that kind of celebration. When it did,
both seemed to know without asking. Tregare could have used
a little more frequency, but after a while he got used to the way
things were.

Now, though, they planned a tryst beforehand. Bran
assigned Turnover to Hain Deverel with Gonnelson riding
shotgun; he and Zelde took the opportunity for sex in free fall.
As *Inconnu* swung 180 degrees while they, in midair, did not,
Zelde laughed. "Never done this way before. Fun, kind of."
When they'd finished, just before Junior Lee—gently, as Bran
had requested—brought the Drive up to thrust, she asked,
"You done it lots of times, I expect?"

Drifting, they thumped softly to the deck. He shook his
head. "Just once before. A long time ago." *With Salome
Harkness.* "My first trip, as a cadet on the *MacArthur*." And
where was Butcher Korbeith now? Would Tregare ever make
good his vow to kill that man? But those thoughts he didn't tell
M'tana.

With decel set at half-max, a few days later the planet's
primary came into view, and then the world itself.

Hailings brought no answer; with the ship in low orbit, just short of plowing air, it took some time to spot where the spaceport had been. Around the flat-lying wreckage of a ship, a few huts clustered. But several kilos distant, Tregare saw a larger settlement. That terrain looked level enough to set down on, so he spread the "feet" on the ship's landing legs. After one more orbit, spiraling down, Deverel landed *Inconnu* safely.

The locals, gathering to meet the groundside party, didn't impress Tregare much. Unkempt, wearing makeshift clothing, they spoke a dialect that had drifted quite a way from standard speech; Bran found it hard to understand. Finally four of the younger men came carrying a sort of rickety palanquin, roofed but open-sided; inside sat a very old person of indeterminate sex, wearing a filthy robe that still bore traces of gold embroidery. When the conveyance was set down, supported by flimsy-looking legs unfolded from its lower frame, the person beckoned and said, "You've come at last. Who speaks for you?"

None of this crowd looked dangerous, so Tregare walked past them to the oldster's seat. "I do. Bran Tregare, captain of *Inconnu*. What's the name of this place? And your own?" And what the hell *happened* here? Well, that would take some asking.

"New Earth, we used to call it, at first when we still thought the ship could lift again. Fell down fifty years ago, it did. But the Nielson was bad, anyway. The Cast Out Ones still live alongside it, radiation and all. Worship it. Grabbed Chira, my great-granddaughter, the other day, for sacrifice." A sniffle, and the person wiped it off with the back of a hand. "I'm Hugh Charlton, last one born aboard the *Conquistador* in space. Or am I? Last one alive, anyway." The old man coughed. "Lots more ships coming out, supposed to be; that's what my daddy said. But none of 'em came here. Not any. Not until you. You going to take us home, are you?"

Tregare looked around him. *Not hardly!* But he said, "We're supposed to conduct an inspection, is all. And make a report. Now could you tell me how the colony is progressing?"

Old Charlton's ramblings took a time, but Bran could put the picture together. After the bad landing, that left the *Conquis-*

tador standing aslant and none too stable, at first the officers
had used the colonists for forced labor, trying to get the ship
repaired while also growing food crops. After a number of
years—Charlton wasn't sure how many—there had been a
bloody revolt. At its end, no technical personnel survived.
Hugh emerged as the prophet of a new religion, devoted to
simplified living and individual freedom. After half the survivors died of famine because nobody had to work if he or she
chose not to, changes arose, but Hugh Charlton somehow
managed to hang onto his—well, high priesthood seemed as
good a word as any.

"What about the Cast Out Ones?" Well, living near the ship
with its malfunctioning, radiating Nielson Cube, the colonists
began having malformed offspring. Hugh vaguely remembered enough to realize that radiation caused the birth defects,
so he moved the colony to its present location and cast out the
defectives, who chose to stay near the *Conquistador*, even
after it toppled over.

"We still get a bad birth here, sometimes. Soon as it's
weaned, it goes to them. To raise or eat, whichever they
choose."

Tregare had had just about enough of these degenerates, but
before he could think how to end the interview, beside him
Zelde M'tana spoke. He hadn't heard her approach. "Charlton!
What's this sacrifice thing you said?"

"Chira?" The old man wiped his eyes. "They shouldn't have
done that, taken her. Not supposed to. We paid them their
dole."

"Wrong answer," M'tana said. "*What* is it, they do to her?
And, they done it already, or not?"

The old head moved back and forth; Tregare felt he could
almost hear the neck creak. "Tomorrow, next day—when the
moons cross. They tie 'em down to the Nielson, to purify.
When their hair falls out, they're pure. That's when the cutting
comes."

During the next few minutes, while Charlton placidly told
what the ensuing rites were, Tregare wished it wouldn't be so
undignified for a ship's captain to puke. Unlike the ancient
Aztecs, the Cast Out Ones didn't cleanly cut the heart out. No,
they opened the abdomen, carefully tied off all major blood
vessels, and emptied the abdominal cavity, organ by organ.
"Then," said Hugh Charlton, "they cast next year's auguries

according to how far the sacrifice can walk or crawl. One I remember, made it more than a kilo." Sniff. "Doped up, likely."

Walking back to *Inconnu*: "Shut up, M'tana! I know we got to get that barbarian kid out of there. What I'm trying to figure, just now, is *how*."

Walking would take too long and lifting *Inconnu* would waste too much fuel, so Tregare used the scoutship, fully crewed. He worried a little about M'tana being in charge of the combat squad, but he'd told her, "Nobody shoots until *I* say so," and no matter how gowed-up she was about this thing, he figured she'd obey orders.

He landed the scout back a way from the toppled *Conquistador* and left Deverel in charge with two guards to watch the ramp. The rest of them, Tregare leading, went to meet the ragged group that gathered around the wrecked ship.

He'd seen some bad things, Tregare had, but this bunch beat all of it. Radiation damage at its worst; after a first look he tried to ignore the scars, the burns, the other obvious mutilations. The one-eyed woman, leading that pack, was apparently in charge, so Tregare said, "We're here for the girl Chira. Where is she?"

The woman's mumblings were barely comprehensible. Tregare repeated himself and lit a drugstick and handed it over. The woman puffed, smiled, nodded, and passed it to the next in line.

M'tana nudged him. "Let me do this, huh?" She seemed to understand the group's gibberish, or else she faked it pretty well, because after a few minutes she said, "I thought they'd settle for a few packs of sticks, but it's more, they want. You got a knife you can spare?"

He was surprised, when he pulled the throwing knife from the sheath at the back of his neck, to find rust on the blade. But the Cast Out Ones didn't seem to mind; Zelde closed the deal.

Chira, led out with chains binding her and no other covering, shouted a constant stream of curses in a voice gone hoarse. Some of the words, Tregare had never heard before, so they must be new inventions. And with words he did know, most of the compoundings were unfamiliar. She tended to

favor combinations of the scatological and the classically
obscene. When she began to repeat herself, he realized she
wasn't necessarily being original.

The noise was getting in the way, so Tregare yelled, "Chira!
You want out of here alive, *shut up!*" When she did, on his
second try, he said, "All right. Take those chains off her." Now
that she was quiet, he looked at her more closely. Built strong,
she was: not tall, but sturdy. No excess flesh at all; her muscles
showed clearly.

She had to be some kind of Caucasian, but dark-com-
plexioned, with a matted mass of curling, almost-black hair.
Still mumbling, he saw, though not loud enough to hear, she
made an occasional snarl as she jerked at the chains.

The one-eyed woman shook her head, and uncannily, Zelde
seemed to understand her mouthings. "Says we take her as is,
Tregare. Afraid if they let her loose she'll bust them up some."

Again Tregare spoke. "Chira." She looked at him. "If you
won't follow orders I can't save your life. You hear me?" Chira
nodded. "I'm going to take those chains off you. When I do,
you come with us. And that's *all* you do. You don't attack any of
these people, no matter how much you think they deserve it.
Or else we leave you here, with them. You got that?"

She erupted again. ". . . shitkissers . . . plowed me every way . . . done every crap thing there is . . ." But finally
she ran down, looked at Bran, and nodded. "You the boss. I
don't kill none."

So the chains came off, and Tregare saw the effort it took
Chira to keep her promise, as he and his people hustled her
into the scout. Once inside, he wished there had been some
way to bathe her first.

Never before had Bran docked the scout onto *Inconnu* with
the ship groundside, but he'd practiced, both in free space and
in orbit, so now he thought he'd give it a try. Making sure that
the bay was cleared and inside-sealed first, he swung near to
his ship, threw a drift toward the opened bay, and cut his
Drive—to give it one impact-softening burst at the last
moment. The landing jar was more than he liked, but it beat
flaming his deck and bulkheads any more than need be.

Then he and Zelde took Chira back to her people.

* * *

"No!" Hugh Charlton shook his head. "If you leave her here—once the Cast Out Ones took her, she was dead. So we'd have to kill her." Tregare's angry protests got him nowhere as the old man said, "*I* never asked you to bring me back my dead."

And thinking back, Tregare had to agree. He turned to Zelde. "This was your idea. What do we do now?"

She shrugged. "There's spare bunks in Hold Portside Upper."

Except for a disgusted wrinkling of her nose, Chief Medic Eda Ghormley took Chira's advent in stride, as Tregare said, "Peace only knows what her health is like. Check on what you can, and fix what you can."

"After she has a bath," Ghormley said, "and a haircut. I can see the lice crawling in that mop, from here."

Chira didn't like it. "Nobody shitfuck Chira. I—"

Suddenly she made an indrawn gasp, and was silent. Bran saw that Zelde M'tana had two of Chira's fingers in her grasp and was exerting leverage: he knew the taming effect of that simple hold, so he waited, as Zelde said, "This lady, she's to help you. Anything she says, you do. Anything she does, you let her. Else you wish you had. You hear me?" From Chira's silent wince, Tregare guessed that Zelde had got her point across.

Washed and sheared, curling hair not much longer than Zelde's, then tested and prodded and inoculated, Chira still glowered. She didn't like all this, not one damned little bit; Bran could tell that much. But so far she was keeping her resentments more or less under wraps, as Ghormley reported, "She's healthier than I'd expect from such a flea-bitten rabble. In the bloodstream, a couple of bugs new to me, but no fever or other symptoms so probably nothing dangerous. I can't think of any other tests to try, so she's all yours, Tregare."

"Not exactly." Tregare didn't laugh, quite. "M'tana? You got time to help me escort our guest to Portside Upper?" He checked his wrist chrono. "It's coming up mealtime, there." He turned to Ghormley. "Would you advise the galley to add one more ration packet from now on?" Then, looking again at Chira, how the issue jumpsuit hung on her, "Maybe you better make that two extra. This one has some catching up to do."

* * *

As they went downship, Tregare noticed that the unfamiliar
surroundings seemed to give Chira no unease. Either she was
adaptable as all hell or had no imagination; he couldn't guess
which. At the hold's door she said, "Locked in? I—"

"Just a place to stay, for now," he said. "You'll have a lot of
new friends here, while we go to another world."

"Friends?" But she went in without arguing.

Then Tregare and Zelde climbed to the galley; breakfast was
a long time ago. He thought of asking her to his quarters, for
after, but didn't. Because he could sense that they were out of
phase; he was in a mood for sex and she wasn't. He didn't know
why, and wasn't sure he liked it, but couldn't put a finger on
how to change anything. At least Zelde had turned out to be
someone he could *talk* with, better than anyone since—
dammit, forget that! So he guessed he'd settle for what he
could get.

At the meal's end he did ask her up for a drink, after all, but
in a way that made it clear he was asking nothing more. So
they were sitting, talking over the day's events, when the
intercom sounded. It was Gonnelson. "Captain! The hold. The
new woman. Trouble."

Jeez—more words than the First Hat usually said all week.
"I'll be right down there. I assume you have a squad on the
way." Hearing the confirming syllable, Tregare signed out, and
he and Zelde headed downship considerably faster than safety
regs allowed. Passing the impromptu guard station at the open
door of Hold Portside Upper, Tregare went in to see a real
mess.

Cherisse Frisco had blood on her face but the wound was
superficial. Three women lay on bunks while Eda Ghormley
and two of her helpers worked over them. At Tregare's quick
question, Ghormley said, "Nothing fatal. But you have to get
that new one out of here." And then Bran saw Chira, a little
bloody herself, and bruised about the face, handcuffed to a
stanchion.

He shook his head. "What the hell happened here?"

"That peacepissing *savage* of yours, is what happened.
She—" Apparently Chira didn't know the meaning of the word
rations—that is, one to a customer, or in her own case, two.
When the packets were brought in and the delivery crew left,

Chira began grabbing as many as she could, and fighting the others for them. Shaking her head, Frisco continued, "Nobody could talk to her; she hit and kicked and bit. So finally the lot of us overpowered her and held her until the guards brought those handcuffs." She quieted while Eda Ghormley cleaned her face and covered the cut with a small bandage. Then, "Damnedest brawler I've seen in a long time. Not trained, though; that was *our* luck."

The group's leader wasn't done talking yet, but Bran's slight wave of hand put her into listening mode. He said, "You think you and she—all of you, I mean—can get along now?"

A frown, and violent headshake. "My people here, they took enough crap already; you know that. Not complaining, Tregare; I know you're treating us as well as conditions permit, and we all appreciate it. But you take that savage out of here or I can't guarantee she'll be alive tomorrow."

And before he could answer, she added, "Several have said, she has to sleep sometime. But she doesn't have to wake up."

No argument with that kind of thinking, and Tregare knew it. He looked to M'tana in time to see her shrug, but asked anyway. "Ideas, Zelde?"

"You can't turn her loose anyplace, and my room won't hold two, even was I willing. I guess you're stuck with her."

He guessed so, too. So he began. "Now look, Chira . . ."

He let her bring along two of the disputed ration packets, and on the way upship he tried to tell her how it would have to be. "You behave yourself, cause no trouble, keep your hands off anything you don't understand, you can stay with me, for now." She nodded, and he hoped the nod meant comprehension and acceptance. "You screw up, Chira—you screw up *any*—and you're down there again with the property. Where they don't like you very much."

Scowl. "I go home. Nobody kill Chira. Just they try, they turdwhackers; I show better."

For a moment he was tempted to turn her offship and forget her. But if he did, Zelde would never let him hear the last of it. So he said, "Too late for that. Ship's sealed; we lift soon." And only by a few minutes was he lying, his reason being that he figured the woman would have *no* chance groundside; she might think she was tough, and be partly right too—but the community Hugh Charlton headed reminded Tregare of a pack of jackals; in the longer haul, no single animal could withstand them.

Entering his quarters he touched her shoulder and she did not flinch. "You're safe here. You'll be fed all you want. We're going to a different world with different people and you can live better, there. All you need to do, now, is be peaceful, not fight, not mess with anything you don't know. You *want* to know, ask and I'll try to tell you." He stopped moving, because she had turned to face him.

She said, "Plow me, I got to let you?"

Carefully, Tregare did not laugh. He said, "No. No, Chira. On this ship, that's not how it is."

The girl wasn't malicious, nor, as it turned out, even stupid. What she was, though, was a damned nuisance. Part of it was her developing curiosity, once she emerged from the shock of her ordeal. It wasn't safe to leave her alone, because without some admonishing presence at hand she *couldn't* keep her hands off things. And somehow she'd decided that Tregare could tell her what to do, or Zelde or another officer, but no one else. Well, except Eda Ghormley. On promise of seeing a Nielson Cube that was safe to touch or stand next to, she admitted Junior Lee to the select company. Afterward the Chief Engineer told Tregare, "Given a li'l book learnin', that ol' gal might *be* somebody."

Ghormley had done some teaching, once, so Bran saddled the Chief Medic with a daily stint as schoolmarm. The assignment took some pressure off Tregare and his Hats, since they'd practically had to arrange duty shifts for watching Chira.

And Tregare couldn't bring himself to lock her up, even if Zelde would have stood still for that solution.

Right away, Tregare figured how to Chira-proof his quarters. His intercom panel and the adjacent console mounted a sizable number of control switches he couldn't afford to let her play with, and there were times when he couldn't keep an eye on her, such as when he slept and she didn't. So he checked the diagrams and found where to insert a key-operated switch in the common-battery lead. Incoming signals weren't interfered with, but without the key, Chira could flip switches until Hell froze, without harm.

In the interests of good sense, though, such flipping was still forbidden.

A week out of Backslid, as Tregare dubbed the ship's most recent stop, he woke feeling feverish and nauseated. He called and asked Gonnelson to take "Chira duty" for a while; oddly, the girl understood the First Hat's monosyllables better than many of his shipmates did. That matter arranged, Bran visited the infirmary.

Ghormley couldn't find any probable cause. She gave him some pills and the time-honored advice: "Stay in bed as much as possible and drink lots of fluids." She scowled. "I don't mean booze, skipper."

Hoping he wouldn't puke until safely back in quarters, Tregare tried to smile. "I figured that."

That day and the next were pretty bad: shakes and fever, and the alimentary canal purging itself both ways long after he felt it had to be empty. Chira wasn't around; he had no idea who had the care of her and was too drained to want to ask. The third day was better; by late afternoon he ate something and it stayed down. And near as he could tell, the fever was dropping, too. But still he was glad the infrequent mandatory reports from Control kept saying his presence wasn't needed there.

That night he woke drenched in sweat and felt the fever gone. He got up and showered and changed the bedding; he ate his first full meal since the bug had hit him. And every bite tasted delicious. But still he was weak, and more shaky than not, as he returned to bed.

He woke slowly and confused, not sure where he was or whether he still dreamed. There'd been a nightmare sequence, something about Butcher Korbeith spacing women out the airlock and bringing them, dead and frozen, back to the Slaughterhouse for the cadets to sleep with. But before Bran could see whether the one in his bed was Phyls Dolan or Tanit Eldon, everything changed—the bed was *real*, and so was someone else, with him. Was this a sex dream, or did he wake? He hadn't asked Zelde to stay over with him, had he? For a dream, this was more than he was used to—the rising urgency . . . He opened his eyes to see Chira moving above him, and it was too late to reconsider, because the Big Train was already rolling, and no brakes.

Judging from the sound she made as she collapsed onto him, she'd made it pretty big, herself.

Still joined, now she lay partly to his side. He said, "I thought you didn't want this." And realized, *hell, she doesn't even have an implant. Can't have. What—?*

With her strong, heavy jaw, Chira would never look delicate. But her tentative smile, the first he'd ever seen on her, had a sort of innocent quality to it. "Not for you, I be dead now." There had to be more, so he waited. "Me here allatime, you got nobody else. So—" She shrugged. "Good, too. Not like *them*."

"Well. I'm glad of that, Chira. And thank you. But now let's get up and go see Eda Ghormley. Maybe it's not too late for a contraceptive implant to take effect." She didn't understand, but she didn't argue, either.

Without explanations, feeling too drained to bother with them, Tregare made his request. Prim-mouthed, Ghormley swabbed Chira's thigh and disinfected the insertor before punching the little capsule into the muscle tissue. Then the Chief Medic couldn't hold back any longer. "Maybe it's not my place to say anything, captain, but I'm surprised and disappointed. Taking advantage of a girl this young! I wouldn't have expected it of you."

Tregare found no answer; the truth, even if Ghormley believed him, would sound like a whining excuse. So he stood, tongue-tied, while Chira looked back and forth between them. Frowning, she said, "Not him. Asleep, him." She jerked her thumb up to point at herself. "Me!"

Eda Ghormley's expression cleared, but only partway. "You mean you already have? Then you'll need a morning-after pill, too." She rummaged in a small, compartmented drawer. "Here." When Chira had gulped the small tablet, the Medic said, "Is that right, Tregare? She caught you, not vice-versa?"

Maybe his grin didn't look sheepish but it sure felt that way. "The fever broke last night; afterward I was dead to the world. Don't remember hearing her come in, even."

Ghormley smiled. "Makes you feel silly, doesn't it? Well, *I* feel better about it, anyway. Not that it's any of my business. And don't you have someplace you should be, now?"

So Tregare thanked her, and he and Chira left.

Up in Control he found everything running on tracks, the way he liked it. The necessary course change had been made accurately by Gonnelson, and Turnover was still a time away. The only bad thing, aside from his own fatigue, was that when it came time for change of watch, Zelde M'tana called in sick.

Bran cut himself into the comm circuit. "You need any help, Zelde? You want to see Ghormley? I can send somebody down there right away, and we'll fudge the watches okay."

There was a pause—he could hear her retching—then, "Same thing you had, I think. I can get up to the infirmary, though, on my own. Better go while I still can. M'tana out."

Leaving Chira to Hain Deverel's care, in Control, Tregare went to the infirmary. Then, forcing his meager strength, he walked Zelde back to her own quarters before returning to question Ghormley. She didn't look happy as she said, "The girl brought it aboard, I'm afraid. Those bugs I noticed, that didn't seem to bother her. Some bacterium must have mutated, there on Backslid, and those people eventually developed immunity. But we haven't.

"I'd better take a culture, and see if I remember how to make a dead-bacterium vaccine. The live kind is beyond me."

Maybe the vaccine worked, partly, and maybe it didn't. No epidemic swept *Inconnu*, but cases of the new disease kept happening, a few at a time. And the bug seemed to grow in strength—Tregare had been flat-out ill for about three days, M'tana over a week, and later victims took longer and longer to recover.

The only good thing you could say about it, Tregare thought, was that nobody had died. Yet.

Turnover came and went; *Inconnu* was on point-seven decel for Far Corner. The worst three weeks were when the "Backslid Flu" hit Hold Portside Upper; nearly all the women caught the bug during that time and the place became a shambles. Even after the repeated moppings-up by crew members, the hold maintained a residual stench that would need draconian measures to clear away. And that grade of fumigation couldn't be done until the hold was empty of human occupation.

Tregare's own worst times came when Gonnelson and Deverel went sick two days apart, and *stayed* sick. Leaving Bran and Zelde, neither of them really fit to pull even a normal shift, to split the watches between them. And short-handed at that. The two had not been together sexually since Chira's advent, and now the whole idea became impossible. Well, he hadn't been doing all that much with Chira, either; he'd told her he needed his rest so she shouldn't wake him in the fashion she first had done. When she disobeyed him, he yelled through gritted teeth that if she had to behave like a spoiled brat, "Peace take you, you get treated like one!" Holding her sprawled across his lap by a wristlock, he took his doubled belt and whaled her butt red for her.

The effort nearly made him pass out. Panting, holding her down, he said, "Just one damned move, Chira, and you're down with the property!" And for a brief moment, he found himself wishing he was Butcher Korbeith.

Surprising him, she smiled. "Real man, you, Tregare. That good. Before, Chira not sure." As she went off to the shower—and thank peace she'd taken to cleanliness, once exposed to the chance for it—Tregare wondered about what had just happened.

He had a handle on her now and he knew it—but it wasn't the kind of handle he *wanted* on any woman; hitting had never been his style, and he didn't want to have to use it.

Finally he shrugged. Chira was Chira; he'd never known anyone like her before, and with luck he never would again, either.

Once more Chira tested the limits of his tolerance; then she settled down, mostly, and behaved herself. Sometimes she'd try a fit of the sulks or a little mild baiting, but nothing that bothered Bran too much. As to sex, she accepted the fact that if he had the energy he'd ask—or say yes if *she* asked. Nowadays, though, such occasions came very seldom.

For one thing, the nightmares. The bout of them following Tanit Eldon's treachery and execution had tapered off over the next month; now with the illness and its aftermath, the damned things were back, full force. Not since the Slaughterhouse, and on the *MacArthur* under Korbeith, had dreams so tormented Bran. Maybe that was why they seemed the worst ever. He could be in the Academy, or shipping with Korbeith, or anywhere else he'd ever been—but maddeningly, the people involved usually didn't fit the times or places.

Airlock drill! Alongside the Butcher stood Plastic Smile, suavely grinning above the handle of the icepick Tregare had thrust under the guard's chin and into his spine. Plastic Smile chuckled—the handle bobbed with his merriment—and pushed Bran's mother into the lock. Korbeith spaced her into vacuum. . . .

Tregare and Peralta were lifting off from The Islands. But wait—someone had been left behind! And running into Peralta's Drive blast, screaming and falling and curling up and frying, was Jargy Hoad.

And then the same thing, except now it was Megan Delange, already blotched and bloated from being spaced by the Butcher, who suffered further mutilation by flame.

Shaking his head, Tregare sat up. It was getting worse; he didn't know what to do. Sedative pills, when he tried them, didn't wear off in time when he needed alertness. One watch, he'd started to move the wrong control lever and caught himself just in time. Zelde, ready to leave but not gone yet, looked at him, until he said, "Sorry. Punchier'n a bird dog, these days. Guess I'll have to drop those peacewasting *pills.*"

"How you figure to sleep, then, Tregare?"

He knew her concern, but stretched to breaking, all he could feel was anger. "Drop a rock on my head, why don't you?"

Her mouth registered a bad taste. "Tregare, was they any way I could do good to you—put Chira with Ghormley maybe, and *me* hold you, and wake you when I feel you going bad—that I'd do. But—"

"But there's only us to run the ship. Thanks, Zelde. Now flag your ass out of here and get some rest."

"Yeah, sure, Tregare. Wish *you* could, too, is all."

He hadn't thought his condition could worsen much more, but it did. Gonnelson and Hain Deverel stayed ill; for some time now they had been in Ghormley's infirmary, too weak to tend themselves. By the time Far Corner's beacon was heard, both Hats were able to be up and around part of the day, but nowhere near capable of standing a full watch.

Far Corner was a small colony; to Tregare's knowledge it mounted no missile defenses and had no organized UET garrison. He wasn't up to rigging a fake log, so he decided to go in as himself and dare anybody to do something about it.

"This is Bran Tregare speaking for the armed, Escaped ship *Inconnu*. Let me reassure you that if you deal fairly with me in matters of trade, refueling and the like, I will do this colony no harm. I can use some extra crew and am prepared to sign on any persons who satisfy me as to their intentions and loyalties." For a moment, he thought. "Passengers are something else. I can't divulge destinations. Tregare out."

He didn't expect much hassle but did figure on some, and was surprised when groundside made no protests at all. So on landing, he was wary. (M'tana did that landing; Bran wasn't fit for it.) But refueling and trade went entirely peacefully.

11. Tari Obrigo

Tregare's surprise ebbed when he tapped the computer logs at Second Site, Far Corner's spaceport town. By no means was his the first Escaped ship to visit this place; apparently the locals were pretty much laissez-faire in their politics.

Bran was pleased to find a coded note from Malloy, saying that *Pig in the Parlor* definitely hoped to make Tregare's rendezvous on Number One. The loose info network was working, all right.

When he began getting into more recent items, Tregare swore. He'd missed Kickem Bernardez, who still held cover by keeping his ship insigned the *Hoover*, by less than a month. But Kickem's tape said, "Should an old squadmate of mine, from Cadre D of our beloved Academy, hear these words, I wish him to know that I shall make all endeavor to attend our planned reunion. Misfortunately I will likely have no chance to obtain a bottle of Irish poteen as would be most appropriate. But no doubt we can liberate something equally suitable." And then Bran had to chuckle. Kickem never changed much. . . .

Always tired, still Tregare dreaded sleep. After a time his mind had learned to give an alarm when nightmare began: if something truly didn't fit, somehow he made a mental twitch and woke up. So he was spared a lot of grueling horror—but he also lost a lot of sleep. Didn't help his disposition at all.

Daytimes, though his negotiations went peacefully enough, a lot of them carried a tedious amount of red tape. To keep his growing irritability within bounds, Tregare took to smoking a drugstick or two before each session; the things didn't help his fatigue, but did keep him short of blowing up in the face of unnecessary delays. Nothing he could do about feeling washed out all the time; as he explained to Eda Ghormley, he'd never been able to handle uppers and this was no time to try. One way and another, he lasted.

He had Ghormley sit in on all recruiting interviews; without questioning under truth drugs he was signing no one from a UET colony. Figuring time and distance, he was close to certain that no counterpart of Tanit Eldon could have reached this place yet. When he read off his list of questions, even one shaky answer scuttled the applicant; fair or not, securing *Inconnu*'s safety and integrity was the name of the game. Sometimes he wondered: was he letting Eldon's betrayal make him too jumpy? Way out here in the boonies, to suspect people of being planted agents rather than merely wanting to get free from UET? Well, maybe he was and maybe not. The hell with it; he was running enough risks already, without any unnecessary ones.

He'd relented enough to disclose to successful applicants that his next stop was Number One, but no one aboard except key navigating personnel knew that world's coordinates—and as far as Tregare was concerned, that was exactly how he wanted it.

At the end of his third day groundside, Bran had his ship full-up with new crew including trainable supernumeraries, plus as many passengers as could be crowded in. Since the passengers were going to Number One and nowhere else, thus were seeing the last of UET, in their cases he skipped the drugs.

When he checked his overall roster against quarters accommodations, Tregare realized he had literally filled the ship; if there were any vacant bunk except the spare in his own digs, he couldn't think of one. He was somewhat chagrined, then, to get a call from a trader named Bret Osallin, a one-armed man not much given to red tape, therefore easier to deal with than most here.

Now Osallin reminded him that he'd halfway promised to give consideration to a passenger represented by the trader, a woman who had been, while waiting for a ship to ride, taking a sort of tour of some of Far Corner's more interesting aspects. "She'd like to talk with you, Tregare. I told her you would."

Impatient, wanting to end the call, Bran considered. Damn it, he knew the background. Osallin had formerly captained a ship for UET, and was known as good to serve under. Then, one way or another, depending on which rumor you chose to believe, he'd lost the arm. And UET, with its usual generosity, had dumped him on this world with a meager and ironically-named "severance payment," to shift for himself.

So for several reasons, Tregare didn't want to turn this man down flat. Earlier, before the ship filled up, he'd hinted that maybe Osallin could use a lift out of UET country, but the man smiled and said, "No, thanks; I have a job to do, here." Well, certainly that was an attitude Bran understood.

But it didn't help him find an answer. Now he said, "I really have a full ship. Unless your client would like to ride in Hold Portside Upper where the bunks are four deep and some sleeping double. But—oh, hell, I owe you, I guess. For being good to deal with. So bring your client out, any time today. Maybe I can discourage the old bat and it won't be your fault."

Even without a screen, Osallin's grin was clear in his voice. "Maybe you can." Then the voice came serious. "But if you can possibly do so, Tregare, please consider taking this passenger. Her reasons are—well, rather urgent."

"We'll see. Bring her."

When Osallin—short, squat, his smile showing three gold teeth and missing one alongside that trio—brought his client into Tregare's quarters and introduced her, Bran saw what the grin he'd sensed was all about. No "old bat" was Tari Obrigo. Somewhere in her early twenties, Tregare guessed. Not tall, slim but somehow not at all fragile—quickly he assessed the identifying details. Clothes weren't anything he noticed much; her dress was a dark orange, fitted well, and wasn't showy. She had an oval face, dark brown eyes, black hair curling down around her shoulders. What else? Front teeth a little prominent, brows arched more than nature probably intended, and at the left nostril a small, fleshy mole. All right—now he'd recognize her. The only thing that bothered him was the way she moved—he remembered that from someplace, but couldn't figure quite where. . . .

Meeting Osallin's awkward lefthanded handshake, Tregare said to the woman, "Passage? I have room for one, only."

"I wish passage; my friend Osallin does not. How much?"

Damn, but she was arrogant. So he said, "What am I bid?" and when she seemed confused, added, "I'm not running a charity, Ms. Obrigo. Highest bidder rides."

"I see. And you have other bids?" Somehow irritated by the precision of her speech, he lied, saying that of course he did. *Why am I letting her get to me?* Her self-assurance, maybe? Or—? She asked to see those bids; sparring, he said everything had been verbal. She wanted to know the amounts; off the top of his head he quoted a sum that should certainly back her away. But all she said was, "And does that include the freeze-chamber?"

Serve her right if he said yes! But, "No freeze on here. The damned things aren't working right. Unreliable." Then, still sounding as if *she* ran this show, she asked how long the trip would be, ship's time. He shook his head, saying he didn't give out that kind of information, but that if she figured on a year she wouldn't miss it too far, either way.

From the look of her, she was ready to drop the matter and leave. But Osallin spoke. "Did I forget to mention, Captain Tregare, that Ms. Obrigo is a Hulzein protege? I believe you occasionally do business with Hulzein agents, other than myself?"

And then Bran knew where he'd seen it before, the way this woman moved. His aunt Erika Hulzein, the one who'd tried to have him killed: the time he'd seen her do combat display. Tregare's eyes narrowed. If *that's* it . . . All right—let's see how far they're willing to go. So he said, "Okay—the price is half of what I just told you. But no less. Not for anybody." *Now we'll see*.

Obrigo raised her arched brows. "What about the other bidders?"

"What you do on this ship is ride it. What you don't do is ask questions. You got it?" If he could drive her away, he would. But irrationally, he found himself hoping that he couldn't.

He saw her hesitate, then rally. "I always ask questions. Everywhere. But I agree—you have the right not to answer. And so do I."

Without intent, he found himself smiling. "We lift day after tomorrow, around sunset. Bring your gear aboard two hours early. No time for last-minute stuff; you see?"

"I understand." So Tregare nodded and led the two people to the door, where the guard waited to take them down off the ship.

Then Bran sat down and poured himself a drink. Thinking, this Obrigo was a wild card he hadn't asked to be dealt. *Was* she an agent of Erika's? In that case, what would she want? *Oh hell, Erika's long dead.* But her daughter would carry the same genes, the same aims. Yet how could anybody know he'd come *here?* In the Long View, a rendezvous planned by only one side simply couldn't happen. But still . . .

His suspicions made no sense; he knew that, but couldn't shake them loose. His parents, on Number One where he was going next: no, there was simply no way they could be involved. Could they . . . ?

His hand moved, as if to brush away cobwebs of fear. This was all garbage; it was the woman herself who bothered him. Something familiar there: not only movement but appearance—yet he couldn't place her. Chance resemblance, probably—but who? Damn, if he could be his real self again, not this stretched-out wreck, he'd put her in her place fast enough, and show her what uppity really meant. Or did he really want to do that . . . ?

Hell with it; he polished off his drink and went upship, back to work.

The next two days went hectic; when Obrigo showed up he was arguing some mistakes with groundside suppliers. He didn't have to argue; he could say "go to hell," and lift off. But he rather liked the idea of Far Corner as a buffer between UET and the Hidden Worlds, so he kept patience beyond his wont. Only at the edge of vision did he notice Obrigo climb to the entrance deck, and Chira go to meet her. He'd told Chira to greet Tari Obrigo, feed her some coffee or whatever in the galley, and take her to captain's digs. Chira, he noticed, didn't offer to help carry the passenger's luggage. Well, maybe that could be a good start. After a while he disengaged the argument without too much prejudice, and went to see how Chira was doing.

* * *

The door to his quarters was open; he heard Obrigo say, "Why must I carry my gear from one place to another, where I will not be staying?"

Entering, standing behind her, he said, "You're staying here, Ms. Obrigo. The rest of the ship is full."

Chira yelled, "Yeah? Where *I* go?" When he laughed, saying she could stay right here and they'd all have lots of fun, she spat. "I don't do that stuff. I *don't*."

"Neither do I," said Obrigo. "Do not worry." And to Tregare, "I have bought passage—only that. Or else I leave this ship."

The whole ploy had got out of hand, but he was stuck with it. Well, sooner or later he had to test the limits; why not start now? He reached out, clenched a hand in her hair, shaking her head slowly from side to side. "Nobody's getting off—and you stay here. Don't crap me how you don't do this or that, either; I know the Hulzein training program. You got it?"

Her only reaction was to say, "Let go of my hair."

He did; she hand-brushed it back from her face, and said, "Erika has more than one training program."

"I know," he said, and left quarters for Control. It was time for lift, and time to see if he could do it.

Liftoff went well enough; bent out of shape Tregare might be, but still functioning. He set course for Number One, waited until Tinhead confirmed that aim and accel were correct within limits of acceptable error, then went downship to quarters.

Tari Obrigo and Chira must have been getting chummy; when he came in they moved farther apart. Chira had a guilty look to her, and Bran noticed a couple of nearly-empty shotsized glasses. So they'd been at his best booze, too. All right . . .

Where to push it? The passenger's luggage. "Inspection time," he said, and saw Obrigo hesitate before she opened the bags to him. He searched quickly, determined that there were no hidden compartments of any size, and came up with a lockbox. "Open it."

She shook her head. "That is private—Hulzein business." And when he said that he was in a lot of Hulzein business himself, she claimed she had no authority in this matter and couldn't even open the thing, herself.

He didn't buy it. "You almost lie like a Hulzein—but not quite."

"Believe what you wish. I cannot oblige you."

He looked at the box and recognized its mechanism—a photolock, keyed to its bearer's retinal patterns. With one hand to her nape he brought the lock to her eyes. "Keep 'em open." But the lock didn't yield. He let her go. "Well, I've opened photolocks before."

"If you try this one, do it somewhere else. Or let me out of here—and Chira, also."

"Booby-trapped, is it? Fine—you can tell me how."

"You know Erika better than that, if you know her at all. Would she allow me to be a possible weak link?" And finally she convinced him she *didn't* know. So he might as well drop the matter.

He said as much, adding, "If you can't open it yourself, I don't have to worry you've got a weapon in there."

Eyes slitted, she laughed. "Is *that* what you were afraid of?"

"Afraid?" While her scorn tore at his gut. "Don't use that word to me, you bitch!"

In flat tones, she said, "Why not, you bastard?" Then he hit her—a slap, not a fist blow—somehow wondering how this woman could so provoke him. Showing no reaction, she said, "I see. You can call names but I cannot? This is hardly a good beginning for a friendly relationship."

"Friendly? All right—let's see you be friendly."

Unbelieving, then, he watched her remove and drop her clothing.

"You see? No weapons on my person, either." Without haste she lay on the larger of the two beds and spread her legs. "Very well, let us get on with it. What are you waiting for?"

I didn't intend this. But I have to call her bluff. "You know something? You're not a very *feminine* woman, are you?"

"I did not have a very feminine upbringing. I am as I am."

"Yeah—well, we'll see." As he got rid of his own clothes he saw her eyes widen briefly—maybe she hadn't seen Slaughterhouse scars before. For a moment he wondered if he could manage sex just now, but it had been a long time; the surge he felt told him that fatigue would not betray him.

Second thoughts might, though. So that they'd have no chance to do so, he simply plunged ahead without preparation, forcing himself into her and hammering away as he hadn't done since he was sixteen and someone taught him better.

At first he could tell she was withholding any reaction whatsoever; then he felt movements that had to be deliberately helpful, before his own overdue climax took away all thought.

Eventually he sat up, saying, "You didn't come?"

"I seldom do."

"Didn't even fake it—try to make me feel good."

"That, I *never* do."

"Chira does." And for the first time he realized he'd done this thing with the barbarian girl watching. Well, too late now, so, "She does it real good—don't you, Chira?"

"Better than her. Any time." Pouting, she said that.

"Well, not right now. Go get us all something to eat."

"You, sure, Tregare. She can get her own."

There was no thought at all, no volition. But his slap knocked her skidding. "You forgetting how to take orders?" Then Obrigo had hold of his arm and was saying to Chira that the two of them could share the chore. Tregare looked at her. "Ms. High-and-Mighty Paying Passenger wants to help with the scutwork?"

"To accommodate one another in small matters, yes."

His hand scythed air. "Oh, get the hell out. And hurry it up—I'm hungry."

Unblinking, she said, "It would serve you right if we ate in the galley and *then* brought your food. Cold."

Effort turned his snarl to a laugh. "Talk all you want, Obrigo. You know better than to do it."

Then she clothed herself and the two women left; Tregare, showering and then dressing, wondered what the hell was going *on*, here. One thing he knew: right now, he didn't really like himself too much.

Dinner, and wine afterward, relaxed him; conversation came easier. After a time, somehow the exchange of information led him to tell Tari Obrigo of the taking of *Inconnu*; she'd mentioned the garbled version that had him gaining command by mutiny against his own people, and he had to correct that.

So he told of the tensions and dangers, the treacheries that could happen with Escape: how after Leon Monteffial assumed command, Cleet Farnsworth's countermutiny had nearly given the ship back to UET. Except that Farnsworth hadn't realized Tregare was working outside the ship in a power suit, and would come back in and "—well, clean house, I guess you'd say. But I wrecked the suit, doing it."

Obrigo nodded. "That is most interesting, Tregare. It explains a great deal."

"Like what?"

"An experience of that sort must not be easy to live with. I will remember, and make allowances."

Draining the latest refill Chira had given him, he said, "Nobody has to make allowances for Tregare. On this ship *I* make the allowances. Don't forget that."

"Very well." But her smile mocked him.

He wouldn't let her bait him again; he said, "You're a smart one, aren't you, Obrigo? I'l keep it in mind."

"And I will keep in mind, Tregare, that you are another."

The talk wound down. Feeling a little mushminded but more alive than he had in some time, Bran said, "Tonight you two can argue who gets which side of the big bed. I'll use the other."

As ship's days passed, Bran felt easier on one level but still anxious at a deeper one. His first thought, that Tari Obrigo was a weapon of Erika's against him, no longer seemed reasonable. But then, what *was* she here for?

The harem thing wasn't an item he was proud of, but he'd begun it without meaning to; he could see no graceful way to ease out. Now that his strength was returning (thank peace for small blessings!) he took his occasional turns with Chira and with Obrigo—though now he tried to have one out of quarters when bedding the other. It struck him that as time passed he was less inclined, though still as attracted, toward Obrigo. Maybe it was the way he sensed that her muscular control, which sometimes heightened his pleasure, could just as easily shut him off. Once, maybe at her purpose or maybe not, that failure happened. Later he said to her, "If I thought you were playing games with me . . ."

She laughed. "We all play games—it is our nature."

"I don't."

"Of course you do. You are playing one now. The name of it is 'I don't play games.'"

Baffled, he told her he ought to space her "and the Hulzeins be hanged!" But later, in bed, she erased his displeasure.

As before, hailing and recognition at One Point One, the planet's spaceport, went easily. And this time there were people on duty, considerably older now, who remembered Bran from his previous visit. One of them patched him through to the appropriate official, and Tregare arranged for refueling to begin as soon as he landed.

He wanted that landing to come when ship's morning was also the port's, so Gonnelson figured the requisite number of hours *Inconnu* should spend in orbit first, and at what height— a little short of synchronous, it turned out. Then, for the last dinner in space, he ordered up a real spread. Chira looked impressed, and even Tari Obrigo expressed appreciation without her usual hint of mockery. At the meal's end he brought out a dusty, oversized bottle of wine. "This stuff I save for special landings, and there's only enough for three more." Going into Far Corner, he reflected, he'd been too frazzled even to think of any celebration.

Sipping, Obrigo nodded. "Delicious. I hope you can replenish your supply."

Chira laughed. "Not hardly, he can't. Comes from UET's main base, off Earth. Armed ships all over, he says."

Tregare found himself explaining how he'd gone into Stronghold with fake papers, for repairs. "That trick won't work a second time. But you never know—someday I may try the place again."

Obrigo nodded. "Yes—with a few more armed ships . . ." *Was she a mindreader?* "What have you heard?"

Nothing specific, she said, except that he'd taken at least one other Escaped ship, maybe more. So he was building a fleet. "Will you take more armed UET ships, or arm your own?"

He glared, but kept his voice low. "Nothing's safe from you, is it? All right—either, or both. I have—"

"You have someone trying to duplicate this ship's weapons. I will not ask where. But the projector unit missing from its turret—not removed for repairs, I think, because the defective freeze-chambers are still in place. And *why*, may I ask?"

"You trying to tell me how to run my ship?"

Now she glared, too. "Somebody should!"

She was sometimes a hard person to agree with. When he

said, yes, he'd offload those chambers, immediately she told him to maintain ownership in case they could be repaired. He yelled a little. ". . . next you'll tell me how to zip my own shoes!"

Chira giggled. "You sure let her get you mad a lot."

Looking then from one to the other, all he could say was, "You're giving her bad habits, Obrigo—you know that?"

"I do not consider honesty a bad habit."

Tregare managed to turn his explosive laugh into a cough. "Yeah. Like she said, you do get me mad. But—you know? I'll miss you."

Surprisingly, she reached for his hand. "Tregare? At the first of this trip, I hated your guts."

"I wasn't crazy about yours, either? So?"

"I am not certain, Tregare, if I *like* you or not—or whether anyone should—but you are important to me. I wish you survival and success."

"Same to you and many of 'em. Anything else?"

"Yes. Tregare, will you sleep with me tonight?"

For some time he hadn't touched her; what moved her now, he couldn't guess. But in the big bed—once, and then again later—she showed him skills she'd never before displayed. Nor, in his personal experience, had anyone else. He didn't know why and he couldn't ask, but he felt deeply grateful.

In the dim light he saw, at the corner of one eye, a tear forming. "What's wrong?"

"This time—this time, Tregare, I truly wanted you. But my body would not believe that want."

There was nothing he could say and not much he could do. But he went to sleep holding her.

When the landing woke him, though—M'tana had the con— he and Tari were disarranged, lying spraddled all over the bed. He worked one leg free from under hers, disengaged other minor entanglements, and pulled the spread up to cover her when he left.

First he stopped by the galley and assembled a snack, which he took with him to Control; if a captain couldn't break his own rules, who could? Deverel was relieving M'tana at the watch. Tregare said, "Good landing, Zelde. If I hadn't been half-awake already I'd've slept right through it." On her way out, the tall woman grinned and threw him a sketchy salute.

The log and instruments were all shipshape. Bran told Hain Deverel, "Except for the usual airlock guards for screening, we don't need Alert procedures here. I think you know what kind of items to handle by the routines, and what to call me for or record for me." Deverel nodded; Tregare took his empty tray back to the galley and went down to the main airlock foyer, where he expected—and found—a group of traders and brokers, all ready to haggle and smiling about it. But it didn't take long for the smiles to vanish and the voices to raise; Bran remembered that Number One was a place for loud and profane dickering.

So, whole-heartedly he entered into the spirit of the occasion.

Some of the dealings went easily, some harder, and some not at all. Meanwhile Tregare heard the fueling pumps start, and made a sort of nod to himself that there was *one* worry covered. Then he put his mind back to arguing with a rather cadaverous elderly man, mostly bald but sporting a thin, grey goatee. The man's nasal whine was irritating, but Alsen Bleeker held the handle on some categories of foodstuffs Tregare didn't want to have to pick up in dribs and drabs from smaller suppliers, so it made sense to make the extra effort. Suddenly the name and appearance clicked; Bleeker was the man who had tried to get cute with his prices on Tregare's earlier visit here. *So watch him.* He'd been on the young side of middle age then, but that was the Long View for you. . . .

A voice broke his concentration; over by the exit ramp, Tari Obrigo was calling to him. His hand waved the argument to a halt. "A few moments, gentlemen. A farewell to say, here." He went to her, gave her a one-arm hug around the shoulders. "So you're getting off. All done with me now."

"Done? Will that not depend on our travels, yours and mine? If I settle here, I may be old before you next return."

The idea hurt him. He looked away, but said, "I might like that. We'd go to bed and *you'd* be the grateful one."

She laughed; a thumb and knuckle nipped his earlobe. "Do not bet on it. But stay in communication when you can, and I shall, too. Good luck, Tregare."

He watched her, luggage-laden, walk to the ramp and down it, out of sight. Then he returned to the dickering. But somehow found it hard to keep his mind to it.

* * *

When he'd settled as many of his dealings as could be managed at this point, Tregare hosted a few of the traders—those who accepted his invitation—to lunch in the galley. Then, he decided, it was time to go visiting. Because the ship that sat down the port a way, easy walking distance, was Pell Quinlan's *Red Dog*.

The ramp guard was officious but not unfriendly. Going by protocol, Bran gave his name and that of his ship, then said of the woman beside him, "This is Zelde M'tana, my Second Hat." Zelde had told him about meeting with Quinlan on Fair Ball and declining his offer of a supercargo passage; in this case, though, there was no reason for her dodging the man.

After a brief talk on his hushphone the guard passed them, and at the airlock another took over, ushering them to the captain's digs. There Quinlan—still lean and tall, wearing a pointed, tawny beard—gave welcome. Handshakes, offer of drinks, then while busy at the pouring, "A long time, Tregare. And you, M'tana—I see you found your way off Fair Ball without help from me."

So they talked, exchanged info and anecdotes, until Tregare decided it was time to make his pitch: the fleet to take Stronghold, then wait and collect successive fleets sent out from Earth, and then—

Quinlan was shaking his head. "It might work—I wish you luck. But I operate solo, always have—and can't imagine doing it any other way." He raised his glass. "I'm sorry, Tregare."

Bran shrugged. "I knew it already. Had to ask, was all. But now—" He leaned forward. "Where you headed next? And how much filled up, with cargo?" The answers suited Tregare quite well. So then he made his *real* pitch.

"I lucked out fine, Zelde." He'd dickered with Quinlan for nearly an hour but now he and M'tana were walking back to *Inconnu*. "Farmer's Dell isn't too far off the course he was planning, and he can free enough space for the women to be comfortable. Well, reasonably." He looked at her. "You handle the workgang that moves the bunks over to *Red Dog*, will you?" She nodded. "I'm glad Pell can take care of the plumbing in a hurry, using his own people to do it."

She cleared her throat. "The women, now. You out to tell 'em the news, or me?"

"Let's do it together. I know you're worried about how it'll work, at Farmer's Dell, but the colony administration has a fund set up; it pays passage rates for any women brought in on the cuff."

"And then? I know, you *said* they're free, but—"

"Everything I've heard documents it that way." He smiled. "Ol' Pell, though. That fake log and ship's ID he worked up. I wish I had time to talk him out of a readout on that. It sounds better than anything I've ever done, along those lines." He shrugged. "Well, I remember enough to give me some good ideas."

"Too bad he's so much a one-man show, Tregare."

"Yeah. I could sure use him on the project. He's just not a man to take orders. Never was. But he'll cut himself some notches."

Upship and in quarters, first Tregare showered and changed clothes. Then he had a drink and told Chira about his latest deal. "So that saves me some worries. And without gouging Quinlan I netted about ten percent over expenses, on the operation. He'll make three times what I did, but I don't have to sidetrack to Farmer's Dell!"

He knew the financial side meant nothing to her, so her frown puzzled him. She said, "I go there, too. With them."

"But—" He shook his head. "Maybe you forgot. Those women down there—last I heard, they didn't like you pretty much."

"Not now, that way. Food runs, I been helping. Talk some. First on here, I didn't *know*. Told 'em, sorry. Nobody mad, now." Her face had a pleading look. "You good to me. But on here—" She spread her hands. "No wind. No rain. No *sky*."

So he said, "All right. You come downship with us when Zelde and I announce the latest development, and we'll see how it goes. Okay?"

So they went down to Hold Portside Upper, and first Zelde and then Tregare explained the situation. The woman Cherisse Frisco looked maybe a decade younger than when she'd been brought aboard *Inconnu;* there was something to be said for decent food and adequate sanitation. She asked questions, and so did others, but eventually they seemed reasonably satisfied. "I wish there were a way you could get us to a Hidden World, not a UET colony," Frisco said, "but I know economics. It *cost* you, to buy us out of that shitbox, and your ship's resources are finite. Besides, Farmer's Dell doesn't sound too bad."

"The place does have a good name," said Bran. "Now one more thing." He motioned toward Chira. "This young woman was yanked out of a backslid savage culture and came aboard here without much in the way of manners. First thing, she got a bunch of you killing-mad. She thinks she's cleared that up, since, and wants to ride with you to Farmer's Dell. Tell me honestly, Frisco—is that a good idea? For her?"

Cherisse Frisco smiled. "Sure it is. So she *did* act like a rotten little savage, then. Thinking back on it, the rest of us weren't too much better. Don't worry; there'll be no problems."

Zelde's work crew was beginning to disassemble bunks, with the women's help. Tregare took Chira back upship to pack the few belongings she'd accumulated. Briefly he wondered why he hadn't suggested simply turning her loose here on Number One, then he realized she couldn't handle herself, alone on a strange world. But as part of a group, she'd be all right.

She went in for a shower. He thought she'd come out dressed and ready to go downship and join the others, but she didn't. Unclothed, she tossed her garments onto a chair, and said, "I told you, you been fine, Tregare. Now I go, fuck you a good one first. For to remember."

This time he was pretty sure she didn't fake her climax. And next day she and the others were off to Farmer's Dell.

With a few things off his mind, Bran got around to checking the Port's computer for messages; maybe his growing data net had some good news for him, or maybe not.

Only a little, was the answer. Jimar Peralta had been here once; his comment was, "You picked the right world, Tregare, for your staging base. I didn't venture to inspect your own private spaceport in person, but on hi-mag it looks shipshape, and having it out away from the civilians is a good idea." And after a brief pause, "I'm off, now, on what you might call a raiding tour of UET colonies; the more they're shaken up, the better. My planned schedule will have *No Return* back here during your rendezvous period." Another pause. "I still feel we need to restructure the administrative side a bit, but I'm sure it can all be worked out." And Tregare thought, *he's still after part of command, Peralta is.* . . .

In the next few messages Tregare found nothing important. Then came a voice he barely remembered and at first couldn't place. But before she spoke it, he remembered the name of Erdis Blaine. ". . . a job in Port Admin, the greeting and querying of ships, before and since your son was born. He's Bran Leon Blaine, by the way." So she'd commemorated Leon Monteffial, her lover killed in Farnsworth's countermutiny. Tregare nodded; the man deserved as much. ". . . leaving now on Keath Farrell's *Spark Plug*, and I hope our destination is a place where Bran Leon can grow up peacefully. Blaine out." Well, he hoped she got her wish.

Alsen Bleeker didn't seem to be a quick learner. Some days later, when *Inconnu's* loading neared completion, the man suddenly tried to change his terms. "Some of that electronics gear you bought," he said. "You have it priced higher than I can sell it." That, Tregare thought, was probably an outright lie, but when he tried to check with Port Admin's computer, the data came out garbled. Cute trick! So the hell with it; Tregare left the trader standing there groundside, went upship and sent an armed squad down to safeguard the rest of the loading.

Only when that was done did he lift the ramp and close ship. And that's when he learned that Junior Lee had found a bug in the Drive; *Inconnu* couldn't lift right away.

Well, all right. He put his downside screens to showing the area around the ship, and opened communications on groundside frequencies to Bleeker. When the man answered, Tregare said, "I'm checking the computations, but I'm having a little computer trouble. Would you have Admin feed me the manifest figures again?" Seemingly relieved, Bleeker agreed, and this time the data came through clearly. Bran wasn't surprised to find most of Bleeker's prices raised considerably from the terms previously set. Well, the best thing, for now, was just plain stalling. Tregare did a rather artful job of it.

Meanwhile he eavesdropped on Bleeker's shorthaul talkset. The man was rounding up an unofficial army, claiming that Tregare had cheated him and possibly several others. "After all, he *is* known as a pirate." Tregare made a face—if he was a pirate, what did that make Alsen Bleeker? But, not to give away his advantage in overhearing, he said nothing.

By the time Junior Lee announced readiness for liftoff, armed groundsliders ringed the safety perimeter around *Inconnu.* "Normal" safety perimeter, that was; if Tregare made a max lift he'd probably kill no one but he could sure bounce a few around. The group's weapons didn't bother him much; besides a couple of two-hands energy guns that might scar the hull at that range, all he saw was standard handguns. They'd make pretty sparks but nothing more.

What did worry him some was eavesdropping on Bleeker's pitch to interdict *Inconnu* with the Port's defense missiles. Only one side of that argument, Tregare got; whatever frequencies the Port was answering on, Bran's comm-tech couldn't find them. So when Bleeker said, "Thirty minutes? Can't you get faster authorization? Well, I guess it'll have to do. And thanks—" When Bran heard that much, he told Junior Lee to lift in fifteen unless delayed by Tregare's personal countermanding. And at max.

"Right y'all purely are, cap'n. Thisyere ship, she gonna show 'em sump'n, you bet my tired ol' tailend."

Before Bran could finish giving Beauregard the usual supportive thanks, Gonnelson pointed at the forward screen. "Aircar!"

The comm-tech hit a switch; Tregare yelled, "You up there! What you trying to pull? Clear off or get shot down." Then to groundside: "*You*, Bleeker—I thought you had better sense. Call off your pipsqueak Air Force—and damned fast!"

As the aircar turned away, still circling the ship but at a more civil distance now, Bleeker spoke high-pitched and fast. It wasn't his, he swore. He knew nothing about it; he'd been right here ever since Tregare closed ship. "All I want is my money, you pirate!"

"You got it—exactly as agreed, beforehand." Bleeker whined that it wasn't *his* fault if prices went up. Tregare snorted. "Your prices always go up; that's an old groundhog trick. And like it or not, most ships pay. But not *Inconnu!*"

Incredibly, Bleeker didn't know the ship was refueled, and tried to use fuel as leverage. Bran laughed and corrected his ignorance. "That's an old *spacer* trick." Then he signed off, and called the aircar again. "Who are you? What's your business?"

* * *

The answering voice came low and sounded concerned, not excited. "Tregare! It is I—Tari Obrigo. I must talk with you."

He shook his head. What—? "Too late; no time. Bleeker'll be programming the defense missiles on me; I've got to lift." He paused. "Glad you came, though. See you someday."

"Wait! Your father is here. He brought me."

"Hawkman? Sorry, but for him it's *years* too late—ever since they left me in that UET hellhole."

"They could not help it; they had no choice! And they—they love you—they want to see you."

"The pirate, the mutineer, in Hulzein Lodge? I doubt it."

"Bran Tregare, the girl speaks truth." Hawkman! "And she cares enough that she would have come here against Liesel's command."

Obrigo would have defied Liesel Hulzein? Somehow Tregare wasn't too surprised. He said, "She's quite somebody, Hawkman. See that you treat her right."

He missed a word or two, then ". . . we miss you. Are we never to see you again?"

For a moment, his guts wrenching, Tregare couldn't speak. Then he said, slowly, "I'll think about it. Next time, maybe."

"And how long? Will your mother live to see that time?"

"I—I hope so." Then, hearing what Bleeker was saying on the other channel, he called down to Junior Lee. "Liftoff coming; sixty seconds and counting." Then to the aircar again, "Scoot hard and fast, Hawkman; this lift is going to make waves. Not like the time with you, Tari." The car sheered away as Tregare got confirmation from Junior Lee. He said a few more words to Tari and to his father, then *Inconnu* lifted.

Before dust hid groundside, Bran saw the armed posse rolled away like rag dolls by the mere blast-outskirt pressures. Then they began to get up and run away.

If Bleeker got any missiles aloft, he wasted them; the ship's backscreens showed no sign. Tregare set course, cutting back to less than half-max accel, and called council. "We've talked all this over, but I want a last-minute check, to see if anybody has improvements to offer." So, in no hurry, they kicked the plan around.

Basically, *Inconnu* was going to be on a combination of listening-post and patrol duty. Number One's sun had a very large planet—practically a grey dwarf—that rolled suddenly around its primary at roughly two weeks' ship-distance from Number One. And for a number of years that world, Big Icecube (though actually it had considerable internal heat), had been and would be in a position to monitor most ship traffic between Number One and other inhabited places. So for the period during which Tregare was hoping other ships would make the rendezvous he'd spent years trying to arrange, *Inconnu* would stay in energy-saving orbit around Big Icecube. Relaying data from incoming ships long before ground-side gear could have detected the signals, for one thing. All right? So far, so good.

"Now then." Tregare waited while Gonnelson, the one-drink man, saw to fillups for the others, who weren't being too thirsty, themselves. When the First Hat was done, Bran said, "Soon as we pass the range a scout could be detected from groundside, I take our scoutship back to Number One, going in on a blindside spiral. The gear's loaded and the work crew's picked, for what we need to do at my bases, across the Big Hills from One Point One."

Zelde M'tana spoke. "Crew's picked, you said. Not all, though. Who's to strawboss for you? *That* ain't said yet."

"You want the job?"

She shook her head; at her left earlobe the heavy gold ring swung. "Makes me no mind. I'll do it or ride here, either one."

Tregare smiled. "It happens I think I need you on here—you and Gonnelson. Pick a couple of bright ratings to help out on the watches." She nodded as Bran looked to his Third Hat. "Hain, I'd like you to help handle things at the bases." And before Deverel's reaction could develop past looking startled, "You and Anse, that is." Then the officer relaxed, and a little later the council convened.

Carrying the dozen that the scout could hold comfortably, that small craft emerged from *Inconnu* and put on decel to head back to Number One. Maintaining a blindside course, so as not to be spotted on his way in, Tregare timed his moves closely. Number One's major, circular-orbiting moon helped a lot.

Gingerly, all senses at max alert, he brought the scout down at Base Two, the rudimentary spaceport he'd ramrodded when he first visited this world. The appearance of the place delighted him—with absentee management he'd tried not to be too optimistic, but he saw no clutter nor plant overgrowth, and the buildings looked shipshape, well-tended.

Since nothing ensured this was still *his* base, he went down the ramp armed and not alone. At groundside he paused until a man and woman, also armed, came out of a quarters building. Tregare raised his voice to carry. "Do you work for MacDougall and Aguinaldo? If you do, you work for me."

Approaching, the woman said, "You're Tregare?" He nodded. "Mac's retired; got a leg smashed, hunting bushstomper. He still does Pete's books, but no full-time work."

"Sorry to hear it." Time for business. "You two here alone?"

"No." The man whistled, and another weaponed couple emerged from behind an innocent-looking scrap pile. *Nice caution.* Everybody shook hands. The woman pointed out the Base office and comm building, then said, "Captain? Now that you're back, do we still have jobs here?"

"Sure. Things'll change, but likely we'll need more people, not less." Inside the office prefab, Tregare saw it was too small for his needs. But a larger one was empty, so he assigned space there for his administrative kipple and left the work crew to see to it while his own people got the scout unloaded. Emila Thorndeck, the stocky thirtyish woman who spoke for the maintenance gang, seemed to have things in hand—so, taking only Deverel and Kenekke with him, Bran lifted the scout for his Base One, the cabin on the higher, gently sloping plateau.

Setting down, he wondered what, after all this time, to expect. Buildings and ground seemed well maintained. Operating his key in the trick sequence that nullified alarms, he found the cabin's interior bare, stark, and dusty, but intact. All the fixtures were there, and so were the stored emergency rations. The attic tank gave only driblets of stale water, so Tregare started the pump and heard fluid surge through the pipe—his well still functioned. Leaving the other two to shake the place down, since they'd be staying there while Bran dossed in the scout, he went out to check the rest of the premises.

It looked good; Pete and Mac had done the job right. Back against the rising cliff his small warehouses were stocked as specified; he was surprised to find two empty crates that had held ships' turret projectors, and couldn't imagine what cooperative act of piracy had brought them here. But gift horses by definition have perfect teeth—so, grinning, Tregare headed for the gully-end of his escape tunnel, followed it to the upward side-exit, and found the projectors mounted in his pillbox. The power switch worked; the units traversed either separately or together, to cover the plateau or guard the cabin. Cutting power to a trickle, so as not to alarm the two men indoors, he fired—the faint hiss and ionization trails said the guns were operative.

Missile control tests showed Ready, too. Yeah, the place was in good shape. Just like he wanted it.

Back in the cabin, Kenekke was cooking dinner. Not "iron rations" but food from the scout. Joining the party, Tregare ate, and had a beer with Deverel. Then at the scout he rigged a relay circuit, so the cabin's intercom could talk with Base Two, below. When he went back to the cabin and tried it, the first thing he didn't like was that Emila Thorndeck had no aircars on hand; one was down for repairs and the other two were across the Big Hills in One Point One. He didn't like his base letting *all* its mobility go someplace else, but he didn't want to start off hassling these people, either. So he asked about the comm situation, Base Two to city or Port, and that was better: the scatter circuit had been down for a while but was okay now. So he could say, "Good," and ask for delivery of an aircar to him as soon as possible, and add, "First chance, I'd like to see Pete. Preferably this side of the Hills, and do the talking over a few drinks I owe him."

Thorndeck chuckled. "I think Pete would hold still for that."

Signing off the call, Bran went to the cabin's front window. Out past the plateau's edge the last of sunlight tinged the horizon, far out on that vast upland plain. *There's nothing like it.* Checking his wrist chrono, he turned to the two men. "Everything else I need to do tonight is from the scout. See you in the morning." So now Deverel and Kenekke would know that even though it was his cabin, he wouldn't be invading their privacy.

Aboard the scout he checked his charts and swiveled the little ship's antennae the best he could figure. Then he set up a loop tape, calling *Inconnu*. Round-trip comm lag had grown to boring length, but he waited. All he got, though, was a rating filling in as watch officer, and confirming that the ship was on course and on sked.

Hell with it. Making a polite acknowledgment, he ended the call. Early still, for sleep. But maybe a little extra would do him good. If his nerves would ease down and *let* him.

Pete Aguinaldo, bringing the aircar next day, didn't look as old as Tregare expected. He was still slim, fluid of movement, his hair black and face unlined. The main difference was that Pete's familiar smile wasn't there *all* the time.

Finally Tregare figured it out. For almost the only time since Bran had first met him, Pete wasn't stoned. There wasn't any way to ask about the change, so Tregare didn't. Well, he had no need to; he knew about "negative tolerance" and could think of no lesser force that would have weaned Pete Aguinaldo from cannabis.

So, with a little bourbon for lubrication, they got down to business. Looking around the scout, Pete said, "You still keep it shipshape, Tregare. And it's been a time."

"Longer for you than for me." *The Long View,* and somehow Bran didn't want to know how long it had been, here, groundside. So he reached for the Base Two inventory readouts Pete had brought, scanned them and made notes. Handing them back, he said, "Back at One Point One, see if you can order this stuff out for me and have it delivered to the Port. I could do it over the circuits, but in-person usually works better."

"Sure. I'll tell you when it's ready for pickup." Aguinaldo frowned a little. "Tregare? I was surprised you didn't get in touch when *Inconnu* was here."

Bran waved a hand. "I wanted to. But too many deals to make in a hurry. And then get the ship out safe. Little problem with Alsen Bleeker, I guess you heard."

A nod. "He's still running around, claiming you cheated him."

Tregare felt his face go rigid; was this man doubting him? "He tried to gouge me on prices, after terms were set. I didn't let him, was all."

The familiar smile came. "I thought so. I've dealt with you and Bleeker both, and what you say fits what I know."

So *that* was all right. Pete accepted one refill on his drink, talking, catching Bran up on events he'd missed here. Tregare thought to order out two aircars for his own use, and Pete agreed. Not long after, while the pass would still hold daylight, Aguinaldo took his leave.

When one scoutsized load of supplies, including an aircar, was ready at the Port, Bran lifted across the Hills and accepted delivery. Part of the stuff was for Two and part for the cabin. And now, with his new aircar, he could shuttle between bases without wasting the scout's fuel.

Next day Aguinaldo called to say the other car was ready, and a pilot could bring it across by afternoon. Tregare said, "I'll be down at Two; send it there. I'll get the pilot back to town on tomorrow's shuttle run." Pete, less talkative than usual, agreed and signed off.

At Base Two, Tregare was rearranging his landing circles; the first setup was fine for safety but not handy for loading a *group* of ships. *And when the hell will they get here?* But he wanted his tractor, towing loaded flats, to have clear runs from warehouses to any ship. And then there was refueling. So he wound up with his circles in a zigzag line, the buildings on one side of it and the tanks on the other.

Done with that chore, he was having coffee in Emila Thorndeck's cramped office when he heard the first sounds of an approaching aircar. No hurry; he finished the coffee, not strolling outside until the car landed.

He got ten paces beyond the door. Then he stopped. Climbing out of that aircar was a very tall man.

Tregare's father, Hawkman Moray.

12. Rissa Kerguelen

Fighting shock, Tregare stood rooted. *He hasn't changed much.* As his father came forward, one hand out for greeting, Bran found words. "What the hell are *you* doing here?" His voice, high-pitched and strained, didn't sound right to him.

Hawkman's smile hadn't changed, either. As Bran submitted to the handshake but glared away any thought of embrace, the older man said, "Why, I brought your aircar. Obviously."

"Pete's letting just anybody come in here? I thought security was one of the things I was paying for. I—" Dammit, if only his head would stop pounding. . . !

"Not just anybody." The deep voice was mild. "And I've never been here before, to either of your bases; I've only seen them from the air, and at a distance. Interesting, though."

"Spying on me? Is that it?"

"Not at all. Bran, *everybody* knows you have something set up out here; Mac and Pete kept close wraps on their dealings with you, but things do leak out. Though your zigzag pass through the Hills—or rather, how to get through it safely—is still largely a secret." Again the smile came, but rueful now. "I know how because I was along on the hunt with Mac when he got bushstomped; he couldn't fly the car himself so he *had* to talk me through. That made me one of the gang, I suppose;

Pete showed me the eastbound strategy, next time *we* went hunting."

With his gut sometimes a lump of ice and sometimes a blazing coal, Tregare nodded. "Okay, thanks for bringing the car. A drink goes with that, so come on in. I'll set you up for meals, and a bunk tonight, and the shuttle can run you back in the morning."

Following into Tregare's own, new office, Hawkman said, "Thank you, Bran. That's fair enough."

Without asking, Tregare poured bourbon. Not very big slugs, because his hands trembled and he didn't want to betray his weakness by spilling anything. The damned *tension!* He tried to analyze it: not fear. Not even anger, as he knew anger—yet he was stretched as tight as even Butcher Korbeith had been able to manage. Now he *knew* he'd been right, all these years, to stay the hell away from his family.

Sitting down, across from Hawkman who was also seated, helped some, but when Tregare raised his glass he needed both hands to hold it halfway steady. Trying to ignore his shame at the loss of control, he said, "Cheers, I suppose."

They sipped. Hawkman said, "Bran? Don't you realize? *We had no choice.*"

"But you *left* me!" He tried to stop, to say no more, but his voice kept going anyway: the Slaughterhouse, the awful brutality. Butcher Korbeith, his filthy ways of piling fear. Megan Delange at Korbeith's airlock, her body spewing as though she were trying to get rid of it. Phyls Dolan—feeling his face contort into pain, Bran saw tears run down Hawkman's cheeks.

As if a maul hit his solar plexus, Tregare doubled over in cramp. He lost hold of his glass and heard it shatter on the hard floor. His belly wrenched and spasmed; grimly he made effort and did not vomit.

But it wouldn't *stop.* He felt arms around him and tried to shake free, but he had no strength. Vertigo struck; it felt like having drunk twice too much and fighting to keep from passing out. The beat of blood in his head brought pain and more pain. He tried not to hear the voice saying, "Bran, Bran—" It was too much; he couldn't stand it; something would break.

And then it did. He heard a dull groaning, half roar and half wail, and knew he made that sound himself but could not stop it.

Slowly the pressure drained; the great, choking sobs abated, and finally, clasped in his father's arms, Bran Tregare was only crying. And so was Hawkman.

When they could sit up and look at each other, mopping away the tears and—Bran, at least—feeling sheepish, Tregare fixed new drinks. His hands, now, were steady. Hawkman said, "Breaking out of armor can be a terrible experience, can't it?" At Tregare's nod, he said, "Why did you need it to be so *total?*"

So Bran explained: at the Slaughterhouse, the seductive dreams of home and family, always ending in dread and shock at waking, until his only defence was to turn against his past, his family, and *hate* them.

Hawkman heard him through, then said, "Do you still hate us?"

"Reflex, yes; reason, no."

The tall man nodded. "Then can we lean toward reason now? Because I have a favor to ask you before I go to my bunk here."

Tregare stood. "Bunk, hell. Come on; we'll fly up to the cabin and stay in the scoutship tonight. We're overdue for dinner, I expect, but Pete gave me some bushstomper steaks for the freezer."

Almost like Earth beef, bushstomper had a special tang to it. After both men had eaten heartily and were tapering down with wine and coffee, Tregare sat back, more relaxed than he felt he should be. Well, *acting* relaxed and businesslike was helping a lot. He cleared his throat. "A favor, I think you said?"

Half-shrugging, Hawkman spoke. "Local politics here. A protégé of ours, Liesel's and mine, you could say. She's in trouble and we'd like to help her, and *not* only because she owns sufficient wealth to become an oligarch and a good ally."

Tregare frowned. "What's the help problem?" He didn't understand, and said so.

"Are you married, Bran? At the moment?"

"Never have been. Why?"

"Then to give Rissa Kerguelen the protection of Hulzein Lodge, through a critical time that's coming, your mother and I would like you to marry her."

* * *

Memory took its time, clicking in. Rissa Kerguelen? Oh sure—back on Earth. The stubble-headed kid on the Tri-V, the one who lucked out in UET's lottery and was buying free of Total Welfare. And taking precisely no crap at all from the Tri-V interviewers. Tregare said only, "Yeah. I know who she is. But how the hell did she get *here*?"

"Why, on your ship, of course." Tregare waited, and finally Hawkman said, "I believe you knew her as Tari Obrigo."

That one, peace take it! Who had put up with indignities, on *Inconnu*, that would hardly leave her fond of one Bran Tregare. Thinking fast, he said, "She might not care for the idea. Anybody ask her?"

Headshake. "Not until the crisis point. Liesel wants her Hulzein-connected by marriage; it's a matter of mutual strength." He sighed. "It's also contingent. Because Rissa must first survive a death duel with Stagon dal Nardo. It seems he tried to bully her, but the end result was his own humiliation."

From so long ago, the name took a moment to register. "That overgrown calf? Yeah—last time I was here, he tried to give *me* trouble."

"A calf no longer, Bran. A bull now, and dangerous; he heads that clan of assassins and has murdered his way to high standing."

Tregare's eyes narrowed. "*I* could take him. So why not—?"

"The rules. You'd need to wait your turn, after he's met Rissa's challenge."

"*She* challenged?"

"She was more or less forced to it. But in any case, I doubt Rissa would allow you to preempt. I've seldom seen such inflexible pride in a young person."

Thinking back to his own dealings with Tari Obrigo, Tregare made a number of reevaluations, and said, "Sometimes it's not all that easy to see what somebody's really like."

Briefly, Hawkman smiled. "I have the impression that Rissa has come to the same conclusion about you."

Wary as always, Treagre asked more questions. *Why* this marriage thing? The answers sounded plausible, but plausible wasn't good enough. Who was going to set it up, and how? Was his own identity as a Hulzein heir going to be revealed? "In short, Hawkman, how phony does this thing have to stack up?"

Tregare's father looked placid enough. "You needn't be named at all, at the time. In fact it's better if you're not. Arrive in hooded garb, if you like."

"Will *she* know?"

"That's up to Liesel, or to your sister Sparline."

His sister—he hadn't thought of her in years. He said, for want of anything else to say, "How old is Sparline now, bio?"

"Perhaps a year older than yourself, whereas the opposite was once true. Does it matter?"

"I guess not." A big difference *would* have mattered.

"Well, then," Hawkman said. "Will you do it? If Rissa survives?"

Tregare thought about it, then nodded. "All right. But don't tell her I know who she really is. I want to do that myself. Assuming she lives to hear it."

Suddenly, to Tregare the whole situation seemed unreal. Earlier this same day he had been engrossed in the problems of his own long-term goals. Now, without warning, his past had struck—and hard enough, apparently, to derail the train of his concentration and common sense. Now he shook his head, not in negation but to earn a pause. "Hold it—I have to think."

Hawkman chuckled. "Surely. And from hearsay, not to mention heredity, I gather you're well equipped to do so."

For moments his father's warm humor took Bran back to his childhood, the safe home he'd lost so long ago—memory bridging the years between and easing them. By effort, Tregare brought himself back to the now that was. "If I do this for you, what's in it for *me?*"

"What is it that you want?" In Hawkman, Bran saw no guile.

"For starters, you might sit on Bleeker a little. And a few others who have the idea they can gouge me on supplies I need." A hand forestalled interruption. "This much I can tell you. I intend to gather some ships here; they'll all need supplying, and it'd save me a lot of trouble, not having to push weight all the time. Bleeker seems to be sparking the groundside traders, to make things difficult."

"Not for much longer," Hawkman said.

"Oh? You're after him already, on your own?"

"To absorb him, let's say, while leaving him nominally in oligarch status. Your mother is gathering power in true

Hulzein fashion." Hawkman grinned. "Her sister Erika chased us off Earth because she feared competition for control of a relatively small country: Argentina. Liesel, if I'm not mistaken, has a good chance to dominate this entire planet."

"But not me." Flatly, Tregare said that. "Not my ships."

The older man shook his head. "Groundsiders can't control ships. Except for UET, and you're part of the living proof that even that tyranny scores poorly over the Long View. No, Liesel won't try to tie *you* down." He leaned forward. "What she might like, mind you, is some exchange of information, and other cooperation."

Tregare nodded. "I could manage that, I expect. But back to Bleeker and his group. What's in mind, there?"

"As a matter of fact, Rissa has more or less taken over that problem. She's inveigled Bleeker into making a bet he can't afford to pay off, without losing control of his own holdings, on the outcome of her death duel with Stagon dal Nardo."

A picture came to Tregare's mind: the slim young woman he'd known as Tari Obrigo, facing the powerful dal Nardo, now grown to full strength. "What kind of weapons will they use?"

"None," said Hawkman, "except themselves. By Rissa's choice, they'll fight nude and weaponless."

Halfway rising, Tregare sat back. "She's insane!"

Hawkman nodded. "That's been the general consensus, but Rissa disagrees. And after she did a few practice sessions with Ernol Lombuno, who's the best unarmed combat specialist we have at Hulzein Lodge, the consensus isn't so solid." He shook his head. "I wish I could stop fearing for her, though. And while Liesel doesn't let on much, she's worried, too."

Abruptly, Tregare made up his mind. "If Tari—Rissa— agrees, I'll do the marriage thing for you, all right. Make it clear that afterward she won't be bound by it if she doesn't want to be, in anything other than legal formalities. As long as *they* may be needed." He paused. "Now then—you say there's nothing I can do about this dal Nardo duel, to head it off, or get to the bastard *first?*"

"No, Bran. If you killed him while he had a challenge pending, you'd be outlawed here." Hand gesture; Tregare held his reply. "Yes, I know you're outlawed on more worlds than I know of, and don't give two small damns. But *here* you want to outfit a fleet. If you killed dal Nardo, unlawfully by our

customs, you'd be totally cut off from supplies. And Hulzein
Lodge couldn't do one thing about it."

No way past that edict; all right: "Then I promise you only
this. If Stagon dal Nardo kills that woman, he won't outlive
her. Not long enough to get hungry."

Near time to bunk down, Hawkman asked if Tregare could
get him a talk circuit to Hulzein Lodge. "Sure." But Bran had
to go through Base Two, then to Port, where a lazy-sounding
operator patched through faster than her drawling voice might
have suggested. When he heard "Hulzein Lodge" he handed
the phone to Hawkman and left the scout's contol room, to give
his father reasonable privacy with his call. A time later, out of
sheer boredom Tregare was preparing to light one of his rare
cigars when Hawkman opened the door and beckoned to him.
So he went in and picked up the handset. "Yes? Tregare here."

"And about time, too." Liesel's voice, his mother's. "All
right, I know pretty well why you've avoided us. Are you done
with that nonsense?"

"Nonsense?" He needed time—time to fight against being
pushed back into his childhood. He said, "That's not what it
felt like. Still doesn't, if you want to know." Inside him,
leaping, came the spark of challenge from long distant in his
past. "Your side of it, I'd like to hear."

More stalling, that was, because she could only say what he
already knew, and that's what came over the circuit. When she
was done with it, she said, "Hulzeins don't ask forgiveness; you
know that much. What I'm asking is, are you ready to do
business?" And that, of course, was exactly how it would be,
with Liesel Hulzein. Looking over to Hawkman, Tregare felt
his breath come shuddering out. "Business, yeah. Hawkman
told me about it, the marriage and all." Oddly, he felt tremors
within him that he didn't understand. So he said, "We've
talked that out; he can fill the story for you. Me, I've had a long
day. The duel, whenever—I'll see you there."

He handed the phoneset back to Hawkman, walked out and
to bed.

Neither the next day nor the day after did Hawkman return
to Point One. He said he wasn't needed there until it came
time for the duel, and meanwhile Tregare found himself
enjoying the chance to show his father the facilities and
planning at both bases: the cabin's defenses, the escape tunnel

and pillbox, the embryonic spaceport down at Two. At dinner in the cabin with Deverel and Kenekke, Hawkman shook his head. "You're prepared, here, for just about anything that could happen and much that can't."

Bran sipped wine. "You think I'm overdoing it?"

"Not at all. Or rather, if you didn't, I'd worry about the entire concept of heredity." He laughed. "But you restore my faith, if it had ever been shaken, in the Hulzein genes."

And Tregare said, "I don't think your side short-changed me, either." The look on Hawkman's face made him glad he'd said it.

The morning they were to leave, Tregare packed a travel bag. Seeing his father's raised eyebrows, he said, "I expect to be gone from here more than just the day."

"I was planning to invite you to the Lodge. Will you come?"

"If I'm alive, I will." *Yes, now it's time for that.*

They went to the aircar; Bran took the passenger's seat and gestured Hawkman to the controls. The older man said, "You want me to fly the pass?"

"Sure. Maybe you can show me some pointers." So Hawkman brought the propulsors up to speed and they lifted from the plateau, making a wide climbing sweep to head upslope toward the pass itself.

Hawkman's technique was, to begin with, neither flashy nor overly cautious; as the summit approached and the cut's walls began to narrow, he maintained a safety cushion of about a hundred meters' altitude. He needed at least half of that, because at the dogleg's first turn he dipped the car into a vertical bank and threw the nose ninety degrees left, broadsiding. His half-roll, then, gave him a few seconds to spare before broadsiding the rightward turn also. The dogleg was on the downslope side, so the lost height in the two maneuvers gave no real risk.

Then the strong westward current caught the aircar and spat it free of the pass, at a height that allowed Hawkman to make another lazy swing and head for One Point One. "Do I qualify?"

What impressed Tregare about his father's maneuvering in the pass was its sheer efficiency. "How many times, you've done that?"

"This was my third experience, piloting westward."

"You're a quick study; I'll say that."

"Possibly I take after my son, who did it first and with no guidance at all."

"I had a lot of luck." Bran laughed. "Maybe that's heredity, too. I hope so."

"Perhaps the heredity factor is the tendency to *make* luck."

Descending on a smooth slant, the aircar bore to the left of the spaceport. Ahead, Hawkman pointed out a small enclosure, alongside an open space where an aircar and two groundcars sat. "The arena's bare dirt. The fence keeps gawkers away."

Tregare said, "Who's all the company, then?"

Preoccupied with landing, Hawkman waited until he'd brought the car to a stop not far from the enclosure's gate. "The aircar's not one of ours, so the dal Nardo contingent must be here first. The groundcars would be the referee's and medic's teams."

"Referee, huh?" Bran began to realize he didn't know much about this situation. "You know who it is? You satisfied?" He was pulling on the hood mask, glad in the day's warmth that the thing was lightweight porous fabric.

"I have no idea. But the officials must be approved by both sides, and I can't imagine anyone slipping a ringer past Liesel." And as Bran started to leave the aircar, Hawkman said, "We must disarm ourselves now. Only the referees may have weapons."

Tregare didn't like it, but rules are rules.

The wooden fence stood about three meters; at the small gate a young grey-robed woman asked for bona-fides. "We're with the Obrigo group," said Hawkman. "I understand there'll be three more—plus our principal, of course."

She nodded. "That's the agreed number. Go on in, please, Mr. Moray." She looked a question at Tregare but didn't say it.

Inside, Bran was surprised at how small the place really was. Roughly fifteen meters across, total, and the dueling ring itself no more than seven. Without asking, he guessed that being forced outside that ring meant defeat, with the loser's life forfeit; that was the way such events usually worked. The dirt surface was dry and solid, with only a few piles of loose dust here and there.

Tregare looked at the others already present; besides himself and Hawkman there were ten. All right—the black robe and two grey were the officials; the man and woman in white coats had to be medics.

Then he put attention to the dal Nardo group. Hawkman was right—Stagon was grown to be a bull indeed. Bellowing like one, too—mostly at the referee and that person's aides. Tregare looked at the man, closely and with heed to detail. Obviously he outweighed Tari—*no, Rissa, damn it!*—by more than two to one, with strong thick limbs and a neck like that same bull. A black beard, trimmed short but not neatly; no doubt the man cut it so as to give his opponent no grabbing handle. The gross belly was probably misleading; the way the man moved, quickly for his great size, the fat hid hard muscle.

Hovering around dal Nardo were five others: two men and one woman (Tregare's instincts dismissed those three as inconsequential), a hulking shape that stood completely concealed by robe and hood, and a slim young man, gaudily clad, who moved like quicksilver. Bran nudged his father. "Who's the Fancy Dan there?"

Hawkman was frowning. "I don't like this. That's Blaise Tendal; he kills for hire and has collected for more than twenty assignments. He's impotent with women, one hears, and hates them for it. Of course he can't be armed here, but still—"

"Course he can't." Tregare grinned. "'tother hand, you and I, one at each foot, shake him upside down a little, we'd know for sure."

Hawkman smothered a chuckle. "I wish we could; I really do. But the referee's duty would be to stop us, at gunpoint if necessary." He clasped Bran's shoulder. "I like your thinking, though."

Before Tregare could answer, again the gate guard admitted a group. Four, this time: in front, Tregare's sister Sparline Moray walked beside a young black man; next was the woman Bran knew as Tari Obrigo and was trying to rethink as Rissa Kerguelen. In the rear walked a man built like a bear and moving like one.

Bran again nudged Hawkman. "Besides Sparline and Rissa, should I know about the others?"

"Ernol Lombuno, up front; he's the one Rissa's been training with. Behind is Splieg; he's here if we need muscle. Splieg once, not too long ago, stunned a charging bushstomper with his bare fist. He's not fast, but not easy to stop, either."

Tregare grinned. "Nice you have some talent on hand. Just in case." But he was looking at Rissa Kerguelen. She was the Tari Obrigo he knew, and yet she wasn't, quite. *What's the difference?*

She moved the same—or maybe better now, with the recent combat training. Not black, today, the tied-back hair, but dark brown—and the sun brought a few reddish glints to it. He squinted, sharpening his distance vision across ten meters or so, and noticed that there was no mole at the left nostril, and that when a brief smile showed teeth, the upper incisors no longer protruded. "Disguise, huh?" Hawkman nodded. "Good job, it was."

"Subtle, Bran. That's the trick of it."

"I—" But now, a distraction. Stagon dal Nardo's raucous voice had receded in importance to mere background noise, but the younger medic called something to "Tari" and the bullish, bullying man was crying foul. Whereupon Rissa shook her head, seemed to shout without raising her voice much, and said, "Claim and be damned to you!" She added a few choice remarks, then turned to confer with Sparline. Hawkman moved over toward them; Tregare followed, but stayed back when his father hugged the young woman and spoke to her in low tones that Bran couldn't hear.

The black-robed referee spoke. "It is time. Tari Obrigo challenges Stagon dal Nardo to the death. Weapons, none. Clothing, none. Seconds and other agreed parties are present. Now, if they wish, the opponents may speak. Challenged party speaks first."

At the Slaughterhouse and serving under Butcher Korbeith, Tregare thought he had learned about cruelty and sadism. But hearing Stagon dal Nardo, Bran decided he'd been playing in a beginners' league. Point by point, dal Nardo detailed the breaking and crushing and gouging and biting-away that would constitute a vivisection, by teeth and nails, of his young opponent. Feeling shock dim his mind, Tregare shook his head to clear it, and was reminded of his promise to Hawkman: that dal Nardo would not outlive this woman. *Not long enough to get hungry.* It helped a little, but he could have used something more. *And what's all this doing to HER?*

Then the roaring man, with one jerk, disrobed the hulking figure beside him: a tall woman who was a shape of horror. Not just the battered, crudely-stitched face—could there possibly still be an eye in that bleeding socket?—but also the bruises and gaping cuts, one arm bending at the wrong places, the blackening breast half torn away, the few broken teeth that showed behind swollen bloody lips. Peace take it, was there *any* part of not bloody? And dal Nardo laughing: "Here's what I do, only in *practice!*"

With no thought, Tregare began a lunge toward the man, but Hawkman pulled him back. "You can't. Not now."

Gasping for breath, Bran let himself be stopped. He saw his sister lean toward Rissa, and heard: "It's a *fake*, most of it." And then, coming to himself a little, looked and realized that most of the woman's mutilations *were* a clever job of makeup. Not the arm, or some of the cuts, but a lot of it. Still, though . . .

His mind leveled out on two imperatives: he would not throw up and he would stay conscious. The rest blurred on him. He heard dal Nardo gloat over the sexual indignities he intended to inflict between the time he rendered his victim helpless and the moment of death; accordingly Tregare decided that if it were his lot to end dal Nardo, the man would not die a functional male.

After dal Nardo's invective ran downhill, calling Rissa Kerguelen "fertilizer" and "mouse," it was her turn. She didn't say much. Bran caught, "If I squeak like a mouse . . . you shit like a bull, but from your mouth." Her face, pale under sun-color, showed no expression as she taunted dal Nardo into obvious rage. At the end she thanked him for the warning of his sexual intent. "I shall make certain you are unable to fulfill it."

Then the seconds began to prepare their principals. Tregare saw Sparline saturate Rissa's hair with grease and then, after discussion he didn't understand, spread the stuff over her entire nude body, leaving only hands and feet free of the stuff. Again dal Nardo cried foul and Bran realized the man had his own hands coated with adhesive and was demanding a share of his opponent's lubricant; the referee gave him short shrift.

Finally the argument stopped; the huge man and slim woman stepped to face each other.

"I see the bull is constipated," said Rissa Kerguelen.

Afterward, Tregare could never sort out the action in sequence. The man charged. True to her word, Rissa in diving aside clawed for the crotch—drawing blood but doing no real damage. First grabbing himself, dal Nardo cursed and waved a bloodstained hand.

Wrong move. She caught his thumb in both hands, braced to slam both feet into his face, and somersaulted backward to face him again. That thumb, now, jutted at an odd angle. He charged; she dropped and tripped him to fall over her, but before she could get up and away he recovered, and hit her across the mouth and chopped at her ribs. He missed a kick as she rolled free; the black man's shout warned her she was too near the ring's edge. She scuttled and feinted, turned at someone's shout and caught a handful of dust, thrown directly into her face. From outside the ring.

The coxcomb! Tregare reached for a weapon he didn't have, then shrugged off Hawkman's restraining hand. "Yeah, I know. But just *wait!*"

Others were crying foul; the big man Splieg had one hand at dal Nardo's chest, the other fist raised like a maul. Rissa wiped knuckles at her eyes. She must have seen the gaudy man skulking back, for her hoarse croak said, "Dig your grave, Blaise Tendal! If I live, you are a dead man!" And Ernol Lombuno shouted that Tendal was dead, either way.

With order restored, again the duel began. Now it was all hitting and feinting and dodging, dal Nardo getting most of the better of it. Rissa backed away, and shouted, "It is time, dal Nardo!" But she was losing; what could she do? With the sweating Bran could see, and the panting he could hear . . .

Feints to eyes and groin, a wrench to the broken thumb. Then a full lunge, stiffened fingers to the larynx. But the thrust slipped off, and his arms closed in effort to crush her slim rib cage.

Hawkman's clutch hurt Tregare's arm; it wasn't needed; he couldn't have moved anyway. He saw her try to kill by concussion, both palms slammed to the ears; it didn't work. The man was bending her backward; the spine didn't have much more leeway before it would break. The heel of her hand punished dal Nardo's smashed nose, to no avail. She clawed for the carotid and drew blood, but nowhere enough.

She had to be close to death; for a moment her hands dropped. Then she thrust a thumb into his right eye and his arms refused to hold their killing grip. Released, she drove her other hand at the larynx again.

This time, Stagon dal Nardo fell and died.

If there was anything Tregare didn't need, it was more confusion. Staggering, Rissa challenged Blaise Tendal. That treacherous man said *he'd* do the challenging. Hawkman shut them both up as Sparline and the medics worked over Rissa and got her into a robe. And then somehow Hawkman was announcing a marriage, as of now, between "our victor, Tari Obrigo," and, gesturing toward Tregare, "one not to be named publicly at this time." Bran heard Rissa mumble, through swollen, bloody lips, something about having the wrong legal identification; apparently Hawkman reassured her.

As they all walked forward, Rissa supported by Hawkman, Tregare saw his battered bride gesture toward himself. "But how can *he* be here?" Whatever his father answered, Rissa nodded.

Bran's own questions gave Hawkman no pause, either. He'd asked if the marriage was to be oldstyle or freestyle. Headshake. "We don't make the distinction here. Now let's begin."

Not one word of that ceremony stuck in Tregare's memory. At the end of it Rissa turned to him; he tasted blood on her abused lips. Then she reached her head up and lightly touched her tongue to each of his eyelids. "If this is all you will show—" and he realized his face was still hooded.

Hawkman was trying to wind things down. While Bran was trying to find an answer for his new wife, Blaise Tendal began to shout, challenging her as "the murderer of Stagon dal Nardo!" Wrenching away from Bran, she shouted an acceptance, but Hawkman in a cold voice negated the entire proposition: as a Hulzein connection by marriage, "Tari" was out of Tendal's status range for dueling. Tendal claimed he was a dal Nardo the same way she was a Hulzein. A short man, one of Stagon dal Nardo's retinue, calling himself Talig dal Nardo and claiming to be Stagon's heir to power in the clan, told Tendal that his nominal marriage to Stagon's prepubescent daughter was annulled. Tendal, red-faced, threw his hat down and cursed the lot of them. "You all hide behind status, don't you? Well, dealing with Blaise Tendal, it won't help you! I'll get her anyway!"

Enough of this shit. I want that one. Tregare stepped forward. "Tendal! If I headed the dal Nardo clan, I'd kill you this minute. If the new head doesn't, he should. Because I'm sure he knows, if you don't, what happens to anyone connected with the fool who harms the wife of Bran Tregare!"

For seconds he thought it would work. Insane and raging, the man was, but Tregare was in position to stop him from getting near Rissa, and moving forward, too. Hawkman didn't hold him back. Bran stepped ahead, slowly. When he saw the man's mouth twisting and knew something was wrong, it was too late. The knife came from nowhere into Tendal's hand—*so much for their damned Security here*—and went far afield of Tregare's frantic grab. He heard a gasp, a shout; he couldn't turn fast enough to see where the knife had gone, but in front of him Blaise Tendal's chest exploded into red steam. The black-clad referee put away her energy gun and said, "I should have done that when he threw the dirt."

The shout had been from Ernol Lombuno; now Tregare saw that the hilt of a knife protruded from the palm of the black man's hand, and the blade out the back of it. But Lombuno was grinning. "Best catch I ever made!" There was blood but not a whole lot, and shortly the senior medic worked the blade loose and opened skin enough to make sure there was no tendon damage, then administered antibiotics and closed the wound.

Later they went out to the aircars. The others—the dal Nardos with the corpse to carry, the referees' group and the two medics (after the younger of those two had hugged Rissa for a time)—left earlier. Hawkman assigned passengers to his and Bran's car. A small man, thin-faced and with a crooked nose, was waiting outside the arena; Hawkman said, "Lebeter, I wish we'd had you inside, there. The dal Nardos had a knifester who got in, armed. Nearly killed our principal."

Lebeter shook his head. "Bad. Who was it?"

"Blaise Tendal. So damn' *fast.*"

Lebeter spat on the ground. "I *should* of been there." And Hawkman laughed, clapping a hand to the little knifeman's shoulder. They both grinned, and Lebeter said, "Your car's crowded. I'll fly Splieg with me. Anybody else?" Hawkman shook his head; Lebeter said, "If you need no more now, I'll leave."

That car lifted; not long after, the remaining group boarded Tregare's car. He waved Hawkman to the pilot's seat; after all, the man knew the way to Hulzein Lodge and dark would be coming soon. Sparline was making Rissa, sedated close to sleep, comfortable on the car's wide rear seat. That done, she turned to face Tregare. "It's been a long time, Bran. Are you reconciled to us now, or—?" He stared at her, and found that all the long hurt was somehow gone. So he hugged her, this tall beautiful sister he didn't really know. "All of a sudden, seems so. We'll talk later; okay?"

"I'd like that. Rissa's said you're not so bad as people say."

He laughed. "I hope to hell not. Go sit down, so's Hawkman can lift us."

Strapping in, Tregare found himself sitting beside Ernol Lombuno, and said, "How's the hand? Hurting much?"

"Some. Not too badly." A pause, and then, "So you've married her. I hope you know what she's worth."

Tregare thought that remark over. "Maybe. Do you?"

Lombuno cleared his throat. "Her worth, I do know." Before Bran could answer, he said, "We had moments. I fought her in practice. Fought *with* her when that Tendal tried ambush, once. Made love together, after." Sidelong glance. "Does that bother you?"

Tregare shrugged. "Why should it? People don't own each other. Never have, never can, never will."

In peripheral vision he saw the other man shrug. "I'm glad you see it that way. Because if you held anything against her, you'd answer to me, for it."

In wonderment Tregare looked at the man beside him. "I think I need to tell you something, Lombuno. Which is, we're on the same side."

Seeing the wounded bandaged hand reach out for handshake, Bran Tregare made his clasp gentle.

As Hawkman, in early dusk, approached Hulzein Lodge, Bran found the place even more impressive at close range. The entire complex sat at the edge of a high valley, with a wooded sweep dropping away below. Landing near the Lodge itself, Hawkman taxied the aircar to the front entrance. Tregare unfastened his harness and went back to see how Rissa was doing.

She was awake, maybe still a bit drug-punchy but not much. He and Hawkman helped her out the aircar's door; then she said, "I can walk unaided now, I think. Let me?" And though she moved as awkwardly as stiffened bruises might justify, Tregare contented himself with staying close in case she stumbled.

As they entered, he spoke softly to her. "On the ship I took you when I had no right to. Now I've got the right—but I won't come to you until you say so."

She touched his arm, then his tattooed cheek. "Be with me now." He must have looked surprised, because she added, "No—only to talk, while I soak out some hurt, in a hot tub."

He nodded—and so, approaching now, did Liesel Hulzein. Bran waited for some unbidden emotional surge within him, but nothing came except curiosity: what would his mother say?

Her response was pure Liesel. She hugged him as though he'd been away for the weekend, and said, "Yes, go with her, Bran. We all need to talk, but that can wait." Quickly she gave Rissa some comforting words and an embrace to match, then asked Hawkman to go with her and give a full report. "I want to hear all of it." Looking after them, Bran shook his head. *Those Hulzein women!* And half his genes were theirs. . . .

Guiding Tregare to her upstairs room, Rissa needed to lean on his arm. Inside, she shed her robe. The marks she bore would have fit well on a Slaughterhouse snotty.

Finding the bathroom, Tregare ran water into the tub, gauging and adjusting the temperature as hot as a person could stand without real pain, or injury. "I look like a gargoyle!" He turned to see her before a mirror, and had to agree: bloody, swollen lips, the purple-bulging right eye above the bandaged cheek. As she touched fingers to her upper front teeth, he saw her wince. "He has loosened a few; for some days I shall not chew well."

Then she entered the tub, sliding down until only her face appeared above the water, and asked him to bring her some brandy, in the flask's oversized cap. The first sip made her shudder; the second brought what she probably meant to be a smile. But not today, it wasn't. Pulling a chair over, to sit beside the tub, he said, "You ever marry before?" Her

headshake was slow and lazy. "Neither have I. It feels
. . . odd."

"Do not worry. Sparline said we need not be bound, after
this crisis." She shrugged. "Whatever that might be."

He tried to explain: Bleeker, the oligarch's reactions to
learning Tregare's Hulzein status, the dal Nardo succession,
and more—but she wasn't interested. Interrupting, "Say
instead how you are here. *Inconnu* was not at the Port—did
you land elsewhere and travel overland?"

She was kneading lather into her hair, and he could see her
wince at working with sore arms. "Here—let me do that."
While he did so, he explained how he had *Inconnu* out circling
the big planet ("almost a grey dwarf") and serving as a relay
station for incoming ships, and that he'd sneaked back to
Number One in his scoutship. "Landed at a place I have, the
other side of the Big Hills, and called Hawkman to come
parley."

And heard what he said: *why did I lie?* Because he wasn't
ready to tell her, or anybody else, how he'd fallen apart, was
why. *Someday* . . . ?

"That is where he has been?"

"Right. Now hold your breath—" And for the next minute or
so, Rissa's attention was distracted by being underwater longer
than she truly enjoyed, while Bran scrubbed away at lather.
When she came up spluttering he apologized; both offense and
apology were horseplay—and meanwhile he could change the
subject. . . . "That thumbnail you tore, there, in the duel—
I'll have to fix it. Might's well cut back those other claws, too.
We need any more fighting around here, it's my job."

"No! Married or not, I do my own fighting. And you forget—
Sparline said the ceremony was for political reasons. We are
not bound unless we both wish it."

He stopped filing the broken nail. Suddenly he knew what
he wished. He couldn't stop his scowl. "Forget politics. You
want free of me so soon, without even trying the marriage?
Without seeing what it's like?"

She looked at him. He was pretty sure what she was
thinking, and that he wasn't going to like it. But he had to
listen. "I cannot know, Tregare, what I will want later. But
mask and all, I recognized you *before* the ceremony. And
now—there will be time, for both of us, to decide our wishes.

"Will you help me out of here? My muscles have turned to

wax." Like his scowl earlier, he had no control over the grin that came now. He aided her to stand and leave the tub, then handed her a large towel for herself and took a smaller one to begin the drying of her long hair. When he stood back, as much done as a towel would manage, she put her own towel aside and again he saw the swollen, distorted attempt to smile. "How can I have such hurt, from blows I do not remember?"

He helped her into her robe. "I don't know. How could anyone your size stand up against the likes of dal Nardo—and kill the bastard?"

"Dal Nardo was not trained by Erika Hulzein." Well, he couldn't argue with that answer. . . . With an arm around her, he walked Rissa into the bedroom and brought a chair so he could sit beside her bed. "Something I didn't know before. On *Inconnu*, any day you could have killed me. The way I treated you, how come you didn't?"

Lying down, it's hard to shrug, but she managed. "First, because no stranger kills a captain on his own ship and survives. Later—as I said before our landing here—I ceased to hate you."

"Ceased to hate? Is that all, Tari?" Tari? His mind had slipped back to the *Inconnu* time with her—and that was all right, because he wanted *her* to do the telling.

Her answer belied her headshake, then—what was she thinking? "More than that, Tregare—but probably not what you would like to hear. Toward the end I felt a kind of sympathy, a precarious comradeship—but also that you were a dangerous man who might still be useful to me."

Useful? She was certainly laying it on the line! "You still feel that way?"

"After what you said to Tendal before he threw the knife? Ah, no, Tregare—whatever happens between us or does not, I will never try to *use* you. Can you say the same to me?"

He found one fist pounding into his other palm. "Peace, yes! But I can't speak for the rest of the family. They—"

Then they came near to arguing, Rissa saying she begrudged no advantage Liesel gained by their dealings, Tregare telling her that to Hulzeins *everyone* was expendable if the stakes were high enough. "*I* sure as peace was." And found himself rehashing the old grievances, until by main will he stopped himself. "Oh, I believe it now, that they had to leave me in hell to save my life." Shaking his head, "*You* wouldn't believe what

UET does to young kids, to weed out all but the very toughest. Either you turn into a kind of monster, or you die."

Staring, he didn't really see her. "I didn't die, Tari—*I didn't die.*"

Her hand touched his; by reflex he jerked away, then came back to himself and clasped hands with her. "There—you see? Thinking back to that, any touch—even yours—is a threat."

"But only for a second—then you recovered quickly enough."

"I don't know. It's been years, and still—"

"To let go of old hurts, there are methods. I can show you, if you like—if you will let me."

"Maybe. If we ever have time for it, maybe I will." At first he couldn't identify the feeling that came to him then, because not since he lost his home had he known it, much. That feeling was, he finally decided, *trust.* He also decided it scared him a little.

She was trying to say something and he hadn't been listening. "And I—" in a small voice, then nothing more. His questions brought no response; she changed the subject to the matter of dinner. "Soft foods, please." The loosened teeth; sure. So over the intercom he ordered up a meal. He thought he'd done a good job of it, so that couldn't be why she was frowning. Then she said, "Tregare? As married persons, should we not know one another by our true names?"

All right, it was *her* surprise; he wouldn't spoil it. Pretending ignorance, he played straight man; yes, the disguise, and so *that* was why the lockbox wouldn't open, and so on. When he saw she was on the verge of exasperation, he said, "You want me to ask, don't you? All right, I'm not married to Tari Obrigo. Who, then?"

"I am sorry it makes little difference to you." She was wrong, there, but he didn't interrupt. "To me, it does. I am Rissa Kerguelen. Now, I suppose, we can talk about something else."

Faking surprise he said, "Sure! I remember now—" and told of seeing her Welfare press conference back at Earth—his glee at the spunk she'd shown and at learning of her later escape from UET. Then his smile faded; he could feel it go. Done with acting, he said, "On the ship—I wish I'd known. I wouldn't have—"

"Ease your mind, Tregare. If you are in dire need of

something to regret, I am sure we can find a more worthy subject."

Their meal's arrival interrupted any further protest. As she looked at the tray he said, "Does my order suit you? Does it—Rissa?"

A nod. "Yes."

"Real names. If they're important to you, mine's Bran." She'd know already, of course, but this was the way he wanted to do it.

"Yes—Bran."

"That's better. Let's eat."

Later they talked more. On the matter of names, Rissa's view was that only in private were the usages important. "Because publicly we use automatic defenses. By ourselves we must discard these or remain strangers." He wasn't sure he followed her thinking, but it *felt* right.

In light of her physical state, at bedtime he offered to leave, but she said, "Not unless you wish to go. I am in invalid status, but if you would like merely to *stay* with me, this bed is large and your presence would comfort me."

"Maybe yours will comfort me, too." Her lips would pain her too much to accept a kiss, so he settled for her forehead. And in bed, knowing how stiff and sore she must be—bath or no bath—he attempted no cuddling.

But once, in the night, he woke to find her snuggling close. Yawning, he smiled, and let sleep come again. Without nightmares.

Next morning, Rissa had a bone to pick. Two, in fact. First, the woman Chira; well, sooner or later he'd have to explain so why not now? He told about it: ". . . bought her for a packet of drugsticks and a rusty knife, because she was next up for sacrifice to their tribal god, a nasty bastard as such things go," and how by no purpose of his own he'd wound up stuck with her. Next, the women in Hold Portside Upper. So he told that, too: the buying and transportation, and the lucky deal to send them off to Farmer's Dell with Pell Quinlan. And that Chira had gone with the rest. Ending, "That suit you, or do you still think I lie to you?"

Smiling, she shook her head. "Bran Tregare, you are too proud to lie—except, of course, in the line of business. You are what my father used to say—a brass-plated sonofabitch who takes no crap from *anyone*. There is much to be said for that kind of person. So I accept you . . . no, not *yet*, you ravisher of cripples!" But his hands were gentle on her, and she laughed, even leaning to touch her damaged lips to his.

"Rissa—how can you fit into the stretched-out life I must lead?"

"How could I know? But for now, while we are here, I think I can. Shall we try?"

Later when he'd run another hot bath to soothe her aches, she lay near-submerged, only eyes and nose and mouth above the steaming water. "Bran Tregare? Now I shall trust you."

"If you do, then except for my people on *Inconnu*, you'll be the first." *But I won't let you down.*

She couldn't have heard him; as he spoke, she had ducked her head under water. No point in saying it again, the said or unsaid, either one. He'd *show* her, was all.

As she sported, lazily, in the steaming tub, Bran did some thinking. It wouldn't be easy, putting together a fleet to go take Stronghold. Then the gamble he couldn't even estimate: lying in wait to take UET's incoming ships, and finally moving against UET on Earth itself. But he had to try—*it's what I'm built for*.

His odds were better now. Looking back, he saw that since the Slaughterhouse had begun to warp him, he hadn't been truly a whole person. *All that waste—walling off Hawkman and Liesel and Sparline. I had to do it, but—if it hadn't been for Krieg Elman's example, I could have turned just as bad. And a paranoid can't do this job of mine; who'd follow him?*

After Tanit Eldon he'd thought he could never trust another woman. How could he accept Rissa so easily? Well, Zelde M'tana had taken the edge off—impossible that *she* could be phony. And Rissa, instead of ingratiating herself as Tanit did, had faced up to him, brought him to a standstill sometimes. That made her *real*.

She'd had her own years of hell—*Total Welfare!* Maybe that was why he and she could respect, and accept, each other. Sipping Rissa's brandy, Tregare sighed, in release of tension.

Dripping, blowing water from her nose and swollen lips, Rissa bounced up sitting. Bran looked at her, and thought: as long as new things were possible, they didn't have to be easy.

Breaking the barriers against his family—damned near broke him in half, but sure worth it. And Rissa, growing up a slave in Total Welfare—what barriers might *she* still have?

He shook his head. It didn't matter. *Because* they knew each other's hellish pasts, they had a handle on something together. And his feeling was, what they had, would last.

Thumbing water from her eyes, she raised her arched brows in query. "Why so solemn, Bran Tregare?"

He couldn't tell her now; it might take years. All he said was, "Come on out of there, will you? Before you turn into a prune, or something."

13. Epilogue: Return to Stronghold

Coming off duty from her watch trick as Third Hat on *Inconnu*, Rissa joined Bran in captain's digs. He cut his terminal screen, where he'd been studying a star chart, and watched her pour coffee for herself, shaking his head as she offered to refill his own cup. "Thanks, though." She sat near him. He said, "What's our latest ETA for Stronghold?"

She sipped, then said, "Six weeks, I would say—give or take a day or so. Within expected limits, is it not?"

He thought about it: t/t∘. "Yes. We're just below twelve percent of c, then." She nodded, set her cup aside and came to kiss him. A time later he put his mind back to business.

He hadn't brought together all the ships he wanted or had expected, only the bare minimum that might do the job. He felt full trust in his captains—Gowdy, Vanois, Derek Limmer, Zelde M'tana and Ilse Krueger. He wished that Kickem Bernardez had made rendezvous on time and that Jimar Peralta's thirst for command hadn't cost—but this was no time for mourning.

Because now it was all, everything, up for grabs.

But for Bran Tregare, when had things been any other way?

ABOUT THE AUTHOR

F. M. BUSBY's published science fiction novels include *Rissa Kerguelen*, the related *Zelde M'Tana*, *Star Rebel* and *The Alien Debt*; *All These Earths*, and the now-combined volume *The Demu Trilogy* (*Cage a Man*, *The Proud Enemy*, and *End of the Line*). Numerous shorter works, ranging from short-shorts to novella length, have appeared in various SF magazines and in both original and reprint anthologies, including *Best of Year* collections edited by Terry Carr, by Lester Del Rey, and by Donald A. Wollheim. Some of his works have been published in England and (in translation) Germany, France, Holland and Japan.

Rebel's Quest, the second of two books concerning the early life of Bran Tregare, is set in *Rissa*'s universe.

Buz grew up in eastern Washington near the Idaho border, is twice an Army veteran, and holds degrees in physics and electrical engineering. He has worked at the "obligatory list of incongruous jobs" but settled for an initial career as communications engineer, from which he is now happily retired in favor of writing. He is married, with a daughter in medical school, and lives in Seattle. During Army service and afterward he spent considerable time in Alaska and the Aleutians. His interests include aerospace, unusual cars, dogs, cats, and people, not necessarily in that order. He once built, briefly flew and thoroughly crashed a hang glider, but comments that fifteen-year-olds usually bounce pretty well.

A Powerful Epic of a New Dark Age
by the Author of JITTERBUG

PURE BLOOD

by
Mike McQuay

In a strange and barbaric time that set human against mutant, the strong against the weak, two brothers clashed in a struggle for the fate of humanity: Ramon, the decadent heir to a dying general's empire, and Morgan, the bastard son who fought for freedom, for a dream that would not die.

Buy PURE BLOOD, on sale January 15, 1985, wherever Bantam paperbacks are sold, or use the handy coupon below for ordering:

SPECIAL MONEY SAVING OFFER

Now you can have an up-to-date listing of Bantam's hundreds of titles plus take advantage of our unique and exciting bonus book offer. A special offer which gives you the opportunity to purchase a Bantam book for only 50¢. Here's how!

By ordering any five books at the regular price per order, you can also choose any other single book listed (up to a $4.95 value) for just 50¢. Some restrictions do apply, but for further details why not send for Bantam's listing of titles today!

Just send us your name and address plus 50¢ to defray the postage and handling costs.

OUT OF THIS WORLD!

That's the only way to describe Bantam's great series of science fiction classics. These space-age thrillers are filled with terror, fancy and adventure and written by America's most renowned writers of science fiction. Welcome to outer space and have a good trip!

☐	24709	**RETURN TO EDDARTA** by Garrette & Heydron	$2.75
☐	22647	**HOMEWORLD** by Harry Harrison	$2.50
☐	22759	**STAINLESS STEEL RAT FOR PRESIDENT** by Harry Harrison	$2.75
☐	22796	**STAINLESS STEEL RAT WANTS YOU** by Harry Harrison	$2.50
☐	20780	**STARWORLD** by Harry Harrison	$2.50
☐	20774	**WHEELWORLD** by Harry Harrison	$2.50
☐	24176	**THE ALIEN DEBT** by F. M. Busby	$2.75
☐	24710	**A STORM UPON ULSTER** by Kenneth C. Flint	$3.50
☐	24175	**THE RIDERS OF THE SIDHE** by Kenneth C. Flint	$2.95
☐	23992	**THE PRACTICE EFFECT** by David Brin	$2.75
☐	23589	**TOWER OF GLASS** by Robert Silverberg	$2.95
☐	23495	**STARTIDE RISING** by David Brin	$3.50
☐	24564	**SUNDIVER** by David Brin	$2.75
☐	23512	**THE COMPASS ROSE** by Ursula LeGuin	$2.95
☐	23541	**WIND'S 12 QUARTERS** by Ursula LeGuin	$2.95
☐	22855	**CINNABAR** by Edward Bryant	$2.50
☐	22938	**THE WINDHOVER TAPES: FLEXING THE WARP** by Warren Norwood	$2.75
☐	23351	**THE WINDHOVER TAPES: FIZE OF THE GABRIEL RATCHETS** by Warren Norwood	$2.95
☐	23394	**THE WINDHOVER TAPES: AN IMAGE OF VOICES** by Warren Norwood	$2.75
☐	22968	**THE MARTIAN CHRONICLES** by Ray Bradbury	$2.75
☐	2?168	**PLANET OF JUDGMENT** by Joe Halderman	$2.95
☐	23756	**STAR TREK: THE NEW VOYAGES 2** by Culbreath & Marshak	$2.95

Prices and availability subject to change without notice.

Buy them at your local bookstore or use this handy coupon for ordering:

Bantam Books, Inc., Dept. SF, 414 East Golf Road, Des Plaines, Ill. 60016

Please send me the books I have checked above. I am enclosing $_____ (please add $1.25 to cover postage and handling). Send check or money order —no cash or C.O.D.'s please.

Mr/Mrs/Miss _____

Address_____

City_____ State/Zip_____

SF—3/85

Please allow four to six weeks for delivery. This offer expires 9/85.

FANTASY AND SCIENCE FICTION FAVORITES

Bantam brings you the recognized classics as well as the current favorites in fantasy and science fiction. Here you will find the most recent titles by the most respected authors in the genre.

☐	24370	RAPHAEL R. A. MacAvoy	$2.75
☐	24103	BORN WITH THE DEAD Robert Silverberg	$2.75
☐	24169	WINTERMIND Parke Godwin, Marvin Kaye	$2.75
☐	23944	THE DEEP John Crowley	$2.95
☐	23853	THE SHATTERED STARS Richard McEnroe	$2.95
☐	23575	DAMIANO R. A. MacAvoy	$2.75
☐	23205	TEA WITH THE BLACK DRAGON R. A. MacAvoy	$2.75
☐	23365	THE SHUTTLE PEOPLE George Bishop	$2.95
☐	24441	THE HAREM OF AMAN AKBAR Elizabeth Scarborough	$2.95
☐	20780	STARWORLD Harry Harrison	$2.50
☐	22939	THE UNICORN CREED Elizabeth Scarborough	$3.50
☐	23120	THE MACHINERIES OF JOY Ray Bradbury	$2.75
☐	22666	THE GREY MANE OF MORNING Joy Chant	$3.50
☐	25097	LORD VALENTINE'S CASTLE Robert Silverberg	$3.95
☐	20870	JEM Frederik Pohl	$2.95
☐	23460	DRAGONSONG Anne McCaffrey	$2.95
☐	24862	THE ADVENTURES OF TERRA TARKINGTON Sharon Webb	$2.95
☐	23666	EARTHCHILD Sharon Webb	$2.50
☐	24102	DAMIANO'S LUTE R. A. MacAvoy	$2.75
☐	24417	THE GATES OF HEAVEN Paul Preuss	$2.50

<u>Prices and availability subject to change without notice.</u>

Buy them at your local bookstore or use this handy coupon for ordering:

Bantam Books, Inc., Dept. SF2, 414 East Golf Road, Des Plaines, Ill. 60016

Please send me the books I have checked above. I am enclosing $_____
(please add $1.25 to cover postage and handling). Send check or money order
—no cash or C.O.D.'s please.

Mr/Mrs/Miss_____

Address_____

City_____ State/Zip_____

SF2—3/85

Please allow four to six weeks for delivery. This offer expires 9/85.